STILL SUMMER

"Mitchard has an astute ear for how women interact with their friends and their children, a gift beautifully showcased in STILL SUMMER . . . Mitchard brilliantly creates realistic, intriguing characters while refusing to settle for an easy or false happy ending."
> —*Entertainment Weekly*

"Entertaining . . . a high-seas yarn with a suburban-mom twist."
> —*Washington Post Book World*

"Mitchard made her mark in the literary world in 1996 when *The Deep End of the Ocean* was chosen as the first pick for Oprah Winfrey's now-legendary book club. Since then, she has written six other novels, but none matches the suspenseful pitch of STILL SUMMER . . . Readers will wring their hands with frustration, weep with sadness, and second-guess the choices these women make. But we can only sit on the edge of our seats and let Mitchard's terror-filled tale wash over us."
> —*USA Today*

"You feel every gut-wrenching second of it . . . Jacquelyn Mitchard is so clever."
> —*Roanoke Times*

"The ideal beach read."
> —*OK!* magazine

more . . .

"Mitchard lays out the series of events leading to the crisis with a sure hand . . . develops the characters in what amounts to a coming-of-age saga for each of them."

—*Seattle Times*

"A finely written tale you will not be able to put down . . . an insightful and moving exploration of the nature of enduring friendship between women. What happens when these ties are put to the most severe test? With her characteristic generosity, intelligence, and warmth, Mitchard illuminates this central question in an utterly compelling novel you will not soon forget!"

—Andre Dubus III, author of *House of Sand and Fog*

"Riveting . . . You'll forget time and place as you become immersed in the terrifying drama."

—*Fredericksburg Free Lance-Star*

"Five stars . . . fast-paced . . . a novel of suspense and adventure. But it also dives deeper into the bonds that bind friend to friend and mother to daughter . . . and succeeds in keeping readers on the edge of their seats."

—*Country Roads Magazine*

"A good beach read."

—*Kirkus Reviews*

more . . .

STILL SUMMER

Other Books by Jacquelyn Mitchard

Fiction

CAGE OF STARS

THE BREAKDOWN LANE

CHRISTMAS PRESENT

TWELVE TIMES BLESSED

A THEORY OF RELATIVITY

THE MOST WANTED

THE DEEP END OF THE OCEAN

Nonfiction

THE REST OF US

STILL SUMMER

JACQUELYN MITCHARD

GRAND CENTRAL
PUBLISHING

NEW YORK   BOSTON

Copyright © 2007 by Jacquelyn Mitchard
Reading Group Guide Copyright © 2008 by Hachette Book Group USA

Grand Central Publishing
Hachette Book Group USA
237 Park Avenue
New York, NY 10017

Visit our Web site at www.HachetteBookGroupUSA.com.
Printed in the United States of America
Originally published in hardcover by Hachette Book Group USA.
First Trade Edition: July 2008
10 9 8 7 6 5 4 3 2 1

Grand Central Publishing is a division of Hachette Book Group USA, Inc.
The Grand Central Publishing name and logo is a trademark of Hachette Book Group USA, Inc.

The Library of Congress has cataloged the hardcover edition as follows:

Mitchard, Jacquelyn.
    Still summer / Jacquelyn Mitchard.—1ˢᵗ ed.
      p. cm.
    ISBN 978-0-446-57876-9
    1. Female friendship—Fiction. 2. Cruise ships—Fiction. I. Title.
    PS3563.I7358S75 2007
    813'.54—dc22   2006033941

    ISBN 978-0-446-69673-9 (pbk.)

For Stacey Kain Sweeney
She walks in beauty . . .

When you were far beyond the sea,
Such thoughts were tyrants over me!
I often sat, for hours together,
Through the long nights of angry weather,
Raised on my pillow, to descry
The dim moon struggling in the sky.
　　　　　—EMILY BRONTË
　　　　　"FAITH AND DESPONDENCY"

Acknowledgments

*T*his is a work of fiction. The author is neither a sailor nor a geographer, and I well know that some of the events described in this book might not have happened exactly how and when and where they did in the fictional world. All the liberties are my own. For their willingness to help make this story real if not true, all my thanks go to Lenny and Michelle Amato, a married couple and the brilliantly skilled co-captains of the sailing boat *Opus*. For their help, I also owe a big *Mahalo* to Patricia Kesling-Wood, as well as several of my other students at the Maui Writers Conference, 2005. By your pupils you are taught, gang. I wish to thank Stephanie Ramierez for sharing her knowledge of Spanish, and Clarice Dewey for global aid. My partners on our research voyage—my cousin Janis, my friends Karen and Pamela—were invaluable comrades. I thank Camille, beautiful young French filmmaker, for her kindness in lending me her description and her name. Eternal thanks to the Ragdale Foundation in Lake Forest, Illinois, where most of the first draft of this book was written in October 2005, especially to Susan Tillett and her loving staff of "writer sitters," who have nurtured my every step. To Jamie Raab and the dedicated team at Grand Central Publishing, a cheer for taking a chance on me and seeing this book through to its debut. To my agent and forever friend, Jane Gelfman, my best love. To those pals who still somehow accept me as I am, my thanks and loyalty. To my children, forgive me my trespasses in taking time from you to write. And a special word to the real Tracy Kyle, who ended up a main character at an auction to raise funds for MS research, but who asked instead that this book commemorate her beloved sister-in-law Tunice and her children, Kyle and Katie; it does. If it's a story about anything, it's grace or disgrace under stress; and Tunice Kyle lived that grace until she died. In her honor, this book is dedicated.

STILL SUMMER

Day One

The three men finished with the small boat before nightfall. The painting had to be done quickly and it was difficult. So afterward they rested and smoked in the drawing dusk, their backs against a massive rock. The boat was called a *yola*. They had spotted it bobbing near an island on a buoy in the natural harbor formed by the embrace of two small spits of land and hauled it ashore. With thick smears of black paint, they covered up its pale blue gray color, its name, *Bonita*, and the white numbers of its registration. Over the lights, they spread a thinner coat. At sea, even if perchance they ran with lights to avoid a reef, this silty covering would make the lights indistinct and fickle; and someone might mistake them for a phosphorescent curiosity of the sea. Now they needed only to replace the engine with the larger one left for them the night before, beneath a tent of canvas concealed with branches and brush. The two older men had lived more than forty years in the same village in Santo Domingo. The younger man, an American barely twenty years old, could understand only some of the words they said. He might have been fluent by now but preferred not to be. Still, he could tell that they were talking about the way the sea always eventually gave up her fish, as well as other things. He heard the words for "weather" and "soup." He knew these men as Ernesto and Carlo; but he suspected these were not their true names. For these jobs, the men lived for a few weeks each year in Honduras, at the homes of people whose names they had been given. They were different people each time, cousins of acquaintances of men who knew *these* men by other names. At each place they stopped for food or rest, they would meet other people with no names. There seemed to be an endless supply of people who would forfeit names and memory for fifty American dollars. He had met them only once before. They disgusted him then. They terrified him now. He did not expect to meet them again.

The young man drew in the sweet smoke, laid his head back, and thought of his sister. The last time he had seen her, she had been seven years old, dressed for Halloween as a carousel horse, in an outfit their mother had made of black tights and papier-mâché. He remembered his father saying that the young man did not need a costume to look like a freak. His mother pivoted on his father and defended him, a reflex on behalf of her cub. But the young man knew that he had disgraced her, too, as his brother, still in high school, had honored her. He had failed to finish high school. His brother brought home trophies and fine grades. His own experiments with drugs and drunkenness had nearly put him in jail and cost his father considerable money and even more shame among his circle of wealthy friends. He did not like sports. After the time for playing baseball in the park was over, he had turned to quieter things. His mother had not minded, but his father spoke of him as a quitter. To the young man, the handsome, rough boys with their wide red mouths were embarrassing, almost frightening. He was not like the sons of his father's friends. Long ago, they had gone off to Brown or Michigan State. His brother would go to a fine college one day also. Still, his brother did love him. And his mother loved him no less than she loved his brother. His mother thought he would come out of the ways he had never expected to go.

The young man sometimes believed this, too.

His thinking of it was interrupted when Ernesto said something conspiratorial to Carlo about offering a puff of their smoke to the owner of *Bonita*. This amused Carlo so much that he deliberately fell over on his back, laughing as only a servile man can, like a dog performing for its master. Carlo was stupid, which the young man did not believe made him any less dangerous than Ernesto.

The owner of the little *yola* sat some distance away with his back also propped against a large rock. He made no comment on Ernesto's offer because he was dead.

Like a rare heron displaced from her environment, Olivia Montefalco high-stepped regally into the heat and blare of O'Hare International Airport. Though it was June, she wore a white wool suit with her high-heeled white sandals and huge diamond-stippled sunglasses. Those she passed were certain they had seen her before, perhaps in a magazine photograph. They fell back to make way. A grandmother rushing to meet her daughter for the Sunjet to Vegas thought that Olivia was that actress, the one from that movie about the artist whose boyfriend was a ghost . . . ? It had been a sweet movie, without all the sex, sex, sex. She had short hair, like Olivia's. A pilot who jumped down from a hotel shuttle—a little too athletically, but in a way he hoped would impress the flight attendants—was sure this woman had been on a charter he'd once flown to Crete. Unlike the gambling grandmother, he was correct.

Oblivious to the stares from fellow travelers and haggard morning smokers, Olivia stood on her toes and scanned the ranks of limousines, SUVs, and police cars. Where was that huge thing Tracy drove? The last time she'd seen it, it had been filled to exhaustion by Cammie and about a dozen of her soccer mates, all chittering and smelling of sweaty socks. Olivia was amazed that Tracy could work full-time and cook for Jim and visit her parents and send letters and coach soccer as well. Perhaps now that Cammie was grown, she had a different car.

Two skycaps trailed behind Olivia, like yoked oxen straining to push the teetering towers of Olivia's turquoise Henk van de Meene luggage. Olivia stuffed their hands with crumpled wads of dollar bills and gave them a smile so candent that they felt something more than a tip had been bestowed. Olivia had shipped most of her belongings, but the bits and essentials that comforted her after twenty years in Italy came with her, in fourteen matching pieces.

Olivia bit her lip—a gesture that, when she was married to Franco, guaranteed jewelry within days—and wondered if Tracy had forgotten her. Olivia hadn't written for months and months, not since Tracy's flurry of phone calls and offerings of help during Franco's illness. She didn't wonder if being left at the airport would serve her right. That was the kind of pondering that Olivia censored.

With a sure hand and her cousin Janis riding shotgun, Tracy piloted her huge van around the arrivals tier.

"There she is! There's Olivia! Behind that weird luggage!" Holly Solvig shrieked from the backseat. "Wonder how much extra *that* cost! I've never seen someone with so much baggage!"

"We already knew that," Janis said dryly.

Tracy remonstrated softly, "Jan. Hols. Come on. If it is Olivia, it's *Olivia*. You knew she was wealthy. What I hope is that I have the right airline and the right day."

Olivia had returned to the United States only twice in twenty years, once for her brother's wedding, once for her father's funeral. Each time Holly and Tracy had come to fetch her, the encounter had been the same: Olivia changed her entire appearance the way other women changed the color of their nail polish. But since neither Holly nor Tracy ever changed, she never failed to recognize them; and she did not now.

"I told you it was her, Trace," Holly repeated triumphantly. "Look, she sees us! She's giving the Godmother wave." Tracy glanced back, nearly colliding with a Saab. It was their wave, the American Sign Language letter y, an extended forefinger and thumb. "Look at those sunglasses. She looks like Mario SanGiaccamo's mother at the country club pool in 1970! She's

Westbrookian all over! Now it's going to take a half hour to come back around again to get her!" Holly felt like a fool, a forty-two-year-old woman making the "y" sign out the back window of a van. She tried to cover by making other ASL signs she'd picked up over the years at the hospital, those for "Not true" and "Talk to me," so onlookers might think she actually was talking to someone who was deaf.

"No way!" Janis cried now. "Whoever that woman is, she's at least ten years younger than we are!" Suddenly, all three women, as if each heard a gunshot at the starting line, covertly found something reflective in the car and began the kind of inventory reserved for buying a bathing suit. Each was thinking variations on the same theme: If this *was* their old friend, then her appearance was more magical than surgical.

"But it is so too her!" Holly insisted, reverting to adolescent language now, up on her knees and peering out the back window. "That's Olivia Seno, the Duchess Montefalco—"

"It's countess," Tracy corrected her. "And you haven't seen her in eight years, Hols."

"She could be the Count of Monte Crisco for all I know," Holly said. "All I know is, she's trying to get you to back up!"

Abruptly, Tracy braked and, through sheer General Motors muscle, with Holly yelling, "There's a very sick woman back there! We need to get her to help! Move!" backed her van through a bleating horde of protesting vehicles toward Olivia. She jumped up and wrinkled her nose in delight. The rest of them smiled with various degrees of moxie. Olivia's shiny appearance, like an advertisement for the benefits of folic acid, made all of them aware of their damp armpits and Thursday morning hair, Jan's and Tracy's yoga pants and Holly's cutoffs, so tight that she would have dislocated her thumb trying to put her hand into the pocket.

Twenty-five years ago, the four of them had been inseparable, a fighting unit with black fishnet stockings under their navy plaid school uniforms, imitation black leather jackets from J. C.

Penney thrown over their shoulders. Unholy innocents, they'd stalked the halls of St. Ursula High, cracking gum and cracking wise. Tough girls who'd never thrown a punch, they posed as scofflaws but never missed their curfews. Twenty-five years ago, they'd baptized themselves the Godmothers (in homage to the movie everyone had seen at least ten times). Even Holly—who, unlike the others, didn't have a drop of Italian blood—had to dye her naturally flaxen hair to the color and texture of a witch's hat. In ninth grade, they'd run a double-D cup up the flagpole. They'd watched from their third-floor math class as Sister Mary Vincent fought the March wind to pull it down, without allowing the flags of the order and the United States to touch the ground, because the janitor, a meek man called Vili, was too abashed to touch it. In tenth grade, once Janis and Tracy had their driver's licenses and Saturday night use of their grandfather's Bonneville, they'd gone to Benny's Beef to pick up rough, bright boys from Fenton High and go parking in the delivery lot behind the golf course, four couples on two leather bench seats. On a dare, they'd drunk whiskey Janis had pilfered from behind the bar at her father's steakhouse as they'd sat on Alphonse Capone's grave in Holy Innocents Cemetery. In eleventh grade, they'd sprayed across the principal's parking space, "We're the crew that brought the brew to the roof of St. U!" By senior year, Olivia was so madly involved with a college boy from Loyola that Tracy got horrible hives, scoring her arms into tracks of welts, because she needed to do both her and Livy's term papers for Honors English and civ. Then the Loyola boy fell for Anna Kruchenko, and Olivia used scissors from art class to cut off Anna's twenty-inch braid a week before prom.

A week after prom, Olivia's mother had a hysterectomy. While the adult women murmured darkly of "C-A," Olivia came to live at Tracy's house for a month, during which Olivia lost twenty pounds, opening huge hollows under the cheekbones that framed her huge eyes. Girls back then wore five, seven, and nine—not two and four. Plu-skinny as rote was not yet ordained. But Olivia's wraithlike beauty drove boys to fight over her like rutting elk, sometimes on the sidewalk in front of Tracy's house. And though Livy had almost never again allowed herself to be anything but concave, she confessed to Tracy that she had made a holy vow to eat nothing but bread if her mother would live, that she had been shoveling peas and pork chops into her table napkin every night. Those nights had been the only time Tracy had ever seen Olivia cry. She had not cried even in the hospital in Florence.

Their principal, Mother Bernard, had to explain to her young sisters (and there were young nuns then, though fewer each year) that there were two kinds of bad girls. One kind did not possess the DNA to turn out bad, and one kind did. The Godmothers were the former. They would grow up to be teachers, parents, and professionals. Perhaps one of them would even have a vocation.

The young nuns prayed that if one of them did, she'd be a Benedictine and cloistered for life.

But in everything but this one matter, Mother Bernard had been exactly correct. Holly was a nurse and the mother of twins. Janis stayed home with her two daughters until they reached high school age and was only now resuscitating her event-planning business, which she ran from home. Tracy taught gym classes in the gym where she'd learned to play basketball. And Olivia! Olivia had made of herself something remarkable, although only by dint of looks and luck. When they spoke of Olivia, it was always Holly who pointed out that Olivia had not discovered radium, she had simply married up.

Still, despite Holly's protests, it was true: The others' lives had been cut from a single pattern—different only because one might have chosen short sleeves, another a scooped neck.

They'd all grown up in Westbrook, a bumper suburb on the hip of Chicago that Holly once called the town without a soul.

All their parents were ten-minute immigrants from the west side, with nothing but blue-collar grit and the best intentions for their children. Janis's father built the Grub Steak and threw in on founding a golf club even before he and the other town fathers got around to building their own church. All the girls were bused to St. Ursula in Belleview one town over, all the boys to Fenton in Parkside. An elementary school was built the second year that Westbrook was incorporated. But no one would have considered anything but parochial school for his or her children.

Janis's and Tracy's fathers were brothers who'd married cousins. Among the two families' six children, Janis and Tracy were the only girls and were raised essentially as sisters. The eight Loccario grandchildren still celebrated their birthdays at Tony's restaurant, the Grub Steak. After a martini, he would recall for them when Westbrook had no strip malls or coffee joints: It was a cluster of houses surrounded by forlorn prairie, with distant moans and grumbles from the freight trains that rattled the china in everyone's hutch and the bewildered hoots of owls perched on bulldozers. There were prairie fires and muskrat. Janis always said Grandpa made the children believe they'd been pioneers in North Dakota.

When the time came, Tracy went to Champaign on a basketball scholarship. Janis went to Triton Junior College and toyed with marketing, as well as with every boy in a twenty-mile radius. Janis was so winsome with her thick auburn blunt cut and her perky rear end that Tracy couldn't believe they'd come from the same gene pool. Janis turned Dave on and off like a faucet until, in dental school, he made a play for a sassy classmate.

Rapidly, Janis had given her hand but, unlike Tracy, not her last name. Dave's surname was Chawson. "It might be dental," Janis opined, "but it's not musical." Olivia, meanwhile, had turned a junior-year-abroad romance in Italy into a romance. Even the ending had been appropriately tragic, hence Livy's triste return to her homeland.

"She's going to have to sit on my lap if we're going to fit that stuff in here," Holly groused as Olivia began the prodigious task of overseeing the loading of her luggage. *Put that there—no, no, that has glass in it—on top, that's right. . . .*

"At least you won't feel her," Janis said. "Do you think she weighs a hundred pounds?"

"*Why* are *we* taking *her* on a cruise?" Holly asked sotto voce.

As only a teacher could do, Tracy gave Holly the Look. She whispered, "Because she's a widow, and we love her, and for your information, she paid for everything except the airfare! Be nice!"

It was Tracy's loyalty, not Olivia's royalty, that inspired this devotion, which drove Holly mad. She had been by far the more affectionate friend, the one who never failed to write Tracy when Tracy was downstate at school, who went to see her play, and fail, in the quarterfinals at state, who welcomed baby Cammie home with a hand-smocked cradle skirt and coverlet, who never forgot a birthday, who co-hosted Tracy's Christmas open house. Yet nothing was too good for Olivia. Holly understood, but she did not accept. . . .

Tracy's daughter, Cammie, would later say that had it not been for the tendency of *everyone* except Holly to oblige Olivia's noblesse, things might have turned out another way. Lives might have drifted on, uninspired, perhaps, but unscarred.

But in that moment, as the three of them piled out of the car and engulfed Olivia, the umbrella of years collapsed over them and bound them close. They were again a complete set. The ineradicable tenderness and surplus of memories they shared were all that mattered.

"Do you believe I've just flown nine hours and I'm going to turn around and fly nine more tomorrow?" Olivia asked. "All because of you nutballs?"

"Is that an Italian word?" Holly asked.

"Nuttaballa," Olivia said.

"But you're a jet-setter," Janis said. "You used to fly to Paris for a weekend to shop."

"Europe is teeny. The sea is big," said Olivia.

"You were always profound," Holly said with a grin.

And they pranced and hugged again.

Day Two

Lenny went home to his family for the short breaks between charters.

It was only fitting. Lenny was the captain, and Michel, though he carried the title of captain for the benefit of their guests, was well aware that this was a fiction. Michel was only working his way toward buying into a half share of *Opus*. And he had a long way to go.

Lenny would jump in the van that would meet him at the harbor and drive him to a meadow outside the town of Charlotte Amalie. There was a meadow there and a dusty track that led to a four-room house, built of stucco and air, where sisal rugs and buckwheat-filled mattresses and pillows made up most of the decor. All that a strong breeze might not blow away were the massive ebony dining set given them as a wedding gift and the love between forty-six-year-old Lenny and his twenty-six-year-old Polynesian wife, Meherio.

After the navy, after having been a master carpenter in Colorado, and a horse trainer, and latterly skipper of a dive boat, Lenny had married the first woman he'd ever actually loved. It seemed to Michel that Lenny had taken his time about it. But he'd made up for lost years. In this place of paper lanterns and passing fancies, Lenny now had the aggregate all men long for: a lifework, a love, a child.

And he had Michel, a partner for whom any erstwhile loner would be grateful. Lenny relied on Michel. Though Michel's experience was shallow, his instincts were keen.

Just before the pumper arrived to flush out the heads, Michel accepted with grace the four one-hundred-dollar bills pressed into his hands by their debarking clients, a retired military diver, his wife, and their two grown sons. He hoped, as he hoisted their luggage, they would not want to linger and chat.

There was so much to do.

He knew that his prescience about a certain sail's likelihood of giving out—in a certain place at a certain time—was clumsy compared with Lenny's. The stitched place on the *Opus*'s mainsail wasn't as long as Michel's fingernail, but Lenny had spotted it and had it double sewn. A new sail would cost the gross revenue of two charters of four guests, twenty thousand dollars. When it came to *Opus*, Lenny was as discerning and alert to every sound and activity as a mother was to a newborn. Although they were betting against the odds, Lenny was confident that the weather would continue to pour forth honeyed days and warm, spangled nights. But Michel knew that June could be dicey, and storms could roar out of navy night skies. Still, the extra six thousand paid by the woman who wanted these dates was needed money. It would help tide them over in the off-season. Lenny and Meherio would travel to Trinidad, where Lenny would work for five months as a scuba instructor. Michel would help Quinn Reilly, running the pub for him while Quinn made his annual pilgrimage to Ireland to see his ninety-year-old mother and father. Michel would live upstairs from the bar in a spartan room. Every penny he squirreled away would put them closer to transferring ownership of the boat from the Bank of America to themselves.

So with determination, and a certain resignation, Michel tied on a bandanna and attacked the boat, grimy and smeared after a week of close-quarters occupancy. It was always an unsavory record of a fine time: smells, spills, hair, and trash. This was okay. The maintenance he did was nothing compared with what Lenny had done on his own, in the restoration of *Opus*. She'd been towed into St. Thomas by a salvager, a derelict, abandoned by her elderly owners after a fire off Tortola. Two days in the inflatable with a handheld radio and a two-liter bottle of Diet Coke had doused the couple's fire for the seafaring life. Lenny had claimed her for dimes on the dollar.

As he bagged trash, Michel watched as Lenny, unable to wait, leapt over the side of the boat and waded up to the place where Meherio waited in the parking lot. She had tied a tangerine-and-violet pareu with a gold ring beneath her breasts. Her breasts were like bronzed pears. Their baby son was hitched on her hip in a sling. Meherio's sister, who owned one of the local van taxis, had brought her to the landing. Michel had to believe that Meherio was indifferent in bed or never washed her feet. Otherwise it would be impossible to live with a woman so radiant and apparently imperturbable and not succumb to worship.

Michel thought of the Australian girl who sold opals at the studio between Reilly's and the outdoor market. The Australian girl was blond and curvaceous and had a grating tendency to hum show tunes, even during sex. Although she gave rambunctiously of her body to Michel, she took care that he left no fingerprints on her heart. This wounded Michel, because although he did not love her, he wanted her to love him.

He shook his head to banish the daydreams of the ways in which Meherio and Lenny would spend their next hours, just as he opened the windows in the cabins to ventilate them.

He checked the battery levels, did a test of the radio, made sure the bilge was dry, checked the amas to make sure the canned goods and batteries were in good order, put the charts for the upcoming crossing in a waterproof zip folder on Lenny's desk in the cockpit, turned all the lights on and off and replaced a few burned-out bulbs, yanked on the jib and ran the sheets, topped off the tanks with wash water. Barely anything had been used on the last charter, since the wife of the military diver wanted no more than to eat restaurant meals each night and toddle between St. John and St. Thomas with their string shopping bags. They would refuel again at Soper's Hole, no reason now. He checked the rigging and lines for frayed places and inspected the ground tackle. Then he began to scrub—floors, toilets, seats, and then, with fresh rags, the stovetop, refrigerator, oven, and, finally, the deep triangular saloon, all furnished in fine maple. He collected his trash bags and leapt out to bin them, vacuumed and brushed the overstuffed cushions, and stripped the beds and table linens for Meherio to launder.

Every time he cleaned *Opus*, he marveled that this gleaming and magnificent creature, a fifty-three-foot trimaran with hulls as graceful as archangels' wings, had once been a crusted wreck. Lenny had spared nothing, bartering his own sweat work and, later, Meherio's sewing for the finest leavings of other wrecks. The cockpit and steps were furnished in teak and brass. The windows were etched with musical notes. The double-bed berths felt like small rooms, not submarine bunks. In a pinch, they'd had a smaller guest, perhaps a child up for adventure, bunk in one of the amas, the side hulls, without ever disturbing the portion Lenny had walled off in one for his emergency locker, in the other for his canned goods. Lenny had taken every opportunity to pull in light and configure space. Even Michel's smaller berth, and Lenny's, which lay aft, could be opened to combine into one lavish suite. *Opus* would run a nimble eight knots with good winds, in flight like the gull she was. Michel had seen her do eleven when only they were aboard.

Michel and Lenny met while both worked on the same huge dive boat. One day, both of them made the simultaneous observation—looking out over the roiling and bobbing sunburned bodies of divers in every shape and size—that this sight put them in mind of the sinking of *Titanic*. In the following days, they appraised and admired each other. Michel envied Lenny his instinctive sea skill, a preternatural sense of what might glide from behind a rock, his scent for a squall that no radar could detect. Lenny valued Michel's utter patience with fools. He had a knack for knowing what people needed before they knew why they were as disgruntled as hungry toddlers: be it a joke, a compliment, some casual assurance, a snack, a word of encouragement. He could jolly an Italian hotdog out of his determination to go down alone, when Lenny had to walk away from the fool's bravado just to keep his temper. He could stop short of coddling the most egregiously wealthy German burgher and remain genial without obsequiousness. At the end of the day, Michel's pockets bulged with tips. Before *Opus* was even seaworthy, Lenny asked Michel to consider throwing in with him. And though Lenny had scores of acquaintances, a year later he had chosen Michel to be best man at his wedding.

Michel finished a cursory inventory of the batteries and winches, the dozens of small rings that could rupture, clips and clamps that could work their way free, whatever could crack or slacken or snap, and sat down to make his list of provisions.

As he gathered food, he would also shop for gossip among his friends. He would have a beer with Quinn Reilly, owner of Reilly's Irish Pub and Hard Goods on Rosalia Street, and listen to Quinn's lamentations about the girl he was trying to woo (in more than one sense) away from his rival at Charlotte Amalie's other Irish bar, The Quiet Man. He would convince the baker, Marie, to trim his hair in exchange for a thrilling tale about two brothers who'd gotten drunk and knifed each other on their rented sailboat. He'd heard that Avery Ben, the jeweler who had crafted a bracelet of titanium and pearl for the fiftieth birthday of Michel's mother, had sold his signature ring to a little woman from Dallas who looked as though she couldn't afford sunglasses. She didn't even dicker on the price, though Avery would have come down from forty to thirty thousand dollars! Abel, the knife sharpener, had just learned he was a grandfather, gift of his beautiful daughter in Arizona.

These were Michel's surrogate family. They looked after the bag in which he kept his grandfather's pocket watch, his books and photographs, his letters from his mother. They thought of him when he was away.

Among island immigrants, Michel was typical.

They said of people who came away from the home of their birth to live rough by the sea that they were either wanted or unwanted.

Michel was one of the latter.

Not quite the scion of a prosperous family who exported lush French designer clothing from Montreal, he had failed to finish high school, done the obligatory stint as a deejay, refused college, and ceded his place at the urbane firm of Eugène-Martin to his brother, Jean. Michel took without pride the proffered handout his father sent him every six months. It almost, but not quite, paid for essentials.

Michel trod a fine line between an established man and a vagabond. He hoped to cross it.

He had not fallen into drug use or filth, like the American boy, Asa, whose parents were millionaires ten times over. Asa stood behind a pushcart with blank eyes and clean hands, selling fruit ices, and would do this until he was an old man. Michel took risks but also cared for himself. He went to mass when he was in port and visited the doctor every six months. If he had to save up to see a dentist, he did. He flew home to his family at Christmas.

His first stop would be Reilly's, where he would trade on that old friendship for a favor. Friendships grew old quickly in these salt islands, where so many stayed for so little time. As he wandered into the perpetual gloom of the tavern, Michel called to Quinn, "You'll have to open the hardware for me. I need can openers. We've let the last one rust up."

"You let it rust or did Lenny?" Quinn asked. "Does he know?"

Michel cast his eyes down, and Quinn nodded in sympathy. Never once would they need to open the tinned food or rip apart the freeze-dried ready-to-eat military meals that Lenny insisted on buying, calling them good nutrition at a great price. But Lenny would be furious if he knew that there was only one working can opener on *Opus*, that Michel had left the last can openers in storage too long without attention. The coruscating air worked away at everything.

Because it was his day off, Quinn was on his fifth pint and it not yet noon, so he insisted that Michel come back the following morning. Michel told him about their charter: four American ladies who'd been friends since school days, a crossing from St. Thomas to Grenada, lots of free sailing, and not much of the boredom of putting in and out for trinkets. The ladies would amuse themselves—reading, sunning, gossiping. He and Len would provide the occasional dive or tale, a board game or a movie on a rainy night. There would be no honeymooners at postnuptial war or carping teenagers.

Michel bade Quinn good-bye and told him to look for his return in a few weeks, give or take. Upon leaving the pub, he began to work his way down Rosalia Street, into the market, and onto Center Cove Road, adroitly hoisting cases of bottled water and wine into the back of Lenny's pitted old Dodge truck. He caught himself hoping that four American ladies could *somehow* provide a bit of amusement. For three months, he'd brought his fluent bonhomie to bear on newlyweds who shook the boat with their moans and spats, family reunions of families who would have been better off dismembered, even six squabbling Boy Guides or Scouts or whatever they were called in the States. He'd laughed when he'd seen one of Lenny's notes in the log they kept in a cursory way: "Weather, sailing fine. Guests loud."

Michel glanced at his list.

"Drinks with little umbrellas," Bridget, the charter broker, had written. Lots of them. To amuse Michel, she'd drawn a little sketch of a lady in a bikini with a martini glass as big as she was. One of the ladies, Tracy, was a vegetarian who sometimes ate fish. All were coffee drinkers. No absurd egg or wheat or peanut allergies. Michel leaned on the truck hood and added liqueurs to the usual checklist and a fierce, good rum, Barbancourt white from Haiti, some Australian wines, shellfish, and chicken. No spices were wanting. In the morning, he would buy his produce, when the market food was new, eggs, bread, and vegetables, just enough for the first couple of days. They would not load up for the whole crossing now, but pick up more stores in St. John, because Lenny was fanatic about quality. Lenny would chart the course, bake cinnamon rolls, make flawless eggs Benedict, poach monkfish in lemongrass and wine, chop vegetables for gazpacho, braise Cuban beef with fried plantains. He would keep the drinks tart sweet and plentiful, snowy with chopped ice. Michel would tell the jokes and lead the dives, strip off his shirt when hauling on the halyards to make it look like hard work and give the old gals a bit of an eyeful.

One of the women was a certified diver.

One had proposed to try a dive.

Ten tanks, and the compressor would do. More than do.

He must not forget the can opener. And peanut butter was running low. He scribbled a note.

Michel picked up the bedding from Meherio.

By the time the ladies were settling into their rooms at the Golden Iguana tonight, Michel would have played with Lenny's baby, Anthony, phoned his mother, spent an hour in the bed of the Australian girl, brought aboard and stored everything but the morning produce and bakery, and have thrown himself into his cabin for a rapturous twelve-hour sleep.

After he made the beds, read a page of Tom Wolfe, and began to drift off, Michel hoped the ladies' swimsuits would not have skirts. This vexed him unreasonably. American women were too fat, as a rule, but Michel preferred the ones who let it be rather than try to hide it.

"We've been thinking," said Cammie, entering the room in one huge step and throwing herself facedown into the foam mattress of her parents' bed. "We've been thinking of taking a semester off and traveling."

Tracy ignored her daughter, except to notice that her hip-hugger shorts, scantily built from gray sweatshirt material, read mau i across the butt in letters nearly as long as the shorts themselves. Tracy made a mental note to pinch her cousin Janis when she saw her in a few hours for bringing the shorts to Cammie from a dental convention.

"Trent and me. We don't have a real plan yet. But Kenny might come, too. And we'd only go to safe places. *Civilized* countries. Ireland, Scotland, Wales, France, India."

India, Tracy thought. Teeming streets, emaciated babies, and portly, protected rats swaggering about, river sluggish with ashes and dung. She bit her tongue mentally, thinking, I just want to get out of the house.

"We were thinking . . . ," Cammie went on.

"Hmmm," Tracy murmured.

Kenny, short for Kendra, was a girl, Cammie's roommate at the University of Minnesota. They'd known each other from Westbrook. Kenny had played volleyball at the public school against Cammie's team at St. Ursula's.

Tracy had heard this song before. The summer after senior year, Cammie and Kenny decided to backpack across Europe, as Jim had "back in the day." That had been an easy one to nix. Cammie wouldn't turn eighteen until early May: There was no way she was going abroad alone. But were Tracy to say now what she thought of the revived plan—which was that times had changed since "back in the day," that backpackers were perceived not as charmed and harmless waifs (if they ever had been), but as prey—Cammie would have her opening. So she gritted her teeth and went on rolling cotton garments, like swaddled babies in miniature, laying each in her open duffel. Through the open window, the shrieks of a few children playing next door in an inflatable pool roused her teacher's warning ear. But soon she heard the lowered tones of a mother. Mmm, she thought, laying aside a bright periwinkle sleeveless shell that was only a year old. "Bring no clothes you'd be heartbroken to see ruined," the packing instructions had read. Cammie sighed gustily and rolled over onto her back, her navel ring winking at Tracy like a drawn dagger.

Kendra was a good, solid girl. Tracy was sure that Kendra's parents knew nothing about this.

Trent was another matter.

They'd met Trent only twice in the six months he and Cammie had been dating, once when Tracy invited him to Easter brunch.

He'd been a boor.

He'd monopolized the conversation, eaten thirds of everything within reach, and had to leave early for his grandparents' annual egg roll on their lawn in Lake Geneva. ("Grandfather started it when he was a state senator, and now it's mostly for the rug rats, but of course, we all have to show the colors!") No *particular* words hinted that Trent saw himself and his cousins as the Illinois equivalent of the Kennedys. It was obvious. They had no idea whether he was nice or simply well dressed and good-looking. He looked like a Viking. Tracy could see the point of the pure hormonal allure. But when Tracy asked after Trent during the weekly phone calls she made to Cammie—which Cammie sometimes returned, often at 11:00 p.m.—all her daughter said was, "He's good."

But that was all she said about anything.

Jim and Tracy agreed that it was irrational for them to have taken such a serious dislike to a harmless kid after a combined total of ninety minutes of conversation. He was just so . . . self-consciously patrician. Jim met guys he imagined were like Trent's father every week—guys building third homes, guys building whole developments of third homes for other guys like themselves. And it would always be all Jim could do to contain his gut loathing. Tracy didn't feel quite so strongly as all that. But the kid was pretentious. Trent's family lived in what he casually referred to as "the slums of Kenilworth," a town where twenty-five-year-old lawyers pulled down twice the annual income Jim and Tracy made together. Trent's former girlfriend had invented a bike seat for women and was already a millionaire. Trent's father had made so much money in the market, he'd retired at fifty and played polo. Trent wore loafers without socks.

"I know I'm nuts, Trace," Jim told his wife, "but I think this little prick is slumming with Camille. I think he sees her as the hot number from the wrong side of the tracks. I mean, for Christ's sake, polo!"

Tracy stared at Cammie's asinine navel ring and thought, What the hell do I care? Why did she let the disdain her exquisite girl child felt for her sweep through her like an infection? Why did Cammie's obvious and even clumsy attempts to push Tracy's buttons never fail? Was it because Camille still seemed like an exotic bird that Tracy had somehow, with paws as clumsy as oven mitts, extracted from a net of complexities and raised with an eyedropper? Was it because it had taken a scant two months of college—only until Thanksgiving—to transform her daughter from a bright, fluttering ribbon into a razor strop and that it had gone downhill from there? Tracy could consider this philosophically. But when Cam still curled herself nonchalantly into the curve of her father's arm (and stiffened when Tracy hugged her), it hurt. That was all there was to it.

I just want to leave, she thought. Let her go to India.

It was all good. Tracy took a nice, cleansing breath.

Cammie had just turned *nineteen*. Most girls rebelled a good three years before that. Tracy was *lucky*. They'd had a long run of mother-and-daughter amity. They had stored memories that would one day make the two of them chuckle indulgently over this awful time. Cammie would come around in time. When she had her own kids. People said so. If Cammie changed her mind as often as she changed her clothes, this was normal. If she longed to break open the door of her lovingly constructed cage, so be it.

Her deskmate at school had a daughter who was a cokehead. A woman in her book group had a son who'd spent two full years making elaborate computer printouts of quarterly grades for a college he'd never attended. Cammie had a future and enjoyed a rather frenetic and modestly alcoholic social life that made Tracy grateful she didn't know more about it. It was all normal. And shitty.

Tracy zipped her duffel closed with room to spare. "You want lunch?" she asked Cammie. "I'm making a salad—"

"Don't you want to make some asshole objection? Or were you even listening?"

"I was listening, Cam. Don't swear. I mean, please don't swear."

"Dad traveled all over the world before you guys got married. He would never have done it if he hadn't done it when he was young. And I'm ten times as streetwise as Dad was."

"No doubt," Tracy said, thinking that Cammie was as streetwise as a gherkin in a sealed jar. *She* had grown up more streetwise than her child. Cammie had been raised as solicitously as a rare orchid. "But you're not twenty, either."

"Why do I even try with you?" Camille asked with a sigh. "Kenny's parents trust her."

"We trust you."

"Uh, sure."

"We don't trust other people." Tracy felt the transmitted thrill of Cammie's triumph. She'd gotten a rise out of her mother.

"Don't you ever get tired of saying that?" Cammie demanded.

Actually, Tracy thought, I do get tired of saying that. She switched leads.

"And you have the money saved for this. . . ."

"But you see," Cammie said, "we wouldn't need that much. A few shirts, a skirt for looking at churches, sunglasses and scarves, a sweater and one of those jackets you scrunch up, one good pair of walking shoes . . ."

On the bitten tongue of her mind, Tracy totted up two, three, four hundred dollars. And that was without bras or underwear. But who would need those?

"I mean emergency money," she said to Cammie.

"I have my credit card."

"You have your father's credit card in your name."

"Can you *think* of anything else to bitch about? Okay, I tried. This discussion is over."

What discussion was that? Tracy thought. But she couldn't rein in her impulse to ask, "What about insurance, Cam? What if you got so sick in one of these civilized countries that you had to be hospitalized? What about the chance our health insurance for you will run out if you're gone one minute longer than a full year from school?"

"A year? Are you deaf? Did I say a year? Or a *semester*? Butt out, Mom. I brought this up . . . just to be polite. I can do this if I want to. Why do you have to stomp on everything until you squash the fun out of it!"

"Cam, nobody wants her kid to drop out of school. You make it sound like prison," Tracy said. "You like school. You always have."

"It is prison," Camille retorted. "And maybe, duh, I'm not the way I've 'always' been. I think three-quarters of school is total bullshit."

"Don't swear," Tracy said reflexively.

"Oh, fuck, Mother. Bullshit is hardly swearing!"

Tracy felt a telltale pulse at her temples. "How's the job going?"

"I love being with Dad," Cammie said sullenly. Jim was a senior partner in an architectural firm. "I even love my hard hat."

"And you don't want to do what Dad does yourself?"

Camille nicked at her thumbnail. "I do, someday."

"Well, then . . ."

"Well, then what? Jesus, I'm not talking about joining an ashram. And I'm not eloping with Trent! Do you think I'd want to end up like you did, twenty with a baby?" Camille mocked her, glee shining from her obsidian eyes. Cammie's magnificent eyes were so dark that when she was an infant, the pediatrician had a hard time distinguishing her iris from the pupil. "Go back to your packing, Mom. Sorry I brought it up. I was under the impression we could talk."

"Cammie," Tracy pleaded, "we can talk. I just think of . . . you crying in some cold street in Edinburgh or Delhi . . . ditched by . . . somebody or other."

"Let's just forget it. Please! I hate it when you turn on the guilt."

"Okay, I'm sorry. You tried to talk to me, and I lectured you. . . ."

"You think? You're always saying, Talk to me, Cammie, talk to me. How's school, Cammie? Anything new, Cammie? Are you keeping up in graphics, Cammie? Just go back to folding. You're a great folder. Look at those . . . Bermuda shorts."

"They are not Bermuda shorts," Tracy said with deep forbearance. "They're ordinary long shorts."

"They're blue-and-purple plaid, Mother! I'll bet you have a purple polo shirt to go with." In fact, Tracy did.

"They're a modest plaid, one pair. The others are solid colors. I have jeans. I have a rain jacket. I have two swimsuits, both with low backs and high necks—"

"Those shorts will make your butt look as big as the garage. And it isn't, so why would you buy them?"

"Because guess what, honey? I don't care. I'm going sailing with my friends, and I don't care who looks at my butt."

"If you don't care, why do you walk forty miles a day on the treadmill?"

"It's cardiovascular. So you don't kill me before my time," Tracy answered, sitting on the bed and smiling at Camille, who promptly popped up.

Tracy wondered if Cammie knew that her mother would go on thinking about their altercation for days. Cammie would forget it by nightfall.

Tracy further wondered if Trent was just a convenient hometown honey. Or was it first love, like a sock in the solar plexus, a virus in the soul, its side effect a kind of luxurious sun blindness? Was Cammie now the queen of blow jobs? Was Trent her first? Jim had been Tracy's first, the summer after high school. And despite two other hapless adventures at college in Champaign, he'd been her last. Tracy looked at the indignant, departing rear end of her beautiful daughter. Cammie sent a histrionic look over one shoulder. Cammie's square chin was softened by lips people now paid to have replicated by cosmetic surgeons. She had lathe-turned shins, a model's rapturous belly, and long, long black hair that glinted blue in the sun. She was so absorbed with making a haughty exit that she nearly fell off her four-inch-thick flip-flops—"guaranteed" to banish cellulite for only $29.95.

What boy wouldn't want her simply on sight?

Yet Cammie was a smart girl. She'd already declared engineering her major, to Jim's nearly fatuous gratitude. Jim had spent hours stroking the left brain of his older child, with math games, dismantling and reassembling phones, and complex wooden puzzles. He'd bragged to his own father that his daughter could fix an engine the way other girls could braid their hair. (Grandpa was not impressed.) It was, perhaps ironically, the way Tracy liked to think that Ted, a high school junior, came by his love of anything outdoor and physical from his mother.

How dull I must seem to my daughter, Tracy thought as she went into the kitchen and began to wash and slice lettuce and tomato. Would she have been so rude to her own mother? Unthinkable. So ruthless with her mother's emotions? Unthinkable. In her sophomore year of college, at the age Camille was right now, Tracy, at least technically, had to have an abortion. It wasn't even her choice. She and Jim had used double protection, not knowing that this was more, rather than less, dangerous. And they would have gotten married right then if they'd had the chance: They had married the following year. But the pregnancy was ectopic, a fairly major surgery that compromised her fertility. Alone in the hospital, with only Jim to comfort her, unable to confide the fact of her surgery to her family, grateful at least that she was not a minor who would have had to have her parents' permission, Tracy had mourned and ached. But still, she would no more have told her mother than have invited her to watch the operation. Her mother had never even seen Tracy's scar. Her mother had never seen Tracy unclothed since Tracy was eleven. Had Cammie needed an abortion, Tracy theorized, she would have *run* home from the University of Minnesota to more fully torment Tracy with the fact.

Of course, Tracy and her mother had more in common. And less.

By the time she was not much older than Cammie, Tracy was married and a mother—just as her own mother had been married and had given birth to Tracy's younger brother, Edward, by the time she was twenty-one. As she'd once quietly explained to Tracy, when Tracy announced her decision to go to four-year college, "Girls in my set went to typing school then." She'd been so obviously and utterly relieved when Jim and Tracy married. And Tracy knew full well the reason why. Her mother feared that Tracy—just shy of six feet tall and as broad across the shoulders as Jim—would end her days as a stereotype, the sturdy maiden phys ed instructor, the basketball coach in low heels and polyester suits, sexually ambivalent, sporting a tight perm and joining bus tours to the Napa Valley.

But though their lenses on life were different, Tracy had never stood toe-to-toe with her mother and cawed insults at her, had never stormed out of the house not to return for two days, never ripped down her handmade Swiss dot curtains and replaced them with mothy black velvet panels too long for the windows or rolled up her eyelet quilt and found a spread that looked to have been knitted from Brillo pads. Cammie would hang up on Tracy in frustration over a single comment. Two days later, just as Tracy's gale of tears had subsided, she'd call back with a chirpy apology and a rapturous description of the strapless dress she'd found at a thrift shop. She announced her decision to smoke, because Frenchwomen did and they never died young. Panicked, Tracy and Jim discussed a way they could reach Cammie and hit on her vanity. But before she could mail off the detailed letter a physician friend had written for them about the aging effects of smoking on young skin, Cammie reported with a sigh that, after three weeks, she'd given up smoking. It made her hair smell.

Cammie had always been that way, a bit like a train on a mountainous track, a little progress, a vertiginous switchback.

But now, her disgust with all things Tracy had spread to Ted, once not only Cammie's adored younger brother, but her best pal. And that seemed utterly cruel. Ted was a mommy's boy, Cammie said behind his back. Cammie could hardly contain her disdain when her brother casually dropped a kiss on his mother's head as he headed out to baseball practice. Tracy still remembered the little girl who'd crawled into bed each morning making endearing whimpering sounds, licking the tip of Tracy's nose and calling her "the mama puppy." At this point, those memories were like a hundred paper cuts.

"Salad's ready," she called to Cammie. When Cammie flounced into the room, Tracy said, "I really am the dullest person alive, Cam. But in a way, it's on purpose." She felt Cammie stop, listening. "Most people look forward to their excitement more than they enjoy it. So I try not to anticipate too much, and I usually end up surprised by how happy little things make me. Now, take Aunt Olivia, she always had adventures. Each one was bigger than the one before. And it seemed to me that she was always bored."

Cammie replied, "At least she was always hot. She's a really sexy Euro woman. She wouldn't wear plaid shorts."

Despite themselves, they both laughed.

"Weren't you ever wild, Mom?" Cammie pleaded. "Like, for a day? You must have had ten minutes of passion when you were twenty. You married Dad. You had me."

"I *tried* to have you," Tracy said, thinking, Yes, I was wild. I was a daredevil . . . of a sort. "And being able to try to get pregnant, instead of being afraid of it, like other girls, probably made me like sex more. I was married. So, yeah, I was free. And who says I don't still like sex?"

"Too much information," Cammie said. But a moment later, and in a different tone, she added, "Look, I know you don't like it when I swear. But you kept hounding me. Anyhow. You tried to have me. You said. But you didn't. Have me."

Cam rarely brought up her adoption. Tracy wondered, Why now?

"No, I didn't," Tracy replied, thinking, This is my chance to lay it out. Be honest. She's asking for it. And she can see my heart, as if she had eyes that performed magnetic resonance imaging; she always could. But it was not a conversation Tracy wanted to start before leaving for ten days. The moment passed. "You know, shorty, I still wouldn't have it any other way. I would never want another kid instead of you. You know that." The unexpected dazzle of Cammie's smile thrilled Tracy. She did still love being loved.

Cutting her losses, Tracy went back into her bedroom to do an idiot check for forgotten items—her reading glasses. Ah, they were on a beaded chain around her neck.

She heard Cammie begin the ritual of her muffled, multiple progression of summer morning phone calls. (Jim was at work, but he didn't care what time Cammie showed up. He didn't care if she showed up at all. He paid her anyway.) Sunlight stippled the old, scrupulously polished cheeks of every wood sprite grottoed in the walnut headboard, once Jim's German grandmother's bed. Tracy had oiled and polished it yesterday, before going to pick up Livy. She liked order in a house, even one she was leaving.

The phone rang.

"For you!" Cammie shouted up the stairs. Jim refused to have a phone in their room, so Tracy had to lean over the railing while Cammie tossed up the cordless.

". . . having a hernia," said her cousin. It sounded like Janis, though Janis's voice was unnaturally hushed, and she clearly was talking on a cell phone with her hand over the mouthpiece.

"Dave?" Tracy asked. "You mean because we're going on the trip? He's having a hernia?"

"I mean *literally* having a hernia. Bent over double. We're at St. Anne's."

Tracy sighed. Her cousin's spouse was the world's most generous man and the world's biggest baby. He'd been whining since Janis first announced she was going *alone* on a cruise with her friends. A devil of a notion needled her: This was a faked emergency. Tracy said stoutly, "Tell him to get over it. It's only ten days. Emma and Alexandra are big girls. They can look after their father. And Auntie Tess is five minutes away."

"I can't," Janis said. "It's either that or he has appendicitis. Here I am, all packed and ready to swill drinks with little umbrellas and bake myself to the bone—"

"Don't say you're not going! Jan, he's got a mother and two big daughters! Come on. Dave's mother can run farther than I can!"

Jan was silent. Then she asked, "Would you leave Jim if he had to have surgery?"

Tracy thought. "Yes," she said. "Unless it was life-threatening. Jim can take care of himself."

"Well, Dave can't," Jan moaned. "I'm so sorry, honey. He wants me to go now that he knows I won't! But he'd forgive me—every day for the rest of my life. It's not worth it!"

"Well, what are we going to do? We can't get a refund!"

"Ask Kathy. What's her name? From your book group. If you go to the airport with a doctor's letter, they'll switch over. . . ."

"I couldn't spend ten days in a confined space with Kathy! I couldn't spend ten hours. She has to have a wave machine and an eye mask. She doesn't know a crayfish from a crayon!"

"Well, there'll be real waves! Don't act like I don't want to go. . . . I'm sorry. . . ." Tracy heard Janis shift voices for an instant. "No, I'm talking to my cousin. . . . Yes, I'm sorry, I'll get right off." Jan's voice dropped. "You can't use cell phones in here. I have to go to the lab with him now—"

"This was for us, the four of us! For Olivia!"

"I can't, I can't, I can't!" Jan whispered, and hung up.

Tracy threw the phone on the floor. The battery popped out.

This day was already shot, and it was barely noon. There you had it! What long-awaited day ever really lived up to its promise? But those tickets had cost big money! Olivia wouldn't fly anything but first class, and though it hadn't been disastrous for Tracy and Jim, it had been a stretch. Jim was setting aside every spare nickel in hopes of starting his own company within a year or two. More than that, a wasted ticket would peck at Tracy's precise nature, casting a shadow over the entire trip. Janis would pay for the ticket. But that wasn't the point. The crew had prepared accommodations for four guests.

Wait. She thought briefly of an alternative, then rejected it. Camille *had* learned to dive when she was nine, visiting Tracy's mother in Florida. She'd dived in Mexico with her girlfriends—a weeklong substitute for the last proposed trek around the world. How could she phrase this to Cammie?

I don't suppose you'd like to go on a sailing trip with me and your godmothers?

I've got a surprise, Cammie!

Cammie, want to see the Virgin Islands, run off from your job for a while?

But did she even want Cammie along?

Yes, a chance for togetherness. But also the possibility of being trapped on a boat with a kid who could go into a sulk as suddenly as a six-year-old.

It was moot. If Tracy made the suggestion, Camille would snort from her deepest recesses. In fact, she was already on her way out. Tracy could hear her moving about, hear the jingle of her keys. "Cam, wait," Tracy called. "That was Aunt Jan. She can't go. Uncle David—"

"I heard," Camille said. "I wish I could leave my job. I'd love to see the islands. As *if* you'd let me come."

Shocked, Tracy suggested slowly, "You could talk to Dad. It did cross my mind. You love Aunt Holly."

"He counts on me, Mom."

Tracy thought ruefully of how long it would have taken Cammie to ditch her mother had Tracy been working, as she often did, in the summer program at St. U's. Cammie would have cut out at the speed of light.

"I guess I could bring it up with him," Cammie went on. "I was just going to run over to the office. But I forgot to check my e-mail. Let me do that first. Let me think about it. I would hate to let Dad down."

"Well, that's good, Cam. I wouldn't want you to."

Tracy sat down hard on the bed. Suddenly she was stultifyingly sleepy. She could barely keep her eyes propped. They were to leave for the airport in six hours and land in St. Thomas after midnight. She had to get a move on. Damn! Yet she had time for twenty minutes. A power nap, the kind for which Jim kept an airline pillow and blanket in the bottom drawer of his filing cabinet. Jim said a ten-minute snore and a huge cup of coffee gave him hours of pep.

Jim was the kind of man who still used words like "pep."

Tracy woke, as befuddled in era as in real time. History seemed to have rearranged itself as she slept.

Next to her lay Camille, not simply on the bed, but on Tracy's side of the bed, so as to be closer to her mother. Cammie's black hair was a vine spread over the snowy linen, prompting Tracy to involuntary thoughts of fairy tales and princesses who slept on and on. Tracy didn't know how long she'd napped. But the clock on her dresser, impossibly, read 2:00 p.m. Jim would be here in an hour. Cammie had lain down next to her and apparently, as Tracy had, fallen asleep like a cat in the sun. Almost without moving, Tracy made a quick visual examination of her daughter. Camille had changed into pink high school sweatpants and an oversize T-shirt that had been Ted's. Depression clothes. A raw, red-fisted place was rubbed under Cammie's eye.

Cam was here for a reason. Tracy shook her shoulder. "I have to get up and get ready, but what's the matter, Cam?"

"Nothing." Cammie feigned a yawn. She hadn't been asleep. She'd been doing what Tracy did when she was down in the dumps, pressing her eyes and mind closed as best she could—trying to make herself unconscious.

"Come on," Tracy urged her. "I have to go soon."

"Well, you don't have to worry," Cammie replied in a tart little voice. "I'm not going to take a semester. I'm going back to school."

"What . . . ? Good. But why?"

"Well, so I check my e-mail . . ."

"And . . ."

"And what he says, Trent, is that it has nothing to do with me, blah blah, I'm perfect, blah blah, if he was two people and could have two lives, blah blah . . ."

"It doesn't get worse if you just say it, Cam."

"He went back to his country club, bike-race rich bitch blond girlfriend, Mama! And not now! Before now! They *talked it over*, and I can just imagine how they talked it over, at spring break, and then he came over and had dinner with us! But he wrote me just now that he could tell I was getting serious . . . about traveling, and he just had to tell me the truth. . . ."

"With an e-mail, the cowardly shit."

"I don't want to talk about it."

"I don't blame you."

"Thanks, Mama," Cammie said, two words Tracy hadn't expected to hear until the day Cammie asked her to baby-sit for her first grandchild. Another switchback.

Tentatively, Tracy put her arm around Cammie, who backed up against her mother's ribs in offhand intimacy and then began to cry. Tracy began to cry, too, careful, precise rivulets from the corners of her eyes that she did not allow to build up into sobs, so as not to let her stomach shudder. That would betray her and ruin this precious parenthesis of intimacy.

"What would help?" she finally asked Cammie.

"Nothing."

"Not even . . . going to the Virgin Islands?"

Camille lay silent. "I don't know. I feel like I'd be a bitch."

"Cam, you could make a deal with yourself to be a bitch after you get back. Come on. Ask your father about me being a bitch. He says I have ten days a year when he'd like to keep me in a box and feed me through the opening. You felt this . . . breakup coming, that was all. Didn't you?"

"Don't bug me about it. And don't be so fucking understanding. It's like you're my guidance counselor."

"I'm your mother. Same thing."

"Not if you were a shitty mother. Trent's mother is a total bitch. She was never home one weekend in his life when he was a kid. Once, she left him with the nanny and went to Hawaii with his father and their friends for Christmas! But he totally adores her."

That's how it works, Tracy thought, riffling in her mind through the dozens of kids she'd known growing up, kids whose parents had treated them as devotedly as farm dogs treated their litters—only to get endless worship from those children in return.

"Let's just find out what Dad would think. He's still at the office. He won't be leaving for a while to drive me to the airport."

"What about Olivia and Aunt Holly?"

"They would love to have you along." Tracy had to stop herself from crossing her fingers behind her back. She had no idea if this was the case. "Here, I'll talk to Dad."

For Jim, it turned out to be hardly worth the price of the phone call. If Camille had wanted to climb K2, Jim would now be ordering snow goggles. While still talking to her husband, who was gathering his things to come home, Tracy gave Camille a thumbs-up. "You'd better get going. You need a ton of stuff on this list. Sunscreen. A wind jacket—"

"Oh, Mom," Cammie said, "I can get everything I need in a carry-on. Can I use Ted's sports bag? One of them?"

"You might need more than a carry-on."

"No, my clothes are small." Tracy's glance was rueful. "Oh, come on. I'll bring a sundress. I'll bring a windbreaker. On the other hand, if you're going to be the clothing police, I don't have to go."

"Of course you will," Tracy said, thinking, Why am I conceding? The spoiled little shit!

A tendril of fleeting regret for things only she and her two friends could have talked about alone—and now would be able to talk about only when Cammie was out of earshot—shot up from her heart. But Cam would probably be out of earshot, stretched out oiled like a sardine with her iPod glued to her head, more often than not. "It'll be fun, honey."

"At least I won't have to sit here and cry and eat Dove bars while he's dancing at the club with . . . Britt. Imagine naming your kid Britt."

"You're resilient, Cam. Or you're faking it."

"I'm faking it."

"I couldn't fake it if I felt the way you did."

"That's because you're feeble," said Camille, but she grinned.

Day Three

Holly had never experienced such abandoned, joyous sleep as she did at the Golden Iguana Hotel in St. Thomas, and sleep was Holly's holy communion. Though the place looked like an adobe-walled restaurant in Juárez, with pink walls and garish, outsize primitive drawings on the walls, the bed was better than at the best Westin, and the room seemed to have been pumped full of some delicious narcotic. Holly didn't recognize the scent, but if she could have, she would have stripped and bathed in it. She said, "I do believe that this is about the third time in twelve years I have not waked to the fragrance of dirty sweat socks. What is that wonderful smell?"

"It's frangipani," Tracy said. "It's more powerful at night. I looked it up while you were asleep." She held up a little green guidebook. "I never saw anyone sleep like you do, Hols. I thought I'd have to hold a mirror to your face to see if you were breathing."

"It's a never fail equation. Holly minus Ian and Evan equals the sleep of the dead. What do you think we do when we stay at a hotel overnight and leave them with you?"

"I thought you . . . you know, caught up on your sex life. You can hardly do it at home, except when they're at soccer. Twelve-year-olds have sharp ears."

"When we go to a hotel, we sleep, Trace. We *sleep*. If we do bump our old bodies together in the morning, we're grateful. If we just lie there and watch the news and get room service, we're grateful. It's the sleep that matters. The Japanese consider sleep a sacrament. Twelve-year-olds don't just have sharp ears. They're as demanding and messy as racehorses. And now, I'm starving. Let's go eat. Do I have to put on a bra?"

"You pay three hundred bucks for nothing but a bed to sleep on?" She tried to remember the last time she and Jim had stayed in a hotel without screwing their brains out.

"Yeah, and I'm going to spend as much time on that boat as I can fast asleep."

"You're crazy! You'd miss seeing . . . the Virgin Islands and the Caribbean to lie on a boat and sleep?"

"In a second," Holly said. "I didn't say the whole time. Just lots of it."

As they searched for the promised continental breakfast, Holly explained that some women's guilty pleasure was reading romance novels. And some women's guilty pleasure was chocolate or recording a week's worth of *Oprah* and watching it all on Sunday. But hers was to sleep as much as possible during the day. She couldn't do it at home. While the boys were in school, she had to study for the degree in nurse administration she was trying to finish. Sleep during the day, for Holly, was like a venial sin, as delicious as it was wrong; and this trip had given her peremptory absolution. When she slept during the day, Holly had the sense that others were taking care of the world. She was temporarily off duty. Nights often left her anxious, prowling, frightening even her own cats. The moment that her twin twelve-year-old sons— great, loud, lolloping things, like human retrievers, towering over Holly—were out of earshot, she could instantly lose consciousness. Her only affliction with Evan and Ian was a surfeit of adoration. She suffered too much on their behalf. Each time one rode the bench during a game, or there was a birthday party to which only one was invited, Holly anguished to a degree she considered pathological. She often told Tracy that the boys had broken her. She wasn't built for the mental torture of motherhood.

"But you adore them. You're a wonderful mother," Tracy

would tell her when Holly confessed this. "I wanted six. I'd have another one in a New York second if I could."

"You could," Holly invariably replied. "Movie stars do, at our age. Even regular people. You could adopt a baby from China. I love being a mother, too. I just can't take the worry."

Tracy had thought about it, about adopting another child. She knew Jim would. With Ted a junior in high school, he was already mourning the prospect of an empty nest. But Tracy had started so young. That baby time seemed to have receded into the sweet bygone. Holly, who'd waited until she was nearly thirty, was still in the thick of middle school.

"Ev is better at most things than Ian," she said to Tracy as they roamed what seemed a labyrinth of halls, more than a hotel with twelve rooms could rightfully contain. "He gets grades eas- ily, and he's more athletic. But Ian has all the friends. When Ian gets invited to hang with some kids, and Ev is left out, I don't just feel sorry for him, I want to murder the little bastards. Like Kevin Wastawicky. Do you know him?" Tracy, trying to listen and navigate, nodded. "The little bastard downloads songs onto discs and sells them for ten bucks to the other sixth graders. He's going to end up in the federal pen. So, two months ago he in- vites Ian to his birthday party. Shit, they live next door. I see Ev looking out the window. I say, 'Do you want to go to the mall?' He shakes his head. He wants to be out there, with all the kids playing with Kevin's new radio-controlled plane. I will give Ian credit. He came home early and went to the park with Ev to kick the ball around."

"So, he's good, too," Tracy comforted her. "They're brothers."

"They're twins. It's different. It's eerie. It was like Ian could hear Ev's thoughts the whole time he was at that party."

"I think I can hear Ted's thoughts sometimes. And what I can't hear he tells me."

"Ted is one of the world's great humans."

"You're just saying that because you know . . . she isn't."

"Cammie? I adore Cammie. What are you talking about?"

"She was . . . on a tear yesterday. Until she found out she could come with us. I guess she had an excuse. Trent dumped her."

"Well, you said he was a pompous ass. I guess if I were nineteen, I'd cheer up over a free trip on a yacht, too."

"Do you mind she came?"

"Why would I? She's not going to get in the way. She's always been like that. She could talk to her toys for hours, remember? Even when she was two? At Christmas, she got down on the floor with Evan and Ian and started building that robot."

"Well, thanks for that much. I asked her because it wasn't just like she was her ordinary bitchy self. She had a reason."

Holly shrugged and said, "She seems to have gotten over it. She was chatty Cathy on the plane. 'Aunt Holly, I got the cutest this. . . . Aunt Holly, do you think Dave would whiten my teeth for cheap?' And I have to say, I thought some of it was funny, Trace. 'Why do engineers have to take English? It's bullshit. Why do I have to read Eugene O'Neill? No wonder he was a drunk. If I was this boring, I'd want to be drunk, too. And oh boy, Virginia Woolf is next. I have it with me. They should call this course People So Boring They Committed Suicide as Public Service.' What I can't figure is that guy dumping Cammie. For who? Lindsay Lohan? Even my boys think Cammie's hotter than a movie star; and they don't have hormones. You should hear them tell their friends, 'You should see our cousin . . . though she's not . . . really. . . .'"

"But as good as cousins. You know, Hols, guys must have changed since we were young, because if a girl looked like Cammie when we were kids, she could write her own ticket. Didn't have to have two brain cells to rub together. I thought it was weird, too, but apparently this was a Pater-and-Mater-wanted-a-royal-marriage thing. Not that this kid is an Astor or anything, but Kenilworth . . ."

"Versus the near west side . . ."

"Exactly, and I had been so furious with her an hour before, because she was on my case about wanting to go backpacking around the world instead of going back to college. . . . It boils down to . . . she can't stand me."

"Trace, she's crazy about you. Otherwise, why would she bother to torment you so creatively?" Holly scoffed, and then pointed out, "This alleged breakfast is mythological. It said it was by the pool. There is no pool."

"She told me yesterday she thinks I've never felt passion. Can you imagine telling Heidi that you thought she'd never felt passion?" Heidi was Holly's mother, dead now for two years.

"Not if I wanted to stay conscious until the end of the sentence. My mother called me a potty mouth for telling her I had a bladder infection. And I was married!"

"I don't expect Cam to be perfect, Hols. And I know it has something to do with that she was . . ."

"That she's adopted."

"That she *was* adopted, Holly. How many times have I told you that I don't think of adoption as a condition?"

"Well, I don't think of Cammie as being adopted. . . ."

"There you go! That's like saying, Oh, I never notice that she limps!"

"Tracy, you know what I mean."

"I do, and I don't like it much."

"You know I don't mean any harm."

"Of course I do. I'm being a bitch. But we were so close. All the way through high school. Cam was a renegade, but, geez, she loved me and Jim and Ted. Now she loves Jim. Period."

"Ted's out?"

"Ted's definitely out. Ted is the enemy because he likes me."

"Ted isn't . . . wasn't adopted."

"Like that's my fault? God, when my period stopped, I thought I had cancer! I never thought we'd have another kid."

"Maybe she just needs some time. Would it help her to . . . know?"

"Do you think so?"

"It's a tough call, Trace. It could make her better or . . . worse. I mean, keeping something like that from her for so long. . . ."

"I didn't really have a choice. That was the condition. That I not tell her."

"Well, I don't want to hear any more about Cammie. She'll grow up and we won't even remember anything but the bikinis she bought on this trip. She was in a great mood this morning," Holly said. Cammie and Livy went for a run and breakfast. After that, Holly said, Olivia wanted to buy a few opals.

"Buy a few opals?" Tracy gasped.

"That's what your daughter said. Livy saw a woman wearing a diamond bracelet last night that she liked, too."

Tracy marveled, "I was so staggered last night, I wouldn't have noticed someone who wasn't wearing anything but a diamond bracelet! You aren't even supposed to bring earrings. The pamphlet says everything gets all tossed around. You're supposed to bring minimal cosmetics, no jewelry, not even rings. I was going to get Ted a necklace, you know, a chain; but I'm waiting until we get to Grenada. I wouldn't want to buy it and lose it."

"Well, I brought maximal cosmetics," Holly continued. "I don't go to SuperSaver without mascara."

"But you'd let your boobs hang out at breakfast."

"I'll never see these people again. That cabdriver last night must have had jugs that weighed ten pounds each, and she was letting 'em rip."

"Why wouldn't they just eat the breakfast here?"

"Breakfast here wouldn't be good enough for Olivia. Not served to her." The hotel was as deserted and silent as if a neutron bomb had exploded during the night. Holly wondered how they'd find a way to pay their bill.

"Oh, Holly. Don't start. You just don't like Livy, do you," Tracy said. "There's the golden iguana," she went on, pointing at a surprisingly large lizard on the wall above her head. It blinked its gemmy eyes at them and skittered away, not quite quickly enough for Tracy. "Can't they keep them outside?"

"I don't think they get to decide," said Holly. "Lizards have their own rules." Her blond hair was standing straight up, in a halo.

Tracy smiled. Holly was a comfort in any situation—the only woman Tracy knew who never stressed a holiday, who could always stretch dinner to accommodate five more boys, simply someone, except for her anxieties as a mom, who knew how to live. Today, she resembled Ian, who had so many cowlicks that he could never get his hair to lie flat even when he smeared it with gel until it was as stiff as the old-fashioned bathing caps Sister Boniface once made them wear into the pool.

"You don't want me to tell you what I think about Olivia, Tracy," Holly said now. "That's why you always change the subject, even when you're the one who brings it up. Wait! I smell coffee. There it is, an oasis!"

Around a sharp turn, and overlooking a beautiful pool made entirely of natural rock, was a glassed-in sunroom. A breakfast bar fragrant with croissants, jam, fruit, and carafes of hot coffee, apparently placed there by elves, was daintily displayed. Tracy gratefully spread jam on a croissant and offered the plate to Holly.

Holly ate half of her pastry before she said, "Trace, when we picked Olivia up the other day, I realized that what really bothers me is that Olivia hasn't changed and we have." She held up a hand to forestall Tracy's objection. "No. I don't mean that she can afford a boob lift—and yes, Trace, I'm a nurse and she *has* had one—and we can't. Or even that we wouldn't if we could—though that is a lie, I would. She never grew up. She never had to. That bugs the crap out of me. I can't hide it. You're right. I don't like Livy. But I love Livy. I just don't romanticize her. The little girl from Westbrook who ended up the Countess . . . whatever. She was even a bitch at her own wedding," Holly said. "Remember? You have to sit here. You have to sit there! I ended up eating next to a guy who didn't speak a word of English and kept sticking his hand up my dress. Forget it, Trace. . . . This is a good pastry, nice and flaky and fresh." She patted her pouch of a belly, visible to anyone else only when she wore the tightest waists; visible, in Holly's imagination, from passenger aircraft flying at thirty thousand feet. "Are you finished, Trace?"

Tracy had fallen quiet.

She was thinking of Anna Maria Seno, Olivia's mother. She was thinking of an ordinary afternoon, when Anna Maria told Olivia frankly, and in front of Tracy, that Joey was wanted but that she, Olivia, born ten years later, had been an accident. Not content to stop there, she went on to explain that women in their thirties didn't have babies then. She, Anna Maria, worried Olivia would come out with two heads and have to spend her whole life in an adult-size crib with the sisters at Mount Carmel. She thought of the stifling small rooms in the Seno house, four rooms crammed with plastic trees in tubs and plastic philodendrons on wood-grained plastic stands, with chairs and ottomans wrapped in plastic like oversize sandwiches, from the lampshades to the golden tufted love seats. ("She could probably hose down the whole house," Olivia once told Tracy. "If she could only figure out a way to get plastic on the walls.") The religious icons in every room. The Sacred Heart. The sere knots from previous Palm Sundays tacked above the beds. The Virgin in her grotto lighted with a blue bulb, her staring ovoid face with its follow-you eyes terrifying Tracy every time she stayed over and had to use the bathroom.

They'd made over a closet for Olivia.

It was a big, deep closet, and Sal, Olivia's father, was a carpenter. He made her a built-in bed, and the built-in drawers and shelves above it were so clever, it was as though he were a New Yorker who'd had access to all the space-saving tricks of an Ikea store. Livy had bins for her books, her own Princess phone, and even high racks for her winter coats. But it was still a closet. Joey had bunk beds, a stereo, red shag carpeting, shelves of Pony League trophies and photos, walls for posters, a big bureau with an ornate cross on the wall above it, heavy silver that could have come from the Vatican. Nothing was too good for Joey.

Tracy remembered the afternoon that Olivia came home to learn that her father and mother had decided that Olivia's dog, Pickles, had dug around the peonies once too often. Sal had taken her to the vet to be put to sleep during lunch hour. When Olivia screamed, Anna Maria slapped her. She closed the windows and made lemonade from lemons, telling Olivia to shut up, the whole neighborhood would hear, that Pickles was dirty and shed and probably gave Olivia allergies. But Olivia continued to scream until she threw up.

Anna Maria and Sal, Tracy thought, who closed their bedroom door after dinner and watched television alone, while Joey and his friends combed their hair in front of the bathroom mirror or, later, teased Olivia and, Tracy suspected, worse. Joey could do no wrong.

All Olivia had to do to get her share of attention was become royalty.

Holly didn't get it. No one but Tracy did.

Tracy remembered helping Anna Maria out of the train at Montespertoli for the wedding, Anna Maria rubbing her legs and saying that Olivia had her nerve wearing white.

"You don't know her like I do," Tracy said suddenly. There was no need to give "her" a name.

"Obviously," Holly conceded.

"I don't mean that. She didn't always have it easy."

"None of us did, Trace. But we didn't turn out like 'Mirror, mirror on the wall . . .'"

"You're jealous."

"No doubt," Holly said. "Or maybe not. Whatever I think, it's between us. I'm not going to wreck the trip. I am grateful to her for it."

Tracy looked at her waterproof watch, with its double dials. She would always know what time it was at home. "The van comes in forty-five minutes. Do you think they're back?"

Tracy and Holly made their way back to their room to gather up their toothbrushes and pajamas. "Before they come, Tracy," Holly said suddenly, laying a hand on her friend's arm. "Don't think anything I said about Olivia has to do with Cammie."

"Look!" Cammie cried just then, darting into the room. "Look what Aunt Olivia bought me! And don't start up about it! I have reasons why this is important. . . ." Tracy and Olivia exchanged glances over Cammie's head. Then Tracy exclaimed over the bracelet, dainty as a double thickness of wire but set with a row of deep indigo sapphires, each bezeled, each slightly different from the others, submerged lights lambent within each stone.

Tracy couldn't imagine what it had cost.

It had never bothered her, over the years, when Olivia sent Camille vast boxes of Italian cashmere and lace-trimmed under-wear. It was sweet; it was extravagant; it was at a distance. Looking at them together there, their dark heads bent acquisitively over the bracelet Cammie was displaying, she felt an old spike stir in her heart, searching for a place to let blood. Olivia had outshone her. Olivia always shined the brightest.

"Get a few opals there, Liv?" Holly asked.

Livy nodded. "Wait until you see."

Unable to restrain themselves, Tracy and Holly leaned in as Livy slowly opened a folded velvet case. The stones, large and small, ranged from rusty to fiery peach and green within, oval and square cut. They gleamed like small planets against the black pile of the material.

"What in the world are you going to do with them?" Tracy asked. "You already have more jewelry than the Queen Mother."

"Earrings, a pendant, maybe. A really big brooch. I'll need

to send them somewhere. I wouldn't trust anyone in Chicago. I know a man in Montespertoli. The Virgin Islands are renowned for opals," said Olivia. "You don't pass up what's there. It's like not bringing home wine from Italy."

They all fell silent out of respect. Franco Montefalco had bottled spectacular wines and olive oil on their Umbrian estate. But Olivia seemed cheerful chatting about her former life. If she was in mourning, it was a mourning of her own variety. She had wrapped herself in a black-on-black sarong, but the skin that showed through the panel carved out of her maillot was flawless, taut, not the sickly white of winter-hidden skin, but a kind of exquisite beige, like fine antique ivory.

"I know a beautiful goldsmith on Rush Street," said Tracy.

"Really?"

"Yes. He made me a ring for our twentieth anniversary, from a drawing Jim did. You could look him up."

"Maybe I will, Trace. I'm an American again now," said Olivia. "Thanks. I don't mean to sound like a snob."

"Even though you are," Holly said. She wrinkled her nose at Tracy and laughed.

"Admitted," said Olivia.

"Well, looks like you've got yourself a find there, missy," Tracy said, turning to Camille.

"A woman should have a few pieces of really good jewelry, Mom," Cammie said. "It's timeless."

"Did you just make that up?" Tracy teased.

"Tracy, I haven't seen my godchild in eight years," Olivia said, genuinely beseeching. "Naturally I'm going to want to spoil her."

"She's my goddaughter, too, and I saw her yesterday," said Holly. "She was bitching because her mother drove too slow. I didn't have the same impulse." Cammie arranged her face in a mock glare of rage at Holly. "Well, admit it, Cam. You sometimes treat your mother like a queen would treat her subject. A mean queen." Cammie stuck out her tongue.

"Admitted," she said. "But Aunt Holly," she added, tickling Holly under the ribs until Holly slapped her hand away, "you *made* me a cashmere sweater for Christmas. I practically didn't have to wear a coat all year, it's so warm and beautiful. That's as expensive as a bracelet if you count the time."

Holly softened, leaning over to pull Cammie's baseball cap over her eyes.

"Well, you can't bring this stuff with us," Tracy said nervously. "We're going to have to ask this fellow . . . here, wherever he is, to FedEx it home."

"No way! I'm never taking it off!" Cammie said.

"I wouldn't trust anything this costly with any delivery service," Olivia said. "Please, Tracy, let her wear it. We shouldn't put beautiful things away, out of sight. They need to be seen, the way pearls need to breathe. Look at it against her arm. It's marvelous, and with her new swimsuit and her hair . . ." The swimsuit had been Olivia's gift also, a full ounce of azure material that mercifully covered critical clefts and hillocks. Between Janis's and Olivia's gifts, Camille would be nude by the end of next semester.

Tracy made a ritual protest. "Olivia! If you're going to give her something like that . . ."

"I never gave her a birthday present when she turned nineteen—"

"You gave her a check for a thousand dollars! And that was a month ago!"

"For college, Mom!" Cammie protested.

"And that wasn't a *gift*! A gift is a tribute to beauty! Franco used to say that," Olivia chimed in. "And I'm taking mine, too. Who knows how honest this innkeeper is?"

They heard the van bleat in the lot.

"I haven't even brushed my hair or showered!" Camille wailed.

"You're just going to get dirty anyway," Tracy said. "It's . . . a boat. And anyway, if we don't go right now, we'll miss it. Aren't you going to put on clothes, Liv?" she asked, grabbing her luggage.

Olivia smiled lazily and asked, "Why?"

They went to a brothel. They had done this the other time. It was a place Ernesto liked to go, the young man guessed, whenever they had these jobs. He bragged that he took at least two girls each time. It was hard to miss the word for "two." Carlo had a wife, but he went also.

A meager place, fouled by years of debauchery, the building was no more than a shack made of planks like broken teeth, the roof tar paper covered with cheap, irregular shingles. The dirt floor looked as though it were raked occasionally. But it had a superb zinc bar and buttery leather bar stools. Drinks were glasses of unnamed clear spirits with no mixer or, curiously, a root beer the owner made.

Some of the girls were so young that they got sick if they drank booze, so they were given root beer before they were led upstairs.

None of them was old enough for this life, the young man thought. No one could ever be old enough for it. It could only make people old.

They were all stolen girls, of many races. He had no idea how they came to be here, on this island, the name of which he didn't even know. There seemed to be houses, with lights strung on poles, Christmas lights of some sort, back among the trees; but he and Ernesto and Carlo did not go farther back, only to this place, on the lip of the harbor. The young man sat there for hours with a book and waited.

One of the girls, a blond child, had come three times to the young American and pleaded urgently in a language he assumed was Dutch. The time before, he had paid to sit alone with her in her four-by-six room and given her a pencil, trying to urge her to draw him a map. She was so frightened and, he suspected, already infected with something that she could do nothing but weep and cling to him, repeating something that sounded like "Mutti? . . . Mutti?" which the young man assumed meant the same thing in any language. He stroked her hair and wished he knew how to buy her and send her home. Perhaps he could find a translator somewhere, at a resort, perhaps. But the owner had come then, before the time he had paid for was up, and with his *pistola* ordered the girl downstairs.

The young man wondered if she would be here when they returned after their drop. There had been another child, blond like this one but taller and older, who had been there the other time but was now vanished. The woman the young man assumed was the owner's wife was kind to him, calling him "Brad Pitts" because he wore his hair cut short and treating him, he supposed, with a sort of maternal good humor. But when he used gestures to ask about the taller, older blond girl, she waved him away. Was there a place worse than this where girls went when their freshness crumpled and their eyes went void even of the fear? He supposed there was a place worse than anywhere. At least here he had seen the older woman, called Alita, dab salve on the girls' cracked lips and lay towels filled with ice against the bruises on their necks.

Why did he think about her? She was, the young man consoled himself, ruined anyway. Was there something of her that reminded him of his sister?

All of them were lost. He was lost. He was done with this mess. The tent pole in his life had passed when he'd gone to state in the long jump. His mother had wept for pride. His father, who'd been the alternate on the Olympic team in the medley relay, had nodded.

He wondered when his partners would be finished here. He wanted only to roll himself in his sleeping bag and mosquito netting and sleep in a hollow near the boat.

The young man didn't have sex with whores. He had been

with only three women, one a good girl in El Salvador, one an American he'd met on a beach, one the girl he loved the summer after she finished high school. Last he'd heard, the girl, who rode her own horse, was at college in Massachusetts. She had always wanted to go to Massachusetts, she'd told him, to see what she could see in the sea, sea, sea. They had grown up more or less together, in upstate New York, near the Hudson River. He sat at the bar, nursing a sugar-rimmed gin and smoking, after Ernesto and Carlo crept up the narrow staircase. His book was boring. The other men began to laugh as the ceiling light swayed.

The young man was through with this.

This run to rendezvous with the man they knew only as Chief would be his last.

Chief, a massive man, perhaps American Indian as well as African, met them in a rich man's boat between New York and Honduras off an unnamed island that was little more than a heap of rocks and scrub, in a cigar boat the young man knew must have cost hundreds of thousands. It soared without ever seeming to touch the water, and the motor was a whisper. Their cargo was double bound in rubber wrap, then wrapped again in the tarpaulin that had covered the engine and stored in lockers meant to hold fish. Once they shifted it over to him, Chief would wordlessly hand them thicknesses of cash, also wrapped in waterproof rubber, and speed away to the deserted spot on the coast where he handed it off to the man who had originally involved the young man in this scheme, a lawyer who knew the young man's father. The lawyer took it to his expensive house on Long Island and then into the city. He sold it to men in garish suits, thousands of miles from the Salvadoran fields where the poppies grew.

It was at that moment, when they turned to make their way back, that the young man believed, the last time, that Carlo and Ernesto would murder him.

But they had not. Perhaps it was because he was quiet and spoke English. Perhaps they thought he would be useful if they ran into the navy or Coast Guard with no papers and a boat painted with grainy black house paint. On the way back, they laughed and drank and grew sleepy and stoned, and the young man took the tiller and steered through a night and a day and a day and a night—it sounded like one of the books he had read to his little sister when she was small—back to Santo Domingo. After they drove a spike through the bottom of the *yola* to sink her, the young man would put on a wet suit. But Ernesto and Carlo, burly and agile as seals, would swim to land, sometimes as far as half a mile. When the time came, they would find another *yola* or a power-boat, a small sailing ship, perhaps this time without an owner who needed killing. After they divided the money, they would part. Some time would pass before Ernesto sent another note and the money for the young man to fly to Honduras to the post office box near the boardinghouse where the young man stayed, in relative luxury by the standards of Santo Domingo. Between these times, the young man went diving and hiking. He loved the quiet green splendor of the land. And the people were friendly.

He remembered the late afternoon, the punishing sun just beginning to relent, when he was walking home from a swim at his parents' summer house in the Hamptons. His father's friend was headed in the opposite direction on the beach road of powdery sand. They had passed each other with a nod when the man called to him. The young man turned back.

"What do you do?" the man asked. The young man shrugged. "You don't go to school. You don't work, your dad says, for more than a month at a time."

"He's probably right," the young man said.

"You're not a big talker. You keep to yourself. Maybe you'd like the chance to make some real money."

"How?"

"I have a friend, a sideline. It's not for . . ." The old man, his father's friend, brayed, a laugh that made the young man's flesh creep even in memory. "For the faint of heart. But it's relatively safe, and it's a chance to get away from Mommy and Daddy and see something. . . ."

"What would I do?"

"I'll explain that later. Come and meet me next week at Circe, say, one o'clock on Tuesday? We'll talk then. Get a haircut first."

The young man had gone to the restaurant. He hadn't known why, but his resolve to do so hardened when, that night after they'd crossed paths on the beach road, he'd overheard the man and his father discussing "the boy's future."

"It's a little hard to see right now," his father had said to the accompanying music of ice cubes chinking. "You might be able to see it with a telescope. It's minuscule. Maybe future perfect."

He'd cut his hair and worn a sport coat over a cashmere turtleneck, though the day was sweltering. And when the friend told him what his "sideline" was, the young man realized he had known this, on some back shelf in his brain, for a very long time. And he loathed himself even as he agreed.

In his room, now, which was clean and sparse, there was a line of books set up on the scarred table, held in place at either end by two beautiful, sea-polished rocks. Behind one book, identical to twelve others in a set, there was a notch in the wall. Beneath the notch was a tiny square of plaster the young man removed and repainted each time he went on a trip. Inside the little square cut, wrapped in a sandwich bag, was seven thousand dollars. With this and his part of the take from this trip, the young man would go and live in Missoula, Montana. It seemed like a good place.

The next time a note came to the post office box near the hostel, the young man would not come to ask for it.

The captain was handsome in his way, Olivia thought, balding but wiry and weathered, as her Franco had been. The young man with the French accent was spectacular, his arms and back rippling through his torn shirt as he tossed their duffels and even her soft-sided suitcase—Olivia did not *own* a duffel bag—into the little motorboat. Olivia saw the young man appraising Cammie and the way that Cammie, full-eyed, looked evenly back at him and then away, extravagantly and deliberately uninterested. Olivia doubted *that*. It was the oldest trick in the book, and Cammie clearly knew that it usually worked. Olivia couldn't blame her. With a body like that . . . and such eyes! But she also caught the minute negative shake of the head from the captain, Lenny, and the younger man's downcast acknowledgment. Cammie wasn't jailbait, but it evidently was policy not to play with the cubs of such a mother bear as Tracy.

They motored out to the yacht. It was beautiful, larger in size but equal in luxury to the one on which she and Franco sailed the Mediterranean with their friends the Antoninis.

"The air is so good," she said in French.

The young man brightened. "*Parlez-vous français?*" he asked.

"*Pas mal*," Olivia replied.

"Welcome to your home for the next ten days, our home for all time," Lenny said gallantly. "Before we leave, even before we toast, I want to give you the mandatory tour."

They put their things away quickly, and gathered on the seats where the life jackets were stored. "*Opus* is a trimaran," Lenny told them. "You're probably more familiar with catamarans, which only have two hulls. She has three fiberglass hulls. So she's really a monohull with little helpers. And if you hear us refer to her that way, as 'her,' it's not because we're sexist, it's because it's a habit, a tradition. Every rope on a boat becomes a 'line' the moment you leave the marina. So when you hear us say to cast off the lines, this is ancient talk. It's like what pilots say to air traffic controllers. We say the prescribed words, even to each other, it's second nature. This is the mainsail, and this is what we call the genny. We'll open them up for you and do some sailing out there, without the motor. Have any of you sailed?"

"I've only traveled on motor yachts. With friends who lived

on them, and a little one we had," said Olivia. "I loved sleeping outside. They had hammocks with awnings over them."

"We have hammocks, kind of, but no awnings," Lenny said. "But there's no rain forecast."

Tracy raised a finger. "I just sailed my grandpa's Hobie Cat when I was a girl; and my daughter has sailed a little. Is . . . Can she dive, too? Do you have enough? I know she wasn't supposed to come. She's a certified diver, too. We brought our cards."

"Sure," Lenny said. "Before we cross to Grenada, we'll go to Norman Island. Norman Island is the real Treasure Island, the model for Robert Louis Stevenson's book. His grandfather went to sea when he was a boy, and they say Stevenson basically copied down his grandpa's diary. You can dive into the caves there and then surface and see where pirates carved their names on the wall. They say there's a cache of gold bars, Spanish treasure, still deep in one of those walls, with the insignia of the queen, Isabella, still on it."

"They say the buried treasure thing wherever you go. I don't mean it's not probably true," said Cammie. "Maybe we'll find it, Aunt Liv. We can buy our own island."

Holly grimaced. "Do you think anyone else has ever thought of that?"

"Aunt Holly! You'd love your own island. . . . You could have a whole soccer team on it. But not little boys. *Big* boys!" Cammie teased.

"Zip it," Holly said, blushing. The way she stared at the boys' soccer coaches was an old joke among them.

"People do," Lenny continued. "Buy their own islands, that is. Hermit millionaires or movie stars own some of these islands. Sidney Poitier owns one. He was born on Cat Island, I think. Mel Gibson owns one. He has his own church there. You can't go ashore on those—except if you're invited or you need shelter from a storm. That's a covenant here. If you need help, none of the privacy rules apply."

"How do you know which ones are inhabited?" Cammie asked.

"The charts say so, the maps," Lenny told her. "The thing is, they change all the time. There's one island out there . . . is it Salt Island? There used to be a whole colony of houses. Now they're all boarded up. The government was selling them for fifty dollars. I should have bought one. If there's a bad storm, sometimes people dump those places. Sometimes they even just leave. Leave million-dollar houses for the lizards. Think of that."

He moved on briskly to a discussion of the safety equipment. Olivia tuned out, offering herself to the sensual rocking of the boat. It was all just in case, as the man said. No reason, but they were required to do it.

Tracy sharpened up, keen as a bird dog. Middle-school teachers followed directions.

"These are the flares," he said, "to attract attention if we should poison ourselves with my cooking. Every seat on this boat is a floating cushion. The radios. The VHF handheld radios. We communicate with each other and closer boats. The SSB. That has a channel for everything, from emergency to gossip. The GPS, not that you'll ever need it, we have the main one right in the nav station. There are batteries, tons of them, in this rubber locker. They're all fresh. The SSB and the handhelds use batteries. They can even run off the solar panel; if you hook 'em up, you'll get a trickle of juice. The life vests are in here. We always wear some kind of shoes because it can get slippery. This is the emergency position-indicating radio beacon, the EPIRB. If you get lost and have to jump overboard in the inflatable, or if we just get sick of you and throw you over, turn this on, and when it hits the water, it'll indicate where you are, so somebody might pick you up." He grinned. "Kidding. The lecture is almost over, kiddies. You'll never have to use it. Here are the beach towels. And sunscreen. If you run out, we have every kind under, well, the sun. And you really need it. Even dark-skinned people do. Here's the first aid stuff, bandages, cold packs, antibiotics we're not supposed to have, painkillers we're not supposed to have . . ."

"How do people really get in trouble, like, fall overboard?" Cammie asked.

"Well," Lenny said, "I hope this isn't crude, but most guys who drown are found with their flies open, because they tried to stand up on the side and take a leak and took a plunge instead. A boat that doesn't even seem to be moving goes pretty fast. And once you're under a boat, you can get your head conked by the rudder . . ."

Olivia's attention drifted back when the tone in Lenny's voice changed—clearly nearing the end of his speech. He was describing the wings of the trimaran, the amas, where they kept the emergency food, knives, and can openers, waterproof boxes of chocolate bars, opening the flat doors that closed with hasps on the outside. "I'll only ask you to leave that one box alone," he said with utmost gravity, gesturing at a padlocked white locker laid two feet by three. "That's my emergency stuff. Otherwise, the boat is yours."

As he surveyed the amas, everyone detected a flat note fall in the captain's voice. Something private had stumbled between him and the younger man, who looked down at his scruffy loafers. They all caught it. "In any case," Lenny said after a thin cough. "We begin each voyage on *Opus* with a toast. Straight Moët or mimosas?" Only Tracy opted for the addition of orange juice. Olivia let one long, perfect finger touch Michel's palm briefly as she accepted the glass, and he didn't flinch. He smiled. White, perfect cubes of even teeth.

"Mom?" Cammie asked, and Tracy nodded. Cammie accepted a glass of champagne.

"Is the young girl your sister?" the young man with the accent asked Olivia.

"She's my friend's daughter, Tracy's daughter. She's my god-daughter. But I think she takes after me," Olivia replied. "I know that's impossible. But her grandfather, Tracy's dad, is a dark-haired Italian. Italian American, not like my husband. My late husband, that is."

"Ah," Michel said, "I'm so sorry for your loss." Olivia inclined her head. To fill space with words, he said, "You should sleep in the trampoline, that's our version of the hammock, on this warm a night, or at least sometime. I do. It's the most wonderful feeling on your skin."

Olivia thought, with sharp pleasure, Is he making a pass? Does he know that Camille is clearly off limits?

Not that she would take him up on it.

But, heaven knows, she might.

Didn't what happened in the islands stay in the islands? Wasn't that what Americans said now? She glanced at Holly and Tracy with sudden affection. She was an American, too, no longer the Contessa de Montefalco. A widow at forty-two. A rich widow, but that hardly mattered. Just a month after Franco died, a quick trip on a spa ship out of Milan had left her, following two weeks of seclusion, looking an easy five or ten years younger. But natural. Not like those horrible Kabuki faces she used to see in the streets of Paris. The physician was a wizard. She had been in seclusion, with no time to answer Tracy's urgent notes, forwarded to her by the villa's housekeeper.

Franco had adored her every line and bump, but the rest of the world's men were not as tolerant as Italians. Olivia did not intend to remain alone forever.

Lenny would save the reprimand for the end of the crossing.

They were only can openers. He would make sure Michel picked up extras in St. John, although he preferred American can openers. He didn't see how Michel, whom he had trained like a son, could make such a stupid mistake. There were no department stores at sea, he had told Michel. Only sailing stores where passing boats could buy rum, crackers, and sweets. It was the first thing he had told Michel. He had read to the boy from Hemingway's *Old Man and the Sea*, the part in which the starving old man wishes he had brought a rock to use with the knife to open the sustenance that sat in his hands, as closed and impenetrable as a dream.

Michel knew that can openers could save lives.

Can openers could prevent a man or a woman from slashing a wrist trying to break open a can of beans by bashing away at it, just as the old man had done.

Still, Lenny would wait.

As far as he could tell, Michel had otherwise done a splendid job, while he and Meherio lay naked under the apricot netting of their bed, diving and plunging together, laughing as Willie Nelson sang songs of longing they did not feel. Anthony had begun to crawl, and in the midst of one of their sessions of lovemaking, he had pulled himself up to peer at them. Naked, they had taken him into the bed with them, their small dolphin completing the pod.

"Do you like this baby, your son?" Meherio teased Lenny. He kissed her soft breast. "Would you perhaps like another just such as he is?"

"Someday," Lenny answered. "Whenever you want."

"Some babies come whenever *they* want," Meherio said, placing her hand on her taut belly, which Lenny noticed suddenly was ever so slightly convex. "There is one in here who wants to come in perhaps five months to see his daddy."

Lenny thought he would die from his immaculate joy. "You are too old a man to have many sons," said Meherio. "But one child isn't a family." Lenny knew that Michel thought Meherio was a beach plum, a fuck bunny in her sarongs and baggy jeans. In fact, she spoke four languages and had a splendid education, given her and her sister and brother mostly by their missionary father, a Brit reserved to the point of parody who had died two years before. Meherio mourned her father, Arthur Midwell, extravagantly, be-

cause, she said, he loved the children with learning, the only way
he knew. Meherio had learned merriment, composure, and music
from her mother, Sela, who still lived happily, but now alone, on
St. Thomas. So he and his wife had many ways to delight each
other, many hopes for growing old in grace.

For this, he had Michel, in part, to thank. He would not up-
braid him. These were kind women—so far as he could understand. He saw how Michel's face opened when he met the young
girl, the unabashed awe, and felt a gentle pity. He was also certain
that the mother would break Michel in two if he even touched
her daughter. Well, a nice, easy charter. He had made and frozen
vegetarian chili and mushroom Stroganoff, as well as several key
lime pies. Tonight, he would make wraps with braised tuna, vegetables, and peanut satay, and the puffs Meherio had taught him
to concoct from bitter chocolate and rum. He would fire up the
blender. He read the computer display. Fair winds at least through
the weekend, open skies.

Lenny loved his boat.

He wrote in the log: "Norman Island. Dive tomorrow at
Madwoman Reef and the caves. Weather fine."

Michel could tell the girl was pissed off and that it had nothing to do with the other women. She was a little impatient with
her mother—but then so was he, he admitted—and all over her
aunts in moments of affection. But she kept mostly to herself. He
caught her leaning over the rail, looking at something on the far
horizon without, Michel suspected, seeing it. Lenny called this
the "thousand-yard stare." When he spoke to her, she answered
politely but in sentences of two or three words. Probably just a
coddled rich kid who thought she was too good to spend words
on a beach bum. Still, he couldn't take his eyes off her. With
her back straight, her shoulders low, as if balancing a weight, she
walked like a tiny queen, even on a deck. And when she looked
at him, it was full on, with an absence of pretended coquetry. And

then she would smirk, as if annoyed or bored. Maybe she thought he was an old man and was disgusted by his obvious awareness of her movements. Well, he was getting to be an old man, out here. Oddly, the girl seemed most interested in the boat and in what Lenny said about it. She asked about weighting the amas, for one thing, and about the size of the motor.

Maybe she was gay.

Most girls at least *looked* at him.

But, in fairness, she was a real girl, educated, not an island girl. If he had chosen another life, perhaps even if he already owned half of this boat, perhaps this would be a girl he could do a real thing with, not a game. No, she was too good for him, except for play. And that would be her call. Playing around never did anyone any harm. So Michel worked hard at ignoring the girl. That usually worked. But she didn't seem to be working at ignoring him.

But it was just the first day. Things could improve.

When she stood on her toes to clamber up onto the bow, he couldn't help feeling those muscled calves tightening around his waist. *Lenny,* he pleaded telepathically, *give me this break.* He watched as the girl slowly, too slowly, applied oil to her arms, her fine, strong shoulders, the space between her breasts where she wore a tiny golden child's crucifix. She saw him watching, lowered her glasses, and turned on a switch deep in the coal of her eyes. But that was it. She was opening her book and actually turning the pages. Michel had to slide down into the saloon. He needed ice in his pants.

For her part, Cammie was trying to figure out how old the man with the French accent was. He could be twenty; he could be thirty. And even when she did the mime business, applying her suntan oil—a trick that usually made boys hyperventilate—he just went right on cutting his jib or whatever it was they did. Well, screw him. He was probably as interesting to talk to as a wet life preserver. She thought of Trent, briefly, irresistibly, as people reconstruct the onset of destructive storms that descend without warning. She had never given in to adages; but, Christ, it might be true that men were all the same—universally hypnotized with their own needs and universally oblivious to the rest of creation.

Michel was wondering if Lenny just *might* be persuaded to cut him a break, if things went well and the girl's mother seemed amenable. He had always ignored Michel's other games—a tryst aboard with a party of bachelorette girls (not with the bride-to-be; Michel had his standards. So, for that matter, he supposed, did the girl—although American and English girls were pretty free). There'd been a German girl on holiday with her aunt who treated the physical transaction with all the passion involved in plugging in a blender, and the most touching, an older widow, not so cool and enticing as the strange, dark, older woman on this trip, but pretty in a soft, open way. She'd come on a charter arranged by e-mail, with a group of women she'd never met. Michel had ignored her age, twice his, and her thighs, twice the size of his, and taken her into his cabin and loved her; and she'd wept and said that it was the first time she'd imagined she could again feel such things. He had a card from her later. She'd married again and had a baby. He felt happy.

Only Lenny knew. There was nothing Lenny didn't know. And he would know if Michel put moves on this girl—with the girl's protective mother, and all her aunts, on board. While appearing to be absorbed in his work, Michel made a point of eavesdropping for a while. The girl, stunner or not, was only a teenager.

Off limits. For anyone.

They motored for a while and moored in Saltpond Bay for an afternoon of swimming and sun, then dinner and overnight.

Tracy took Lenny up on his offer to motor into town and send postcards to Ted and Jan; but Michel took Cammie diving at Rhone Reef, where two coral caves lay only twenty-five feet down. She wore a wet suit over a black one-piece, but Michel was mesmerized. She didn't act like a fool, the way women did to charm a man, to invite him to touch them in the guise of helping. She had a steady, strong, horizontal stride in the water, and despite her childlike delight when a sea turtle flapped lazily past them, she didn't move to disturb it, as so many others did. He pointed out the corals, their riot of minarets and turrets, their eerie pastels, meant for no one human ever to see.

"Thank you," she said when they surfaced.

"You're a good diver."

"I've only done it a dozen times or so."

"You're a natural islander," said Michel.

"Uh, sure," Cammie said briefly.

"Where are you from?"

"Illinois."

"I've never been there."

"It's not exactly a destination," Cammie told him, toweling off. "Most people only see the inside of the airport."

"I'd like to see Chicago."

"It's okay. It's a great shopping town."

Shit, Michel thought. She was a dumb, spoiled kid.

"Are you at school?"

Cammie laughed, and to his relief, it was a nice, munificent laugh. "Is that the French way of saying college? Yes, I am. I'm studying to be an engineer." She sighed and went on, "I'll end up working in Chicago in a big building that looks exactly like the big building next to it."

"Do you want to do that?"

She laughed again. "Actually, I do! Ignore me. There's just something I can't keep out of my mind, and it puts me in a foul mood."

"This is a good place for forgetting," Michel said, listening to himself sounding like a travel poster.

"That's what I'm counting on," Cammie replied with the pursed-lip parody of a smile.

A guy? Michel thought. A serious family thing? "So why engineering?" he asked, to keep things moving.

"Well, it's like, people think of 'the environment,' that needs protecting, and they think of this. But a city is part of the environment, too. It has to be cared for. The neighborhoods have to be kept up. It has to be planned. It's not really that interesting. . . ."

"No, it is," Michel said quickly. "You're right. You don't think of a city as needing protection."

"You would if you saw the Robert Taylor housing projects," Cammie told him as she stripped off her wet suit. Michel swallowed hard, a fact Cammie noted, from the corner of her eye, with satisfaction. This guy was . . . really, really hot, whatever his age. She'd never let him know . . . but on the other hand, if she . . . whatever. Well then, next fall she could see Trent and think of his clothing-line-inventor debutante and think, Go swing on it, Trent. Maybe she could sink Trent like a shipwreck.

She slipped below to dress for dinner and came out with her hair straight and wet, without makeup, in shorts and an ordinary UM T-shirt. Michel observed that she ate with a lusty appetite. He couldn't stand women who pretended that they had no appetites so that men would find them delicate. Later, after they'd polished off the last of the key lime pie, they gathered with their mugs of coffee like children around a hearth and asked Lenny for war stories.

Before he began, Lenny said, "I want you all to know that tomorrow I'm going to have to go in and bring all your passports, because we'll be leaving the United States. By the time we get to Norman Island, we'll be in British waters. We'll go in for passport inspection twice more on this crossing. So if there are any items you need, tell me now or come along tomorrow. Okay?"

"Okay, but let's have a story. Tell us about swashbuckling and walking the plank and all that," Holly begged.

"They never did, for starters."

"What?"

"Walk the plank. It would have been a waste of a plank. If you were going to kill someone, you'd just tie his hands and feet and push him over. I don't know where the legend of the blindfold and the plank came from, unless it was personal for one of the crew, and they wanted to make it torture, to set an example."

People always longed to hear the same things, Michel thought as he began washing the dishes, politely refusing Holly's offer of help. And if you hadn't heard them before, the tales of these mysterious islands, tossed among cultures for hundreds of years . . . he had to admit they were beguiling. They wanted to hear if anyone was ever tempted to roast and eat a shipmate, about ghost ships and buccaneers. They were disappointed to learn that modern pirates were the equivalent of L.A. gangsters and that most of the illegal activity in the islands was drug smuggling.

The good part was that the islands had been filled with layer upon layer of characters out of legend since Columbus's time. They still were. And most of them were real. Blackbeard was real.

"Actually, some of the really weird things that have happened aren't written down in books," Lenny began as the women finished their second bottle of wine. Michel knew what was coming.

Lenny never tired of telling the story of the sailing ship *Annabeth,* which came alongside and hailed Lenny's friend Lee Wikowsky in 1994 on a bright, cloudless night. Michel thought Lenny was jealous of Lee, a man as plain as brown bread—that it had been he instead of Lenny who saw *Annabeth.* The moon shone so clearly, Lenny told them, that Lee could read her name and all but see the face of the man who called out to him—a man, he noticed, who was wearing suspenders.

"My wife is ill," the man called, according to Lenny. "Can you help? She's giving birth. Do you have a cook aboard?" Lenny said his friend was puzzled: a cook? He fell silent, letting the suspense simmer. Then he went on.

"Lee told them he'd been a medic in the army," Lenny finally went on. "He said, 'I can help you, if the baby's not breech, if there's help to be had. Is she bad off?'"

"'I don't think so,'" said the man. "'But she's in great pain.' That was what he said. Now, 'great pain' is a formal phrase. It's not something you hear out here every day. And Lee noticed that."

The women leaned forward, spellbound, as Lenny described how Lee ran downstairs to get his first aid kit and sharp scissors, twine, blankets, a pot for boiling water.

"I'm cold," Cammie said, though the night was warm.

"Do you want me to turn off the air conditioner?" Lenny asked.

Michel, drying his hands, slid in next to her and put a shawl from the cedar chest around her shoulders.

"Thanks," she said, reaching up. Their fingers met, his rough as horn, hers soft as petals. Damn, Michel thought. Cammie later would swear she'd seen the brief shake of the head Lenny gave— and wonder if this was his way of laying down the law to his partner. As it was, she didn't know if Michel was gay or if Trent had busted her antennae. She could usually feel the chemical jolt when a guy touched her. This guy was taking pains to treat her the same as he treated her mother.

"Are you okay now?" he asked.

"I was okay before," she said. "But thank you anyway."

"The long and short of it was," Lenny went on, "the night was dead calm. Not a breath of wind. Nowhere. And if the boat had a motor, Lee would have heard it starting. But when he came up, the boat was gone. Entirely gone. Now he was out there, where we're going to go after tomorrow. There were no natural harbors or structures the man could have slipped behind, at least slipped a whole boat behind. As far as the horizon, he couldn't see a thing, not a shadow."

"So, who was it?"

"That's the thing. We talk out here all the time, gossip and so on, using the SSB radio the way long-haul truckers do. Channel twenty-three is for emergencies. Next morning, Lee raised a guy we both knew, though he's dead now, poor soul. I was there when he had his heart attack. Tried everything. We got a portable defibrillator that season."

"Come on, come on!" Holly cried. "Not that, forgive me, I'm not sorry about your friend. I am."

Lenny smiled that smile Michel knew so well, delighted he had set the hook, that tonight they would all crane their necks at the windows to seek the black schooner *Annabeth*. "Well, this friend of ours, Jack Trijillo, Lee swears he heard him get pale over the radio when Lee mentioned the man in the suspenders. And he said, 'Let me guess, his wife was having a baby?' And Lee says, 'Well, did he come to you? Was the baby okay?' And Jack says, 'He never came to anyone. Not in this life.' Lee sort of whispers, 'What are you saying, Jack?' And by then Sharon and Reg and half of us were listening in. Jack said, real slow, 'Lee, that man is not real. Or he was, but not now. That ship sank in 1890. Check the *VI* files'—that's our newspaper, the *Virgin Islander*. He said, 'Check the files if you don't believe me. Went down with all hands—Charles Quillen, a textile merchant, his sons and their wives, his five-year-old daughter . . .'"

"And his pregnant wife," Holly said.

"And it was like . . . what? You've heard of the boat *Mary Celeste*. They found *Mary Celeste* adrift, the table set for breakfast, the food warm, the deck just covered in blood—"

"Oh, my God! I can't sleep now!" Olivia was breathing hard.

"Well, I can, and don't think you're leaving the light on!" Holly cried. "It's just a bunch of nonsense. Like the farmhouse with the lights in our neighborhood, that was there before Westbrook was a town, where the traveling preacher murdered the whole family on Thanksgiving night—"

"I'm going to sleep in the hammock," Olivia said. "Do you have a . . . what do you call it?"

"A tether?" Lenny asked. "Sure, but you might wake up all wet if we run into some waves."

"I'm pretty sturdy," Olivia said.

"Whose blood?" Cammie asked. Lenny shrugged. "It all smells to me. How could two ships so far apart see the same sailboat on the same night?"

"Were they attacked by pirates?" Holly asked.

"Nobody knows," Lenny said, clearing the glasses. "That's the most logical explanation. But, you see, it wasn't the same night, Cammie. Jack Trijillo saw *Annabeth* a full *year* before Lee did—"

"Oh, come on," Cammie said. "You just tell that to the tourists. It never happened, and you know it!"

"I only know what I was told," Lenny replied with a shrug. "And Lee, well, you'll meet Lee. He's the bartender on *Willie T.*, the most famous floating bar and restaurant in the Virgin Islands. Big freighter made over into a restaurant with a dance floor. We'll stop there tomorrow after we dive. You ask him yourself. Lee never takes a drink. Never did after that. Never known him to lie. It was just the following spring that he sold his boat and went to work on *Willie T.*, named after the pirate William Thornton. As far as *Annabeth*, this is no ancient legend. It wasn't that long ago. She was a real enough boat. And Lee's not the only one who saw her, either. I've talked to three or four people who did. Same story."

"I'm completely creeped out now!" Tracy said. "Cammie, are you ready for bed? I'm not going anywhere alone!"

Cammie and Tracy settled into their cabin quietly, and Michel saw their lights go dark within half an hour. Holly's never went on. He brushed his teeth and lay down on his neatly made bed to read.

Then he figured he should check on the countess and make sure she hadn't gone overboard. So he edged his way silently out to the foredeck. She was leaning back on both hands, her bare back long and pale, her swimsuit top hanging loose where she had opened the knot.

"Are you okay?" he asked.

"I'm fine," Olivia told him in her husky voice. "Do you smoke?"

"No one's supposed to know. One, and only once in a while."

"Me too. Do you have one?"

He sat cross-legged beside her, and she held the blanket to her chest as he cupped his hands and lit the match for her. "You should, really, I'm not having bad manners here, but you should wear a sweatsuit or something. You might get chilly," Michel said.

Olivia smoked her cigarette delicately and didn't answer. She combed her thick, wavy hair back from her face and looked up at Michel from under heavy, artfully smudged eyelids. Finally, she flicked the butt over the side, turning a quizzical face to him.

"It's biodegradable," Michel said. "I use organic."

"Now, you could lend me your sweatshirt there. I'm sure you have ten," said Olivia.

"That's fine," Michel said, reaching over his head to slip it off.

"Or, well, there are other ways to stay warm." She drew the blanket back and was naked.

Michel knew before he smiled that he would regret this. But he was nothing if not polite; and she was alluring, this odd woman, not beautiful like Cammie. It was Cammie, off limits to him, who had him unsettled in his skin and yearning. This was being offered. . . . He pulled his sweatshirt over his head, but then folded it to use as a pillow.

Day Four

Cammie woke first and set about making her own coffee.

Lenny, already dressed in a T-shirt and cutoff shorts, overtook her, guiding her to a seat in the saloon.

"You're supposed to relax," he said.

"It's so beautiful. The boat. Even the air. Where does the water come from? In the taps?"

"We have tanks filled with fresh water. Why do you ask?"

"Can you make fresh water from salt water?"

"We have a water maker, but it'd take you days to make enough for a shower."

"The salt must get to your skin."

"It does." Lenny smiled. "But my skin's shot anyhow. I didn't even wear sunscreen till my wife made me. She made me go to the doctor and get checked for melanoma before we got married. She said she didn't mind marrying an old man, but she did mind marrying a dead one."

They both laughed.

"I think you've got it pretty good."

"I do, too," Lenny said. "What do you want to do?"

"I'm studying engineering."

"Must be hard."

"It's okay. I don't like the other crap I have to do. Poetry and stuff."

"That's weird. I see a lot of college kids on our charters, with their friends or with their parents. They're all stressed about jobs. Stressed about school," Lenny said.

"Hmmm," Cammie said. "Well, I have a guaranteed job. My dad and I are going to start our own company after I'm finished."

Lenny said, "I like that part. I like being my own boss. I worry about the boat too much. And we want to make it perfect, me especially. I go nuts over it. I can't tell you how we do it. It's hard work, though I know it looks like one long vacation. But we love it here. And doing this lets us stay and have the boat."

"Yeah. But you work in paradise."

"There's a dark underbelly," Lenny told her, smiling, trying to draw her eyes from the sight of Michel, silently slipping down into his cabin. Damn, he thought. What he had heard in the night, with that third ear of his, had been genuine. Even for Michel, this was unprecedented, the first night out. Lenny didn't want this kid to know. It was distasteful. He tried to distract her by showing her where to find sugar. "A lot of people here who want to use people, or have people use them."

"Sounds like an Annie Lennox song," Cammie said. Lenny had no idea who Annie Lennox was, but he nodded.

"Do you have kids?" Cammie asked as the rich, dark blend began to drip.

"I have one kid, but not your age," said Lenny. "He's about this big. He thinks I'm king every time I give him a graham cracker." He made a two-foot span with his hands.

"A baby!" Cammie said. "My mom loves babies."

"You don't seem so bad."

"Ah, I have a dark underbelly. See, my mother and her friends? They were like this gang in high school. They have pictures of themselves with their beehives and black mini-skirts, like Catholic Goth girls. They called themselves the Godmothers. You know the movie *The Godfather*? Well, they wanted to be these total rebels. But they were these little suburban girls. I don't think any one of them ever even got a speeding ticket. When they tell stories, it's about running a stick along the metal fence at St. Dominic's monastery to make the Doberman pinschers that the monks kept there go nuts. They're ridiculous. I make fun of them."

"So your dark underbelly isn't so dark."

"I could go either way," Cammie said, pouring about half a cup of milk into her coffee.

"Why?"

"Well, for one thing, it drives my mother crazy. She never gets mad. I've been trying for nineteen years."

Lenny wondered why she was so confiding. Then he remembered being seventeen, leaving Iowa for boot camp, spilling to an old woman on the bus. There was solace in the stranger on the train, who would never see you again—like the psychological harvesting of bartenders. He could only imagine the tales Quinn Reilly collected at his pub.

"Maybe you need to cut loose for a year after college, hike across Australia, go in the Peace Corps, come here and hire out as crew. You don't appreciate a warm bed and four walls until you're soaking wet, trying to lower a sail in a hurricane."

"I was thinking about something like that. You think I'd learn my lesson then, right?"

"I did. I never felt so lonely. And free."

"You've really been in a hurricane?"

"You think?" Lenny said, and then repented. "Anyone who's spent any time here has. I've watched it suck the water up into itself and then bounce like a ball, blowing up houses everywhere it touched. Bands of clouds were pulled down into it, too. And us all the while in complete calm, all hell breaking loose two hundred yards away."

"Jesus Christ," Cammie said in a breath.

"But exciting! And once, before I was with Michel, I crewed on a boat that was in a TD-two, that's tropical depression two, and we had eighteen-foot seas. You'd just rise and fall, flip and fall. And it was a catamaran. It's pretty easy to flip over a catamaran, because when they get going, they go up on one hull. Stuff was flying all over, charts and papers, food, cupboard doors coming off, cans of food rolling around."

"Wow. What a memory to have. If you live," Cammie said, but not fearfully, more as if she were rolling the idea around in her mouth, tasting it.

"What's a memory if you live?" Tracy asked, ducking her head as she picked her way from the riotous bright of the sunny morning into the shadows of the saloon. "I slept like the dead."

"People do or they don't," Lenny told her. "Me, I like the rocking. It comforts me. Other people say it disorients them."

"Mom, Lenny has a little baby," Cammie said. "Does your wife come out with you?"

"Not very much. Meherio likes her ocean three feet deep and warm. We'll sail to Trinidad this winter, though. When it's just your family, it's easier."

"That's a beautiful name," Tracy said as Lenny thought, What nice people. Except the pretty twist up in the hammock. Who was, for all he knew, nice as well. She just didn't strike him that way. Tracy was what his mother would have called a "handsome woman," strong and attractive without any of her daughter's glamour. "What does it mean?"

"Meherio? In Maori, I think it means a mermaid or one who brings gifts. She's brought them to me. We're expecting again."

"Congratulations," Tracy told him, accepting her coffee.

"Can we dive right after breakfast?" Cammie asked.

"Not right after. As soon as I do the paperwork and we moor, though," Lenny promised. "You two go up now. I'll bring up some cinnamon rolls in a few minutes."

Left alone, he scanned the horizon again. Something felt odd to him. Nothing was there. He called out on the SSB to find Lee, partly to see if the bar would be open and partly to ask if Lee had heard of any weather.

"You're going to make me tell that story again," Lee accused him. "Well, come on over. For the one supernatural experience in all fifty-five years of my life, it sure gets a lot of attention. And no, there's nothing out there, Len."

Still, Lenny called Sharon Gleeman, his favorite captain, next. Sixty years old and still sailing with her partner, Reginald Black, Sharon was coming in to take her boat to the Hamptons for the season after a three-week charter. Sharon had so much money, she had no need to do charters. But she loved the business. Reginald was queer as a limerick, said Sharon, who had spent her younger years with the proverbial lover in every port. But they had co-owned *Big Spender* for thirty of them. Her house in the Hamptons, where Lenny had visited, had seven bedrooms. Nothing's out there, Lenny, she told him. But she warned him not to provision too much. She had scads of food left over from a charter that was cut short by a family emergency for one of the guests.

"What do I owe you?" Lenny asked, ritually.

"A visit at Christmas," Sharon replied. "It's you or the sharks, Len, for the food. I don't mind giving it to you."

They said good-bye fondly. It must be the news of Meherio's having the new baby that had him edgy, Lenny thought.

Olivia wandered out of her cabin. She wore loose white pants and a see-through white shirt over a bathing suit. She gulped down two cups of coffee and picked at a roll.

"Did you sleep well?" Lenny asked.

"In a sense," she said, looking him right in the eye. "This boat agrees with me."

"I heard you lived in Italy."

"My husband died six months ago. He had pancreatic cancer."

"I'm sorry," Lenny said, his mind shying from the image of any life without Meherio.

Olivia said, "I'm glad he's at peace. There's that, at least. His partner bought out the *fattoria,* and I came home."

"Does it feel like home?" Lenny asked.

"Not yet. But then, I've only had a day there. We came here the day after I arrived. I've only seen my mother for an afternoon."

"Do you think you'll ever feel as though it's home?"

"I don't know," Olivia said thoughtfully, breaking off another crumb. Holly had emerged from her cabin and thrown herself down on the banquette next to Tracy. "If it doesn't, I'll go back. Or somewhere else. I'm fortunate to have the choice. But when you're lonely, you want your friends around you."

"She wouldn't let us come for the funeral," Tracy said.

"Because there was no funeral. Franco was buried on his family's land, by a priest we barely knew. There was no reason."

"We could have been there for you. And brought home all that wine," Holly said, her voice muffled.

"You don't know how many cases I've sent you! Dozens and dozens! I took all the best stuff," Olivia said, and Holly pantomimed clapping her hands. Then she lowered them to her lap.

Making sure Tracy observed her generosity, Holly continued, "You should have let us come, Livy. I know you didn't have *friend* friends there."

"I was fine. We had some good acquaintances and a private nurse. It had been such a horrible death, even with all the painkillers, and he was such a happy man . . . I considered staying on and running the business. But Franco's partner bought the business and the villa from me. Franco had an ex-wife, too. Did you know that? She was very beautiful and stylish. Andrianna. She sailed. She had her own boat. *Felicia.* Happiness. She died in a storm off the Italian Riviera. She was alone."

"Sounds like Rebecca de Winter," said Holly.

"Who's Rebecca Dee Winter?" Cammie asked. The three older women sighed.

"Didn't they make them read *Rebecca*?" Holly asked.

"I have a copy," said Lenny. "I'll give it to her."

"Did she die in a sailboat?"

"Yeah. Sort of," Tracy answered.

"Ladies, if you have to make phone calls home, now's the time. After we head offshore, all that will work are the radios."

Tracy called Jim and Ted. Ted asked to speak to Cammie, and Cammie said cheerfully that she'd bring him a T-shirt. What did he want on it? She rhapsodized about the weather and told her father that she loved him and to have the temp file the building permits for the Serranos' lake house. Tracy called Janis. Dave was fine, of course, sitting up and eating tapioca pudding. It had been a smoking appendix—hardly the end of the world.

"I told you so," Tracy chided her.

"You don't have to," Janis said. "If you can take any pleasure in it, I'm absolutely miserable. It's so hot that if you were here now, you'd want to buy a condo in hell. The *dog* has a urinary tract infection. What are you doing?"

"Finishing homemade cinnamon roles and Mimosas. Then we're going diving at Norman Island, the real Treasure Island."

"I hope you drown. How's Livy?"

"She's fine, really, she's fine. I think she had time to come to grips with Franco's death before. It probably was sort of a relief. I should run. Love you, cuz."

"Love you, too. Have a ball, Trace. I mean it."

Michel appeared, looking hangdog. "Len, I've checked everything. So, should I get the tanks ready? Two are diving? One snorkeling?" Len shrugged and looked at the women.

Holly said, "I'll snorkel."

To her credit, Michel thought, she pulled a terrycloth cover-up over her head and was wearing a discreet two-piece with a veil around the middle. She wasn't like some women, who came out here and forgot they were twenty pounds overweight.

Tracy slipped out of her shorts. She wore a bright red maillot from some sensible catalog. Michel was surprised. This woman was all muscle. A moment later, Cammie emerged, glorious in her aquamarine thong bikini.

"Will I have to wear a wet suit today, Lenny?" she asked.

"Most people do. You could get scratched or stung, and the sun out here is stronger than you think. But you don't have to. I do. I'm always cold."

"I'll try without, then. I was hot in mine yesterday," Cammie said. Lenny shook his head.

"Well, sit tight. We have a little trip first. Michel will take you down. You'll see some beautiful things. Like an aquarium where all the tropical fish have grown up. Rays. Maybe a reef shark or two. Definitely. Beautiful day."

"I'm up for it," Olivia said. Michel looked more miserable. Serves him right, thought Lenny. Then Olivia added, "But I'm too tired. I need a sleep."

"I thought you said the boat agreed with you. Maybe you need some ginger pills," said Lenny, and he loped down two steps to extract a big bottle from a cabinet. "Works rings around Dramamine."

"It's not that," Olivia answered. "I just got distracted by the stars." She directed a wisp of a smile at Michel and disappeared below. No one except Cammie noticed.

Cammie stared at Michel with a slight sneer. Michel was the first to look away.

By the time they had motored to Norman Island and moored on a white day sailing buoy, it was late morning. They'd passed up Madwoman Reef as it was crowded with the last of the tourist sea-son party-hardies, and Lenny abhorred foolish divers. The sea was a mirror. The women were geared up, and Michel had gone over the cursory modes of entering the water, the rules about avoiding coral and never touching anything, except perhaps a sea cucum-ber he would give each of them to hold for a moment. Olivia was still sleeping. They opted not to wake her.

Cammie was obviously angry. She took her wide stride into the water before Michel gave her the okay and rolled over to wait, looking away.

Michel fetched his camera. "Is it okay to take some pictures of you underwater? We can send them to you and maybe use them in our new brochure. We don't usually have divers who are so . . . uh . . ."

"He's trying to say beautiful," Lenny called.

"I don't care," Cammie told him. "Whatever."

Thankful for Olivia's exhaustion, Michel was grateful that he didn't have to deal with dual hormones seven fathoms down.

While Holly snorkeled happily above them, Michel, Tracy, and Cammie lowered themselves on the rope, three feet at a time, to fifty feet. He pointed out parrot fish, clowns, a barracuda longer than Cammie was tall. A reef shark crossed the sun slowly above them. When they came upon a massive ugly grouper, Michel motioned to tell them this was a good eating fish, along with the kingfishes they saw. He handed each of the women a sea cucumber to allow them to handle its deceptive, foamy heft. After he eyeballed each of their tanks, they rose slowly and then entered one of the caves. Within a few feet, they were able to stand. Tracy shoved up her mask and could barely pull out her regulator before exclaiming, "This is the most amazing dive I've ever had. Better than Mexico. I've never seen so many fish."

"No one can catch them. That's why they're so used to people. If you had a spear gun, you could," Michel said.

"Did you ever?"

"We have. Not around here. Lenny keeps one in his room, with the real gun."

"Ah, a real gun," Cammie said. "Very macho. What's that for?"

"It's a rifle. It's just for safety. He doesn't load it. You never know. People have been attacked out here, raped or robbed. But we were talking about the spear gun. It's easy, like operating . . . like a slingshot. Shoot and reel it up. Like a popgun that's sharp. You wear gloves and you work in a team, and you have to have a net ready and grab the line fast, before they dive."

"Why?"

"Well, you saw the size of that thing. And it would be bleeding."

"So you wouldn't want to prolong the agony?"

"I wouldn't want to attract the sharks. But the fish are protected here, and they know it," Michel said. Cammie turned away, looking out at the horizon.

Tracy wandered back on a ledge and slipped off her fins, inserting them carefully in a crevice. "Imagine people trying to hide things here hundreds of years ago," she said, creeping farther along the wall. "Michel!" she called, reveling. "There actually is writing in here!"

"Don't go too far in, Tracy. You could slip. Yes, some of it is just graffiti. But some scholars say some is genuine, from the time of the explorers and the pirates." He went on to say that no one could write on anything or touch anything anymore, because two-thirds of St. John was national park. "Of course, people sneak in and do things, the way they do anywhere."

"People are always sneaking around doing things," Cammie whispered suddenly.

Michel felt like the complete ass he was. He had hoped she wouldn't get it. But she had.

"Look," Michel told her, turning his face fully toward her, brushing back his tawny hair. "I'm so sorry. That was rude."

"Oh, do you think it was rude? Is sex part of the package deal? My aunt was just widowed this year, you know."

"I didn't know."

"Look, I couldn't care less, but don't pretend you didn't know."

"C'est la vie," Michel said, shrugging elaborately. "Seems as though this conversation is a waste of your time."

"I couldn't agree more. I'd rather hear about the caves."

They sat, self-consciously turning their backs on each other. Cammie spat in her mask and rubbed it carefully. The minutes crept past. Her voice muffled, Tracy exclaimed over another scraping on the cave walls.

Finally Michel said, "You really are the most beautiful girl I've ever seen."

"Whatever," Cammie snapped. "Please stop it. You're making me uncomfortable."

Tracy approached, and to cover his own discomfiture, Michel pretended he was finishing off a travelogue: "Now, Blackbeard, he used to put fuses in his beard and light them on fire to scare people away, literally burnt his beard. They would all drive other ships into the narrows and attack them there, grab on to the ships with these big grappling hooks. They never had to shoot anybody. People would just give their stuff up. Some went with them to go pirating. Actually, one of the most famous pirates was a guy named Dingdong Wilberdink."

"Oh dear," Tracy said, putting her fins back on. "He probably became a pirate out of self-defense. They'd have killed him in middle school!"

"He was involved with the brothel for pirates on the island called Olago, which used to be called Love and Go, you see."

"Like Ojibway became Chippewa over time, the name of the Indian tribe, from people's way of saying it," Tracy pointed out.

"Exactly. Well, this Wilberdink, he started up bars, a hospital if you got a taste of your own wickedness, or a case of . . . well, you can imagine, and he started a boatyard—a body shop for pirate ships! Are we ready to go back down now?" The women nodded.

Cammie muttered, "Finally."

But once below, they again marveled at the eels that darted out at them and were gratified by even fifteen more minutes. They examined a nurse shark, asleep far below them. Then Michel motioned for the surface, and they made their slow ascent.

"Did you have fun, Holly?" Michel asked when they broke into the dazzling light to find Holly floating lazily on her back.

"I could see all of you as if I could reach out and touch you," Holly said happily. "And I'm as warm as I am in a pool. I think something stung me, though. I have a bite."

"Did you see it? It wasn't a jellyfish, was it?"

"Can you see them?" Holly asked, laughing. "I thought they were transparent."

"Let's climb out," Michel said. "Hand me up your things, Holly first; I'll remove the tanks. We can go again after lunch if you like. Lenny should take a look at that bite and see if it needs a doctor when we go in."

"I don't want to go to a clinic. I want to see this bar where the man saw the ghost," Holly said.

"I thought maybe we'd go to the Bight for the afternoon," Michel said to Lenny when they returned to *Opus*. "It's a great little—"

"Little chop around here, though," Lenny said.

"It could just look that way. It does that," Michel told him. "Is the paperwork all done? Weather?"

"No events. We'll see about the Bight. It's a nice place to go in, Pirate's Bight, a pretty cove with this wonderful bar, my favorite bar, on a little beach. Why don't we have a little something to eat? You've used more energy than you think. Call Olivia, Michel. Maybe we'll go to the Bight. We'll definitely take the tender over to *Willie T.* when it's nearer sundown."

If Holly hadn't been bitten and then fallen, Michel might never even have kissed her, Cammie thought later.

She would be tormented, bitterly, by what happened to her aunt Holly. She would recall it with a dank misery that she could never tint with philosophy. And at the same time, afterward, she was also perversely grateful, to the point of prayer, that Michel had the chance to kiss her.

Aunt Holly had thrown out her back at Christmas and gained weight. So she wasn't as agile as the rest of them, stepping down into the little motorboat. "Now, is it a tender or a dinghy, Lenny? I've heard you call it both."

"It's a tender. We should call it a tender. I don't know why we slip up sometimes. I guess because people are more familiar with the word *dinghy*. Up there, the life raft that's lashed on to the mast is an inflatable boat. Inside it, there's more MREs."

"And those are . . . ?"

"Meals ready to eat, like in the army?" Lenny slapped his forehead. "Other people think they're crap. I like 'em. And water and blankets and you know . . . A person could live in it for a while, some days, really, if a shark or a coral didn't slice it. It comes that way. Oars and all."

"So you can never die on the *Opus*, like the people on the *Annabeth*," Holly said as she prepared to make her way down into the tender after Olivia.

"Well, you can die, but there'd have to be an awful lot that would have to go wrong. She won't capsize, for example, unless the mainmast is broken and pulls her over. She's a safe boat."

"I'll assume she is," Holly said. "And you have to give me the name of those ginger pills, in case I decide to have more kids and get morning sickness, or any sickness. They're a miracle. Except they aren't working right now. Lenny, Trace, I'm sorry. I just feel lousy." She made the step down into the tender and then slipped, barking her shin and opening a nasty scrape. "Christ almighty! God that hurts like hell! Can you imagine that just two million years ago I was the flier on the cheerleading squad? Now I'm going to have a grapefruit on my leg to go with the bite!"

"It could have been a scrape on coral," Lenny said. "We need to get some ice on that, Holly. And maybe just ditch this and find a clinic—"

"No, if you have butterfly bandages, it'll be okay. I'm a nurse, Lenny. Most things look worse than they are." With cumbersome care, she climbed out of the tender. Her wound was bleeding freely.

Lenny said, "I'll stay with you, then. Hydrogen peroxide. Ice. Gauze. Big drinks, huh? Michel, you can take the rest of them."

"I'll stay with her," Tracy insisted.

"Mom! Lenny can handle this! Come and see the ghost guy. We don't have to stay long," Cammie urged her. "Aunt Holly, I don't mean that in a bad way. But she knows how to take care of herself, Mom." Cammie's anxiety about going anywhere alone with Olivia and Michel was palpable but opaque to her mother.

Tracy insisted, "I heard the story. I think Holly and I will play gin. As I recall, she owes me money."

It was a standing joke. Holly had cleaned Tracy out of her birthday money one night during Christmas break in college, tucked two hundred bucks into her bra, and walked away. Tracy had been furious, calling Holly over and over the next day, insisting she get a chance to win back her money. Holly had listened politely and then cruised blithely to the mall and bought a real leather jacket with a fringed purse to match it. Tracy could never bear to see her wear it. She would say, "That's my coat, you whore."

Olivia pouted. "I guess this means I have to stay, too," she said.

"Yes, it does," Cammie told her with cloying politeness. "With your lifelong friends."

"Wait a minute, no," Lenny interrupted. "No one has to . . . Olivia, come on. Go ahead and go with Michel." But the situation was fraught. He could sense, now, that putting Michel in the tender with Olivia and Cammie was like putting calcium carbide in water.

"Never mind," Olivia said. This was, she supposed, her penance, to watch beautiful Cammie motor off with beautiful Michel. Still, she was annoyed. Olivia was a vain woman, and vain women often make more mischief than they intend—although they often intend more mischief than they realize. Mischief with Michel had not only made a diversion, but proved a point. As a young wife in Europe, she was allowed certain latitudes; but now she was without the courtly protection of Franco's name and stature. And being neither young nor older, she teetered on the slack in the wire. It would have been difficult for a woman like her to age in any case. But Franco's death had flanked her, left her a chatelaine without portfolio. Her face literally had been her fortune. She had no skills, nor had she any need of them, and few interests beyond herself. Each year would be more than subtraction, it would be an amputation. Olivia's need to be desired was prodigious. And now, to be consigned to sit here and fumble with sticky playing cards, while Lenny stroked his balding and sunburned head, was oppressive. Olivia had been looking forward to the bar. There would have been someone interesting there. Ah well, there would be other bars. There was no way that Michel would dare to try anything with Cammie. Tracy would eat him alive.

There was that satisfaction, at least. She had bested a girl half her age, a girl more beautiful than Olivia had been.

It would be impolite to dash off and seclude herself before a seemly interval had passed. Fifteen minutes? A whole half hour? Olivia glanced again at Michel and Cammie, both grimly silent as he stepped into the tender and prepared to help Cammie descend. Cammie had slipped into a sundress no longer than a man's shirt. Both of them looked as though they were on the way to donate blood. When Olivia glanced up, she saw Holly, her face deliberately bland, reading Olivia's own expression like the face of a clock. Holly had always been able to make Olivia feel as though Holly had pulled her over and were running her license plates.

The four of them left behind draped themselves on chairs and benches in the saloon while Lenny mixed a paste of antibiotic and baking soda and applied it to the welt on Holly's thigh. He then—quite skillfully, Holly thought—cleansed and thoroughly bound the cut on her shin, attaching a pack of ice with Velcro straps.

Christ, Olivia thought, my kingdom for a book. She asked if she might later go down and peruse Lenny's library. Distracted, he agreed. Telling the others she'd be back in moments, Olivia slipped away to Lenny's cabin. The pictures of Meherio took her breath away. What had this girl seen in . . . But then she herself had married Franco. There was a television canted above the bookshelves and hundreds of neatly labeled, alphabetized DVDs. But the bookshelves were filled with fucking classics. She'd done classics. *Anna Karenina*—now there was a book that took all the fun out of adultery. The short stories of Grace Paley. A biography of Lyndon Johnson. Erudite legal thrillers. Olivia wanted a breezy murder mystery. Discouraged, she slouched back up to join her friends.

"Now I know what you need," she heard Lenny say to Holly. "It's my specialty. Len's Libertine. My own recipe."

"What's in it?" Tracy asked. "And why's it called that?"

"What's in it is whatever's on the boat, plus pineapple," Lenny replied. "And it's called that because after one, it's what you become. I usually save it for anniversary couples. They need a jump start."

They all laughed. Olivia sighed and decided then to treat herself to three Valium and a long, restorative sleep. It wasn't that she didn't care about them; she did, in abstract. But she could already feel the slow, inexorable contamination of suburbia. Shorts with blubbery knees tucked beneath. Quiche and quilting. Golf and garage sales. Welcome mats outside the door that read bless this mess! She would soon be filing coupons and hosting a bunco club. She shuddered. More than any of them, she was still the girl she had been twenty-five years ago in Westbrook. She longed for things these women had forfeited decades ago. She had liked them; she had never been *like* them. Round, muscular Holly, even though tiny enough—then—to toss into the sky as a cheerleader, had always been about as agile as a Shetland pony. And as a sturdy little pony, she went through life. It was practically a metaphor. Tracy bounding down the court in three strides, sweaty, mocked, blithely unaware. Janis, just short of a tramp and only a few rungs above dim-witted, her lashes caked with mascara that looked as though it could be weighed on a scale.

Olivia had written for the literary magazine.

Yes, she had been a greaser like the rest of them, but better read and, she suspected, gifted with a subtler intelligence than any of the others. It had been she who hatched the escapades, the others who carried them out and were grateful, even if they later were punished. It was she who mesmerized the chemistry teacher—a boy probably no older than Michel—into giving her "just one look" at the previous year's exam, pleading parents who would "really punish" her for a C. He had left her alone in his room, probably because he'd had a hard-on, and Olivia had copied all the answers onto the inside of her left arm. Holly was right: Olivia would have been a brilliant Mob wife, except for the obedience and the babies that had hung like hooked fish to her friends' boobs until they lengthened into the equivalent of the *National Geographic* photos they'd all once studied with such hilarity and terror. She had attended mass regularly in Italy, but only for the social diversion: She was stunning in her long black silk skirt, a shawl thrown over her splendid shoulders, and raised her chin when she heard the village women, in their flowered frocks, whisper of *"la contessa."*

Olivia's own breasts, tucked just an innocent tad by the physician, still perked. And her thighs were as lean as any college girl's—yes, by dint of a suck, but what was money for? However much she'd scoffed when Holly confided that she weighed 150 pounds, Holly was right: Olivia would have killed herself, or fasted for a month, if some calamity caused her to pack on that much lard.

Tracy was the only fit one, but she was no longer nimble and adventurous. And now, *this* was their idea of a big getaway. Olivia had foreseen a great many more opportunities for clothing and jewelry to ship back and men to entice—beyond the ship's boy. And still, there had been that. Not one of them would have done what she had last night. Not one of them would have transgressed her vows or been able to please him. Olivia sighed in satisfaction. She supposed relaxation was a kind of gift. She turned again to her friends. They were chuckling now, a drink tucked away by each of them—Olivia didn't drink anything but the scant flute of champagne—*chuckling*, the way her mother did with Aunt Tina, over coffee and cannoli.

"I didn't do anything in high school," Tracy was saying. "I was sort of a lukewarm student. None of it made sense. I had no idea what I liked. I played basketball. People thought I was nuts."

"They did not," Holly replied. "They thought you were gay."

"You were the elite. You were a cheerleader."

"Oh yeah. But *Janis* was a pom-pom. We were considered part of the team. They were the Dallas Cowboy girls. Janis had the first bare midriff in St. Ursula's history."

"Not counting St. Ursula, of course," Tracy added. "I'll bet she had some wild outfits."

"But not maroon knee-high boots. Can you believe we let them call us the Teddy Bears?" Holly turned to Lenny. "You know, Ursa? Bear? The football team was from the boys' school, Father Fenton. But you can hardly make a good team name from Fenton. The Fighting Fentons. It sounds like my next-door neighbors. So they used our school for the name. The Battling Bears."

Holly's monologue made this sound like one of the high points of her life. I will never, ever give in to such dreary wifeliness, Olivia thought. Life was a ripe plum, and she would suck it to the pit.

"Take the radio, Michel," Lenny shouted, his voice booming over the still water as the tender slid away. And Michel dutifully looped back. "Take the GPS, too."

"I can see *Willie T.* from here, Lenny."

"Take it anyhow. Be safe," Lenny told him.

So Michel and Camille set out again, the splutter of the motor the only sound. Michel finally spoke. "Are you going to ask him about *Annabeth*?"

"Why else would I be going?"

He could see the even picket of her smile in the darkness. "To say you'd been here. With me. With Michel Eugène-Martin, captain."

"Well, at least I'll be able to say I've been there. What a shame my aunt couldn't come!"

"It's probably better," Michel said uneasily.

"You really think so?" Cammie asked. "Jesus, weren't you the guy who promised he wouldn't talk to me?"

"Fine," Michel said, revving the engine. They approached the floating bar. To his astonishment, he couldn't shut up. "It's dead here now. You should see this place in the middle of tourist season. You can't get on. People are dancing with a Piña Colada in each hand. They're hanging off the railings. They'll close down this week for the season. Not so many boats about now. But usually this place is a floating meeting of . . . what do you call it . . . Triple A?"

"Alcoholics Anonymous? AA?" Cammie asked. "Why do you put on this act? I'm not an old lady who'll fall for it. How long have you lived in the United States?"

"Six years. But I studied English."

"So they get stinko. And then they go back to their boats," Cammie said. "Big deal. It looks like a shithole."

"The captains don't drink," Michel answered. "Not ever."

"Uh, that's good," Cammie answered, her apathy elaborate.

Lee hailed them as they tied up at the dock. "Michel, where's Len?"

"A passenger had a little accident," Michel explained. He tied off the tender and handed Cammie up onto the floating boardwalk that led to the barge.

"Well, Sharon tells me he's going to be a daddy again!" Lee boomed.

"Hey! I didn't even know until yesterday!"

"You didn't! Well, jungle drums and all. Meherio spoke to her. She wants Sharon to stand godmother. Think we should have the baptism out here?"

"I think it would be the first baptism on this platform," said

Michel. "But perhaps not the first conception." He blushed and glanced at Cammie. "I'm sorry."

Camille said nothing. She gave her hand to Lee Wikowsky and shook it firmly. "I'm Camille Kyle. Lenny says you saw a ghost. But I don't think you did."

Lee was more than willing to tell the tale again. Near the end, his voice quieted. "And the odd part was his shirt had no buttons. He would have had to put it on by pulling it over his head. I heard him as plain as I hear you. I saw the water barrel on the deck. Now that I think of it, that should have . . . Who has water in a barrel?"

"You could see that in the dark, I'm so sure," Cammie teased him.

"In the moonlight I could! I thought there was something odd about a man in a three-masted schooner wearing suspenders in the night!" Lee said. "Now, who's for a drink? This is a tavern."

"I didn't bring my money," Cammie said suddenly.

"Your first Piña Colada is on the house," Lee said.

"The next is on me," said Michel.

"I'm nineteen," Cammie said, and Michel felt his stomach capsize. "Last month, I was eighteen."

"It's okay, if you're with Michel. No one to bust you out here," Lee said. "Not that I'm pushing liquor or agree with underage drinking, though technically you're legal in British territory at eighteen."

"What the hell, then," Cammie said.

Michel got out his wallet. "For her. And let me pay, Lee."

Cammie drained her drink as if she were slugging water on a tennis court and asked for another. She was halfway through that one when Michel said, "You might want to slow down."

"You might want to shut up," she answered softly, thinking of Trent's perfectly bronzed face with its outthrust, patrician chin. For a moment, she longed to be gay.

Lee busied himself at the other end of the bar. Cammie drank four drinks, and when she stood to use the washroom, Michel saw her sway, just slightly. But the boat was also moving, as the wind was picking up slightly. She was probably used to drinking.

A few other couples, in advanced states of inebriation, sat on rudimentary stools, stroking each other and murmuring. One woman seemed undecided between two men.

"Bareboat cruisers," said Michel, gesturing with his chin, when Cammie returned.

"What's that?"

"No crew. They'll run their boats aground tonight. We'll be over hauling them off."

Cammie wandered to the edge of the boat, to a dark corner, and leaned over. "Are we going to cross the equator?"

"No, we are not going quite that far, but we will be close to it," Michel said.

"Huh," she said. "Well, as far as I'm concerned, I've seen the *Willie T*. We can go now. Let me ask you one thing, though. Why are you reading Dickens? I saw *Bleak House* on your bed."

"I like it."

"I wouldn't read Dickens except for school unless someone paid me. So you're not as stupid as you act." Cammie went back to the bar and took a long last swallow of her drink.

"You think everyone who lives this life is stupid?"

"I didn't say that. I'm not a fucking snob, you know."

"No. I didn't say you were. You're just spoiled. Like every other college kid I've ever met. You wouldn't know how to do a day's work to save your life."

Michel had no idea why he had said this. It was probably easier to see her mad at him than indifferent. But she didn't rise to the bait. So he paid Lee and shook his hand. When they descended to where the tender was tied, Michel said, "I'm sorry. Really. Let me help you into the tender. It can get slippery."

"I'm fine on my own," Cammie said, but it was apparent that she was not. "And I'm not spoiled. College is no picnic. You might know if you tried it. Engineering is basically majoring in math, geometry. I've worked every summer of my life and saved what I earned. What do your parents do?" She faced him with her fists on her hips.

"They own a clothing factory."

"They own a clothing factory. What do they make?"

Michel sighed. "Cashmere. Sweaters and coats."

"Okay, well, ooh-la-la. My dad is a small-time architect, and my mom is a teacher. I go to school because I have to. No one is going to take care of me. I bet they take care of you, their little rebellious boy. . . ."

"No," Michel lied. "Well, yes, a little."

"So who's spoiled?"

"I only meant don't look down on me."

"Then you should have said that instead of calling me spoiled. You don't even know me."

"You're right. I just said it because you make me nervous, and it was easier to have you angry with me than treating me like you're a princess and I'm a servant—"

"I never did that!"

"I know," Michel said. "Look, this is my problem, okay? Forget I said anything. Let me help you. This is my job, Cammie. If you fall, you could sue us. So let me help you, please. The same as I would anyone else." But he did not help her as he would have helped anyone else. He stepped into the tender and held it steady by planting his legs wide, and when she reached down, he took her waist in his two hands and lifted her into the boat.

She stood looking up at him.

She was so tiny.

Michel bent down, and thinking she would push him away or avert her face, he kissed her. She allowed it, her lips smooth, the taste of her like a lollipop from the syrup. He kissed her again, and she opened her mouth and let him pull her against him. They kissed, rearranging pressures and positions, testing each other.

"I can't believe you did that," he said.

"Neither can I," she said.

"Well, you had a lot to drink."

"I'm not drunk. I had a huge meal."

"I'm sorry for what I said, and even more, I feel like an idiot for—"

"Look, I know you do," Cammie said, and then laughed with unexpected kindness. "You should."

"You've probably never done anything you regret in your life."

"Honestly, I haven't," she said. "Not very much." She sat down and ran a finger under the strap of her sundress. "I got some sun . . . ouch," she said. "You do burn here. You weren't kidding. I'm dark. I never burn. I wonder how Holly is."

"Lenny would have radioed me if she was really bad off. If she'd been stung by a big jellyfish, she'd have to be in hospital now. If it gets worse, he'll take her to the doctor right away. They are all your aunts?"

"No, they are not all my *ahnts*," she said, laughing indulgently, but not in a mean-spirited way, at his pronunciation. "My real relative is my aunt Janis, my mother's cousin. She was supposed to come."

"But her husband . . ."

"Right. They are all my godmothers, though, like in *The Sleeping Beauty*, Flora, Fauna, and Merryweather? And all their husbands are my godfathers. Except Olivia's—"

"Let's go," Michel said. "I'm perfectly sober, Cammie. Want to go back?" He swallowed once and then again. "Or we could go lie in the sand and look at the stars, like teenagers. Well, you are a teenager. I won't touch you, I promise."

"I know you won't," Cammie said. "I don't care. It's a pretty night."

They motored to the far side of the island, opposite where Lenny had moored *Opus*, and hauled the tender onto the sand.

Michel pulled a big rug from the waterproof box. "We keep it for picnics," he said.

They lay side by side on the rug, five inches of carpet between them. Finally, Cammie said, "You could get lost here."

"I did."

"Where's your family?"

"Canada," Michel said. "They're wealthy, but I'm poor. I'm the black lamb."

"Black sheep . . ."

"Black sheep. They're nice about it. I see them in the fall. I always go home for Christmas."

"You don't think of real people living here."

"Not many do," Michel said. "Lenny's not the usual kind of man here. He has more substance."

"He seems like a good person." Cammie reached up and ran her hands through her long hair.

Michel propped himself up on one arm. "Do you think I could kiss you again?"

"Sure," Camille said. "Why not? Because none of this is real anyhow."

When she didn't push his hand away, he pulled her to him, elated when she pressed her hips so hard into his, he could feel the twin knobs of her bones and the pulses beneath them. Knowing he shouldn't, he lowered the straps on her sundress and kissed her neck, the hollow of her throat with its tiny crucifix, and finally he let his lips brush her small breasts with their fiercely hard nipples. Her sharp gasp delighted him, and when she kissed him again, over and over, it was every time with more confidence and less fear. It made him uneasy, how clear she was about what she wanted. Finally he said, "You aren't going to believe me that what we're doing right now has nothing to do with last night, no matter what I say. You'll think this is part of the service of the boat, like you said. But the truth is, I only did what I did last night . . . because of you."

"Come on," she said. "Don't try to make some half-assed excuse. All we did was make out for five seconds."

"It's the truth. I wanted to be with you, and I knew your mother would . . ." Michel made a slicing motion across his throat with a forefinger. Cammie seemed to consider this.

"I'm an adult," she said. "My mommy doesn't tuck me in at night."

"I know. But it's a small boat," Michel said.

Cammie laughed. "Please shut up," she said. "I'm enjoying this. I'm pretending we're in a movie."

They kissed again, and unable to help himself, Michel slid her dress down over her hips. In the moonlight, with only a triangle of silk against her dark skin and the tiny cups of white where her bikini top had rested, she was so beautiful that Michel thought she might vanish like a new moon. He had never felt at a loss with a woman. And it disconcerted him. Enticed, he had felt, and satisfied and avid, but never protective, protective to the prohibition of his own desire.

"What do you want, Cammie?" he asked.

"Who knows? It's not that big a deal," Cammie said, but her face, blurred by desire, contradicted her. She let the back of her cool hand trail along his face. They kissed, intentionally and with more mastery, and she let her hands skim his ribs, under his shirt, down to the ridge of his belt. He could feel her giving up her trust to him, for no good reason. Instead of igniting him, this made him hesitate. But they were finding it difficult to separate. When she lifted her hips and pulled him to her, both of them began to shiver. If an eighth inch of cloth had not separated them, he would have been inside her. Michel opened his shirt and made it a tent around both of them, as if a storm threatened; and Cammie slipped out of the last of her clothing. Michel laid his hand lightly on her belly, and she opened her legs slowly, looking steadily into his eyes so that he would understand this was not a bit of girlish mischief.

"Are you . . . ?"

"A virgin, you mean? Yes, I guess. More or less," Cammie said, biting her top lip. "Pathetic. I'm nineteen."

"I think it's wonderful."

"Jesus. My roommate thinks I'm retarded. And just a minute ago, I was pretty sure I didn't want to be a virgin anymore. But you keep stopping. And now I just keep . . . going back and forth. There's just . . . come on . . . there's no good reason except the obvious to do this and about ten good reasons not to."

"I don't want you to think I'm taking advantage of you. It's not like that. If it would make a difference, listen. We'll stop. I'll . . . I'll come to where you live when the season is over and I'll visit you."

"Do you think it would be the same? Wouldn't it feel like . . . a fish out of water?"

"I don't know," Michel said. "But I know you could meet a hundred women, and then the woman of your life, and you fuck it up the night before."

"You *could* come and see me at school, I guess. You know you're not like . . . you said, a beach bum. That's just your poor-guy act. You'd need a coat," she said with a nervous laugh. "It's Minnesota."

"I have a coat."

"I guess I wouldn't mind." Cammie thought of Trent and indulged in a tight, secret smile.

"But it's not that I don't want to . . . right here and now."

"I guess I do."

"You're not sure, though. You don't know if you would want to if it was the real world and I had on a coat. Or a tie."

"I believe you have a coat," Cammie said, burrowing into Michel's shoulder. "I don't believe you have a tie."

"I don't have a tie," Michel said. "But I like you. And I'd rather wait until I had one than have you think I'm such an ass."

"I don't think that. See, I don't really want to think about anything right now. Do you get that?" Cammie asked. Then she added slowly, "Because we are here, now. You didn't kidnap me. We are here, now."

This time, while they kissed, she put her lips to his throat and reached with her hands, roaming in the pockets of his jeans. Wanting her to lead but knowing she would not, Michel reached to open his belt and ease her way but said at the same time, "I don't think I should be trying to make this your first time. And I haven't got anything along with me. For protection."

"Well, shit!" Cammie said, stifling the impulse to knee him, feeling angry tears leap into her eyes. "What kind of crap game is this? You're trying to make me feel like an idiot *and* a slut."

Michel felt his heart compress. It was he who was clumsy, an idiot.

"No. Wait. I'm not making myself clear. This isn't an easy subject to discuss," he whispered. He took Cammie's hands and turned them over, so that her palms lay open in his. He kissed each palm, closing her fingers around the kiss. He cradled her until the tension melted from his shoulders and her chest and their bodies softened into the clefts and attitudes for which they were created. "I didn't say we should leave, only that we shouldn't have sex. Full sex. I didn't mean we shouldn't do anything."

"Oh," Cammie said, still uncertainly. "Oh. Well then . . ."

Lenny heard the radio crackle and a distant voice he thought might be Sharon Gleeman's. But Holly's leg was still swelling, and he wanted to keep pressure on it. He glanced at his watch. It was midnight. Damn Michel. *Willie T.* was dark. He could see Tracy anxiously looking out over the bow.

"Probably stargazing, Tracy," he said finally. "You can't blame them. They're young. It's the tropics."

"He's not that young," said Olivia.

"He's only twenty-five," Lenny told her. "Didn't you know that?"

"He seems . . . older. She just turned nineteen, Lenny."

"Nineteen is old enough for most purposes," Holly put in.

"He's been on his own for a long time. And out in the sun. That's why he seems older. But it's not his fault, Tracy. He's a good boy. His father wanted him to be a bigwig in the clothing trade. He wanted to be an artist. It ended with this. He's happy, and he's a wonderful sailor. But I don't want you to think he'd take advantage of her. He's a well-brought-up—"

"It's actually not him I'm worried about. She's, uh, going through her hellcat period, Lenny. She's more than a match for him. I just don't want, you know, a grandchild right now."

"I wouldn't worry."

"I would," Holly said. "I remember going through my own hellcat period. . . . I'm *kidding*, Trace. I'm sure they're talking. You know, about what if the stars have planets just like this one around them that are inhabited. . . . Maybe they're smoking dope."

"That's a comfort, Hols," Tracy said. "I feel better already."

"I see lights." Holly pointed off the starboard.

From somewhere in the darkness came the shout, "I'm a goddess!"

"Oh, Camille," Tracy said softly. "She has to be drunk."

"What if she is?" Holly asked. "It's not like we didn't get drunk. Younger than her."

"Look, I can see her. She's standing up!"

"Queen of the world, Mama. Nothing like a good boff to put you in a fine mood," Holly said.

"That's even more comforting," Tracy murmured. "Quit while you're ahead, Solvig."

"Oh, Tracy Ann! You quit! I mean being such a mother hen."

"Like you wouldn't be."

"Fortunately, my boys are in sixth grade."

"They do it in sixth grade now, too, Hols," Tracy said, laughing, as the tender drew closer.

"They do not!" Holly insisted. "Ian and Evan wouldn't know one end—"

"Don't be so sure," Tracy teased.

Lenny said, "I'll tell her not to stand up in the tender. Those little boats, they start in gear. If you're standing up and you fall out, and someone goes in after you, the boat can just come back around and cut you up. Even with a life jacket on. But see, Tracy, she does have a life jacket on. She's a good kid. It is the tropics, the stars look closer. They make everyone crazy." He glanced up. The stars were gone. "Does anyone need another drink? More ice for your leg, Holly?" They shook their heads. "Then I want to check something." He walked up into the cockpit and shut the door.

When Michel tied up the boat, he insisted on lifting Cammie onto the ladder. He gave her a final kiss. All three women saw it. When they walked up to her aunts, Cammie said, "I was just horsing around. In the boat."

"So I see," Holly said, punching Tracy, whose lips were pressed tightly together.

"Mom, come on," Cammie said. Olivia, like a shadow among shadows, got up and slipped silently into her cabin.

"You could leave, too, Holly," Tracy suggested.

"I'm enjoying this, though," Holly said. "I'm drunk and in pain, and I deserve a good laugh."

"Tracy, I should explain," Michel began, ignoring Holly. "It's not what it seems. . . ." Camille reached for Michel's hand.

"I don't think that's any of our business," Tracy said, and Cammie shot her a blazing look of gratitude.

Lenny returned, took in the scene with a single beleaguered glance, and drew himself up, as if to glower. All he could finally muster was little more than a shrug.

"It's all fine here," Holly said.

"It's fine here," Tracy repeated.

Lenny took off his hat and ran a hand over his head. "Well, there are no storms anywhere," he said.

"Good," Michel answered, as eager to be out of his partner's sight as he was to stay beside Cammie. "I'll say good night now."

"Good night," Cammie said.

Michel woke in the middle of the night remembering that Lenny would choke him to death for leaving the radio and the GPS in the tender. Fucking simpleton, he thought. Well, he would wake up before Lenny and recover them. Tonight, he would dream.

Cammie got ready for bed, slipping into her pajamas and doing pas de chats on the floorboards. Power radiated from her like an aura.

"Are you drunk, Cammie?" Tracy asked.

"Not so much now. I was earlier. It's legal here," Cammie answered. "We just had fun, is all. It's so beautiful here. Thanks for bringing me."

Tracy sat up in her berth, nearly grazing her head. "Now I know you're drunk."

"Okay, okay. But I talked a lot with Michel. He's really interesting."

"I can see *that*."

"It isn't just that, Mom. Although, it is that. We didn't do anything."

"Cammie, you don't know him. . . ."

"And that is why I just said we didn't do anything. And as you so nicely put it up there, it's nobody's business. Even yours."

"Well . . ."

"Mom, you don't have to grow up on the same street, like you and Dad and Aunt Janis, and go to the same school, and have Thanksgiving dinner together your whole life and play cards on Friday night. You can just know someone you meet wouldn't ever hurt you on purpose."

Tracy smiled. "It's theoretically possible."

"And that even if they made mistakes, you'd forgive them?"

"That's absolutely possible."

"Well, I had a great night, and now I'm going to have the best night's sleep I ever had, okay? I'm not even going to wash my face." She threw herself down, her long hair tumbling, to give Tracy a kiss. "I can't wait until morning," she said.

Tracy lay quietly in the dark, surrendering to the soft roll of the boat. There were worse things than a shipboard flirtation. She punched her pillow and snuggled into it. Much worse, she thought. And she knew they'd done something. No one did a few ballet steps before bed over nothing. But if it had been just around the edges, Tracy thought, well, there were worse things than that, too.

A few miles off the coast of Africa, from the direction opposite that from which tropical storms come, the wind did not know that what was forecast were partly cloudy skies and perhaps a thunderstorm later in the week. So a wave traveled across the North Atlantic and crossed the warm water of the Gulf of Mexico. And then the admixture of warm and cold water generated a vortex, a depression, that began to spin. Energy was created. The summer had been warm and the water was warm and the wave became a tropical storm that had no name and no one's eyes upon it. But Lenny felt it on the back of his neck. And so did the three men setting off in the *yola* from Santo Domingo; and each of them thought of the reefs behind which they had crouched while water swept over their heads, on the last trip; and the wind had seemed to turn personal, directly upon them. All of them hoped the wind would change its mind.

Day Five

*N*ow, I'll run in and top off the fuel tank," Lenny told them as they finished their Caribbean eggs Benedict, with horseradish, arugula, and, except for Tracy, chorizo sausage. "Anyone need anything?"

"I'm going to pop in, too, after you get back. I need a few things, and I can get groceries if you want," Michel said, smiling quietly at Cammie, who looked down at her breakfast and promptly lost the will to eat it.

"No need to do that until tomorrow morning. Everything will be fresh on a Tuesday. It's market day. All I really need is bread. I'm getting some fish and meat from another boat. Tomorrow, it's going to be a bit of a tedious day in terms of diving and so forth," Lenny said. "You have to watch for structure. . . ."

"That's . . . what?" Holly asked.

"Reefs, rocks. It's sort of a narrow passage. But once we're out, we're out, and out there, you're in deep water really quick. Don't let it scare you. It doesn't feel any different from thirty feet. And you can look down forever and see amazing things. We'll moor tonight off Skull Island; but it's just a little piece of scrubland, nothing on it. Then, we'll hopefully pick up some breeze and do some real sailing. We'll rendezvous with my friends Sharon and Reg, because they have food for us from their last charter. So get out your cards and a good book. . . ."

Olivia said, "I need a book. I couldn't find one in there. I didn't have room in my luggage, and I like mysteries. I've been reading everything by P. D. James. Can you possibly get me one?"

"I'll try," Lenny told her. Olivia wore a sleeveless beige silk shirt and wide-legged capri pants, and Cammie thought, Who's she trying to fashion model for? Not that I can't guess. . . .

"Livy, you can read anywhere," Holly said. "Let's sit in the sun and catch up." She'd put on her bathing suit and a huge straw hat.

"Okay," said Olivia, bored already by the thought. "Tracy?"

When they'd clambered up the swim ladder and spread out their towels, they all noticed that in addition to wearing a scarf over her hair, Olivia wore a hat with wings that tied under her chin.

"How do you stand having all that on, Liv?" Tracy asked.

"I have to protect my face," Livy said. "And I have to protect my hair. It probably looks ridiculous. But the result is not having sun damage. In fact, I use a serum that actually isn't a sunblock, but keeps the sun's rays from ever reaching your skin. As far as my hair, if you color . . ."

"I don't," Tracy said.

"I do," Holly said.

"Mine's still naturally this color. I just touch up one corner," Olivia said. "Once you dye it, it seems to get more porous."

Holly smeared a palm filled with a fat dab of cream on her face and neck and lay back to allow the sun to embrace her. "Sounds like a hell of a lot of work."

"It is, but it's worth it."

"I guess. You look great. I personally think it's all genetics. My legs are like Norwegian firs. Meant for the plow."

"Well," Olivia replied, honestly puzzled, "then I don't know what mine were meant for."

Holly's laughter was gusty. "The plow, too. Only the other way, Livy."

"Oh, Holly," Olivia said, preening secretly. "How are your children? How old are they now?"

"They're twelve, and they just about have me worn to the nub," Holly said. "Evan's a good student. It's effortless for him. Ian's like I was, slow and steady, always a little bit below the curve. He asked me last week what the book was they were supposed to read over summer for seventh-grade English. It's the beginning of summer break. Evan read it over a weekend in May, to get it out of the way."

"Sounds like a hell of a lot of work," Olivia said.

"Touché," Holly admitted.

"But I'll bet Ian's more popular," Olivia said. "You were."

"He is, and it kills me," Holly said. "And Ev, he's glad Ian has so much fun. If we went to church enough, he'd end up a priest. He'll come into his own after they're in high school and I'm dead from worrying."

"You worry about them too much, Holly," Olivia said. "Do you remember our parents being like that?"

"Hey, mine weren't. As long as I was perfect. My brothers, too. Only three siblings ever to be named Student of the Year at St. Ursula's and Fenton. I remember senior year. Homecoming *court* wasn't good enough. I had to be queen! Heidi wouldn't speak to me for the whole weekend!" Holly said.

Silently, then, Holly forgave her mother. She had only wanted the American dream for her girl. And being queen was what Heidi understood as requisite to the dream. It was like the old show *Queen for a Day* that Heidi had watched with her own mother. Grandma Haldaag learned English from Monty Hall and Bob Barker. They all sat back in the thrall of memory. Their parents hadn't *worried* about them! Their lives were so censored from their parents' reckoning that their elders would have been lunatics to *worry*. As far as anyone knew, the girls wore their uniforms to school with white knee-high socks (the fishnets didn't come out until they hit the girls' bathroom before class) and went to dances with boys whose hair was still marked by the comb. No one went to "rehab." There was no "date rape" drug. Their parents assumed their children would grow up to be just like them and have martinis before dinner every night. Drinking wasn't a sin. Even priests drank. And though Tracy never got the hang of smoking, all the rest of them did, just as their parents had. Not one of the others had quit until she became a mother. Olivia still smoked.

The few girls who wanted to go all the way did, and the rest of them petted their way to aching ovaries and kissing chins. When Carol Klostoff got "in trouble," she became Mrs. O'Sheridan and graduated with a big belly under her pleated maroon gown. Everyone thought it was cool. Carol would get to go to Germany with her husband, who was in the navy. None of the girls' parents knew about the nights Janis climbed down the drainpipe and met Olivia on the corner. None of them knew how the two of them then drove off in a car with two older boys they'd met only once—both of them "making out" *lying down* for the first time at the vacated house of one guy's parents. No one wondered whether those guys would murder Janis and Olivia. Kids, in the Godmothers' era, paid more attention to their parents than their parents paid to them. And they paid more attention to each other, or so it seemed to Tracy, than she and Jim did—each of them consumed, week to week, with one child's success or distress.

Tracy couldn't remember a Friday and Saturday night in sequence, not ever, that her parents stayed home with them. Either her father and mother worked at the restaurant or, if they could trust the current manager not to dip into the till, they went to a dinner dance at the club (Polish night was a special favorite). Everyone turned up for mass on Sunday morning and then went swimming in the summer at Janis's pool. The parents drank and drank. They weaved their way home, somehow always without incident.

What they got away with was almost anything.

She and Janis baby-sat by scaring their younger siblings silly with tales of callers who turned out to have tapped into telephone wires in the basement, slaughtering everyone on the first floor before the police could arrive. Their little brothers didn't come downstairs after that. And once the kids were asleep, they had boys over and divided up the rooms. They didn't "do" anything, not any more than Cammie had, but that same Mikey Battaglia once had to climb out a second-story window and, holding his pants, jump for it when Tracy's parents arrived home early.

The knowledge that Cammie had quite probably taken even more awful risks than she had, though not in her house, gave Tracy palpitations. Why the risks she had taken seemed somehow more innocent than what Cam and Ted faced, she didn't know. The world was crueler, for one thing, the consequences of chances not legal but lethal. Her parents' ignorance was rightly described as bliss. At the end of the last great era—when college was still a possible dream for every kid, when restaurants and retail stores didn't go belly up after eighteen months, when a man might spend his life under his own shingle and a woman work part-time only if she wanted to set aside money for a cottage or a cruise—less seemed to happen. Serial killers didn't cruise the Internet. The only kids who smoked "pot" were poets, headed to Bennington on scholarship.

For her part, Olivia, the only childless one among them, was hard-pressed to keep herself from nodding off. She found her pals' chatter not dull, but meaningless. She had shopped at Chanel, they at Marshall Field's. She had re-created herself. They had only grown into the bodies puberty had given them. Jolly Holly was still cowlike and complacent. Tracy—whom everyone called the Tree behind her back—was still the rock, the only thing approaching a true friend Olivia supposed she had on earth. Janis was still pretty, but pedestrian in her Eileen-Fisher-from-consignment, the dutiful hausfrau staying home to bring puddings to her husband's sickbed, toying with her event-planning business. Did they not crave adventure? Olivia's life was only half-over. She craved antithesis. The unexpected. It was the only thing that made life bearable.

"I'm surprised we weren't all expelled by then," Tracy was saying. "Listen to this: I was in the chemistry lab for something, to bring a note to a kid who got injured on the uneven bars? And I remembered the glue on the Bunsen burner valves?"

"But that was one they never nailed us for!" Holly crowed. "Poor Mary Brownell got it. And she didn't dare rat us out. . . ."

"She was an associate Godmother, like a utility infielder. If we had a party before homecoming, she got to come," Olivia said. "She had to make some contribution." She said this matter-of-factly, without any special remorse.

"But we were so mean," Tracy recalled. "You know, Mary Brownell is a professor at Smith now? She's written poetry that has won these big prizes? And look at me. I'm a gym teacher at my own high school. My daughter thinks my shorts make me look like Eddie Albert."

"Your shorts do make you look like Eddie Albert," said Holly.

"Well, why do they put them in the catalog if they're not fashionable?" Tracy complained. "I thought they were, you know, preppy."

"They're, you know, ugly," said Holly.

"Oh, shut up. Like I care."

"You don't, do you?" Olivia asked wistfully. "You really don't care what you look like. I mean, your hair has a good cut; you have a killer smile; but the rest of it is just, take me as I am or leave me. You have freckles, Tracy! If I had eyes like yours—green eyes, without contacts!—I would have line cream under them all night and half the day! You were always like that. And I was moving the scale around in the bathroom and putting my hand on the windowsill before I stepped on to make it read one hundred and two instead of one hundred and five. I still am."

"Now, that sounds like a hell of a lot of work!" Tracy said. "What are you going to do now, Liv?"

"Spend months with my mother and remember why I thought it was okay that she only came to Montespertoli once a year. Maybe go to see friends we have in Switzerland, perhaps spend the winter there and ski. Do some writing. I do a little writing. I thought perhaps some essays, or maybe even a novel, about our life on the vineyard. I had a few little things published in Italy. . . ."

"You never told me!" Tracy scolded her.

"I said *little*. It wasn't worth telling."

But it was, and Olivia deflated when Tracy slipped back into reminiscence, as if her achievement had been, well, what Olivia had pretended it to be. If they knew, she thought. If they only knew.

"Guess who left the convent? Mother Bernard," Tracy told them, apropos of nothing. "She was a college president by then. Where was it? Mount Mary in Milwaukee? She's got to be sixty, no, more like seventy! She called me a couple of years ago."

"We thought she was as old as Methuselah when she was principal of St. U. She was probably forty," Holly said.

"Why would you quit if you were already . . . ," Olivia began.

"Too old to get a man?" Tracy asked. "Uh, no. Actually, she has one. But she said it was political. Now, her name is Sylvia Venito. I used to think of her like Rosalind Russell in *The Trouble with Angels*," said Tracy.

"I was obsessed with *The Trouble with Angels*," said Holly. "I didn't even care that their clothes were out of style, even then."

"I was obsessed with *The Nun's Story*," Tracy went on, "but Mother Bernard told me it was just like that movie. She said, 'Call me Sylvia.' It was like God saying, 'Call me Big G.' They make you go into a room and give up your wimple and rosary and that whole deal. . . ."

"She was still wearing the habit?" Olivia asked.

"Maybe she saw *The Trouble with Angels*, too."

"She was a good woman," said Holly. "We aged her."

"No, she liked us," Tracy said. "She said we had spirit. But she was worried you'd marry into the Mob, Livy. . . ."

Olivia laughed. "I'd have been a great Mob wife. All that cash. All those mirrors with gold etchings on them and tight capri pants . . . just like Italy! Remember the ushers with guns under their coats at Jodie Camorini's wedding?"

"It's another world," Tracy said. "The mobs now are poor kids who sell drugs and sing about shooting cops. It's not like organized crime anymore. It's unorganized crime."

"Was there that stuff in Italy? Did you have faithful family retainers who were actually hit men?" Holly asked.

"God, we had a maid and a cook, like most people do."

"Well, *we* do, of course. And a butler. You can't do without one, especially at the holidays," Holly said, crooking her pinkie.

"Come on! *Everybody* did. And workers on the *fattoria*. That's it. No one thought of me as a countess except my mother. It's a Communist government, for Pete's sake. It was just an old, inherited title," Olivia said, waving a hand. "*Basta*."

"But you used the crest on your Christmas cards!" Holly teased her.

"I showed Cammie her baptismal gown a couple of years ago, that you had made there?" Tracy said. "My God, Livy, it was the most beautiful thing."

"Venetian lace," said Olivia. "The tradition is, that same lace is supposed to trim her wedding gown. . . ."

"One world at a time," Tracy said.

"Is she giving you a run for it, Tracy?"

"Kind of," Tracy said.

"And what did you expect?" Olivia asked coolly. She had an overwhelming desire to sleep again. Perhaps tonight she would lie out again in the hammock. But nothing would happen. She yawned. Her abdomen tingled at the memory. Why couldn't Cammie wait her turn? she thought. Poacher.

After Lenny set off in the tender, Cammie concentrated on not noticing Michel's every move. He uncovered the sails, carefully stowing their coverings, and attached the whatchamajigs to them, running them up and down experimentally. As it grew warmer, he slipped off his shirt. Cammie lowered her baseball cap and concentrated on Mrs. *Dalloway*. She read the first sentence on the page six times.

"It's just a treat for the older ladies," Michel said to her softly as he stalked the ledge of the ship, sure-footed and feline. Was that why they called it a catwalk? Did they call it a catwalk? Or was that modeling? Was he modeling? Cammie concentrated on her book. She'd read the same half page six times.

"I loved Virginia Woolf," Olivia said, coming up from her berth and settling down beside Cammie. "I had the most glorious nap! I'm not used to schedules," she added. "Now I can sleep outside again tonight." A spurt of irritation possessed the girl, but she dismissed it.

Olivia was attractive. Michel had admitted he was wrong. She could still feel his . . . She blushed. Olivia noticed, and Cammie thought she saw her godmother actually grow taller as her back stacked itself up over her hips, her posture transforming from lounging to imperious.

"Odd to see a handsome man with his shirt off in the middle of the day, huh?" Olivia commented.

Cammie thought, She doesn't think I know. She's trying to draw me out about him. "Yes, I guess," she said. "Though they don't seem to wear many clothes here. You are dressed up, Aunt Livy."

"I try."

"Well, as for Virginia Woolf, I . . . don't," Cammie said. "It's all so downbeat. I don't see the point of why the artist has to die. He's just thrown in there to die."

"Well, in the novel, it's a sacrifice. A metaphor. The artist has to die, like Christ. But she was foreshadowing her own death. Don't you think? She wrote all that in longhand, over and over, three hours at a sitting."

"And then she committed suicide. Didn't she want to enjoy it? She worked so hard. Can you imagine wanting to die so much you'd fill your pockets with great big rocks and—"

"If there was no hope," Olivia said. "There was a moment, when Franco was diagnosed, that I thought, I can't live without this man, who's taken care of me so long. I don't know that Virginia Woolf ever knew she'd be famous. I don't think she thought she could ever live up to all the talent of her siblings. . . ."

"But she's the only one anyone remembers."

"That's the irony."

"Mmmm," Cammie said.

"And she was truly ill. Depression is an illness. I was never that way. Only terribly, terribly sad."

"Oh, Aunt Liv," Cammie said politely. Olivia was so old. She was so lonely. She might look younger, but she wasn't. She was old, like Tracy and Holly. Sympathy overtook Cammie's pique.

Olivia said then, "Your mother told me luck could be bad, but life is good."

"She got that from Holly. Holly says that all the time."

"Well, maybe she does, but Tracy is the most purely good person I've ever known, Camille. She's done a lot for me. I've done a lot for her. She might be stern . . ."

"Stern is the word for it. But I know she loves me. Us."

"You confuse uprightness with uptightness."

"I just called her that. Something like that. Just a couple of days ago."

"When we were young, there was no dare your mother wouldn't take. She rode the wildest horse at my uncle's stable. She drank the most shots of brandy quickest. In high school, mind you. She was the Michael Jordan of St. Ursula's. She brought home a state championship twice."

"I don't think of her that way," Cammie admitted. "Can you imagine? Teaching in the same gym you played basketball in when you were seventeen?"

"I can't, but your mother . . . she's like the North Star, Cammie. We were all over the place. First, we were greasers. Then, we were metal heads. Then, in college, we all let our hair grow out and got political. But Tracy was always the same. If you asked her today what she wanted, she'd say the same thing she said then."

"What?" Cammie put her finger in her book and tried to clench her legs to ignore Michel, who was climbing the mast.

"To have a happy home, a good man, and be of service. She would say that. Be of service." Olivia felt pleased with herself. She had done something nice. She'd made up for whatever perceived slight was airborne between them.

"To what do I owe this lecture, Aunt Liv?" Cammie asked.

"Just, nothing. Franco was totally needy. And I was ready to give up. Just leave, go, give up. He didn't know I was there half the time anyway." Olivia found any kind of demand debilitating. She had never been able to grasp the yearning for children, who embodied the worst of human characteristics, being both demanding and boring. At the end, Franco had been like that. Waking if she let go of his hand, asking for his rosary.

As if clairvoyant, Cammie said, "Are you very, very sad now that you and Franco didn't have children? Could you not, like Mom, or is that too personal?"

"God, no! I could. I wouldn't. He had grown sons. From a first marriage. I rarely saw them. They lived in Rome and had their own families."

"Didn't you want to know them? They must have been . . . my age when you got married."

"I did, in a sense, but they were their mother's sons."

"Well . . ."

"And Franco wanted me to be his little one. His *piccola*."

Cammie found this creepy. If she had been more given to the precision of words, she would have called it "precious." She mused, though, "You could have had nannies. You probably would have had an exotic child and sent her to some Swiss boarding school."

"I don't like children. I like you, Cammie. But I can barely do all it takes to look after myself, much less another person."

Cammie thought privately, It's a good thing you don't have children. They'd be in trouble. She felt a stitch of regret for the way she treated her own mother but then said, "I do respect my mom. I'm more like my dad, though. To me, she's just my mother. She's a gym teacher. She didn't exactly cure cancer, Aunt Livy. Oh, I'm sorry. That was dumb."

"It's okay," Olivia said. "But, Cammie, not all lives have to be comets in the sky." She smiled wickedly. "Just some of ours do."

"And you're still on the way up, huh?"

"I hope so!" Olivia said

"You're making me sleepy. I'm going to go lie in the hammock. Was it comfortable?" Cammie asked with a tang of malice.

"A little hard on the back," Olivia said.

I can imagine, Cammie thought, and got up to get her towel.

A few hours later, Michel woke her. She had fallen asleep, numbed by the tranquillity of sea and sun, the breeze that kept everything from ever feeling too hot. "You'd better turn over. You're done on this side," he said. "Do you want to run into town with me?"

Cammie jumped up and threw on her maui shorts. "If they're British, do I need a shirt? Is it more formal?"

"Not from my point of view, but probably. For the sun if nothing else," Michel told her.

"How do you stand it here? Is every day like this?"

"Mostly. Not always. There are filthy, foggy, rainy days. Storms.

Crud. And you can get tired of . . . you know the saying. Just an-other shitty day in paradise."

She chose modest denim shorts and a cotton shirt that tied under her breasts.

They spent two hours wandering narrow streets in the little town. After the first hour, Cammie, with a comic graciousness, allowed Michel to hold her hand.

He was twenty-five, and holding a teenage girl's hand made him feel as though he had a winning Lotto ticket.

"I want to buy you something," Michel said. He reached out, plucked a blossom of bougainvillea from a trailing vine, and tucked it behind Cammie's ear. "Now you look like a native girl. You need a bauble."

"That's dumb," Cammie said.

"To remember me."

"Okay, whatever," she said, and meant more than she would say.

"I want to."

Michel chose a necklace made of the tiniest identical shells, lion colored, interspersed with hematite beads. It was pricey and would mean a week of beans on toast this winter. But there was a mad thrill in seeing how the shells caressed the hollow of her throat, just above the cross she never removed. "I have to keep my cross on. It was my baptism gift," Cammie said. "I wear it for luck now. I'll wear this always, too."

"Don't wear it always. You scratch those shells up and it's ru-ined. If you take care of it, it will last forever," said the woman who owned the little store.

They had a drink—Cammie a Hurricane and Michel a Pepsi—and then Michel asked her to wait while he darted into a phar-macy. "I need . . . uh, toothpaste." And a can opener, he thought. He would have to get a can opener before they went back out to the boat. He had to remember. But then, the radio crackled.

"Okay, get some toothpaste," Cammie agreed, wondering if he

really had run out of toothpaste or meant what he seemed to be signaling, wondering if anyone could go crazy from sheer horniness.

"You stay here. Don't walk off. We have to get back," Michel said.

"I thought I could get some cheese and bread. We could have a picnic."

"Later," Michel said, and kissed her lightly. "Lenny radioed. He wants me back. Work before pleasure."

As they motored back out to *Opus*, Michel reached over, touched the necklace, and took her hand lightly. Cammie was sure then. You could go crazy. She sent up her sweetest prayer: *Thank you, God, that my uncle is fine, and that he had to have an operation. Thank you.*

Day Six

*O*kay!" Lenny said. The women didn't know it, but his voice on this, his twentieth voyage on his own boat, was as elated as it had been on his first. "Today, you're going to see her under sail! You aren't going to see much of me, because I want this to feel wonderful and make good time, too. But Michel will fix the drinks."

Michel asked Lenny, "Did you get anything else? More food?"

"A dozen eggs and some fresh bread for French toast. Sharon has more than enough of the rest. She's coming in loaded. The group they had fished, but they won't be able to take the fish home. Emergency back in Texas. And she's got a ton of stuff I said I'd take off her hands. I'll call her in a bit."

"She won't take money for it."

"So she already said. You know Sharon."

"Well, I'll take her and Reggie out for a big dinner if I stop in New York on the way home for Christmas," Michel said.

"I'm going to go and see them then, too," Lenny said. "Maybe we'll make a week of it, if you want." He nodded absently, busy with other tasks. Michel noticed that Lenny had not mentioned the can opener. Damn it, Michel thought. Next stop. But he wasn't about to bring it up.

The women watched as the two of them unfurled the genny and raised the mainsail, which thrust themselves up like massive flags, towers of white. Lenny cut the engine; Michel unfurled the sheets to sail with the wind.

And *Opus* did what she was built to do. She threw out her

wings in the way that sailing ships do, inspiring immoderate ecstasies in painters and poets as such boats have for centuries, even among those who've never set foot on one.

"Lenny is a real sailor," Michel said as they sipped rum punch and nibbled on mango salsa. "I can do it, but he has the lightest touch. He'll barely have to touch the wheel. It's called bearing away. The wind's running over the side of the stern, see how the mainsail is filled? It's like he said. The wind is pulling us. The mainsail is set on the opposite side of the wind. She's running now, until the wind changes."

"It's not what you'd think," Holly said.

"We're pretty free with what we can do this late in the season," Michel said. "The important thing is that either Lenny or I always keep watch. We change every six hours or so."

"It does feel like flying."

"It feels like my guts are flying," Holly said suddenly.

"Ginger pills," Michel said, leaping lightly down into the galley.

"It's funny how one person can feel nothing and the other everything," Cammie said.

"It's your ears," Michel said. "I've seen these big, burly guys go green the minute we leave the harbor. It has nothing to do with whether you're weak or strong. Maybe some leftover nausea from her bite."

"I'm sure that's it," Holly said. "I'm still not . . . right. I'm a nurse, so I know this is a little . . . something."

Michel set out to eyeball oncoming vessels. He held Cammie's hand so she could stand up beside him. "See out there? A cruise ship. It looks a million miles away, doesn't it? But we could get to her faster than you can imagine. We can make more than a hundred miles a day if we want to this way. You can make fifty even drifting with the current. The likelihood is that the captain might not see us even in broad daylight. I have to go tell Lenny about that ship, though I'm sure he's already seen it. They'll talk to each other, and most likely, since we're going faster, the ship will stay clear until we pass. We'll be the stand-on vessel, in that case. That's what we call it. It would be different if they had nets in the water for fishing."

When he returned, Tracy asked, "Is there any land out here at all?"

"Tonight we'll drop the anchor by a couple of tiny islands, hardly islands at all, really. Just little spits of scrub and trees. They don't have beaches, hardly any shallows around them," Michel said. "The only reason to go over onto them is to go crabbing or something. Or if you just have to feel land under your feet or take a swim or something and you don't want to go around the boat. Our boat."

"Like the kind of island you'd get marooned on?" Cammie asked.

"Only if you were the unluckiest lub alive. Or if you wanted to be . . . like alone to meditate."

"Like a monk," she said.

"Yeah, or not. As for us, we'll anchor off one," Michel said, averting his eyes. Why was he as shy as a kid in sixth form? "If we go in, we'll motor in the tender. You could swim over there easily. You could never expect an anchor, or even two huge anchors, to hold a boat overnight. But usually, it's okay here. You don't get in trouble the way you would other places. You get in trouble drifting around." Michael felt abashed. He was babbling.

"So I hear," said Cammie, rescuing him and running one fingernail down his spine.

Tracy watched the minute adjustments Michel made to the sails at Lenny's instruction. The angles were understandable. It wasn't so different from a massive version of her grandfather's little Cat. Michel detached the sheet and cleated it off. She imagined the rudder underneath, keeping the boat out of a skid, the flow of water under the keel. She remembered what her grandfather had taught her. If she put her hand outside the car window when the car was moving and cupped her hand, all the wind did was blow her hand back. But if you turned your hand, technically, your hand would be blown forward, not back, by the wind slipping over it. She remembered nothing of what he'd taught her about sailing upwind, except that it required ducking her head when he moved the boom to the other side of the little boat. Magellan, Grandpa had told her, had to have his sails set at a ninety-degree angle to the wind; and still he went around the world.

Just as the sun began to drop, she heard the sails flap against the mast as Lenny lowered them and folded them neatly, tied to the boom. She felt a leveling off in the forward motion of the boat. Michel readied the motorboat to tie to a big tree on a tiny island. While Lenny held their place, Michel zipped across and tied off the line.

"If there's no wind, you could make a fire out there tonight," Michel said when he got back. "It would be nice."

"I could do that. It would be like camp," Cammie said.

"Not really," Michel said softly. "Not like the camps I went to."

Oh well, Tracy thought, overhearing them. She felt a sudden pang of longing for Jim, his reddish burr of hair and long limbs. Was she longing for Jim or for both of them, her and Jim when they were young? Or simply the liquor of being young, a single potent glassful that was supposed to fuel a lifetime?

That night, while Lenny prepared the makings for baked mussels with spinach and wine, Michel took the tender, pulled it up onto the sand, and walked over to the quiet side of the island, to shore-cast for a fish to quickly fillet and grill. Stealthily, in her bathing suit, Cammie hopped over the side of *Opus* and swam the thirty feet to join him. Her stealth was invisible to no one.

"She likes him," Tracy said to Olivia and Lenny. "She only had her first real boyfriend this year. And then *that* one went back to his rich sweetie. She generally thinks men are thick."

"Men are thick," Lenny answered, laughing.

"So what's he fishing for?" Both of them smiled at the double entendre. Olivia lowered her hat.

"He wants a barracuda," said Lenny. "Then I can broil it and you'll never taste anything like it, when it's straight from the sea. You would be surprised at how good it is."

"Will he catch one?"

"That's the problem. He probably will, but he'll have to cut five lines before he can bring one in."

"Why?"

"Because barracuda can be monsters. Not only would he need to drag the fish, we'd waste it. We'd cut off a few fillets, and it would be shark food. What we want is a nice little barracuda, ten, twelve pounds. We can have dinner, and I'll freeze the rest. We have all this food coming from another boat."

On the other side of the island, Michel's fishing pole was thrust deep into the sand. He had Cammie pressed against a tree. She had her leg twined around his hips, their hands exploring each other's every curve and cleft, outside their clothing.

"You are going to get me fired," he said. "I really, really have to catch a fish."

"You can say there weren't any."

"He knows there are."

"You can say it got away."

"I wouldn't do that."

"You can say a beautiful woman swam through treacherous waters for you."

"That, he would understand."

They knelt, then lay down. He kissed her throat. She unbuttoned his shirt and kissed his chest. This was impossible. He was being offered a lush box of sweets. He wasn't going to pass it up. This script had not yet presented itself in his life. Sex had been great fun, like great exercise, no yearning afterward, each woman a memory that crossed his mind if he heard a particular song or saw a particular place. No more than that. What he felt about this girl, an acquaintance for two days, was odd and uncomfortable. She was so shy and so bold and so very young. He helped her remove the top of her wet bathing suit. "There's nothing here but sand, Cammie. You'd get scratched up."

"There's your shirt. And the rest of your stuff. And the rug is in the tender, isn't it? Are you . . . Shit, listen. I'm not trying to give it away," Cammie said, her eyes suddenly thunderous. She slapped her wet top against her chest and began tying it up.

"Wait . . ." Michel's line began to sizzle. "Looks like dinner! I didn't mean it that way," he said. "I just meant I had to catch this fish. I don't have to catch the fish and rush it back out to the boat! Let me just catch it and wash my hands off. It's not bending the rod enough to be too big. . . ."

"Okay," Cammie said, still dubious. "Here's an experience, I guess. This is good. I've never seen a barracuda outside an aquarium." She fastened the strap of her bathing suit around her neck. "We can come back later and make a fire, like you said."

"I don't want to wait until later, Cammie," Michel said, struggling to have as much poise as possible while working the fish from side to side.

"You'll be all fishy."

"I said, I'll wash up. I have anisette." Michel planted his feet on either side of the pole and hauled back. "It's not a barracuda. It's a jack. Maybe ten pounds."

"How can you tell?"

"By the way it's moving."

"Come on, Michel. Haul it in!"

"You're distracting me."

"You're just afraid you're not going to get it and you'll look like an idiot in front of me," Cammie said with satisfaction.

Michel leaned back with all his strength, and the fish came flying onto the sand. Quickly, he threw it into a nest of bushes, where it lay, thrashing. Then he waded out and washed his arms and hands and splashed his hair and reached into the tender. He took the bottle of licorice-smelling drops that were supposed to deceive fish into taking baits and rubbed his hands with it. He removed the rug.

"There," he said, making his way back to shore. "I could have done this from the boat, you know. I didn't have to come over here. I convinced Lenny there might be fish playing around little reefs underwater."

"You knew I'd come over, I think," Cammie said.

"No, I didn't. Of course, I hoped you would. I didn't take it for granted."

"Did you really buy toothpaste?"

"No," Michel said.

"Do you have what you really bought with you?"

"No," he said.

"And so we can't do anything. Everything."

"We could, but we should wait until the right time."

"You probably have ten tropical diseases."

"No, I wasn't thinking of that. I know I don't have any," Michel said.

"So you're concerned about pregnancy."

"Aren't you? You're nineteen years old."

"I am and I'm not. Concerned. I don't think I'll get pregnant."

"What if you did?"

"I don't know. What if I did?"

"I wouldn't like it if you had an abortion. I'm a Catholic. And between us, I feel that wouldn't be right. So you have to think about it. If you got pregnant, would you have me?"

"What do you mean, *have* you?"

"Would you have me as your husband?" Michel had no idea why he was asking such a thing of a girl whose existence he'd been unaware of thirty-six hours earlier. But then, he thought about having a baby, as Lenny had a baby, and a wife, as Lenny had a wife. His wife, Camille. He thought about his mother's face when she saw Cammie. Nothing he thought corroborated any image he had of himself. In fact, Michel thought, he had not entirely considered, until now, his own image of himself, or reflected on his private concept of who he was. He had simply seen himself in others' eyes.

"How I feel at this moment, I would have you," she then said. "I was thinking about this last night. I know that you're supposed to think and make lists and compare the person's way of life to your way of life and see if they match. And they don't. But I still . . ."

Michel felt that he might inflate and, if untethered, float off earth. He felt like a diffident superhero, a stud whose stomach threatened to rebel, a humble child. He had to conclude that this was what people meant by love. He knew he had never felt it. He expected that if he were to measure it, he would be running a fever. He put his arms around Cammie, and they lay down together.

That was the moment Olivia appeared out of the brush.

"What?" Cammie cried out. "What's going on?"

"I swam over. Lenny was wondering about you. Michel," Olivia said, shaking her head, "she's a child."

"What are you really worried about, Olivia?" Cammie asked, her voice low and combustible. "Protecting me?"

"Not really," Olivia said. "Lenny says to bring the dinghy back. He says there's wind coming."

"You must like to swim, like your niece," Michel said coldly.

"My *niece*!" Olivia spat. "Camille, this is ridiculous. Your mother would hardly—"

"My mother trusts my judgment."

"I don't."

"Well, you're not my mother."

"Camille," Michel said warningly, "we'll just go back. We'll come back when it's dark. We planned to. Let's not ruin it for the others."

"Go ahead and tell my mother, Olivia," Cammie said, getting to her knees, then her feet. "Then I can tell her what I know about what you did, too."

"This is absurd," Olivia said wearily. "You don't even know this man."

"How can you say that? You of all people . . ."

"It's an entirely different . . ."

Michel tried to intercede, quietly. Then he gave up hope. He noticed something even more important.

Lenny was right. Weather was coming. The water, so quiet moments before, had begun to lap and churn.

"We need to go," he said quietly. Olivia had turned her back. Cammie was red-faced. "It's best not to take this . . . back to the boat. It will make Tracy unhappy, and Lenny unhappy. Olivia, this was private. I'm sorry if this seems offensive, Olivia, but it meant a great deal to me. She means a great deal to me. I know it seems impossible, like . . . at first sight. I don't know why."

"Because she looks like a fashion model and she's giving it to you like a whore, which she isn't," Olivia said in brittle cadence.

Cammie turned to him, and he held her face against his chest as Olivia whirled and picked her way back to the tender, her spine arched. His gut lurched again. He would not be able to eat. It's okay, he thought. He could feel this living girl in his arms, feel her lean into him, trusting, longing, grateful. He felt proud of this. He thanked his patron, St. Michael.

Water was slopping in great willful fistfuls against the hull of *Opus* as they approached. Lenny always thought, at times such as this, of how old sailors were careful to be respectful toward gods they didn't believe in. The weather was not threatening; but it felt stealthy. Lenny didn't like surprises.

"Idle until I pull them in and we'll tie up," Lenny said, leaning over for Olivia's hand and then Cammie's. Cammie's hand slipped out of his on the first pass. Michel putted in a circle and threw the fish on board. "Cute," Lenny called. "Jumped right into the boat. We'll just drop anchor and let her drag. I think there's going to be wind. If I was smart, I'd bring her around the other side. We're exposed. But I think we're out of time."

"Let's get Cammie on board," said Michel.

"I'm ready," Lenny called back.

But the wind had other plans; and the tender bucked as Michel made his second approach. Michel cursed in French.

"What should I be doing?" Cammie asked.

"Nothing. I'm just not the prince of the sea today," Michel said, tension stiffening his voice. He drew alongside again.

Cammie stood and a wave lifted the bow of the tender out of the water. Leaning precariously to reach for Lenny's hand and the overboard ladder, Cammie stumbled instead, knocking her hip on the oarlock, dislodging the oar, falling backward and disappearing under the water. Before Tracy could open her mouth on the cry that ballooned there, Cammie surfaced, spluttering.

"It's okay, sweetheart," Michel told her, his hands secure under her shoulders. He pulled Cammie over the side as the others watched, breathless. Another wave broke, soaking both of them. Holly groaned.

Lenny noticed *Opus* was drifting faster than he had imagined.

"Here's a rope," Olivia cried out, kicking the first coiled length she saw into the water.

Lenny watched the fifty-foot stern line unfurl into the water with dismay. But this was like a car wreck in slow motion: He had no time to point out what a rope that length could do to the propeller on the trimaran's single engine. He could only hope for the best.

"Let's get the tender secured," he shouted to Michel.

"Her first," Michel said, bringing the tender alongside, idling. This time, Lenny was able to pull Cammie, soaking wet, over the side, where her mother waited with a towel. "Okay," Michel said; "Len, I'm sorry about the oar." But he had barely finished when the tender motor began to cough, bicker, and then died.

"No way!" Michel shouted.

He pushed the starter again. The motor turned over but sounded odd. As Michel took hold of the tiller, the engine coughed and died. He grabbed the can. Was it too light? No. He grabbed at the other can. It was full. He reconnected the hose and started the motor again. It bickered and died.

". . . fuel!" Lenny heard him shout.

"Pump it!" Lenny called.

"I'm trying!"

"Try harder!"

Michel stood up. He pulled the engine up and checked for anything that might be tugging at the propeller. As he did, the wind shook the tender the way a naughty schoolchild shakes a soda pop can, and Michel hit his knees, hard, on the bench seat. Unable to hold himself balanced, he fell forward and struck his forehead.

"Michel!" Lenny yelled. "Double shit!" Lenny cried. "Michel! Michel! This is nuts! It can't be happening!"

Michel didn't stir. His arm flopped ominously with the motion of the small boat. The tender drifted.

"Michel!" Cammie screamed, struggling out of the towel, making for the side, as Tracy fought to hold her back.

"Oh, shit!" Lenny cried, kicking off his shoes. "I'll grab him and row it over . . . I'm sure he's fine . . ." *Oh, please God*, he thought, *and I was pissed about a frigging can opener.* "Hang on!" Lenny's flat dive cleaved the churning water neatly and he made for the tender with sure, economical strokes. But the wind was watching; and *Opus* was drifting away, too fast. Lenny noticed the snakelike length of the stern rope, and treading water, he looped it around his chest and knotted it. There was enough length. He could still make the tender . . . easily. But how fast was it moving? He was caught between the boats, unsure. Lenny began to swim, harder now. The sky was darkening overhead, the clouds heaving. Soon the sun would set.

Abruptly, Lenny turned back, now swimming for his boat and, he realized with almost comic import, for his life.

"Cammie," Holly said, "as soon as he's close enough, you throw the life ring . . ."

"What about Michel?"

"He'll come to his senses and row right to the nearest boat and be back by tomorrow. I saw him hit. It wasn't a skull-fracturing blow," Holly said, with more hope than conviction. Cammie looked at her, a kaleidoscope of panic in her great eyes.

The sun lay down a line of rose and gold, a child's crayoned horizon, as they struggled to keep Lenny in sight. By dint of his strength and the line, he was making time. Tracy flipped on the huge light.

"Lenny!" she shouted. "Come on!"

"Come on, Lenny. You can make it!" Cammie cried. Lenny's head was a point in the sudden utter darkness, his arms working up the rope. Hand over hand, he closed on the side.

Then a wave lifted one of the wings of *Opus* as if it were a loaf of bread. The women tripped and slid on the slick deck. Lenny felt the wave's approach and struggled to free himself from the stern line. Why had he tied it around himself? The wet knot was intransigent; Lenny kicked backward. But the line seemed . . . it was hung up on something, but nothing he could see in the dark. To his horror, he saw his beloved hull rise, a monolith above his head. Involuntarily, he turned away. He heard Cammie scream-ing. *Meherio*, he thought. He felt the great silent gust of air that preceded the impact, and he felt the impact not at all.

At nearly the same moment, all of the lights on *Opus* flick-ered for a moment. Even at so great a distance, Michel could see it. His head thundered. He tried to sit up and fell back again. There came the first bite of real fear. Where was Lenny? He could not leave Lenny. Or had Len left him? Michel searched the figures behind the lights on *Opus* for Cammie. He could not make out for sure which was she. So he chose one figure, fixing on it like a star. Because he did not die quickly, as Lenny had, and the night was long, he imagined, during his intermittent moments of consciousness, that Cammie had married him in that last moment when he glimpsed her silhouette, and felt for Cammie what Lenny felt for Meherio. What a man knows, Michel thought. He had felt at least that. Then at last the field of his vision was as blank as the night that surrounded him.

Day Seven

The sheer jolt of the disappearance having subsided, Tracy shoved her mind into gear. It was necessary. The others' faces were like blank sand after a tide.

"We have to start looking for them right away," she said firmly. "There's a good chance we can find them. We have a motor and they don't."

She bounded up to the cockpit and turned the key. The motor shuddered and turned over. And then it stopped.

"What's wrong with it?" Cammie called, her voice dull as a dropped coin.

"I . . . don't . . . know," Tracy answered, huffing, struggling with the key, as if it would matter, as if it had ever mattered when what turned out to be a minor thing—some minute wire or drop of oil in the wrong place at the wrong time—caused her car motor to fail her, for no apparent reason. She removed the key, reinserted it. This time, when she turned it, there was no response. Well then, Tracy thought, I will . . . raise the sail. Urgencies called for urgencies. It was a sail, after all, a bigger sail than she had raised as a girl, but a sail with a boom, and . . . it was only a sail. She could tack in a widening circle, while all of them looked for a trace of the tender, and worry about the motor later. It would be one of those drops of oil or loose wires, and the fact that it had happened now was not a hideous, portentous grotesquerie, but only a coincidence, an ill-timed coincidence.

"Help me, Cammie!" Tracy shouted. "I'm going to raise the sail and look for them."

And for the next hour, she did just that, with Cammie and Olivia using the handles that operated the floodlights on the railings to sweep the inscrutable, unbroken surface of the sea.

None of them noticed the wind rising. It was subtle at first, just a small freshening that gave Tracy a little more challenge in managing the boat's turns—nothing she couldn't handle, though it quickened her heart.

And then the squall came, so quickly that Tracy wouldn't have been able to lower the sail even had she known how. Abruptly, she found herself fighting to keep her windbreaker from billowing off her back as she fought her way down to the saloon.

"What do we do?" Olivia called over the wind.

"I think these sails are made to take this," said Tracy. "Don't worry. We'll just ride it out and hope we don't go too far." She knew that they would go too far, but panicking Olivia seemed to her as unnecessarily unkind as wearing a ghoul's mask into the bedroom of a jittery toddler.

And the gusts buffeted *Opus* sharply, regularly, but for a surprisingly brief time. There was no rain, only the fist of the wind. The mast shuddered, and a few metal clips tore free and clanged mournfully. The sail bellied outward, but the women didn't see. They didn't know that they should have fought the wind at almost any cost to rush and lower it. It was a rule they hadn't needed to learn.

Instead, they clung, hand to hand, in the saloon.

Opus no longer felt like the kind, cradling, big-bellied mother who'd rocked them in her palm as they slept. Cammie wept until her face was swollen; and Olivia crawled up the stairs and over the deck on her knees, only to fetch her cloisonné box and extract a Valium. Over Cammie s protests, she made the girl swallow it with a sip of water from the sink. She then took a pill herself. Olivia saw that the water came in a slow trickle, not in a gush, and wondered if it had something to do with the boat's pitching. Whatever it was, Tracy would fix it.

The weather seemed to pause for a breath. And then it stopped altogether.

They wobbled up onto the deck. The sky was impassive, blank of stars.

Holly found the flashlight and shined it around her. Loose things had been taken apart with abandon, as if by an angry, rough dog. The top half of a swimsuit lay on the stovetop. A long-sleeved T-shirt seemed to have thrown its arms around one of the supports of the canopy, a leg bent like an old man's shillelagh. Life jackets bobbed in the wake behind the boat, tethered by the lines that still held them. Two loaves of bread, flattened like matzo, lay on the stairs, and glass from broken bottles of wine and mugs crunched under her feet. Because it was what a person should do, Holly found a dustpan and whisk, secured by magnet to the inside of a cabinet door, and began to sweep up. She winced as she did it, because her leg, though wrapped tightly, still refused to support her fully. She was making headway with the mess when she heard Tracy say, "Mother of God." She followed Tracy's eyes upward.

The sail, plucked apart first at its carefully mended fingerling tear, had then blown to bits like an overinflated balloon. It flapped in gigantic shreds from the mainsail.

"How could that have happened?" Tracy cried.

"And so fast," said Holly. "That sail was perfect."

"Thank God for motors," Tracy said. "Lenny's beautiful sail . . ."

"They're out there, Trace," Holly said. "The wind might have blown them away from us, but they've got the motor started by now." Tracy's rueful glance told her that she didn't believe for a moment this was true. "Well, they're strong men," Holly went on. "If anyone can make it, they can. They know this area like the back of their hands. We have to think of us, right here, now."

"Yeah," Tracy said. "Well. It was my fault. I brought the boat around too fast."

"You've had a lot of experience steering fifty-foot yachts," Holly said.

"Don't kid about this," Tracy told her sharply, and Holly shrank back. She was always the one who was good for a laugh. Always. And it was lousy, yes, but for her part, she was grateful that she was soon going to be walking on dry land and gathering Ian and Evan in her arms. She imagined Chris, her husband, hauling her butt to a hospital. Action and forward motion had propelled Holly her whole life. She rarely had the patience for reflection; and if she sat down too long, even in a movie theater, she fell asleep. She was, she supposed, more like her mother than she would have liked to believe. Heidi's maxims: Do not throw good money after bad. What can't be cured must be endured. Her impulse was to worry about her sons; but they were not here, not at this moment. If she was to cast the line of her mind out far enough, she would be sweating the dark line that proceeded, half a centimeter at a time, up her thigh from the site of her wound. Holly had blood poisoning. She knew it, but what good would it do to tell the others? How could they help? Even with her knowledge, how could she? A few handfuls of amoxicillin wasn't going to cure septicemia. If she didn't get help quickly, she would go into septic shock. She already felt intermittently feverish.

So lost in thought was she that she didn't notice Tracy, bagging trash and, with her strong hands, straightening out the bent leg of the canopy.

"Mommy!" Cammie screamed from the cabin.

"I'm here," Tracy called back.

"Mom! Is Michel back yet? Is Lenny here?"

"Honey, I think the boat drifted in the night. I'm sure they're fine, but we can't see them. It's still too dark. Wait until dawn. Then we'll see what's going on with the motor and go looking for them."

"We'd better just go back to St. Thomas," Olivia said, unscrewing the lid on a bottle of Evian. "We can't go looking for them, Tracy. We don't know where we are. That's what they'd do. They'd go back."

"You know they wouldn't. They'd come for us. Or send someone for us," Tracy said.

Olivia poked her head out of the saloon, scanned the sky for weather, and protested, "At least someone there will know something! What the hell happened to the sail?"

"Mom, what if they're dead?" Cammie clambered up the stairs. "You! Aunt Olivia! You did it with him! You came out there to the island because Michel was with me! And now he's dead!"

"What are you talking about, Cammie?" Tracy looked from one to the other.

"She did!"

"What does she mean?"

"She slept with him. She slept with Michel! Ask her! And it was her idea! She asked him to!"

"I did not," Olivia said, sipping her water.

"How? What?" Tracy said. "This isn't making any sense."

"I mean she slept with Michel, Mom! She had sex with him!"

"Surely, she's . . . honey, you don't mean that."

"Ask her! Ask her!" Cammie tugged at her hair. She looked like a supernatural creature, with matted, angled dark locks and chalky lips. Her cheeks were the only stain of color on her face. Pallor that extended down to her throat seemed to have overtaken her tan. Holly limped past Tracy and put her arms around the girl. She convinced Cammie, as much with susurrant sounds as with words, to calm down, that they didn't have the luxury for a temper tantrum. Not for any reason.

"This is nonsense," Olivia murmured, and then asked, "Why did the motor cut out? I don't mean their motor, on the dinghy. I mean ours, the big motor."

"I'm sure I did something stupid to it," Tracy said. "That's the first order of business. We have to find out what's wrong."

"No, the first order of business is coffee. Coffee is proven to raise your IQ a few points. I can get around. I'll make some coffee," Holly said. "The stove's propane. We have to think this through. Did anyone try a cell phone?"

"I just did," said Tracy. She shook her head. "No luck. Look," she said, her voice dropping to a purr. "Come on, Cammie. Holly's going to make us something to eat, at least some bread and coffee. And, Olivia, you're going to come with me and get out the flares, and I'll find the generator and turn it on. It runs on diesel, that much I know."

An hour later, as the boat drifted, they ate bread and slices of cheese. "Can you stand on your leg?" Olivia asked Holly.

"It just hurts. It looks worse than it is. Honest." She lied fluently, but then she always had. Her mother and father had been stricter than the other girls'; and Holly had narrowly escaped social annihilation at their hands when she'd insisted, with a blue-eyed opacity she practiced in front of the mirror, that all they did on Saturday nights was watch Eddie, Tracy's brother. How many nights had she strolled out of the house with her mini-skirt, the length of two hand spans, rolled at the bottom of her gigantic purse?

"Please, Holly, Cammie, eat something," Tracy said.

"I'm not hungry," Cammie said. "I don't see how you can be."

"I think it's fair to say none of us is hungry. But for right now, we're safe," Holly said. "Let's eat because we have to work. We have to get back, to your dad and Ted, Cammie." Tracy nodded and swallowed her bread with visible effort. "That's the reality."

Cammie whispered, "This is the reality, too. This is real. And it's the most horrible thing I could ever imagine, Mom. It's like an awful nightmare, but you don't wake up. It's like being dead but seeing yourself dead."

"I imagine it is, Cam."

"You know, Mom, if it's anyone's fault it's mine," Cammie said. Her rage at losing Michel spent, she looked the way she had as a child when she was coming down with something. But she was the only one among them who could possibly make the motor work; and in the anemic dawn, Tracy could see that even the little island where Michel and Cammie had gone, probably to make love, was invisible. They had drifted that far. "If you think back to the moment, Michel was trying to do his job and I was distracting him."

"Cammie," Olivia said, "I know you won't believe me. But I'm sorry, about Michel. I'm sorry for being such a fool."

"It would be okay now, if you said that and he was here," Cammie told her flatly. "Because he isn't, it sounds easy. It sounds like you're rubbing it in."

"Will someone tell me what the fuck is really going on?" Holly asked. "I mean that in a polite way."

Olivia sighed. "It seems that I—"

"It seems that the first night we came out, Olivia fucked Michel," Cammie said. "He felt sorry for her. He felt sorry for the poor widow."

"I'm sure that's not true, Cammie," Olivia said, squaring her shoulders.

"Tell me you're kidding, Olivia. I thought Cammie was wacky. You didn't have sex with that kid." Holly pantomimed gagging. "*Très* tacky."

"It wasn't all my idea."

"He said it was," Cammie insisted. "You took off all your clothes."

"It takes two, Cammie. That's why I didn't want you to—"

"It was different for us, Aunt Liv. It was two young people who might have been sort of trying to really be together, not a mercy fuck. . . ." Cammie was animated by grief and confusion. It felt almost exhilarating.

Olivia snorted, "Love at first sight!"

"You never loved anyone but yourself!"

"Stop, Camille. Whatever happened, please don't talk to Olivia that way," Tracy said.

"I don't know," Holly said. "I think I'd talk to her that way, considering. I think I just have."

"Aunt Holly is right! That's what it was. Yeah, he did it. But he felt like crap about it! He thought you'd kill me, Mom, if he laid a hand on me! He was a nice boy, a nice young man! I cared about him. For her, he was just a way to prove she could screw someone other than her hundred-year-old husband."

"I assure you, I have had plenty of other—"

"Stop it!" Tracy cried, putting her hands over her ears. "Both of you, stop it! You're bickering about a boy who may be dead, and we also may be dead if we don't get this boat back to St. Thomas or find a way to get someone to come for us."

The sun burst gloriously through a gray band of clouds.

"Adventures in paradise," said Holly.

That night, Olivia had offered to do something nice. She supposed it was her obligation. At first she tried reading, but she quickly tired of the way the bounce of the boat made the page blur. She needed reading glasses. She would never get them. She went to get another bottle of water, her second in two hours. She was astonishingly thirsty, dehydrated and edgy. She was eating Valium as though they were Pez.

Somehow, along the way, she must have developed a tolerance.

When she was young, a single pastel pill could put her under for an entire night. All she'd had to do to get a bottle filled was gesture at her tummy, indicating period cramps, and the local physician quickly scrawled a prescription. Soon, she was swallowing one every night as she applied her Bugati cream. She would waken when the sun was high and the workers already in the shade with their late morning snacks. She'd rise slowly, as if still in the arms of her dream, wrapping herself in her kimono, then taking a long bath before she came down to the ground floor.

Often it was noon before cups of strong espresso had restored her and she was ready for a languid swim or a consultation on the evening's menu.

Franco simply considered her delicate, in need of a great deal of sleep. He liked a wife as easily bruised as a blossom. In truth, after the first thrill of its ancient charm, Olivia, as a new wife, found Italian village life dull. Against the monotonous lowing of cattle and the dreary punctuation of church bells, there was always a feud boisterously brewing or tearfully on the mend, another baptism, a fashion show, the wheel of the religious holidays and the harvest. While they were rarely on the estate in the winter, Olivia was not, as were her few transplanted British or American friends, charmed by the light that outlined the frozen vine, the comic snowcap on the stone garden god.

One of these friends, Eliza—who also had been a child, a student who fell under the spell of a man with an ever present silk ascot and manners so courtly that they were invisible—said she painted away the summer and slept away the winter, particularly on those nights when her own husband, Mario, hinted at amorous intentions. The weeks Eliza and Olivia spent in Paris—red-cheeked under the lights in their furs, with bottomless checkbooks, their parcels bulging with so many pairs of shoes that the women had to throw away the boxes, the sly flirtations with boys their own age—were the charms on the bracelets that locked Olivia to the gates of the Villa Montefalco.

Cammie would get over this bullshit idea of love.

Cammie was doing something Olivia had never done, romanticizing a fling.

Olivia was certain that Michel had not "cared for her," as he had said. That was only a way to get into Cammie's pants. Love, Olivia had observed, was either an adjective trotted out helplessly to describe the throes of a strong attraction or the bond that outlasted that attraction and translated into the interdependency of age.

Had she loved Franco? She was almost certain that she never had, even when she was most grateful for his generous protection. Would she have loved him in time, if he had lived to be old? She thought not. She had seen her parents together, Sal and Anna Maria, side by side in the car, her mother sitting on the middle of the bench the way girls sat next to their boyfriends before bucket seats, side by side holding hands on the couch, side by side in bed. Never once had she been allowed to sit next to her mother in a restaurant booth or crawl into her parents' bed on a stormy night, though she had stood at their door and knocked. They had certainly been close, doing everything together, even the laundry and grocery shopping. Now that her father had died, Olivia was certain that her mother described theirs as a great love, to her friends from church, to her sister, to anyone who asked. But even this was a riddle. Olivia had watched her parents eat whole meals without speaking to each other or to Olivia or to her brother. Was this because love conferred an understanding that didn't require words? Olivia doubted it. Her own happiest times were spent in the occasional stunning conversation or in the company of books. Having never loved a child, or felt loved as a child, having never loved a sibling or felt protected by a sibling, never shared confidences in quite the way she knew that Janis and Holly and Tracy had, she had observed the world in a puzzled silence until she became old enough to realize that she was beautiful and needed to be no more than that to have power over others.

On the other hand, she didn't like discomfort or the feeling that something was expected of her.

She was again alone, the observer; and she didn't want the blame for any part of this calamity, minor as it was.

She imagined the Coast Guard would come soon, and she would be relieved, but Olivia wanted to walk off this boat with her friendships, the only bonds in her life that had truly lasted, intact. Whatever frisson of excitement she had felt about the drama of the crew had long since dissipated. It was sad about the men, if they really were lost at sea; but would the world be poorer for two footloose sailors—though hadn't the older one had a young child? The Canadian boy, well, it had been an affirming interlude, but she had been with more adroit men. She hadn't really known them. And now, while she was not frightened, she was physically spent from hauling around this and pulling up that. Tracy's unwonted demands, along with the nervous tedium, were ghastly. This couldn't last for very long; it was too awful. The others, she knew, had worked harder physically than she had.

Hence Olivia's solitude. She'd offered to do something nice. She volunteered to sit alone and steer while all the others caught a few hours of sleep, until the fogs cleared off. She scanned the murky, seamless verge of the ocean for some sign of light or life. There was nothing. A far-off airplane. A star that seemed to bob and recede—a trick of her eye, Olivia thought. Finally, just before a smudged dawn broke, she knelt and placed her elbows on the storage seats and prayed, "Oh, heavenly Father, forgive me my manifold sins and wickednesses which I have committed against Thy divine mercy. Please have mercy on the souls of Lenny and Michel, and guide them in Your great sea, where our boat is so small. . . ."

It sounded right.

Cammie slept and dreamed of Michel, of lying on the rug in the sun with Michel, of his dark, slender face, his cheekbones that lifted when he smiled, his hair streaked like a lion's mane, gold and dark, the touch of the stubble on his cheek the last time she'd touched him. She woke crying and saw her mother, still awake, watching her. "I'm okay, Mom," she said.

She dropped off again and less than an hour later woke again. She had been dreaming that she could not sleep. "Even in my sleep, I can't sleep. My mind feels like I tore it, Mom. Can't use it. Can't rest it."

"It's natural. Cry it out, Cam."

"Did you ever cry this hard? Until you were so worn out?"

"Of course," Tracy said.

"But you've never been unhappy, not really unhappy. You've never had to live through a tragedy. Grandma and Grandpa are still alive," Cammie prompted her.

"I cried when I had a miscarriage, and other times. Everyone cries, Cam. Cries herself sick. Everyone's hurt is as real to that person as another's. You can't compare the tears of someone who's had cancer to the tears of someone in mourning, even mourning an accident. They're the same and not the same. It's not as though you have to have a right to them."

"He was so gentle, Mom. He was the most gentle boy."

"I hate that this happened to you."

"Can I sleep up by you, Mom?"

"Mmm, come ahead."

"I've been a bitch to you."

"That's forgotten, Cam."

"Do you think God's punishing me?"

"I think God has better things to do."

"Mmm," Cammie said, drifting, her attention unreliable.

"What's that?" Tracy asked, and called out, "Olivia?"

"Yes?"

"What's going on?"

"I'm moving over to Lenny's cabin. There's an open wall there, between their two berths. I don't feel well."

"If there is, Holly should have that, Olivia. She needs room to really get that leg up."

"Well, tomorrow, okay?"

"Go back and take the wheel, Olivia. We could be about to hit a freighter."

"I will in a minute."

"She's completely selfish, isn't she," Cammie said.

"No, Cammie. Not completely." Tracy wondered if she was lying to herself now, willfully. She thought she might need to pin the burden of her heart's debt, like the tail on the donkey, on a hopeful fiction about Olivia's nature. She had seen Olivia five times in the past twenty years. Her own wedding. Livy's. Sal's funeral. Joey's wedding. One other time and now. How could anyone say she knew someone at that remove? Moreover, Tracy thought, she was certainly blindfolded, spun around, and left alone. She couldn't see a damn thing with any clarity at all.

Holly drifted and wakened, drifted and woke again. At night, the pain was only irksome. She thanked God once more that she was a heavy sleeper.

To distract herself, she let the album of her life fall open to a room filled with floral arrangements and a tiny bundle of boy at each breast. Chris was beaming with immoderate pride, as if he had won the claiming race for studs, calling out to total strangers in the hallway of St. Anne's. She flipped ahead to the year they were two and still biddable, and she had dressed fair Ian and dark-haired Evan in matching outfits for Easter. Bow ties as long as her thumb. Tiny velvet jackets. Then to cheering on the sidelines from her folding canvas picnic chair when Evan, entirely by accident, scored his first goal. How small they had been, no more than six? Spelling drills at the kitchen table. Moans from the moment the door opened and the boys smelled Tuesday meat loaf. Muddy tracks on the foyer floor. Stepping over the bodies of half a dozen boys on Saturday mornings after sleepovers. The heavy silver frame into which she slipped each year's school photos. The portrait they'd spent hundreds of dollars on, a painted photograph: the four of them, shiny and sedate in their best clothing . . . Ian at her side, Ev standing next to Chris. Why hadn't they waited to take that picture until just before the boys left home? Because they were still children, she thought. Next year, they would be chrysalids of young men.

Well, she thought. Just as well.

Olivia sighed and hoped it wouldn't take very long for Tracy to wake. Dull as she was, Tracy usually had ideas.

It didn't occur to Olivia to try actively to turn the boat's wheel, though she kept a hand on it when she could remember to do so. She waited for Tracy to wake and tell her what to do, and what would come next if she did what Tracy asked. If Olivia approached life with the greed and thoughtless hunger of a child, it was perhaps because all her adult life someone had always been there to guide and buffer her way. When she truly was a child, no one ever had.

Day Eight

When Tracy did wake, with the first light, Olivia had already made coffee for them.

"Thank you, Livy," Tracy said, genuinely touched. Holly accepted her cup with a benign smile as well and, Olivia noticed, with the absence of a single observation about butlers and silver tea services.

"What should we do first?" Olivia asked as she waited for the others to nibble on some bread and apples. She could never abide food before noon.

"Well, I'm sure we can find the generator, and running the generator should charge the batteries. Cammie's good at that, if we can get her to . . . I have to go down and talk to her. She's really upset, Liv, not that all of us aren't."

Olivia nodded but then shrugged. "Really, Tracy, getting her going would be the best thing for her. A teenager's broken heart is the least of our worries. And then?"

"We'll . . . motor to . . . back. We'll read the locator, the positioning device thing, and go back to St. Thomas or St. John, whatever island we come to first. We'll stop when it gets dark, if it takes us more than a day, though God knows how we'll tie up to anything. But if we should run aground, unless the boat sinks, well, all the better. We'll set off the flares. Someone will see us. It's good we didn't get very far. What a swell notion for a trip I had, Liv. I'm sorry."

So you should be, thought Olivia. But, still feeling generous from her night of sacrifice, she said, "Well, don't worry about it. I'm not angry. If it hadn't been for the crew and all, this would actually have been more of a distraction from mourning my husband and leaving my, well, my home than . . . any old trip. I've been on dozens of those. As Lenny said, it's exciting, in a horrid way. Do you think they're all right?"

"I don't," Tracy said, trying to move her mind aside from the small thud she had felt, felt with her entire body, that night as she'd turned the boat. She prayed, briefly but earnestly, that it had not been what she feared. "I hope with all my heart that they are, but no, I don't think so."

"They had no fuel."

"Maybe there was fuel. Maybe the motor was just flooded," Holly suggested.

"That's probably right," Olivia said. "Want more coffee?"

Holly said then, "Livy, you're so nonchalant. How can you be? That girl in there is . . . Cammie. It's like you're not upset for her, or about what happened. It's like you don't care."

"I care," Olivia said. "But I can't do anything about it. So why spend time talking about what I can't fix?"

For a moment, Tracy saw a montage of mental snapshots, of Olivia's closed eyes and slackened face, her black hair spread, dark against the pillow as a vine, of the borrowed assurance of white jackets. Olivia had been curiously unmoved then, as well as now.

"Drink up," Olivia said. "I'm going to bed. You've all slept, and I've been up for hours. You take over now."

They watched as she crossed quietly to her cabin and closed the door.

"She's so damn odd," Holly said.

"I want you to take a couple more of these antibiotics," Tracy replied.

"You just won't talk about her that way, will you?" Holly asked.

"And I can take all the antibiotics on earth, Tracy. I don't think I have an infection that they can touch."

"Antibiotics never hurt," Tracy said. "Take them, and take half that painkiller thing."

"I'm the nurse," Holly reminded her, amused. She watched tolerantly as Tracy slapped the bubbles out of one of the syringes Lenny kept in the first aid kit and, after gathering up a fold of Holly's healthy thigh, gave her a tentative injection. What Holly suspected was only lidocaine still spread like a balm through her, allowing her to relax her clenched neck for the first time in hours. "Thanks, Trace," she said. Tracy looked white around the lips. "What's wrong?"

"I've never given anyone a shot. I was scared to death."

"Well, you did a great job. I'm going to rest now for a moment."

"Well, then I'm going to get Cammie. Olivia was right about one thing. Getting her moving is going to be the best thing for her."

The men lay up for a day when the winds came. They meant to stop only for a few hours, to refuel. Fuel was sometimes left for them at this place, sometimes at another. The young man didn't know this, but he went along dumbly. He did not know that they did not usually see the people who lived in the house near the dock. There was no need. When they approached, the young man sometimes caught a glimpse of a child disappearing into the shanty, like a small furred thing into its den. This day, however, there was no use going on. They would hardly have made any time at all, despite the size of the motor. The winds were brief, but they gave Ernesto and Carlo a chance to drink again. And when they drank, the young man was guaranteed that they would be insensible for twelve hours at least. The young man thought their livers must by this time appear brined and stippled, like ugly fish.

The house was the home of an acquaintance of Carlo's sister. The man fished and was gone for long periods. The woman seemed to have no discernible personality. She made strips of beef for them and hard corn bread with peppers. Carlo made her sleep on mats on the floor, with her two feral children, a little boy and an even smaller girl. In the night, the young man heard Carlo grunting as he had sex with the woman. She made no noise at all.

The young man slept in what he assumed was the rope bed that belonged to the little girl. In the night, she wandered out to use the toilet, and when she returned, she crept into bed beside him. "*Frío*," she said. He could see the lice shining in her dark hair. But he held her close anyway, and he began to cry. Two days more, he thought. Nothing was worth this.

"This is hopeless," said Tracy, letting her hands drop to her sides as she surveyed the generator's smooth, opaque planes. "Even looking at it scares me."

"Mom, I'm mechanical, I'll figure it out. I'm more worried about Lenny and Michel," Cammie said. Her eyes were swollen from crying, and though she had rallied enough to try to help, Tracy could see, with pity, the distance in her eyes.

"Honey, it's not going to change anything, you worrying," Tracy said, trying Olivia's tack.

"You do it. You're, like, the grand master of worrying."

"But I know it isn't a solution. And neither is carrying around whatever happened with Olivia and Michel, while we're at it. That stuff poisons you."

"Trust you to lecture me about my psychological state, Mom, when we're stranded in the middle of the ocean. I'm not going to kill her. She's just cheesy. And I didn't appreciate you telling me to let her alone."

"What you were saying was so vulgar."

"Mom, I was *with* Michel. There was a lot of mutual . . ."

"Attraction."

"And interest. He's mysterious. He's smart. Anyhow, whatever. I can't think of it now."

"Let's assume they're alive," Tracy told her, squeezing her daughter's hand in response. "It would make for at least some kind of happy ending to a crappy ending. Let's hope Michel's at some billionaire's house on some gated island and he's sending the Coast Guard for us now." She was careful not to mention Lenny.

Holly spent the next few hours, while the painkiller was still working, at the stove, cooking. She was good at cooking plain food, and what food there was would spoil if she didn't do it now. The electrical system was, at least temporarily, defunct. And despite her growing apprehension that she could lose her leg at the end of this voyage if it didn't end pronto, she felt better being useful.

So she fried fish and baked it.

She used Lenny's dough and baked cloverleaf rolls.

She contemplated what looked like a pork roast but thought it probably had already gone over. When she threw it into the water, she saw sharks rise, like snakes the circumference of her thigh, green as the water, tearing and worrying the bloody lump. Tracy had told her that Cammie was determined to try to fix the motor. Cammie would have to go down there. But not now, not at the intersection between afternoon and evening, when the sharks glided back and forth like racing sleds, making use of the rhythms of the other creature, of their hierarchy on the food chain. Holly shivered in the dull heat and made the sign of the cross. Olivia had awakened briefly, for water, but gone back to bed, pleading a migraine. What a horny bitch, Holly thought idly. She wondered what circumstances would prompt her to cheat on Chris. The guy would have to be younger, she decided, and Australian. And a soccer player. Pro. Despite herself, Holly smiled.

At last, Tracy came down.

"I was fantasizing about screwing an Australian soccer player."

Tracy grinned. "Do you have a fever?"

"I think I probably do, but it's not bothering me. I started by wondering if I'd ever have done what Olivia did, even if I had the chance. And then I got to thinking about how Olivia was like the proverbial cat in heat—"

"Oh Jesus, can we leave that alone now? Do you have to keep blaming her! You're gossiping like we're all still in high school."

"And you're so loyal, it's like a mental illness. You're acting like you and Olivia wore the matching French braids on Spirit Day."

Tracy blew out her breath in what could hardly be called a sigh. She said, "Cammie's got the wheel now. She's steering straight on. At least we have the compass and we know we're pointed in the right direction." She paused. "Listen. I don't want you to think I condone this. I think she's a lonely person, Hols. And she was when she was the belle of Villa Montefalco, too."

"That's such crap, Tracy. Could you see the good side of John Wayne Gacy? He could draw nice pictures of Bambi, you know. This isn't the *Queen Elizabeth*! It's so totally gross to actually fuck someone with five other people twenty feet away."

"Well. We're not talking about some big sin! They're both single. He did it, too."

"Granted, let's stipulate. Men are pigs. But did you see the little necklace Cammie has, that he gave her? He wasn't a total asshole. No, your friend—"

"My friend! She's your friend, too, Holly."

"She was my friend for a very short time a very long time ago, Tracy. Yeah, we were the Godmothers. It was all fun. It was fun to go to Italy after she dropped out of school and watch her, in that train twenty feet long with all the little Italian girls in white dresses, marry the old guy. Nice guy. But you think she really loved him? Or do you think she wanted the money and the big villa?"

"I think she really loved him. She was distraught after he died, Hols."

"If I had to bet, I'd bet she was distraught because his partner had the percentage power to put her out! If he hadn't, she'd be there now, stomping grapes and telling the locals to eat cake."

"I'm not listening to this."

"And you know why she had sex with that kid? She thought of us as a bunch of over-the-hill cows and she some rare filly who never got older. She had to prove it as fast as she could!"

"Stop. Just stop. Let's get home. Holly, I love you. You're my best friend."

"Janis is your best friend."

"Janis is my cousin. Let's just get home."

"Next time we go to Vegas."

"I'm with you."

"Mom!" Cammie shouted.

Holly watched her friend lope up the stairs two at a time and gave herself the small pleasure of sitting down. She wondered if Tracy and Jim fought.

Everybody fought. She and Chris sometimes bickered so darkly that Evan said they should go to a marriage counselor. They never had, but that was because Chris could never sustain a grudge more than overnight; and it seemed small of Holly, much as she actually enjoyed a good bout, to bait him about the silly stuff she did, and in front of the kids. The last time, it had been over his mother installing electric shoe racks labeled in colors, which presented her mother-in-law, Karin, with a dozen pairs in each color at the touch of a button. It was none of Holly's business. But it was so nutty, and so was Karin. Try as she might, Holly couldn't even *imagine* Tracy bringing something up with Jim like the automatic shoe rack. It would be beneath her, beneath them. Jim occasionally drank too much at a party or a barbecue, drank himself to the point of singing old songs from his college glee club. The worst Tracy had ever done was give Jim a reproving smile and put out her hand for the car keys. Holly wouldn't have let Chris live down a stunt like that for months.

Except that now she would.

Once she got home, she would.

She would stop being a hobby bitch, stop thinking that it was funny to tease Chris and even ever so slightly embarrass the boys.

She wouldn't do that anymore. It had been only a game anyhow, a way to let Chris and the kids know that, yeah, they had her, but, boy, they'd better not take advantage . . . but it had been silly.

Holly got up stiffly and hauled herself onto the deck.

"I don't want to wait anymore," Cammie was saying to her mother. "It's driving me nuts."

"You don't have to do it this minute!"

"I don't want to wait anymore. Someone's going to have to go down, and I'm the logical one, Mom," Cammie said.

"I don't want you down there."

"Look, I'll be ten feet underwater."

"Alone!"

"She'll be safe, Tracy," Olivia put in, emerging from her room with a cloth held to her head.

"No one asked you," Cammie snapped.

"Let's not start," Holly said. "Let's talk about it over dinner. I've made dinner for an army."

They all dutifully sat in the saloon.

Her appetite briefly revived, Holly devoured most of an entire pie, forkful by forkful, while Cammie pulled a piece of bread into bits.

"Mom," Cammie finally began again, "listen to reason. Daddy taught me how to fix car engines. He taught me how to fix the rotors on the dishwasher when I was five. He taught me how to do oil changes. I was the *only girl* in auto mechanics in high school,

Mom! If there's something around that prop, maybe I can get it loose. I admit, it doesn't look good, but we have to try."

"I don't want you to. I will."

"And what are you going to do, Mom? Will you be able to take the propeller apart and clear it?"

"Okay, Cammie, okay. But you'll wear a tether, in case you get in trouble?"

"Word of honor," Cammie said. "I don't want this boat drifting away from me. I'm not interested in being a hero."

"In the morning, then," Tracy said. "It's almost sunset, Cammie. You know that's when the sharks come up. It's when they feed. Let's please all try to sleep tonight."

And they all did try.

Holly's leg throbbed. She could smell her leg. It seemed to stink beneath the gauze. Gritting her teeth, she used a hot steak knife to lance it, sponged away the pus with alcohol—which hurt so much that she nearly swooned—and replaced the bandage. Thank Christ they were going home, one way or another. She would not alarm Tracy. Tracy already believed that even planning this trip had brought down the curse of the cat people on all their heads. Holly lay back and tried to think about her Christmas knitting, which she'd already begun, complicated argyle sweaters for Ian and Evan, who had decided to dress prep in the future. She dozed and watched her own sturdy hands coax and flex the soft yarn, and a certain peace stole over her. Ian's sweater was almost completed. Holly never finished anything if she didn't start ages in advance.

She had never been sought after. Boys called her to ask advice about wooing Janis or Olivia. She was popular as a friend, a girl everyone knew. But until Chris, no one had ever looked at her with the kind of helpless adoration she saw in boys' eyes when they looked at Janis.

Holly could never quite achieve a look. It was only just before she lay down to go to sleep that her pageboy curled in identical commas against her cheeks and her skin looked translucent and pure, not mottled with excitement or exertion. So Holly adopted the role of the clown, the buddy, just a tiny bit off the pace, not the butt of jokes about herself, but the originator of the jokes. Olivia was the leader, the untouchable. Jan was the sexpot. Tracy was the alibi. Holly felt fortunate just to be able to rely on the conferred status. It no longer mattered. It had been another life. But seeing Olivia again, up close and arrogant, set it rankling within her. And she felt like a fool being unable to pull her own considerable weight because of a sting, a minute incident, an assailant too small to fight.

The important thing, Holly thought as she lay, trying not to pick at her leg, was Cammie.

Cammie had to get home. Michel was already lost. Lenny had at least experienced a taste of a fortunate life. Ian and Evan were presumably safe. But Cammie hadn't had a chance for all that she, Tracy, and even Olivia had known.

She thought of the deer that awakened her one summer when the boys were small and they had picnicked in the Brezina Woods, the three of them falling asleep on a leaf-strewn blanket in the October sunshine. Of making spritz cookies at Christmas. Water-skiing at the cottage she'd inherited from her parents, far up in the north woods of Michigan, veering and leaping for hours before her strong legs even quivered. Roistering with the boys in their backyard pool that Chris had built from a kit. Smoking dope two years ago with Tracy, for their fortieth birthdays, on an abandoned green at the golf course. Swing dancing with Chris at his niece's wedding—after weeks of dutiful classes at the local community college. Clearing away snow from the heads of her first crocuses. The sunroom that had been her tenth anniversary present from Chris, all glass and green plants, a cloister of oxygen and scent. She thought of huddling next to Chris, as if their spines had been magnetized. In fifteen years of marriage, they had never slept "apart," as couples did over time, not without some bit of her body, if only her hand against Chris's shoulder on a hot night, touching, linking them. She was so glad of that now.

Well, Holly thought, well.

She was not afraid of dying. She was afraid of missing the knowledge of how things turned out. Quietly, with firm certitude, she believed in the survival of the soul. But she could not envision herself as some sort of Tinker Bell–like creature in a white nightgown with gossamer wings, fluttering about her children's headboards, breathing the correct definitions for the ACT test vocabulary section into their ears.

You'll be fine, boys, she thought. *Except for a few brushstrokes, you're both of you finished. You have all the confidence and approval I could give you; and you have something I gave you only accidentally: each other.*

Her leg pounded, thrumming like a machine whose product was misery. She had never felt worse pain, even in childbirth. But still she kept a corner bright for hope. She had seen worse things get better.

Day Nine

With Tracy watching anxiously, Cammie carefully pulled up her wet suit and zipped it, slipped her weights into her belt, and fastened them, settling herself, physically and mentally, as if she were getting into an airplane seat. She tested her buoyancy vest and peered at the gauge in the tank to make sure it was filled. She did a good-girl check.

Water was water. But diving down into five hundred feet of it, even if you were just going to skim, felt different from diving in the controlled confines of an underwater park or with a dive master by her side at a showy reef. She breathed in through her regulator and allowed her mother to help her hoist the tank onto her back. She had ninety minutes. Although she did not confide this to Tracy, Cammie didn't believe she would need that long. She thought the motor was damaged beyond repair; but if she could repair it, if there was even a chance they could get it to limp, they would be saved, before anything got worse. Cammie sat while Tracy balanced the tank and attached the tether around her. Then she rose and made her giant step off the port side.

Once she had adjusted her vision relative to the boat, it was difficult to follow the propeller. The boat seemed stationary when they were on it, probably because the water was calm and they had no landmarks to measure their progress. But it was moving, and she had to kick her way to it. Soon she could see the prop shaft and glimpse all manner of shredded garbage hanging from it. Cammie kicked in great stiff scissors, her hands clasped beneath her breasts.

Letting air escape the vest, she lowered herself and caught hold of the fore rudder. She worked her way down the boat. The hull was slick and sound, pocked only with tiny seaweed. She could see the propeller in front of her. There was the shredded bright green rope from the tender. It was just as she had imagined. The rope had wrapped around the propeller before the propeller cut the rope in two. The rope dangled, and a thickness of rags and weeds, too . . . and a shoe . . . a hand.

A hand.

A bone and a hand. There was more. Cammie jerked her head away and kicked for the surface.

She had to get up and out, fast, into the real air, to howl and howl.

Cammie broke the water shrieking into her mouthpiece.

It would have taken reason to remove it from her mouth. She had none.

Hers was an unhealthy cry, not of anger or even fear, but of something mortally injured, not sane. Still floating, making no attempt to haul herself up the tether toward the boat, she reached up toward Tracy as if supplicating, like a child begging to be carried. Tracy leaped into the cockpit and slammed the boat into reverse before she realized the boat wouldn't move. The boat would take her nowhere.

She shouted, "Take out your regulator! I can't hear you!"

Cammie bobbed and rose, screaming, the sound muted by the equipment. She was growing smaller as the current seized the boat.

"Cammie, pull yourself in!" Tracy yelled.

Holly asked, "What is the matter with her?"

"I'm going in after her," Tracy said. "I don't want her to get dragged against something."

"No more of that," Olivia cried. "None of us can do a thing

without you! We'll get her! It's really going faster than we thought, though, isn't it?"

"Cammie!" Tracy shouted. "Honey, look at me . . . Camille, look at me." Cammie quieted and looked. "Drop the vest and the tank. I'll throw you the life ring." Tracy threw the life ring, and Cammie hooked both arms through it, hanging limp.

Tracy yelled, "Good!"

"Help me, Olivia!" Tracy commanded, and together, they hauled Cammie hand over hand. "Throw the ladder over!" When Cammie got to the bottom rung of the ladder, she held on to the step and vomited. Tracy crept down and held her head, washing off her neck with seawater. Holly, her leg now wrapped tightly in a clean new Ace bandage, brought a towel. Cammie leaned over and vomited again. Olivia fetched a Coke from the cooler. It was warm, but Cammie rinsed her mouth and spat with it.

"I have to lie down," she said. "I don't mean in the bed. Right here. How do you feel when you faint, Mom?"

"I never have."

"Like the world is getting louder and smaller and then . . . blink," said Olivia, who had fainted during Tracy's wedding.

"I'm better now," Cammie said, taking hold of her two elbows to stop her quaking. Holly dropped a blanket around her shoulders.

"You are better, Camille. You're safe, and you're with us." Cammie shuddered. Holly continued, "Look at me. You're safe, and you're with us, and you're going to go home." They all handed Cammie up onto the deck, and then Holly somehow found a way to ease herself down and pull Cammie onto her lap. To Tracy's surprise, Cammie relaxed, trusting as a child, as Holly rocked her. "Do you want to tell us? Or wait until later?"

"Now," Cammie said, her face half-turned against Holly's shoulder. "But not get up."

"You don't have to get up," Holly told her.

Cammie drew a deep breath and aligned her face. Tracy had seen her do this before—when she danced as a child, when she tried a sport, when she solved a math problem. She had asked Cammie what she was thinking when she made her face so serious, expressionless, and Cammie had told her, "I'm thinking, I can do this."

"Mom, the propeller is hopeless," she said. "The stern rope that Olivia kicked in was wrapped so many times around that it actually displaced the prop shaft out. The shaft is bent, so I can't put it back in. I'm afraid the stuffing box is letting seawater into the . . . the . . ."

"The bilge," Tracy prompted her.

"Long story short, what I'm worried about is that maybe seawater is getting in. What I'm afraid of is that it'll get high enough that it's going to do something bad to the electricity. Will it, Mom? What if the lights go out?"

"We'll . . . that's not going to happen," Tracy said.

"What if it did?"

"We'd . . . use the candles and the lanterns that run on batteries. Don't worry. The bilge pump is on. It's going to be okay."

"It's not going to be okay," Cammie went on. "Mom, there was something else."

Tracy wanted to run. This wasn't about a motor. But she said, "Cammie, I can hear it. Whatever it is."

"Lenny is . . . Lenny was . . ."

"He's down there," Holly said calmly. "That's what she saw." She went on rocking Cammie gently. "Do you want to go on, Cam? Because we can wait."

"I'm thinking of what to say."

"Okay, then. You're safe," Holly said.

"Mom, he had the rope tied around him. He drowned. I hope he drowned. Maybe he hit his head on the boat in the waves. But I'm sure he was dead by then. The rope got tangled in the propeller. The fish must have done the rest. What is left of him . . ."

"Oh, poor, poor Lenny," Tracy said, dropping her face into splayed hands. "All of it happened so fast."

"No, Mom. If it was anyone's fault, it was mine. Mine and Michel's. We played around when we should have come back. The weather was getting rough. It was just seeing . . . his hand. I flipped out. But I decided when I got back on the boat that someday I'm going to think of all this and fall apart. But not now . . ."

"That's sensible," Olivia told her.

"Livy's right. We could run that tape forever. I just wish there was a way we could . . . bury Lenny," said Tracy.

"Mom, he is buried, where he would want to be buried."

"He loved his wife so much."

"There won't be much left of him, I'm sure, at all, by the time we get back to St. Thomas. But maybe there's a medical examiner who can collect enough so that she can bury him. They do that."

"Why are we talking about this? It's all so theoretical. Let's get the hell away from here," Olivia said.

"Shut up and go steer," Holly said.

"Lenny's wife, of all people, will understand. Not his death, but the rest of it. There was no trace of Michel." Cammie pressed her lips together and shook her head.

"I'm going to try the radio again," Tracy said. "I've been trying every hour, on every channel, and I haven't been able to raise anyone." She went up into the cockpit. Olivia came down.

They listened as Tracy identified them, the sailing ship *Opus*, said they were headed north, and spoke the ancient French-derived words for help.

"Wait!" they suddenly heard her say. "Yes, this is *Opus*. We are passengers, not the captain. . . . I can't make out what you're saying. What's the name of your boat? Passion? Fashion? . . . I'm sorry. I can't understand you. We have no sails or motor. Can you please call the authorities for us? Over. . . . I can't hear you. . . . Please repeat. Over." She could not hear anything else.

Tracy walked down the stairs.

"I don't know if they heard anything I said."

Day Ten

*H*olly found some Excedrin PM in Lenny's medicine cabinet and fell asleep, again trying to send a message to her sons. *Oh, I should never have spent so much time trying to escape from you and rest! I thought we had all the time in the world. And I thought it was funny. It was funny. I always could make you laugh. Remember that.*

Holly Solvig was not given to sentiment. She hadn't even cried, only grinned with pride, when her sons, in kindergarten, had shyly presented her with twin ceramic handprints, with a verse about how soon these hands would outgrow her own. But now tears slid from the corners of her eyes and wet her pillow. But then she prayed to St. Anne. She didn't mince words as she confided that she certainly wasn't ready to be through with her own life, but that if she had to be, then, please, could the patron of all mothers cut Camille a break? Holly would consider it a special favor, and so would Holly's mother—whom Holly was sure St. Anne knew on a first-name basis.

Cammie woke just before she hit the floor, sprawled on her stomach, blood from her mouth spurting onto the floor. Her mother was trying to get to her feet, one hand on her berth, one on the wall.

"We hit something," Cammie said.

"You're hurt."

"It's nothing, Mom. I nicked my lip with my tooth. I'll put a clean rag on it."

"But what did we hit?"

Cammie grabbed the flashlight she kept under her pillow, and by its wavering beam she found the stairs, which were canted at a forty-five-degree angle. Using her fingers as feet, she walked her way up them. Abruptly, the boat righted itself with a shudder and thud. Olivia screamed. Holly called, "Liv! Be still. Let's figure this out. No one can hear you anyhow."

Olivia said, "I wasn't screaming for help! It was involuntary."

Cammie shined her light around the deck. "Check the bilge, Mom, and see if there's water in it. See if whatever we hit damaged the side of the boat and it's leaking."

"It's basically dry," Tracy called back.

"So we probably scraped a rock underwater, but it didn't come through. Why wasn't anyone steering? Olivia, you were supposed to be on watch."

"I don't know how to make this thing go straight!" Olivia complained.

"I thought you had a lot of experience steering boats," Tracy said.

"Boats with motors! Plus, every muscle in my body aches from pulling her out of the water!" She pointed at Cammie. "I just lay down in the saloon for a few minutes."

"So *no one* was steering?" Tracy seemed to grow taller, outstripping her six feet. Holly thought, with delight, that Tracy might finally haul off and deck Olivia. But Tracy forcibly controlled herself. "Olivia, listen. I can't do everything. Holly's sick, and I'm worn out. You don't have a choice here. You let us all down by leaving that cockpit. We could have run into a cruise ship or a freighter." Tracy brought Olivia up to the cockpit and put her hands on the wheel. "I will tie you here if I have to. I mean it."

But it was no good. They were hung up on something. It would have to wait until morning before Cammie could again dive to investigate or until the shifting currents or winds simply lifted them off. Holly thought, Tracy will never let Cammie go down there again. And I wouldn't, either.

Perhaps someone would come along. Didn't she use to tell the boys that? If you ever get lost somewhere, stay there? Don't move or let anyone make you move? One of the freighters, Holly thought. She indulged in a grim laugh. It would probably mow the lightless *Opus* down like a newspaper sailboat in a storm gutter.

Tracy went back down to sleep.

It had to have been less than an hour before Holly heard Olivia screeching. "Tracy! I see something! I see something!"

She heard Cammie cry, "It must be one of those ships! The ones we're supposed to call!"

So extinguished with weariness that she wouldn't have cared if Olivia had seen a party barge with dancing pool boys and ice-cream drinks, Tracy slid out of bed. Holly came limping out of the stateroom, carrying a sealed package of flares and the last box of kitchen matches.

The ship was a mere shape, distant, gray, and indistinct. They couldn't tell how far away it was or figure out, quickly, which function of the navigation unit in the console would allow them to measure the distance.

"Okay, I'm going to call them on channel twenty-three and hope this time I get good sound. And when I do, Holly, you set off three flares, one after another. Okay?" Tracy asked. "Ready?"

Holly lit the first flare, and they watched as it arced over the stern and died in the water. Tracy shouted, "This is the sailing ship *Opus*. We are . . . well, without power at . . . Do you hear me? This is the sailing ship *Opus*. Mayday. Mayday."

"Give us your position, *Opus*. This is the U.S. merchant vessel *Cordoba*. We are at sixty-eight degrees latitude and thirteen degrees longitude, approximately three hundred miles northwest of Grenada. Over," a faint voice replied. The rest of them began to cheer loudly until Holly shushed them.

"We can see you, *Cordoba*. We are the sailing ship *Opus*, captain Lenny Amato, out of St. Thomas. Lenny is dead. Our captain is dead, and our co-captain is missing."

"*Opus*, can you maintain your position? Over."

"We are stuck on something. We won't be moving soon, I don't think. We are passengers. We have no experience with sailing."

"Can you see a landmass? Over."

"No landmass at all."

"Try to maintain your position, *Opus*, or raise sail at full light. Over."

"We have no sail. The sail is torn apart," Tracy said mournfully. Holly lit another flare.

"We will send in a report about your position."

"Do you see our flares? Do you see us?"

"Negative, *Opus*. But we'll find you. . . ."

The lights went out, and the console went black.

Cammie was dumbfounded.

She had expected the last of the power, but not when they were so close, so nearly within the perimeter of safety. The irony pummeled her chest like fists. She drew back her foot and kicked in Lenny's precious glass liquor cabinet. The remaining bottles clonked together.

They stood crowded in darkness, in the cockpit. The boat rocked, but without any forward progress.

"Okay, look. This is bad, but I just thought. Janis will report us missing. She will expect us to call. We can wait that out. It can't be long now," Holly told them.

"That's the spirit, Holly," Tracy said, ruffling Holly's salt-stiff hair. "Always the cheerleader."

"What's my choice?"

"You could have taken to your bed, like the countess," Tracy said, and Holly, unable to restrain herself, beamed. "I'm going to need that handheld GPS and to use the VHF radios—"

"We have a radio," Cammie told her. "I saw Lenny use it all the time."

"And Lenny showed me the handheld GPS."

"Mom, he made Michel take one of the radios and the GPS in the tender that day. Remember?"

"No! I completely forgot both. But now that I think of it, I'm sure . . . it was just the radio."

"No, he had the GPS, too. I was there. I saw it. We have one radio."

"But the GPS is gone? He would have brought it in that night. . . ."

"He lifted me onto the ladder. And he came right after me. We were all over each other. I didn't see him bring them in."

"Check around, though."

"I will," Cammie promised.

"Yeah, well, at least maybe he can navigate himself somewhere," Holly said pensively.

"But as for us, we can sail and sail if we ever move. . . ."

"We have the ordinary compass. We have the maps, charts, whatever. We'll have to try to steer by the stars or something."

"Cammie, I've sailed across a lake in northern Wisconsin. I know where the North Star is, and the Big Dipper. That's it."

"Well, I'm going to try to decipher the navigation charts today. Maybe I can figure out something useful."

"I wish one of those big winds would come and blow us off whatever's holding us."

"We still have the SSB," Cammie said. "Damn it. I never imagined there was so much about mechanical stuff I didn't know."

"We only have that thing when it works," her mother replied.

"That's what pisses me off," Cammie said.

Occasionally, they heard a word or a barrage of chatter on the

SSB, but when they answered, shouting, madly depressing whatever button there was, no one seemed to hear them. Cammie could not for the life of her figure out why. It was a straightforward mechanism. When a plane flew over, they shouted and jumped and tossed out a flare; but the plane never acknowledged them.

"*That* is not going to happen again," Tracy said, swearing under her breath. "Cammie, here's what I want you to do. First thing in the morning, I want you to find the crowbar and pry loose any pieces of wood or fiberboard that you can."

"From where?"

"From the galley, the saloon, wherever you can find it. I'll find some paint."

Day Eleven

The roof of the saloon was made from pristine panels of button board, snow bright and smooth. Starting at dawn, and using the claw end of a hammer, Cammie ripped them all down. Tracy used markers and waterproof blue paint Lenny had stored in the ama on Holly's side and wrote in letters five feet high: sos.

Cammie nailed a panel to the roof of the cockpit, ignoring the ugly splintering of the fiberglass sheathing. It read: hel p. t he opus! She made two more exactly the same. These, she threw overboard—one just after they ate, one at noon. Later, as she was applying some previous passenger's aloe to the burns on her shoulders that had blistered and broken, she felt movement.

The wind shifted, and suddenly the boat was again adrift. Despite its disabilities, it seemed stable. It could be steered. In the cockpit, Tracy steered out toward the color band that signaled deeper water.

Elated to be headed somewhere, anywhere, Cammie later settled in for her watch.

But time passed slowly. The lantern's glow bounced, making reading more irritating than diverting. She brought up the CD player, put in a CD, and softly sang Patsy Cline songs. She sang the theme of every movie she could think of. Finally, she nearly dozed at the wheel.

When she woke, she thought she was dreaming.

Just in front of her face, seemingly feet from the windshield, she saw what she thought was a dark cliff. But the cliff had numbers on it, high above her.

Cammie wrenched the wheel with all her strength, and had the boat proceeded another few yards, it would not have been enough. They missed the freighter by mere feet, all the while unable to hail it.

Frantically, Cammie jiggled and shouted into the SSB, and then the VHF, then the SSB again, her hell-bent determination to be heard temporarily banishing the knowledge that the freighter could have crushed them and that its pilot would have felt that the boat had nudged a reef, if that. He'd have gone on, carrying cars and cabinetry, statuary and stainless steel ovens, tiles and tires. They would spiral down, like Michel and Lenny, their hair like trendrils of seaweed among the corals, their open eyes as impassive as the eyes of the gliding fish.

Cammie watched the huge city of a ship churn loudly into the distance and tried to restore her calm. Her chest was heaving as though she'd run ten miles. She needed flares. She needed to have them with her on watch at all times. They had to have a watch along with whoever steered, someone who could look off the stern. It was just too much for one inexperienced, weary, frightened human. She found a box of flares, and as the freighter retreated, she lit and tossed out two. The SSB crackled, and a voice said, ". . . nightfall." But no one responded to Cammie's increasingly hoarse calls. One day, she would tell her mother what she had almost done and how close salvation had come before a nightmare.

But not tonight.

The freighter had made a noise, passing, like a great wave. Its engines pounded, louder than any train. She couldn't imagine how her mother and the others had slept through it. And then Tracy, her voice sluggish with sleep, called, "What?"

"Nothing, Mom. I dropped something," Cammie called. "Go back to sleep."

Then, behind them, just off the stern, Cammie saw what looked to be a dim light. She shouted, "I see something! Everybody!"

"What is it?" Tracy called back, alert now.

"I think it's a . . . I don't know, but it's moving," Cammie said as Tracy scrambled up the stairs. "I can see the lights going up and down."

"Get the big flashlight!" Tracy called to the others. "Cammie thinks there's a boat of some kind back there. Maybe a fishing boat! We need to signal them."

"Now," Cammie said. "While it's still dark. They won't see the light otherwise." They all willed the sun not to rise.

"You keep signaling," Cammie said. "It might not even be a boat. It could be nothing but, what do they call that stuff? That phosphorescent stuff? St. Elmo's fire? Or some kind of glowy coral?" They were all awake and huddled on the stairs to the cockpit by then. "I'm going to check the bilge. Aunt Holly, can you steer for a while?" She crossed the deck and lifted the hatch to survey what she could see. "Mom, there's water down in here. A lot of water . . ."

"No!" Tracy shouted angrily. "Not enough to sink us!"

"I don't think so, but stuff is floating. Stuff is . . . It would come up to my knees."

"Well, you're little. We're going to have to hand-pump it, then. The manual pump is up in the cockpit."

"How do you know this stuff?" Cammie asked in wonder. "I'm proud of you!"

"I just . . . I don't know it. I looked at it," Tracy told her daughter. "I look at everything. I read owner's manuals. You didn't get all that precision from your father." To their mutual surprise, they were able to manage wry smiles. Holly gave up her position to Tracy, and they worked steadily, taking turns, to make sure the bilge was relatively dry.

The others could not go back to sleep. The sky turned gun-metal, then the familiar striations that signaled the appearance of morning.

It was Olivia who finally asked, "Why hasn't that boat caught up?"

"I don't know," Cammie said. "Maybe they can't see us very well. It's just a flashlight. Damn, if only we had the lights. The lights ran off the diesel. Lenny said we'd never have to worry about the refrigerator or the toaster or anything. Maybe one of the tanks is low. I'll have to try to switch over or fix it somehow. Why aren't they working? The motor and the generator, they don't have anything to do with each other. Or maybe they do. Maybe running the motor does something for the generator."

"I don't want you mucking around electrical stuff. I'll do it," Tracy said.

"Mom." Cammie gave Tracy a level look. "You can't check the oil on the van with the dipstick. At least give me the respect of treating me like an adult out here. You got full-on aces with the bilge pump."

Tracy looked away and said, "Fine. Whatever."

Cammie examined the mucky quagmire belowdecks. There were more tools in cases like fishing tackle boxes, but more sturdy, and even some of Lenny's MREs—though no longer RE, by the look of them. Still, she handed them up to Olivia. Now, a broccoli-and-noodle casserole, a box of cereal, a packet of crackers, and some nuts were the sum total of their food—except for the tins of beans and tuna stored on little gated shelves in the ama.

"Maybe these are salvageable," Cammie called up.

She located the generator and wished she had been the one to examine it sooner, instead of standing there holding the light while her mother screwed around with it. The operation was straightforward enough. She fiddled with it, sure she would be successful, but to no effect. When she emerged, she said as much. "Either it's just busted, and I can't figure out how, or we . . . or we used up the fuel we had. That's impossible, though. But I don't think I can do anything with it."

"How could this have happened and us lose the sail, too?" Tracy mused.

"It's not possible," said Olivia, her voice on the verge of a squeal. "Two things like that couldn't happen at the same time."

"Except they did," Tracy told her dully.

"What do we do now?" Olivia cried.

"We could eat that casserole," Holly said. "And when all we have are a few gallons of bottled water and whatever trickles out of the faucets, we're going to wish we had it."

The noodle casserole was cold. None of them could stomach it, although they were hungry from all the activity and the paucity of rations. All of them opted for handfuls of raisin bran and nuts. As they sat down to eat, Cammie apologized. "I'm sorry. I can't find a manual or any notes about the generator in the old logs. They just say, 'We dove today.' Or, 'The temperature was twenty-five Celsius.' Or, 'We made fine time.' Or, 'We have good luck with family groups,'" Cammie said. "But I know how to work the little manual water maker. It's going to take a hell of a lot of work to make a little fresh water from seawater, just like Lenny said. But a person can do it. I'm not worried about that." Her face was unreadable in the gloom, but something thrummed in her voice.

"What are you worried about?" Tracy asked.

"That boat. If I shine the light right on it, I can see that it's a boat. It's still back there. It's like they could come up beside us, but they're not. And the lights on it are funny. They're smudgy. They're like fog lights, but only just."

"That's what I thought," Olivia said.

"Maybe they're poor people. It doesn't mean they're bad," Tracy said.

"I found an even bigger flashlight, bigger than the one Cammie has, a humongous flashlight, in Lenny's things. We could try signaling with that," Holly said. "I'm going to take a nap, Olivia, so come with me and get it and bring it back. Let me know if anything happens."

As soon as Olivia returned, Tracy turned on the big light. Blink. Pause. Three rapid blinks. A blink. Then three rapid pulses.

Still, the boat seemed to keep its distance.

On the *yola*, Ernesto was sweating and swearing, his wolfish stink overpowering. Exertion made it worse. The young man thought Ernesto would beat Carlo to death. If he had not needed Carlo's back and hands, the young man was sure Ernesto would have killed his cousin. On the island, at the home of the woman, they had been left a cache of fuel. And then Carlo, whose job it was to fill up, had left the fuel behind. Until now, he had not told Ernesto, and unaccountably, Ernesto had not noticed the gauge. When he did, he began to scream.

They would not make it to their meeting with Chief. There would not be enough diesel. A boat so painted as *Bonita* could not slide into any harbor and refuel, even here, where few questions were asked of anyone. Even had there been a harbor or a ship to hail for help.

And then Carlo saw the light. The blinking light. Three times. Then again. Then three rapid blinks.

The young man saw it also, the clumsy attempt at Morse code. He saw it with a faltering heart.

Carlo chortled. He raised his binoculars. It was the same big three-hulled boat. They had lost sight of it. Now here it was again. *"Mujeres blancas,"* he said—the young man understood no more than he wanted to—and *"mala."* He assumed Carlo was suggesting that the women they could see plainly on the boat, whenever the big lamp they held up shined on them, would want it badly. Thus, he soothed Ernesto. Drink, rape. The things the women would have, food and fuel, perhaps valuables to be sold. The boat itself.

Maybe, the young man thought, they would be satisfied with the boat, the big yacht, to drag somewhere and then claim on the way back. A boat such as this one could be restored and sold for a great deal of money. The hope was faint that this bounty would satisfy his partners. The young man looked down at his hands. He was astonished by them. They still looked like a boy's hands. As if he had never grown up. He had never been good at reading or writing logically, but his mother said he was good in a crisis. He could solve problems. But he felt too young. He would need to be a sorcerer, like the men in the fantasy books he had loved as a child when his sitter read them to him, to make these women invisible to Ernesto and Carlo.

If the women were invisible, they could survive.

A big freighter had passed an hour before. Ernesto had killed the lights as they'd watched it slide by. So they'd waited until full darkness had fallen to make their move. No longer needing to worry about wasting fuel, Ernesto opened up the huge motor. The boat reared up and, instantly, was upon *Opus*.

"I guess they're not poor fishermen," Tracy said to Cammie through the open cockpit door.

"They could be. That's a shitty boat, but the engine . . . ," Cammie said.

Ernesto was not discouraged. The boat was a prize.

Now that he was close enough to examine it, by the light of the lanterns the women switched on, he could see that only the mainsail was destroyed. Perhaps these women were too stupid to run the motor. He almost laughed aloud. Americans were stupid, but all rich. There would be good things on this boat. The men were cramped, their clothing stiff with dirt and sweat. They did not mind the filth, but they minded the jerky and rough flat-bread they carried to eat. On this boat might be steaks and choco-lates. Where there were boats in trouble, there sometimes were watches, wines, and women cowering beside spineless, chinless hombres. Perhaps the men were working belowdecks. The men could die quickly or be bound and thrown down to watch as they fucked their women. When he saw the girl who had been waving and throwing flares, her body supple as a fluid under her brief clothing, he felt even better. Here was another prize, to have and even to sell. Perhaps even more valuable than the big boat. If the old bitches were left to live, they would not remember him.

Ernesto had learned that Americans thought all men who spoke his tongue looked like one man.

He shifted to let Carlo steer. After grunting and gesturing at the young man to pick up the gun and take it from its case, but to keep it low, out of sight beneath the seat, Ernesto lifted a hand and waved. With simple words and gestures, he told the young man not to bother to load the automatic rifle. They might need ammunition later for something serious. The sight of the gleaming big blue gun would suffice.

Once, years before the young man had joined them, Chief had given them extra cash for a canvas bag of fat-faced watches with jangling bands, watches a man such as he could never wear. No man could wear such a watch without the rattle of its metallic band like a signal of his approach from yards away. Americans walked about like animals at a fair, braying and jingling. Still, Chief had warned them not to kill American citizens, and though this meant little to Ernesto, it still crossed his mind. He would think this over after a time. The long-haired girl was very beautiful. A woman who stood beside her was also beautiful.

A few hours lost would do no harm.

A good meal, maybe even a sleep and a fuck. Then they would speed all the way to Chief and plead bad weather for their tardiness.

Cammie had motioned the motorboat to come alongside before she noticed the black paint smeared all over it, smeared in streaks and blots, like a little child's school project. But the boy smiled at her. He was blond and young, certainly not much older than she. Cammie was confused.

Fishermen, after all, she thought. She put out her hand to him, and he took it.

"Thank God you came," she said to him as the motorboat purred alongside. "We've been out here for . . . ages. Well, it seems like ages. A freighter just passed us by. I can't believe it didn't hit us. I'm from Illinois. Where are you from? Do you have a working radio? Because ours is wrecked. It only sends or we can't answer . . . and we have only the one VHF. . . ." She attached the ladder and threw it over. "Maybe you can help me work it. I'm usually very good at stuff like that—"

"They can't understand everything I say," the young man told her softly, cutting her short, his voice grim as an omen. "Especially complex sentences. Do precisely what they ask you to do and maybe we'll go away."

Cammie jerked her hand back.

She saw the big, dark-skinned man pull himself up from his bench seat in the little boat. He tugged his shirt down over his immense belly. He motioned to the young man, and the young man handed him an enormous shining rifle.

Cammie tried to wrestle the ladder back into the *Opus*. But the big man was up over the deck like a fat shark with its gaping mouth, pushing her against the wall of the saloon so that her head pounded from the impact. He motioned to the young man to follow him. Another man, smaller but not young, motored in circles around the *Opus*. He threw a rope, and the fat man caught and secured it.

Carlo climbed aboard.

In Spanish, Ernesto told the young man to greet the women in American and to tell them that no one would be hurt if they acted *con mucho cuidado*. The young man said, "Listen to him. Pay attention. He will murder you. You have to do what I say, even if

I, uh, make a pretense that I'm hurting you. I'm trying to speak in sentences they won't comprehend."

"What do they want?"

"The boat, I hope."

"You *hope?*" Cammie cried.

"They desire you as well," the young man said.

"What? Why?" Cammie cried. "Are you thieves? Who are you? Why did you smile at me?"

"Because I don't want any unpleasantness. I'm not an evil person. I'm trying to use words they won't grasp, you see? They can comprehend some English, but not the idiom." He glanced over his shoulder at Ernesto, who was examining a scrape on his hand. He whispered urgently, "What's a long word for, um, forcing intercourse?"

"Forcing intercourse," Cammie said.

"Sexually molest," Olivia called.

"This man would sexually molest the Virgin Mary," he said.

"Oh God, no, please help me," Cammie whispered.

"I'm, uh, attempting that."

"Cammie?" Tracy called from the saloon. Cammie came down the stairs, pushing her arms into the sleeves of a shirt she wore over her bathing suit. The sight of the dirty men and Cammie, cringing, struck Tracy mute and motionless. Olivia stood at the stern, wide-eyed, her back flattened against her closed cabin door.

Ernesto sat on the storage seats and pulled Cammie onto his lap.

"*¡Mi hija!*" Tracy cried.

Ernesto muttered something to the young man as he pawed Cammie's shoulder, pulling down the strap of her bra.

"That's my child!" Tracy cried.

"He knows she's your daughter," said the young man. "Can you . . . can you make a diversion of any kind to let me concentrate? Otherwise he'll force her right here." Tracy nearly yelped but choked it back. "That's good, that's okay. You have to behave as if I'm ordering you around." Tracy rushed down into the saloon. "Do you have booze? Do you have food?"

"Not much," Tracy whimpered. "But some. Here and . . . here."

Cammie was moaning, hugging herself, rocking her body side to side. Carlo approached as Ernesto nudged Cammie's shirt up with the handle of his knife. Carlo tugged at her bra. Her breast, exposed, seemed to gleam in the dim light. Then Ernesto pointed his knife at Carlo, warning him away.

"Mama!" Cammie bleated, pulling down the cup of her bra to cover herself.

"Mama!" Carlo bleated. "Ma-ma!"

Olivia said, "Shut up, Cammie! Tracy, come and help me."

"Is that your sister?" the young man asked. Cammie said nothing.

Baring her teeth at Carlo in a mask of a smile, Olivia pushed past Cammie. While Carlo held Cammie's arms back to placate him, Ernesto stuck a thick finger into the waistband of Cammie's shorts. He rooted until he touched the shaved line above the tendrils of her hair. The young man winced. Tracy flew out of the saloon with a full bottle of Chivas. Ernesto saw the label on the Scotch. This was expensive American liquor. He could do the girl later on. He let Cammie step aside and made his way down into the saloon.

Cammie fell to her knees and scrambled away like a crab into the corner. She pulled a beach towel around her.

"No. Steer," Tracy told her sternly. "Get up now. Go steer."

Ernesto grunted a word.

"He would like to request drinking glasses," the young American prompted Olivia.

Olivia brought three glasses and smiled with what she hoped was a hint of seductiveness, a hint she hoped did not betray play-acting.

"Listen," the young man said, "do you have anything . . .

dangerous to give them, to put into the spirits? I don't mean cyanide. . . ."

Olivia hesitated as Carlo grabbed her wrist and began to stroke her thighs. Olivia smiled and swiveled her hips. She knew that the young man had taken her hesitation to mean no, there was nothing. But she was thinking that it would be unwise to let the young man know that she had anything, tranquilizers, sleeping pills, whatever remained in her enameled boxes.

"Well, then let them drink. They drink like you breathe." Ernesto downed a full glass, then another. Ernesto nearly smiled and then said quietly, "Fuck."

The young man asked Olivia, "Where's the captain? Is one of you the captain?"

"He's dead," Cammie said. "He got hit in the head. The other captain got swept off in the tender. The tender is gone." The young man motioned at Olivia. "That's my aunt. The man who died is still tangled in the propeller. His body is tangled in the propeller."

The young man spoke to Ernesto in brief, halting Spanish.

Carlo said, "*¿Un hombre muerto? Mala suerte.*"

"He thinks this is a bad omen, a dead man on the boat." The young man spoke again. "That's good for you. A woman on a boat is a bad omen as well. They might want to get away. I told him we should get fuel. We are out of fuel."

"We have fuel, but the engine doesn't run. It's damaged."

Ernesto motioned for more drink, banging his glass on the table of the saloon.

"Olivia," Tracy whispered, her lips barely moving, "get Holly to give you the canned food. I'll give them the bread and the noodles. Get her to give you the MREs." Olivia crossed like a ghost to Holly's closed door. "Ask them if they want a meal," Tracy told the young man. From her college Spanish, Tracy understood the offer of food. "I told you, Camille. Go away now and steer the boat." Cammie slipped up into the cockpit. "She has to steer the boat." Tracy made her hands into the shape of a great wheel. "We'll run onto a sandbar."

"Don't say that again. That's what they'd like. Then the boat would be stuck until they can come back," said the young man.

"*Comida*," Tracy said.

Ernesto shrugged. Then he nodded, his eyes lidded.

Tracy jerked her chin at Olivia, who bounded down into the cabin that had been Lenny's, where Holly slept. But once inside, she could not find Holly. She opened the closets and the bathroom door. "Are you fucking hiding while we get murdered?" she whispered.

"I can hear you. I can hear everything that's going on. Just take the canned food. It's mostly tuna and beans. A can of rice and a can of corn. Make a loud noise. Drop the cans," Holly said. Her voice was muffled. She was in the ama, inside the hull. She opened the small door and tossed the food out to Olivia.

"Why? Why are you in there?"

"I don't want them to hear me lock the door."

"Lock the door? You stupid cow! Come out there and help us," Olivia seethed.

"Olivia, do just what I tell you, now, or you won't have to worry about them because I'll kill you myself," Holly said. "Shut your fat mouth. I know what I'm doing. There's no reason they have to know that I'm here. I'm better off doing this."

"Whatever you mean by *this*!" Olivia hissed.

Holly didn't bother to answer. She climbed out and knelt, the pain from her wound like an electric shock, to help gather the cans into an apron Olivia made of her gauzy shirt. As she left, turning back to bare her teeth at Holly, Holly nudged the door closed, slowly, behind her. She waited. In a moment, she heard the clatter of the cans falling. She slipped the lock and crept into the ama through the small door near Lenny's headboard. She went back to work. One thumbnail ripped off at the quick. Holly winced and sucked on her thumb until most of the real bleeding stopped. Then she breathed deeply and forced herself to keep at it.

Back in the saloon, Olivia held out the beans and canned fish, the tin of rice. Carlo nodded. The young man extracted a Swiss Army knife from his belt and opened the cans. Ernesto caught up one of the water jugs and swigged from it. Tracy swallowed her reflexive gag, then brought spoons. Both Carlo and Ernesto began to eat. The young man watched. "You can eat, too," she said, for no reasons he understood.

"No, thank you," he said. He drank a large glass of water.

Cammie came down the steps from the cockpit, wringing her hands as she watched her mother serve the men. The young man raised the gun and pointed it at Cammie. "Don't be frightened. Look as though you are horrified. The gun isn't loaded. They want the boat. See? Maybe they'll let you, uh, escape in the lifeboat. Make a motion like you're asking for spectacles. Eyeglasses."

Cammie made two circles of her index fingers and thumbs. In Spanish, the young man told Ernesto and Carlo that the young girl couldn't see well. Carlo shrugged. He downed another glass of whiskey. The young man said, "If they think you can't see them, maybe they'll be more likely to let you survive, because they're not supposed to kill Americans."

Olivia disappeared into her cabin, and Ernesto roared for her to return. She did, pulling on over her translucent top a long sweatshirt that had been Michel's.

Carlo said, "*¿Qué pasa si usan su teléfono para llamar a alguien?*"

The young man said to Olivia, "Give him your cell phone."

Olivia ran lightly back into her cabin. Carlo smiled approvingly at her behind and pointed at it, for Ernesto. Olivia brought back her cell phone. "It doesn't work," she said.

The young man translated.

Carlo ground the tiny silver phone under his bare foot until its spine split. "*Todo,*" Carlo said. Tracy produced her cell phone and watched as Carlo and Ernesto mangled it and then tossed it over the side. When Carlo asked for Cammie's phone, Tracy haltingly explained that she and her daughter had only one. Cammie's phone was tucked safely inside the inner pocket of her duffel.

Then the SSB crackled.

Cammie froze. They all did, the worst possible choice they could have made. The men were drunk. Tracy thought later that she might have chosen that moment to punch the button on the CD player and turn it up, loud. But the player wasn't in its customary spot on the shelf. Cammie had taken it into the cockpit. Cammie sprinted for the cockpit. A second mistake.

"Tell them she just has to steer, that no one can hear us," Tracy pleaded with the young American, who began to speak. "We've been trying for days."

But it was still possible to hear, faintly, a voice that said, "This is Captain Sharon Gleeman, over. Lenny, you rascal. Where have you got yourself to now? Did you forget we were to rendezvous for the food exchange? . . . Lenny . . ."

Ernesto got up, staggering with the drink and his heft, climbed out of the saloon, and, after pushing Cammie roughly against the steering wheel, smashed the SSB into shards. Angrily, he took his knife out of his belt and stuck it into Cammie's thigh. She screamed, and Ernesto sighed, jerking his knife away. He then delicately made his way back down into the saloon. He sat down and asked for the young man's small knife. Using the corkscrew, he opened a bottle of red wine and drank a glass.

"*¿Qué pasa si hay otra radio?*" Carlo asked.

"He wants to know where the other radios are," said the American man.

"The electricity is shot. The console doesn't work," Tracy told him. "You can see that. We have no lights." Ernesto put his great head with its tangled snakes of curls on the saloon table. He gestured to Carlo, a wide, swinging arc with his thick arm, and mumbled a command.

"No!" the young man said. He explained very slowly, and simultaneously to Cammie, that Carlo had been instructed to smash the control panel. The young man had told Carlo not to do this, because it would lower the salvage price of the boat. If it didn't work, there was no reason to ruin it.

"He stabbed my daughter's leg!" Tracy cried. "That's a deep cut!"

"Don't you have bandages?" asked the young man. He said in Spanish not to cut the girl. A sick girl was bad.

Ernesto lay back on the bench seats and began to snore.

Tracy got out the first aid box and found butterfly bandages. She pressed a gauze pad to Cammie's leg. When that soaked through, she grabbed a double thickness of gauze, cut it with a kitchen knife, and pressed it so the pressure slowed the bleeding. Then she applied a line of butterfly adhesives across the cut, smearing it with antibiotic ointment and taping a layer of gauze across it. Christ knew where that knife had been. She was about to slip the knife into the back of her shorts when Carlo strode across the deck, took it, and tossed it over the side. As Tracy watched, he did the same thing with the rest of the knives in Lenny's immaculate rack above the stove. Tracy fetched a pair of blue jeans for Cammie to slip on. They were Tracy's jeans, and she would have to belt them tightly around Cammie and roll them up, but at least they were so loose that they would not touch the wound.

Carlo told the young man that now he needed to get fuel. Tracy noticed that the young man didn't obey Carlo readily. He waited a moment before he said, "We're going to have to siphon from your engine down into ours. Hold still. Carlo will do it." Carlo half slipped, half fell into the *yola*. He caught up a length of ragged garden hose and climbed back onto *Opus*, then staggered toward the stern. He attempted to make a link and begin the siphoning. He asked for tape and sucked the hose until the fuel rose. But the hose was far too short. It popped out of the *yola*. Diesel leaked into the sea.

Cammie said quickly, "That hose is too big and too short. You would have to use plastic piping and hand-pump it in."

"He's drunk."

"Cammie could do it," Tracy said. "She's an engineer."

"She should do it, then, if she knows where the things are, the quicker the better," the young man told her.

"But you have to make them promise to leave her alone," Tracy said. "They can have me."

"They don't want you, ma'am," said the young man. "I mean no disrespect."

"I take none, for the love of God! But if they don't leave her alone, then they can't have the fuel. She won't show them where the piping is."

"They can kill all of you and look for it."

"It's in a locked case. I have the key," Tracy said. She in fact had no idea where the plastic piping was, or if there was any at all.

"A *ella*," the young man said, and continued, with a combination of gestures and words, to point out that Cammie could transfer the fuel. Carlo grunted and nodded. He poured himself a glass of wine. When he beckoned to Olivia, she crossed the room stiffly.

Carlo said, "*Pecho*."

Raking his hair, the young man mumbled, "I'm so sorry. He, uh, would like to see your breasts." Olivia shook her head. Carlo pointed at the weapon that lay limp, like an offering, across the young man's upturned hands.

"Can't you stop him?" Olivia begged. "Aren't you a man?"

The young man shook his head. "I don't . . . ," he began. "I don't know what to do."

Panting, Olivia slipped out of the sweatshirt. Mesmerized by the grim striptease, Tracy watched in exquisite disgust. Olivia began to remove the light blouse she wore over her bathing suit top. But her hands, trembling and sweating, slipped down onto her belly. Carlo became impatient. He got up and yanked the cloth until the elastic bra snapped up beneath Olivia's chin. Her hands fell to her sides, and she looked away, out at the sliver moon, while Carlo pinched her nipples and chuckled as they hardened.

Tracy began to cry.

Quickly, the American man told Carlo that he must hold the gun. The girl could fool them and put water in their fuel lines.

But as soon as he and Cammie were out of earshot, he said, "He'll drink more now. He has to hold the gun. He won't be able to do anything to her."

"I won't do it," Cammie said. "What's wrong with that man?"

"Don't tamper with them," the young man whispered. "Don't do that."

"I won't do it unless he lets her put her shirt down."

The young man barked at Carlo. He would take this chance because Ernesto was asleep and Carlo thought that the young man was wealthy and he knew that the young man knew the Big Man who gave orders to Chief. Carlo reluctantly nodded his head and turned away. Catching a look from Cammie, Olivia jerked down her blouse. Carlo asked for food. Tracy pulled back the covering on the casserole. Like a dog, Carlo leaned over to sniff at it. He knocked it from the table, and the glass broke into large pieces on the floor. After motioning for the young man to open more beans and tuna, Carlo made gestures that told Tracy to give him cigarettes.

Tracy's mouth parched, instantly.

None of them smoked.

But then she remembered the cigar box Michel had kept in his cabin. A dim picture flickered. She had seen him, only once, with a black French cigarette in his hand. He had been about to leave the marina. "Olivia," she asked urgently, "did Michel smoke?" Olivia nodded, her mouth slack. "Get his cigarettes now." Olivia scampered, slipped and fell, but got up and was back in a moment. She lit a cigarette for Carlo and placed it between his lips.

"*Bueno,*" Carlo said. He spread his legs, the hair of his crotch springing through a rip in his canvas trousers. He pulled Olivia between his legs. The young man was about to begin opening the tins when Olivia, holding up one finger to show Carlo she would be gone only a moment, got up and ripped open one of the MREs with her teeth. She added water. Then she opened a fresh bottle of wine with the boat's corkscrew and poured him a glass. Carlo smiled. Olivia lit one of the cigarettes for herself.

Tracy brought down the CD player, inserted a CD, and Emmylou Harris sang about a teenage wedding and how the old folks wished them well. Carlo rocked and moved his hips. Then the batteries in the player slowed, and Tracy rushed to load new ones. Carlo finished the cigarette and stepped on it with his bare foot. He began to eat. After a few bites of the MRE, Carlo said, "Shit." He began throwing the open one and all of the others over the side. Tracy took the moment of his sightless rage to nudge a jug of water under the seat in the saloon with one noiseless foot.

The young man opened a can of tuna and two cans of beans and one of corn. Tracy emptied all of it into a bowl, and Carlo ate, the gun propped inside his elbow like a child. He threw the opened cans into the water.

"Do you really know where there is piping? If you do, maybe we can show them we're filling the tank and I can talk them out of . . . this."

"This. By 'this,' you mean murdering me. You are a coward. I know where it is," Cammie said.

"Then get up."

"I want a shirt. From my mother." Tracy pulled off her shirt and gave it to Cammie. "And no one is steering this boat."

The young man pointed to Tracy, and Tracy, reluctantly, looking back at her daughter, ascended the steps to take the wheel. Cammie said, "Follow me. It's near the small toolbox, up there, where the life preservers are. Some of it is, that is. It's all over the place. They use it for the plumbing and if they bust a water line."

"What happened to the sail?" the young man asked. Cammie didn't answer. She unwrapped a twisted tie from a loop of tubing and proceeded back to the tank. Carlo called for her to put on one of the lanterns so he could see her.

"I don't have it. Go get it," Cammie said. The young man looked frightened, indecisive. "What the fuck do you think I'm going to do? Jump in while you're gone? There are sharks down there." He went to bring back the lantern and switched it on. By the dim light, Cammie sucked until the fuel was primed, then began to pump by hand.

She stopped.

"Why did you quit?" asked the young man.

"It'll work, but this isn't long enough," she said. "I have to find a longer piece. And when I do, and get it connected, this is going to take until morning, you piece of shit." The young man looked as though she had struck him. No matter how ugly things were, this boy was nothing to worry about, Cammie deduced. He looked more distraught than she did; and he was the predator.

Cammie set about searching for more pieces of piping, lifting, unrolling them, and measuring them against the side of the sailboat until she found one that would stretch between the motors with room for motion. She could not decide if she should hurry or if hurrying would only hasten what the men would inevitably do to them. Buying time meant that Sharon Gleeman, or someone, could possibly show up and interrupt this gruesome show. But for days, no one had. Cammie finally decided that she would proceed with as much speed as she could, which wouldn't be much, and chance that the men would need to leave or miss their connection. However, their leaving didn't mean that she would not be raped and her mother killed. Those things would take only moments, and Ernesto had the impassive eyes of a grizzly. He was neither more nor less interested in them than he was in eating or taking a shit. He would not reflect, before or afterward, on her blamelessness or his blasphemy, any more than a grizzly would think about the morality of eating a fish. The only bargaining card Cammie had possessed over the matter of the fuel was already played. Whatever happened next was buried in a deck, facedown.

"Go tape it on," she told the young man.

"They told me to watch you."

"Are you their puppet?"

"I suppose," he said. "But I'll help you."

"Yes, you help me. What a good idea."

They pumped without speaking, trading hands when Cammie's cramped, for half an hour.

"What happened to you? Did playing pirates in the bathtub get out of hand?" Cammie asked.

"Your mother loves you."

"Are you suggesting that yours didn't? And you do this because you didn't get the right bike when you were nine?"

"No, I just said she loves you."

"Are you suggesting that I don't upset her by getting myself murdered? Your mother loves you, too, if she's alive."

"I know she does."

"Even now, she would love you."

"Yes," said the American boy, deeply ashamed. "She would. Unless this went any further."

They looked at each other, for a moment only a boy and a girl in a serious jam.

Then they heard a slithering plop as Carlo slipped off the seat and onto the floor of the saloon.

Olivia jumped away from him and said, "Valium."

Day Twelve

*J*anis's husband, Dave, went back to the office on Monday, eager as any war hero to show off his scar. The staples wouldn't come out for a few days. The four-inch pucker that snaggled along above his hip looked particularly lurid. Jan hoped he didn't have the impulse to whip up his white coat and show his patients while he tapped their fillings.

He kissed Janis at the door. "I'm sorry you had to miss your trip. I really am," he said.

She shrugged.

"Don't be mad, Jan. I told you to go. I wish you had."

Relenting, she gave him a hug. "Go on. I have about sixteen loads of laundry to finish that no one did during your confinement, and I have to get a press release out for the Boo Bop," she said. Slowly, now that the girls were in high school, Janis was resuming her work, one event at a time. For this gig, a masked Halloween ball to benefit the local blood bank, she was in charge of publicity and collecting local celebs. What fiery hoop did you not have to jump through to get a richie who'd drop six hundred bucks on a coat in an afternoon to write out a fifty-dollar check to charity? Well, she had some friends among the local newshounds, a couple of athletes who'd grown up in Westbrook, too. In fact, she wanted to get the laundry in and jump around a bit on her little trampoline, maybe lift a few hand weights, in part to burn off the aggression.

The half of her who wasn't a dutiful and sympathetic wife was still fuming. Dave would indeed have been just fine had she gone on the cruise. Men were such infants when it came to any sort of illness. He'd lain there, moaning and calling out for juice and broth . . . while her friends . . . While her friends . . .

Sunset drinks, she thought. Old stories. And water, water, water, and sun, her natural elements. She fantasized about them all, tipsy on tropical ambiance and pure sloth. No need to dress up for stuffy dinners, as she had in Hawaii at the dental convention. Just lying about like louts, as they had when they were seventeen. Janis let herself slip back to the nights when the four of them cruised from Pepe's Taco Stand, past Holy Innocents Cemetery, around the corner to Miller's Meadow, to shine their lights on whatever couple was parking there. They'd end up with their butts parked on picnic tables at Custard's Last Stand (was political correctness unknown then?), their faces bathed in flamboyant green-and-pink neon. And school. Olivia with her uniform rolled over twice at the waist to make it shorter and her boots with the Ur stiletto heels. Tracy with a man's baggy sweater (in the regulation navy blue) that hung down to her knees and was cuffed to her elbows. Holly with her black lipstick.

How perfectly awful they'd all looked. Like living trailers for some badly outdated horror movie.

And how cool it had been.

Janis figured her friends would be in Grenada by now, buying Spanish trinkets, handmade jewelry, and duty-free cologne.

The sluts.

She called Tracy's phone. No answer. She'd wanted to leave a message, liberally peppered with four-letter words, but even the answering function didn't kick in. As she gathered the sheets, she flipped on the Weather Channel. Tropical Storm Eve was making its way across the Caribbean and might make landfall in Texas as soon as the end of the week. But they were already on land, so it was fine. Janis made a mental note to check the channel again later. That had been their one worry, the remote chance of getting stuck crosswise of a hurricane.

Emma called down, asking for her double tank tops.

"In the dryer!" Janis called.

"I have to go *out!*" Emma cried. "Can't anyone ever do anything around here except me? I already used up half of June, my only vacation, bringing Dad lemonade—"

"Look, they'll be finished in ten minutes," Janis said wearily. "Take Nubs out."

"Oh, my God, I just said, can't anyone do anything . . . Alexandra, Mom said to take the dog out!"

"I told you, not your sister. I'm going to bring Uncle Jim and Ted dinner tonight, so if you could make your bed, too, please. I'm making beef Stroganoff. Is that good for you, too?"

Emma flounced past, carefully donning her white and then her black tank. "You could walk the dog, Mom, I mean honestly. You're jumping on the little thingie and not going anywhere."

"It's my little thingie, and it's your dog, Emma Rose! Please, hurry up. . . . If that dog pisses on the rug again after I spent the whole last week with Spot Shot—"

"Oh, my God!" Emma huffed. "Nubs! Come on! Let's go for a run. I can't handle the stress. God."

Janis took the laundry into the living room and sat down again. She called Dave's office.

"Dave?" she asked when he picked up. "How do you feel?"

"Weak," he said. "A half day will be enough. You were right. I shouldn't have come back so soon. I feel like I could fall over."

"Everybody does. It's only been a week. It's mostly the general anesthesia that's the killer. Honey, I want you to do me a favor. Before you come home, call that guy at Channel Five you know, the one who's the meteorologist?" Dave had put porcelain veneers on everybody from the local news anchors to several outfielders for the White Sox. Until they grew old enough to be embarrassed by it, he would arrange for the girls to meet his famous patients at car shows and the opening of car dealerships.

"What's up?" Dave asked.

"I'm worried about Tropical Storm Eve. I'm worried about where Tracy and the girls are."

"The *girls*," Dave said.

"What do you call the dental hygienists, David?"

"Uh, sorry," he said.

"I'm sure they're fine," Janis went on. "But I'm surprised Tracy hasn't called me. I'd like to know what the status of the storm is in the Caribbean. Grenada is the Caribbean proper, right? Not the Atlantic?"

"I almost failed geography. Ask Emma."

"Well, your friend, he could just make a call."

"I'll do it right away. Next call I make," Dave said. "Second thought, don't tell Em and Alex, though. Don't scare them. It's probably nothing. Don't you think? But let's put your mind at ease. I'll call right away."

He rang Janis back twenty minutes later. "There's no weather out there, Jan. So rest easy."

Janis began to jog on her trampoline and tried to relax. But she could no more relax than cause the hands on the kitchen clock to spin forward until Tracy was at her kitchen table, drinking coffee and nagging Janis to get a treadmill—that cheesy little thing was going to ruin her knees.

Holly knew it had to be close to midnight. She had no way of measuring time, but the small, battery-operated lantern had begun to dim.

Lying on her stomach, trying with all her strength to ignore the shrieking of her leg and focus her efforts, she used the claw hammer alone until the hasp of the lock broke entirely away. But the lock was still fast. If she used something else, someone on deck would hear the pounding and know there was another person on the boat. With a long nail, she poked at the guts of the lock, to no avail. She heard no clicks, no tumblers sliding or shifting.

But then she heard music.

She raised her head.

What was this? The music was loud. The CD player was battery operated. Why were they playing country tunes? If it was a signal to her, she couldn't imagine what it was. Through the crack under the door, she had watched as Olivia's breasts were roughly flipped out of her bra by the man with the grimy hands and had seen Olivia cringe. She didn't have to be a rocket scientist to know that Cammie was next. Holly decided to believe that the music was intended to cover up the sounds of her maneuvering. She reached behind her into Lenny's tool kit and found the smaller pry bar. With the corner of one edge of the tip inserted into the lock, she swung her arm back as far as the limited space would allow and bashed at the lock. Nothing happened. She hit it again. The lock seemed to loosen slightly in its metal wall.

Steadily, Holly pounded and pounded, harder, surer, and with greater abandon. Emmylou Harris sang of breaking her heart and making believe.

"I thought you said you didn't have anything like that," the young man called, accusing Olivia.

"I was thinking of poison, and then when I thought of this, he wouldn't let me get off his lap," she said, shrugging.

"How did you get it, then?" Cammie called to her.

"I sent your mother," Olivia answered.

"Will he wake up?" Cammie asked the young man, referring to Ernesto.

"Probably not, but if I were you, I would ask your mother to put some of her pills in the whiskey just in case."

"She's not my mother."

"I didn't mean the little woman. The tall woman, your mother."

"Fuck you," Cammie said.

"Yes," said the young man.

"Where are you from?" she asked.

"New York. The Hudson River Valley."

"Long way from home."

"We both are."

"My hand is tired again. You pump," Cammie said, rubbing her palms. "I'm going to tell my mom about the pills."

While the young man pumped the bulb, Tracy slipped down from the cockpit and forced open Olivia's cloisonné box, dropped three Valium into Ernesto's glass, then covered it with three fingers of whiskey. She shook the box.

The pills were all but gone.

The whiskey was going down.

"Who is that boy?" Tracy asked.

"Mom, take the one VHF radio up with you and keep calling. Keep calling for anyone."

"No, you do that," Tracy said. "If he wakes up, Olivia is here."

"I'll give him more booze," Olivia assured her.

Ernesto groaned, and his mouth lolled open. Then he sat up, keen as a serpent. "¿Se acabó?" he roared at the young man, his head weaving in slow, metronomic sweeps, until it fell again to the tabletop. With difficulty, Ernesto sat up again.

The young man shook his head. He pointed at the small bulb of the hand pump. Olivia held out a black cigarette and lit it. She sat down and lit a cigarette, too, and crossed her legs. She poured herself a glass of wine and put it to her lips. Ernesto drank a glass of whiskey, a huge draft, and shook his jowls, setting it down long enough for Tracy to slip another pill into her hand. She watched anxiously to see if it would dissolve before Ernesto drank again. Olivia threw back her head as if she were swallowing. She stood up and allowed the knot on the sarong she wore around her waist to seem to slip, then hastily covered herself again. Ernesto winked at Olivia. She regarded his glass. The pill was a tiny wafer, hardly visible in the golden liquor.

But they were down to the remnants of one bottle of whiskey and a single slender bottle of wine. Who could be awake after taking thirty milligrams of Valium?

Was Holly dead? Tracy thought. A part of her prayed that Holly was still wisely hiding. She must have heard this—the rough voices, the weeping, the shouts, and the music. She would have come running to help. Nothing would have stopped her. Another part of her prayed that Holly was dead, that she had died in her sleep. For the rest of their deaths would be much worse. And unless she could reach this strange, clean, broken young man, they would also be prolonged.

She approached him slowly.

"The gun isn't loaded," he said softly. "They didn't think they would need ammunition for this. But Ernesto has a big magazine of ammo. It's around his belly in a belt."

"Why are you here?" Tracy asked. "Why?"

"I work with them," said the young man.

"How? You don't seem like the kind of person who would do this."

"I am doing it, so I must be that kind of person."

"Are they forcing you?"

"No."

"Then what?"

The young man rubbed his eyes with the backs of his hands. "Listen, I don't want you or your daughter to get killed, or your friend, either. I am trying to think of a way out of this, and getting this fuel into our motor is the best thing I can think of."

"Where is your mother?"

"Please don't," said the young man.

"Where is she?"

"She's in New York. In a house by the ocean right now, because it's summer."

"So your family is well-to-do."

"Yes."

"So you don't have to do this. What is it that you are doing? Do you rove around and just steal from people?"

The young man pointed to the bouncing *yola*. "There is heroin in that boat, and these men bring it to another man who brings it into New York City. That's why we have to get the fuel in a hurry. We got held up by the wind that popped your sail."

"But you said 'these men,'" Tracy pressed him. "As if it weren't you also."

"It is me also."

"You bring drugs into New York?"

"I do this for money, a great deal of money for me. I've only done it once before, and I won't do it again if I live."

"Are you a drug . . . user? Are you a drug addict?"

The young man laughed. He looked hard into the woman's green eyes with the gold flecks. "Of course not," he said.

"Then why?"

"I want to move to Montana," he said. "I always have."

Tracy laughed. It was as if he'd said he was studying piracy for a role in a movie. "Why doesn't your father just give you the money to move to Montana?"

"He doesn't know where I am. Neither does my mother, really."

"Nobody does this to move to Montana! People move to Montana and get jobs. What's the real reason?"

"It is the real reason," the young man continued. "If there are other reasons, I don't know them. . . ."

"How did you even meet them?"

"Why does that matter? Look, this is the last trip. I'm going away from here in just two weeks. Then this happened. But if I'm lucky, they will only want to come back for the boat after we drop off the cargo and then you'll be gone. Please be gone when we come back in three days."

"Why do you care?"

"I don't want to hurt anyone."

"Drugs hurt people."

"I don't know them! It's their choice!"

Tracy sank back on her heels to think of a way to take advantage of this deep well of vacillation. If he was a young man from a wealthy family, someone had driven him away, and since mothers did not do this, it must have been his father. But if his mother knew about this, she would be distraught. His mother—this might be the reason, beyond their common nationality, that he was eager to escape without damaging her and Cammie and Olivia. Gangsters wept over their mothers. This kid was deep in bad company. But perhaps Tracy could mine whatever vein of his recent past she could uncover. *All* his past was recent—perhaps closer to the surface than Tracy thought.

He shook the fuel can. "This is taking a long time," he said, glancing at the maw of the saloon, where Carlo and Ernesto slept.

"You can take the gun and shoot them," she said finally.

"Yes."

"You've thought of that."

"Yes."

"Why don't you? You'd be free. You could go home."

"I can't go home," he said.

"Your mother would welcome you home."

"Yes."

"So would your father."

"No."

"He would, even if he didn't say it. He may be a fool or proud, but you're his child." The young man grimaced. "Would you let them kill us?"

"No," said the young man. "But I don't want to kill even them unless I have to kill them. I hate them. I hate what we've done. But killing them would make me one of them. I don't mean entirely that. I am one of them. Killing them would make me worse than I am. I just want to get out of here without being worse than I am."

"And . . . ," Tracy prompted.

"There's the matter of prison, not only my conscience. They haven't done anything to you except threaten you. If you kill a smuggler while he's asleep, that doesn't make it something, like, nobler than murder. People would know, because you would know, and eventually someone who knows my family would know, and I would be . . ."

"Unworthy?" Tracy asked.

The young man smiled, a smile that had seen orthodontia. "No. Unsalvageable."

Tracy looked for the riddle. Why hadn't they simply gunned them all down, raped Cammie, and pushed all of them over the side? Wasn't this game of threat and reprieve just that, a game— as Lenny had told them, something pirates didn't do, the waste of a good plank? There had to be a reason that all of them were not already spiraling down among the sharks, and it had to lie in the balance of power among these three men. This boy, no less handsome or vigorous than her own Ted, and not much older than Cammie, was a drug smuggler, with an automatic weapon, in the company of criminals. He was himself a criminal. Why did he turn to her with crucifixion in his eyes? Did she only imagine it? Because he spoke English? Because he didn't smell of offal and pitted teeth and rancid oil? Was she such a pure racist that this boy's veneer of politeness and concern, not to mention his wide blue eyes, had convinced her that he was a handhold of hope? Did he have the same intents as these others, and was his as-signed role only to present the face of civility?

Unsalvageable, she thought. He said he wanted to be saved.

"There isn't a soul for miles around here," said Tracy, pressing him. "Why haven't you hurt us?"

"I don't want to," said the young man. "I've said so."

"Why haven't they? Are you afraid of them?"

"Yes, I am. But for them, if the man above us were to tell the man above him that they killed American women, it would be certain death. Or if they were caught, if this boat was to be found and identified. There is no appeal in a Central American prison. They will hang or be put against a wall and shot. They have to think this over." Tracy thought of the scales' delicate equilibrium. "This boat, it could be made unrecognizable with some easy work. But time is a factor."

"But how would you ever get it to . . . wherever it is you go? The motor's frozen. You can't sail it."

"Oh, you can make a sail from anything. You still have the genny," the young man said, pointing to the small, furled sail. "You can use canvas. Bedsheets. If we made another sail and set both of them, even halfway decently, we could make good time. It's the time before you get there, until the boat is hidden and painted so it looks like another boat, that's the fear. Because people might already be looking for you and your family."

"They are," Tracy said rapidly. "My cousin called the Coast Guard. The American Coast Guard. And I assume they'll cooperate with the navy in Grenada. . . ." She had no idea, especially with Dave's illness, whether she would be on Janis's mind at all.

"Grenada, you are not even close," said the young man. "If they think you are near Grenada, then they are looking in the wrong place. You're headed for Honduras now, or you were. They'd have to know where you are to find you. Don't let them know people are looking. It might make them feel reckless."

"What can I do to save my daughter? What would your mother do to save you?"

"I want to try to talk them into going to bring the drugs to . . . the man we meet. And to convince them you will be here when we return. I don't mean you. I mean the boat. And maybe your . . . sister, the younger woman, and the girl. They're no good to them dead."

"You mean sexually."

"I mean that and other things."

"What other things?" Tracy's voice ratcheted up. The young man's hand slackened on the pump.

"There are places that women are sent. You don't want to know."

"What would your mother do to save you? Because you'll go down, too. You said prison. Your father will know. Or they'll kill you. You speak English. You could tell the police that you were forced at gunpoint. They know that you could do that. You could betray them and they wouldn't even know it. You could die and your mother will never know what happened to you. No one even knows your name. Would your mother want this to be the end of your life? Would your mother want you to end the life of another mother's child? My child?"

"No. That's what I'm trying . . . I'm trying to stop this. Stop talking. I'll try to explain this to them. You could offer them . . . your rings, your watches. Maybe they'll take them."

"You don't think so, do you? You think they'll take them and then they'll kill us anyway? Or take the rings and watches and earrings and liquor and then drug them and sell them and kill me?"

The young man looked at her, and his eyes were horrible. "You, and me, too," he said. "I wish we had never seen this boat."

"Olivia," Cammie whispered as the sun moved overhead and the men still slept, for what Cammie imagined was by now the eighth hour. "Do you think we can lift them?"

"We could try with the smaller one. Your mother could help us," Olivia said. Carlo's phlegmy snores were punctuated by a snort and a sigh.

"She's with him," said Cammie, indicating with a brief nod the young man. "If we ask her to help us, what do you think he'll do? What I think is, I think he'll help us. Or he'll just keep pumping the gas and try to get out of here, because he said when he got on the boat that he was going to try to make sure they didn't hurt us. . . ."

"What if that was just to get up on the boat? What if he was just trying to jerk you around?"

"We have to try."

"He'll drown," said Olivia, nodding at Carlo. She gave him a nudge with the toe of her sandal, and he did not stir.

"I hope so," Cammie replied.

"What do you think Holly is doing?" Olivia asked. "She told me not to say a word about her being in there."

"She's hurt. They'd hurt her worse. She can't help us."

"If we can push him up the stairs and onto the side, we can roll him over."

"We have to get him up the stairs first. He's heavier than we are combined, and he's deadweight."

"Why don't we just take *their* boat and run for it?" Olivia asked.

"I thought of that. We have to wait until that thing down there has fuel. At least enough to get us far away from them. And we'd have to take the one radio and life jackets and flares. Blankets or something to cover us from the sun . . ."

"We're not planning a picnic, Cammie. We have to get out of here. It should be full now."

"No, we wasted so much time messing around before I could even start to pump that it'll take longer for it to have enough to go more than a few miles. That's a big motor." She looked up at the sky. "How long will that Valium keep them out?"

"Hours. It would knock down an elephant. I gave him two ten-milligram tablets and another one, and your mom gave the other guy the same, plus what they drank. . . ."

"Okay, then. You stay here. I'm going to go get my mom. You go up and steer. They won't notice."

Cammie crept up onto the deck, keeping to the shadows as

if the passage were an alley and she a scavenging cat. When she saw her mother sitting folded back on her heels, the way an old Chinese woman might, her hands on her knees, deep in conversation with the young man, she paused. She saw her mother reach out her hands, not quite touching the young man but caressing the air around his shoulders. Cammie knew that she was arguing, pleading for Cammie's life, offering her own in exchange, begging the young man to help them. She crawled forward on her knees.

"Mom, we need you down there," Cammie said. "Aunt Olivia is sick. She's throwing up. You can do that yourself, can't you?" she asked the young man sharply. He nodded. Then, impulsively, she whispered, "Why can't you help us? Why can't we push them over? You could take the boat yourself and go and meet your guy. You could take us with you if you wanted—"

"It won't hold four," the man said. Cammie thought, Five. With Holly, five.

"Well, you could take me, for insurance—"

"Cammie!" Tracy warned her.

"And then we could send someone back for my family!"

"He would kill me. The man we drop it with. Like you swat a fly." The American paused to consider what he had said. "At least, I think he would. He might not. Yes, he would. Because I could tell others about this thing they do. He'd kill me."

"You could just go yourself, then, and tell him that they tried to double-cross you and that you left them somewhere you stopped, in self-defense! Or you could just not show up, you fucking asshole! Can't you think for yourself? Just help us push them over while they're out cold and get the fuck out of here!"

"He's known these men for fifteen years. He knows they'll show up."

"No!" Cammie whispered. "What if you hadn't seen us? You'd have run out of fuel. You wouldn't have shown up at all. Don't you see that? Are you a retard?"

"Look," the young man said with wretched certainty. He

thought of the money in the patched plaster behind the books in his room. He thought of the great gorges in Montana. "I have to get back to where I came from, just once more. I won't let them hurt you. I promise. Just please help me get this tank filled. I don't want to have done so much wrong for nothing. Please."

For another half hour, while Tracy paced, clasping and unclasping her hands, Cammie squeezed the bulb.

And then they all heard an angry rumble that built and built; and, blinking, Ernesto stood up.

"Is the tank filled, at least enough?" asked the young man.

"Yes," Cammie lied. They would not find out how filled it was or was not until they were too far away to turn back. They would be stranded.

"Good. Now I'm going to try to get them out of here. Nothing will happen. Stay quiet."

Cammie sat cross-legged, miming the pumping of the fuel, as the young man spoke urgently to Ernesto, pointing at the watch on his wrist. Ernesto shook his head and pointed at Cammie. "*¿Por qué no guardamos a ella?*"

"*¿Por qué?*" the young man asked. "*Solo queremos el barco.*" No room, he said in English, pointing at the *yola*. Ernesto shrugged and pointed briefly with a thick finger at the crumpling surface of the water.

They were talking about her, Cammie realized. Talking about taking her along with them. If they needed her, it would not be for very long, she realized. She began to consider what she would do if any of them made a move toward her. She would run to her room, on the opposite side of the saloon from where the men stood. She would lock her door. By the time they had broken down the door of her cabin and the lock on her bathroom door, she would have pried the blade out of her little disposable razor and cut the artery beneath her own ear. She would not die with their filthy hands on her and then be thrown alone into the impassive depths. She would be brought home, to be buried by her father and her mother. Hugging her knees, she willed herself not to cry. She sensed that if she cried, Ernesto would be elated. Cammie tried to make herself small. She tried to shrink into nothingness.

The music had stopped, and Holly could hear the sound of raised voices. The fucking lock would not give. All around it, the metal of the box was dented and pocked. Her pounding had opened a hole in the white metal. She could easily poke through it with the pry bar, but there was no way to get anything out. She had no choice left, though. She opened the ama and crawled out, wincing, lying with her ear close to the thin edge of light along the bottom of the cabin door.

"I'm telling him that Chief will never let him live if he shows up with this girl," a voice was saying, a strong, young American voice. "¿Por qué no la llevamos con nosotros?" the same voice said, and then added loudly in English, "I'm convincing him we can come back for the boat, and find it with our locator, and then take the girl back with us to . . . the place they go. They'll pay mucho for . . . ella linda. Of course, you'll have vanished by then," he pleaded, whoever he was. "Get into the lifeboat. It's made to hold four. Just get in and get as far away as you can. Try to find land. You have to have a device that shows where you are. . . . You're not far from Honduras now. . . ."

Holly crawled back into the ama. She despaired. She alternated the claw end of the hammer and the pry bar to enlarge the hole. Two inches. Three . . .

Impossibly, the lock fell backward into the box. Holly threw open the lid.

Ernesto spoke. Slowly, almost lethargically, he hefted the magazine off his chest and, as Tracy watched, began to load the gun.

The young man cried, "¿Matar a todos? ¿Por qué?"

Ernesto gestured again at the water. Tracy understood some of what he said. In the sea, he'd said. They will never be . . . seen? Found? The young man argued that the boat would be grounded on rocks, that possibly it would sink. What a stupid thing to do, he told Ernesto. Waste the girl and the boat. Why not . . . just the older woman? "They can't even sail it!" he told Ernesto urgently, pointing up at the shreds of canvas, forgetting in his haste to translate. "They don't know how!" He began to repeat all of it in halting Spanish.

"*Por favor,*" Tracy pleaded. "*Mi hija . . .*"

"*Si hagas eso, no vas a la cárcel. Te ahorcarán,*" the young man said quietly.

"What are you telling them?" Tracy asked.

"That if he kills Americans, he's going to hang, because people already know you're out here."

Ernesto squatted as if to think. He mumbled to the young man.

"Tell your daughter to get undressed," the young man told Tracy. "I promise you, I won't let him touch her."

"No!"

"I promise you."

Tracy looked down the length of the deck at Cammie, impossibly small, wedged into the corner. She walked over and knelt down. "You heard what he said," Tracy whispered, touching Cammie's shoulder.

Cammie pulled away. "Mom, you'd let them see me? You'd let them touch me?"

"Honestly, yes. I would to save your life, Camille. It would be a disgusting, filthy memory. But—"

"He probably has AIDS, Mom!"

"Oh, my God. Yes. You're right. But it won't come to that. The boy promises he won't let them touch you."

"How do you know he won't? I would rather die, Mama."

"No, you would not rather die, Camille. No, you would not.

You can survive humiliation. You're not going to have to survive rape. It's our only chance, my precious. I won't let them touch you. They'll have to kill me first, darling."

Her eyes streaming, Tracy helped Camille to her feet. As she had when Cammie dressed for preschool, she held her daughter's arms over her head and pulled off her sweatshirt. Behind her, she heard Ernesto's lascivious yodel of appreciation. "Let Mama help," Tracy, sobbing, told Cammie. Tracy undid the belt on Cammie's jeans and lowered them, helping Cammie step out one leg at a time.

"Why are we doing this, then?" Cammie whispered.

"To buy time for him to convince them. He's trying to tell them that they could . . . sell you." She stopped and held Cammie, who was now wearing only her bra and underpants, against her, with her back to the men, shielding her as she listened to a dispute that seemed to have erupted between Ernesto and the young man. Carlo, still asleep, only moaned as they raised their voices. The young man said, *"Nunca nos van a ver de nuevo."*

Ernesto replied, *"Muerta."*

The young man spoke again, this time roughly, pointing at Olivia. Ernesto's eyes widened. He nodded.

"¡Joyas y relojes! Díles."

The young man said, "He needs you to give him your jewelry. This can stop right here if you do. I'm pretty sure."

Tracy took Cammie's hand and unfastened her bracelet of sapphires. Leaving Cammie bent double, arms across her breasts, fumbling with one hand for the towel, Tracy brought the bracelet to Ernesto.

"Okay?" the young man asked. "This is *muy*—"

"Okay," Ernesto said. *"¡Traela y ven aquí! Rápido."*

"No vale la pena," the young man repeated. *"No americanos.* My father . . . Chief will shoot you down like . . . *un perro."*

"Haz lo que digo," Ernesto said, motioning at Cammie again. He pointed to the gun barrel.

"We have opals!" Tracy shouted. "Thousands of dollars of opals!"

"All of it, then," the young man pleaded. "Right now. *¡Rápido!* He has to think I'm ordering you around." The young man made a motion with his hands, miming precious stones, in a ring, in a necklace.

"I'll get them!" She leapt down the stairs and tore open Olivia's door. "Olivia! Come in here. Give me the opals you bought," she said.

She grabbed Olivia's purse and ran out onto the deck, dumping over the contents, sending lipsticks rolling like tubular marbles. The velvet bag was in a zipped pocket.

"Here they are. Give me your ring." Olivia stared. "Give me . . . Are your earrings real?" Olivia, motionless, nodded. "Give me the earrings," Tracy told her. Olivia, tears spilling from her eyes though her face remained expressionless, removed them from her ears and dropped them into Tracy's callused hand.

Quick in the deceptive way that a bear is quick, Ernesto crossed the deck and pulled Cammie against him, dragging her backward across the planking. She was insubstantial to him, light as a bundle of rags. He did not like these skinny women. But she was beautiful. And all women had the same holes.

"Mama!" Cammie screamed, thrashing, her feet lifted off the deck. The welts her nails raised along Ernesto's forearms popped forth beads of blood. This seemed to affect him no more than it would have had Cammie stroked his arm with a feather.

"We have gems!" Tracy called, holding up the opals and allowing them to sift through from one hand to the other, letting the light flash through them, displaying their miniature rainbows. "But tell him I won't give him these diamonds and gems until he lets my daughter come over to me. I'll throw every fucking one of them over the side of this boat, right now! I'm talking tens of thousands of dollars here. I'm holding that in my hand."

"Let her go," the young man said to Ernesto.

"*No. Dije no*," Ernesto said. "*Haz lo que te mando, ahora mismo.*"

The young man pulled Cammie away from Ernesto. She stumbled, and he jerked her to her feet. "Fool," he said to the older man. "I'm pretending we can have her and the opals, too, you see?" His voice was harsh but his words imperative. He crossed the few feet between him and Tracy and took the bag from her hand, scraping the jewels from her palm into the sack. For Ernesto, he opened it and spilled the opals onto a deck chair. He let Ernesto paw them, showing how many and varied they were. He saw as Ernesto's eyes lighted up.

"He likes this," the young man said cautiously. "*Diamante grande*. What is a big diamond like that one in the earring worth?"

"Five, ten thousand dollars," Tracy said. She had no idea.

Ernesto said, "*Bueno. Ven aquí.*"

He put the jewels back into their sack, pulled the strings tight, and stuck them into the ragged pocket of his pants. Then with the rifle he struck the young man under the chin, not a hard blow, but enough that the young man staggered. He put his thick arm around Cammie's neck.

"Mama!" Cammie cried, writhing, kicking backward with her hard soccer player's nimble heels.

Ernesto spat on the deck. In English, he said, "Kick balls." He pushed Cammie back at the young man, who held her loosely while she tried to reach his arms, her mouth open to bite.

"*¡Carlo, que cochino eres! Ven aquí*," Ernesto called. When Carlo did not stir, Ernesto grabbed a jug of water from the shelf and poured all of it onto his cousin's head. When Carlo, spluttering, hit the floor of the saloon, Ernesto kicked him in the stomach. Slowly, as though he had been awakened for school by his own father, Carlo got to his feet and climbed the stairs. He shook back his wet hair and grinned. Ernesto heaved himself down, heavily, into the *yola*. "*Vamanos!*" he muttered to Carlos. "*Ven aquí*," he told the young man, gesturing at Cammie. "Fuck *tu papá*."

"*¡Ya!*" Carlos grunted, attempting to mimic his cousin's tone, as he slipped down into the boat.

"*No es, uh, necesario* . . . ," said the young man.

He thought, I promised them. I promised the mother. The mother was fused in his mind with his own mother. All of the bitter, good feelings that bringing the drugs had briefly given him last time, feelings of victory because his father bowed every day to the man who had involved his son in this business, were depleted, released like air leaking from a child's water toy. It was as though the young man could see it deflated, spinning beneath him. Ernesto would leave this girl ripped and bleeding. None of it had ever been meant to come to this. He had known how deficient these men were, how savage. He had seen them fight, seen the young whores they punished. But he had never imagined himself part of a murder. The young man had counted on their fear of Chief and the man above him. He had known them to be rapacious but had not counted on greed making them so fearless. Like all bullies, Ernesto and Carlo were cowards. They would not, in his experience, have taken such risks before.

The young man realized that he had still somehow believed that being his father's son, with his blond hair and his well-brought-up accent, would act as an invisible shield, keep him from being truly befouled. Now he saw himself for what he was—a blue-eyed, soft-cheeked monster who would soil his family now so absolutely, his character turned inside out to show what had grown inside him, that he could never again enter anyone's heart.

He pointed out at the ocean and made a gesture to Ernesto that encompassed the horizon. He still believed that Ernesto would not kill him, but he had run out of ways to keep his promise to his mother to never do anything really wrong. "*¡Policía!*" he cried. The gun lay on the deck, its magazine loaded. Ernesto ignored him. He reached up awkwardly from the *yola* and motioned for the young man to give him the gun.

The young man hesitated. He told Ernesto in Spanish that they needed to leave now.

The young man did not want to die. He did not want the girl to die. He pulled Cammie to him with a show of great roughness.

"When I tell you to, run," he said into Cammie's ear. "Run and pull your mother down into the cabin. The man is fat and old. I can stop him, I think, if I kick the control of the motor out of his hands. And I will shoot him if I have to. But you have to move fast." Loudly he said, "*¿Comprendes?*" Cammie nodded.

He could kill Ernesto. If Ernesto killed the young man, Chief would shoot him in the mouth like a dog. But Chief would not kill the young man over Ernesto. There were hundreds more like him to take his place. He thought that he knew this for a certainty.

The young man pulled Cammie backward, as if to take her over the side onto the ladder, down into the *yola*, where Ernesto stood, reaching out to steady the rocking ladder. The wind was ruffling the water. Ernesto told the young man to hurry. He turned to position himself to make the step down, dragging Cammie.

"I'm going to take one single step onto the ladder and then let you go," the young man whispered, pretending to grab Cammie harder around the waist, as if about to lift her.

A crash from the stern of *Opus* made him jerk his head and look up.

The blast took him full in the left chest. His shoulder burst, festooning the deck, and Cammie's face and hair, with bright ribbons of blood. He fell backward, his blue eyes open as the sea, thinking for a moment of a poster he had kept above his bed as a boy, a big photo of Wayne Gretzky, then of his sister's first lost tooth, and then nothing more. His head hit the stern of the *yola* with a hollow *thwack* before his body slipped slowly beneath the surface. Cammie keened like a rabbit as she knelt.

Ernesto leapt and caught the gun before it fell.

"Throw your gun over," Holly told Ernesto, stepping up to the side of the boat and gesturing with Lenny's rifle. Tracy loosened the rope, and the *yola* began to drift. Holly fired again, opening a hole in the side of the *yola*. Water sprang into the hull of the smaller boat. Carlo slipped across to plug the hole with rags. Ernesto began to raise his gun, but Holly did not move. She fired again, grazing Ernesto's shoulder, and said, *"Muerto."*

Ernesto let the big blue automatic gun drop into the water. Holly saw him motion with his hand for Carlo to give him something else. She took aim and shot Carlo in the thigh. Carlo wailed, his voice louder and higher than Cammie's cries. *"Pistola,"* Holly said, sending another bullet into the hull of the *yola*. Tracy counted.

Holly had a single bullet left.

Ernesto sprang for the motor, and the *yola* lifted nearly vertical as he wheeled it up and away from *Opus*.

Fewer than two miles away from the yacht, when he could barely see it, he pushed Carlo, still sobbing and drenched in blood, over the side of the boat. Carlo begged as he flailed and finally sank below the surface. Ernesto quickly left him behind. He would be lucky to make it to the rendezvous. Now he was alone. He knew that Chief's boss had something to do with the father of the blond boy. This was bad business. He would say the boy was gone, a coward, that he had not been able to find him at the boardinghouse. He tucked the bag of gems into his shirt for safety and wondered if he should go on at all or simply turn back and run for home.

Swinging wide of the *Opus*, with the murderous bitch aboard it, he chose to do just this. He would slice the packages so they would splatter into pieces and then sink. The blood was bad enough. But he could swim to shore with the jewels in his mouth. There were times when the best a man could try to do was defeated by fate. He would save what he could. This blood-covered and useless boat would disappear, like all the others.

Day Thirteen

*T*hey had not slept or spoken since the shooting.

Through the dark hours, Tracy watched as Cammie, her eyes wide, stared at the wall of the saloon. Olivia steered, and Holly gave herself a shot of painkiller and slept.

The gun lay on the deck like a serpent until Tracy carried it down and set it quietly on the floor in Holly's cabin.

The moon had set, and the tincture of the darkness changed, slightly, toward gray. Finally Olivia called, "I've got to lie down for a little while, Trace. This took a lot out of me, too. It wasn't you they were after."

"I don't want to leave her alone," Tracy said.

"I don't think she's going to do anything," Olivia remarked. "We have to clean her up, though. Do you think that would help?"

"We can try," said Tracy.

"Okay, I'll get some clothes and you steer. Just leave her there for a moment."

Opus, broken, floated in sunny silence through a sea that would never have a shore. The surface, tufted only by the occasional tiny wave, white over turquoise over green over gray over white over turquoise, was objectively so divine, which made their state all the more repugnant. They knew only from the compass that they were now pointed west, and the sun burned in the sky like the business end of a soldering iron.

Sadly, Tracy wakened Holly, who dragged herself up to take the wheel. "We won't be long," she promised.

Cammie did not speak while Tracy and Olivia slipped off her clothes and burned them. They washed her with soap and shampooed her hair until no traces of blood or blue tissue remained on her anywhere, Tracy standing beside Cammie in the trickling shower. She was as pliant as a doll when they dressed her, in Olivia's own delicate embossed underwear and cotton gaucho pants, under a clean green T-shirt that had been Michel's. Cammie spat into the sink when Tracy brushed her teeth. Tracy braided Cammie's long, tangled hair as best she could. Finally she sat on one of the deck seats, with one of Olivia's huge hats tied over her face.

To avoid looking at the unbroken water, Tracy tried reading to Cammie. She read aloud from *Rebecca*. She read aloud from *The Once and Future King*. Holly glanced back and watched Tracy read aloud to her child. She was reminded of the faces and postures of the impossibly elderly women she had changed and dressed, propped and bathed, crooning cheerfully to them, at her first job. She had sat them out in the sun just this way, and they let themselves be put into chairs, with eyes that gazed serenely back into time. When an arm of their sunglasses fell askew from one ear, Holly put it gently back in place. Their hands were as beautiful as lilies and as fragile as the pages of a Bible.

"Leave her alone," Holly said finally. "Give her one of the shots."

"You need those," Tracy said.

Tracy and Holly looked at each other. In Holly's eyes was only regret, no fear; and a dart of anguish pierced Tracy's exhaustion.

"Give her a shot," Holly repeated. "She needs it now."

Although she clung wordlessly to her mother's hand until consciousness slipped away, the shot knocked Cammie out. It must not have been lidocaine, Holly reasoned, but something stronger. She wondered about Cammie's weight and the dosage but . . . Cammie would not die now.

When Olivia woke from her nap, Holly and Tracy sat in the captain's chairs. Olivia steered.

"This must be what post-traumatic stress feels like," said Tracy. "I can't stop replaying the whole thing."

"Yes, and you can talk to your physician about it, but the remedy has been shown in studies to result in possible side effects such as dizziness, insomnia, flulike symptoms, joint pain, nausea, headaches, stomach inflammation, occasionally severe—"

"How can you joke?"

"Because that's how you get through a trauma. That's what soldiers do in hospitals. And crime victims. And cops who shoot the wrong person."

"You didn't shoot the wrong person."

"I didn't shoot *a person* at all."

Tracy chose not to bring up the young man's grief and confusion. "How'd you learn to shoot?" she asked instead. "Or even load a gun?"

"Chris taught me, in his macho period. We went pheasant hunting. No pheasants ever suffered."

"But you were so good."

"That was adrenaline. It was building all that time in the ama, while I was trying to break the lock on Lenny's locker. It was a bitch."

"You're not taking credit. You saved our lives."

"I'm taking credit," Holly said. "I'm a good credit taker. I'm just describing a biological fact. Things you can do under the influence of adrenaline, you can't otherwise. I've seen it, in hospitals. Wheelchair-bound patients who get up and walk to their son when he comes back from a combat zone. Mothers who have lifted cars off their kids' chests."

Tracy put her hand on Holly's and was amazed how light-boned and small it felt. "I love you, Hols. I loved you before. But now I owe you my daughter's life."

Holly smiled. She looked out at the twinkling water. "You'll make sure that they knew I wasn't a chicken?" she asked softly. She laughed. "I just want my boys to know I wasn't a chicken."

Tracy saw how yellow her friend's skin had gone, how slack the skin under her solid jaw. "That's not going to happen. We'll tell them this story ourselves," she asserted stoutly.

"But if anything should happen, you'll tell them?"

"That you're the bravest woman I ever knew. But it's not going to be like that."

They clasped hands and intertwined their fingers. And they sat un-self-consciously, like old lovers on a beach, watching porpoises frolic in a pod, for more than an hour, neither with the impulse to give a parting squeeze and withdraw her grasp. Tracy wondered if friendship was at all like being in love and if she had ever consciously preferred Janis or if their closeness had been only because their family connection tumbled them constantly together. She wanted to weep for all the mornings she had almost called Holly to go for a jog or run out for coffee and then neglected it because going alone was quicker. Holly wondered if the boys knew yet who their teachers would be. But no, they wouldn't know yet. It wasn't even the Fourth of July. They loved the fireworks at Navy Pier, and all fireworks. Holly hoped her boys would not miss the fireworks.

"This is Janis Loccario," Janis told the Coast Guard operator. "Can you hear me?"

"I can hear you, Miz Loccario."

"You sound very far away."

"There's a slight thunderstorm here, ma'am. We tend to have sluggish service in these conditions. Where are you calling from?"

"I'm calling from the United States, from Illinois. Well, of course, you're in the United States, too. I mean the mainland. My cousin and my friends left from St. Thomas ten days ago, and they were to be in Grenada by now. But I can't reach my cousin. I know she would answer me if she could. So I want to report a vessel missing."

"It's a little soon for that. If they were only supposed to be there today."

"Yesterday."

"It's still a little early. Sailing isn't precise. They may have decided to stop for a while somewhere. They may have tied up for two nights instead of one. I wouldn't worry."

"I just want you to check. Have you . . . Don't sailing boats check in every day?"

"Yes, they do. They report their positions every day."

"Well, will you check on transmissions from the charter boat *Opus?*" Janis asked.

"That's Lenny Amato's boat, Miz Loccario. I definitely wouldn't worry about them now. I happen to know the fellow. Lenny knows these islands like the back of his hand. So does his mate, Michel Eugène-Martin."

"I still want you to check. Will you please do that?"

"Of course I will," the operator said. "Do you want me to call you back?"

"I'll hold."

"It could take some time."

"I'll wait. Now that I've got someone on the line."

Janis fiddled with the purse she had found at a garage sale and was making over for Tracy's birthday. It was nearly finished. She had only to affix the antique button and a trace of gold braid. It was purple. Purple was Tracy's color. God, help Tracy, she thought. Help Cammie. Jim and Ted had not heard from them, either. In his innocence, Ted suggested his mom and sister were simply having too much fun. But there was a deep line between Jim's eyes that morning when he returned the dish in which Janis had given them the Stroganoff. He'd asked her, "You do think they're okay?" And she'd told him, "Of course." And neither of them had believed the other. Janis had no idea how to call the Coast Guard, but it was surprisingly easy, right in the Blue Pages, just like the fire department. The number was different for St. Thomas, of course, but the woman who answered her had located it in no time as well. So, once Dave was off to work and the girls to school, Janis gathered her craft bag and her courage and made the call. Now she waited, measuring the braid. Too long. She snipped it. Just right. Rakish. She cradled the phone receiver on her shoulder and began to stitch.

"Miz Loccario?" said a male voice.

"I'm here."

"I'm afraid we haven't had a transmission from the sailing ship *Opus* in . . . seven days. But that doesn't necessarily mean trouble. Lenny Amato had a conversation with Sharon Gleeman, another captain, on . . . let's see, on the fifteenth. And there could be weather out there that might be interfering with their transmission . . ."

"So you'll file a report? You'll send out a message to look for them?"

"We take this very seriously, ma'am. We don't start a formal rescue operation, which is huge and expensive, until we've already done that. But we'll send out a bulletin immediately."

Later, Tracy began to pick up glass—the glasses and the shattered casserole dish, the leaking, stinking cans, and the bottles that the men had smashed. Unable to think of what else to do with the evidence of their presence, she tossed the trash overboard. However long they had to wait or however long they . . . had left, Tracy knew none of them could survive and look at the staging area of the massacre. After pulling on Lenny's thick rubber fishing gloves, she used a mop and a bucket of salt water to wash down the deck. She tried to keep herself from thinking of the boy's once innocent blood, scrubbing harder and harder. She tried not to think of how his mother slept, unknowing. It was useless. Her mind went to dwell there. Did that mother stir and for a moment murmur his name? What was his name, and how, if ever, would his parents know that they no longer had their blond-haired son? Would Ernesto give up his name if he was caught, as he surely would be, bobbing about in a leaking boat with insufficient fuel?

Tracy finished with the mop and then used the towels she found in a locker to clean the blood out of the crevices where it had been driven deep. Her empty gorge rose as she forced herself to continue. Her mind buffeted her back and forth with each motion of the towel. The boy had not been good. He would have let Camille die to save himself. The boy was caught in an impossible place, for what reason Tracy would never know. He had died to save Camille. Swipe, swipe, swipe, she worked and sweated, until at least the inside of the boat was white again, as Holly and Cammie slept on. She wrung the towels into the water bucket that went pink, then rosy. She poured the water over the side, unable to stop herself from murmuring a prayer for the family of the boy.

And next, unable to still her nervous hands, Tracy decided to create a new, tiny sail. There was not a puff of wind; they sat rocking in what Lenny might have called the doldrums. Today, the sun would be as punishing as a blowtorch. Tracy did not believe she would ever see the sunrise again with anything except dread. But if she was lucky, her makeshift sail would work. She would sew it and then unfurl the genny and set them both. She would do just what the young man had said to do.

She would not think, over and over, not any more, of the hole opening in his side, just below his top rib, and the long, impossibly protracted shower of blood.

Briskly, she fetched the bedsheets from the room where Olivia had slept until the smugglers had come on board. Olivia had since moved back in with Holly, drawing the partition between their beds. Using the only needle she could find, a huge upholstery needle she imagined the men had used to mend canvas, Tracy sewed two bedsheets together lengthwise and poked a hole through one thickness of one of the top hems. Through metal lines that had sprung from their fastenings during the blowout she chopped away with the wire cutters until she had a thickness she could loop through one of the eye hooks on the mast. Then, using a strong new piece of line, she affixed another corner of the makeshift sail to one of the cleats along the side of the boat.

When the wind came, Tracy would be ready.

When Tracy took the wheel, Olivia reluctantly threw out the last of the sealed tray of desserts, which had spoiled beyond what she said even Louis XVI would have ingested, their creams and light fillings a straightforward invitation to food poisoning. In the one MRE she could find, the macaroni and dried beef swarmed with small white insects—the origin of which Olivia could not imagine. She tossed that mess over the side as well. There was a half-filled box of cereal and a bag of almonds left. Where had the crackers gone? She didn't remember the men eating them. The only water was the single jug Tracy had hidden. Four cans of ginger ale remained. Olivia drank one. She lined up two others next to the water jug. She filled a paper cup and she brought ginger ale to Holly, who swallowed it gratefully and then promptly threw it up. Olivia called Tracy, who washed the outside of Holly's mouth with seawater and supported her like a doll to her bed, helping Holly to change into a clean shirt. She promised Holly she could come up again once the sun was not so punishing. "That kind of heat would make anyone sick," she chattered brightly. But having accomplished all it took from her to break the lock and assemble the gun seemed to have extinguished something in Holly. Please, oh, please, Tracy prayed. Let me have another chance. Let me have more time to give Holly. Let Holly go home to her family. She is so much better than I am, Tracy prayed, knowing full well that this rationale had never sufficed as a cause for vouchsafing survival. Not ever, in human time.

At dusk, Cammie woke.

When she did, Tracy led her up from the cabin and sat with her in the saloon. She poured Cammie a glass of ginger ale. In vain, she tried to explain that Cammie needed to speak about what had happened. Cammie, Tracy noticed gratefully, at least shook her head. Tracy persisted. What she didn't purge would haunt her, sleeping and waking, she insisted. Cammie took her cup into her own hands and drank the rest of it. Tracy put a few nuts on the table and encouraged Cammie to eat, which she did. But she went back to bed without saying a word. When Tracy looked in on her, her eyes were open, but she lay motionless, the sheets tucked neatly under her mattress, her sunburned face immobile as a doll's. She did not even blink.

That night, after they had washed down their cereal with ginger ale, Tracy jotted down a water schedule. Each of them would be allowed a finger's width of water twice a day until the jug ran out.

"That's absurd," Olivia told her. "A person can't survive on that."

"A person can," Holly replied softly. She had told Tracy that she felt better when she kept moving. But she was wrapped in her blanket, and when Tracy touched her forehead, it was as hot as a spatula just out of the pan. "And a person can live four or five days without any water at all. And if you have to, you can drink the water from the slop tanks. And if you have to, you can drink your own urine, because it's sterile."

"Jesus Christ!" Olivia said. "Like an animal."

"We are animals," Holly said. "We'll do anything to survive. Do murder. Eat our young. Maybe not our young. But become cannibals."

Olivia cringed and told them good night. Tracy went up to begin her watch.

Day Fourteen

The next morning, after an hour's sleep, Tracy searched every cranny of Opus to try to find a single bit of tinned food that had not been consumed by the pirates. For two hours, she scoured the bilge, the cabinets, the lockers and shelves. With flour and salt, she could have made an edible dough, but she could not spare water to congeal it. Finally, far back in the ama next to the bed where Holly slept, she found, beneath all the gear and tools Holly had tossed aside in her frenzy, a single can of tuna.

Pulling back the top of the can, she divided it into fourths, carrying Olivia's portion to her on a saucer. Olivia turned up her nose, then ate the few bites.

"I need water," Olivia said. "Will you hand me up some?"

Holly appeared at the bottom of the stairs. She was, Tracy noticed, using Lenny's unloaded gun as a crutch, a deeply unsettling sight.

"I'll call the media," she said to Olivia. "We all need more water. But you don't get another bit until tonight, unless you want to use up your ration."

"Fine, I'll use up my ration. This is bullshit. I'm sweating it out as fast as I'm drinking it," Olivia snarled.

"So is everyone," Tracy said. With Holly settled in the saloon, listening quietly to music, Tracy brought Cammie her portion of tuna. To her immense relief, Cammie stuffed it all into her mouth, using both hands.

"Honey, do you want to get up now?" she asked Cammie.

"I need you. I have to get the water maker started. I can't do it alone. If I don't get the water maker to work, then we'll all die. And we didn't go through . . . that to die out here. Please, Cammie. Help me."

Cammie opened her mouth as if to experiment with her voice. No sound emerged.

"Cammie, I need you to help me. I've slept one hour in two days."

Finally, Cammie said, "Yes."

Tracy held out both hands. Cammie said gently, her voice still raspy from her screams, "I'm not hurt, Mom. Nothing about me is physically hurt. How is Aunt Holly? I . . . blanked. I never thanked her and told her how much I love her for what she did. Is she okay?"

"She's right down in the saloon."

Cammie flew out of her cabin and down the steps to nestle into Holly's arms. Although Tracy saw Holly wince against the impact of Cammie's abrupt embrace, her friend tried to conceal it by shifting position.

"And here you are, back from your coma," Holly said.

"I never thought I would be the kind of person who would ever see or feel anything like that," Cammie said. Tracy felt an unwonted pang; Cammie had not confided in her. "When it was happening, all I wanted was for them to die. Then that boy did die, and he was trying to save us. Until last week, I'd never even run over a squirrel. And now I've seen people die."

"Cam," Tracy warned her.

Cammie glanced up, confused. "He was, Mom. You know he was whispering to me the whole time that as soon as he walked down one step, he was going to let me go and grab the motor from that fat pig and I was going to run for it—"

"Cam, stop!"

"No, Tracy. Let her say it. The boy I shot, the blond boy, he wasn't a part of this?"

"Of course he was," Tracy said, sitting down and slapping her hand flat on the table. "He was just as responsible as any of those men. He had been smuggling drugs with them for years."

"Mom!" Cammie protested. "That's not true. . . ." And then she seemed to gather up a handful of loose threads into the fist of her mind. "Aunt Holly! You didn't do wrong. He wasn't a . . . professional killer, like those other guys, but they would have forced me into the boat. He couldn't have stopped them. . . ."

"Did I kill a kid who was trying to save us?" Holly asked Tracy.

Tracy said, "He was trying, but it wasn't going to work."

"Mother of God," Holly said with a long breath.

"You couldn't have known!" Cammie told Holly, stroking Holly's face. "He wasn't a good person!"

"He was someone's child."

"So were the other ones," Tracy explained.

"You know what I mean. But when I saw Cammie in her underwear, and with him pulling her over . . . and saw her leg . . ."

"Of course!" Tracy said soothingly.

"Mother of God," Holly repeated. "Trace, help me up. I want to go and lie down."

"We have an active search in progress, Miz Loccario," the Coast Guard officer told Janis. "Of course you can come, but it's not going to change anything. We're doing everything possible to find them, everything. We can't raise them on the radio, so we assume they're out of reach of a VHF handheld. The freighter Cordoba out of Costa Rica is actively searching for them."

"If there aren't so many boats out there now, and the storm passed them, shouldn't they be easy to see?"

"It's a big mass of water, ma'am. But I guarantee you, we'll find them."

"Will they be dead by then, though?"

"No. Most every boat has emergency rations. They should

have plenty of food for a while, and if they have a water maker, they will be set for fresh water. No worries there."

Janis looked up at the clock. "Okay. I'll wait. And you'll call me tomorrow, you promise?"

"I'll call as soon as we see anything, anything at all. Or hear anything."

Cammie felt terrible about what she had said to Holly.

She made it her new mission to get the water maker to work. It was nothing but a big filter, she reasoned, that ran on batteries. She filled it with seawater and let the treated water drip into empty jugs. She tasted it. It had a funny metallic edge to it, but it didn't nauseate her. If Lenny had it, it must be safe, simply a long time unused. It took forever, though.

They watched as the level of the jug diminished. It was Cammie's idea to alternate "good water" with "yuck water" for the daily ration. That way, a handful of almonds and a few swallows of spring water would seem like a treat.

So that afternoon, Cammie gave Olivia her scant ration in a Dixie cup. It was water that Cammie had made. Olivia immediately spat it out. "What's in that crap? Some kind of sanitizing pill?"

"No, it's safe water. It's just made from seawater. The water maker takes out the salt."

"Well, I don't want any more," Olivia told her. "I can't handle it."

"You have to," Cammie told her, a slow boil commencing deep in her stomach. "We all have to. The jug water is for special—"

"No, the last bottle of wine is for special! I'm not drinking crap."

"Then you'll be thirsty," Cammie said.

They all gathered at sunset for their "good" water and ration of nuts and cereal. Holly reminded them again: People could live for thirty days without food and need only minor medical treatment afterward. It was liquid that counted. Any liquid that wasn't seawater. She vividly described the torments of those who, in desperation, drank seawater. Even Olivia was chastened.

Cammie spoke up. "I know that the water from the maker is gross. And on top of that, you're going to have to wait for what I make. It goes so slow. You have to wait forever for, like, a pint."

"Can't you make it work faster?" Olivia asked.

"Livy," Holly said, slumping deep into one of the padded benches in the saloon, "if you want it done faster, do it yourself."

"It's battery operated. It does what it does," Cammie said.

Not long after sunset, a small plane buzzed low over their heads. Cammie lit and threw flare after flare, and the pilot, whose head she could see, dipped a wing in response.

"Did you see that, Mom?" Cammie shouted in ecstasy. "He saw us. If he saw us, that means he might have seen the SOS on top of the boat. He knows we're in trouble! He'll send someone!"

"Probably not, but I pray to God," Tracy said.

"Can you boost me up to the top of the cockpit? I want to make sure the paint is still good. It's waterproof, so it should be fine." Tracy helped Cammie, who felt alarmingly light in her arms, to put her elbows on the roof of the cockpit. She felt Cammie slump in her arms.

"What's wrong?" Olivia called from within the cockpit.

"It's gone," Cammie said.

"What is?"

"The sign is gone. It must have been knocked off."

"Cammie. Stuff happens."

"Not over and over. It's happening over and over, like I deserve to die."

"I know I don't!" Olivia snapped from the saloon, where she was drinking a thimbleful of red wine.

"She didn't mean it that way," said Tracy. "You're overreacting, Liv. You too, Cam." I am sick to death of playing peacemaker, she thought. Let them get along or punch each other out. This isn't a drama. It's real. The first thing Tracy intended to do when she returned to Lowell Street was run for miles, run until she was breathless, exhausted. As soon as all the bruises and cuts she had not noticed when they happened healed, she would run and run. She would climb to the top of a hill and breathe deeply of the ordinary air of life. They were trapped, like hungry rats in a cage, eyeing one another with malice and ill will—confined in the midst of a ceaseless, breathless expanse of sky and ocean. The irony was too vast for Tracy to make out all its contours. She willfully tuned out Cam and Olivia's low-level bickering, and Holly's occasional barb, until the talk evaporated, meaningless as mist and less substantial.

Holly shivered in the heat. Darkness brought no relief. No amount of aspirin seemed to break her fever, and each night she used her flashlight to examine the dark line creeping inexorably up her thigh, perceivably longer day by day. She tried to turn her attention to the others, away from her own troubles. Nothing else had ever worked. Holly tried to examine the degree of selfishness that had marked her life. Yes, she had been selfish—too much the tease, too eager to claim the stage. But she had been no more selfish than any ordinary person and less so than many. She had forgone pleasures for her children's sake, and frills for her and Chris's dream of a vacation cottage. But was this charity? Had she ever really given of her self, her soul's muscle tissue? Not until this trip, Holly thought, and then it had been to do murder. She drew her blanket closer around her.

"I can't just sit here! The only thing we can do is find more wood and make another sign and nail it up there," Cammie said. "Let's get going. There's wood paneling all over the walls of the cabins."

"You get going," Olivia said. "I'm tired of getting going. I'm tired of hauling and steering and pumping and staying up all night. This trip was your idea, Tracy." She took her last sip of wine and stuffed the cork back into the bottle.

"Olivia, is this really an act?" Holly asked suddenly, her examination of her soul interrupted by a sudden quirt of rage. "Or could anybody really be such a simp?"

"Oh, shut up. . . . Except for your big moment, you haven't done anything but sit on your fat ass and whine about your leg for two weeks."

Her voice dangerously soft, Holly replied, "Look, Livy. Face facts. I happen to be hurt. Badly hurt. You might have noticed if you gave a damn. You might be used to people catering to your whims. But guess what? You're the same as us, Countess. My leg is infected. Cam's heart is cut to ribbons. Tracy killed a man. I killed a man. And you come tripping up every day as if you're ready for your close-up. I hear you use the shower. Where do you think that water's coming from? The rest of us have had two showers exactly since we left. You take one twice a day, while they're too busy and I'm too out of it to stop you. And now you want big, strong Tracy and Cammie to do the work that could save you. That's not going to cut it right now."

Olivia sighed. "You seem as though you can handle any crisis. You certainly showed that. You hardly need my contribution."

"Will you talk normally, Livy? You're Olivia Seno, a kid with a nice ass and a B average from the west side of Chicago. Get down off your high horse. Your best friends are in danger. *Camille* is in danger. If you had so many bloody fucking friends in Italy, you'd never have come home anyhow. Your mother lives in the same little house in Westbrook she lived in when you were twelve. Why hasn't *she* got a villa, Countess?"

"I've given my mother trips, clothing . . . not that she ever did shit for me."

"But she lives in a dump," Holly continued. "So does your brother and his wife. Joey works in a bindery, Liv. Why? Could it be because you never offered to help them do better?"

"Why would I?" Olivia asked. She whirled, stomped up the steps from the saloon, and made her way by moonlight to her cabin.

"Look, we're tired," Tracy began. "They really never did do anything for her."

"Maybe she was always like this."

"No, you don't know. Her family was like a pack of wolves, and not very nice ones."

Holly snapped, "Well, my mother slapped my face if I chewed with my mouth open. Your parents were drunk half the time. We don't act that way. No. I'm tired of her, Trace. I don't owe her."

"Please."

"No! Listen, Trace. Remember how cool and daring and gorgeous Olivia seemed to us when we were kids? She was so 'what the hell'? And we just loved it? She'd do anything. That's why she was the queen of the queens, the capo of the Godmothers. We were really just ladies-in-waiting, her underlings, her little people."

"What are you getting at?"

"Well, what I think is that Olivia is a sociopath."

"Holly!" Tracy stared. It was unseemly, disturbing, to seem as . . . eager as Holly seemed in sharing such information. But that was exactly how she seemed, avid—as though she'd been carrying an object around for a very long time and had finally figured out its use.

"No, listen. I'm a nurse, Trace. Most sociopaths go through life like everybody else does. They don't become mass murderers or even poison their neighbors' cats. They just don't give a damn. That's the difference between us and Olivia. She didn't give a damn for anyone but herself then, and she doesn't give a damn for anyone but herself now. Sociopaths are very charming and attractive. That's because they can tell what everyone needs. They have, like, an instinct for it." Tracy glanced at Camille, who was listening, her attention captive. "And they give them what they need so people will fawn on them or do what they want. That's one thing when you're a wild kid and you want some boy who's got a fake ID to buy you beer. It's another thing when you're a grown woman who's supposed to have a conscience. Olivia doesn't really care if we all get out of this alive, as long as she does. She doesn't care."

"You don't believe that really," Tracy said, aghast. "You're angry."

"No, I do believe that really." They heard a rustle as Holly ran her fingers through her stiff hair. "I do."

"Well," Tracy said slowly. "Even if what you say is true, then she'll have to do more to help or she's going to be out of luck, just like the rest of us."

"You'd think so," Holly murmured slowly, her tone maddeningly cryptic.

"Let's make the sign," Cammie said. "It's creepy, and we've had enough creepy shit to last ten lifetimes. Let's talk about practical things. Aunt Holly, the box you broke into. It was waterproof, and all the batteries we have are in it. You broke it open, and now it's not waterproof. So what if the boat turns over or something?"

Holly shrugged. "Then it's not going to matter if the batteries are wet. Is it?" she asked.

Tracy was silent for a long interval. Then she asked quietly, "It wasn't really the bigger bed you wanted, was it, Hols?" Holly said nothing. "It wasn't just that, was it? You wanted to be the one in charge of whatever happened with everything that was in the box." Holly didn't reply. "Holly?"

They heard her get up and listened to her uneven footfalls as she walked away. They heard her cabin door click and then a subtle tick. The sliding lock.

Day Fifteen

With wood ripped from the walls of Michel's cabin, Cammie and Tracy made another sign and nailed it to the roof, this time using twice the number of nails they'd used before. As they worked, they heard a small plane buzz high overhead, but neither even bothered to look up. Cammie was distracted. The sight of Michel's books, his shirts, his picture of him with his mother at an outdoor restaurant, his sunglasses on a hook, all these still turned her heart. She slipped the sunglasses off the hook and put them on. They were huge but somehow comforting, protective. She felt better, as if Michel were somehow closer by.

When they were finished, they were famished, so each of them counted out a dozen almonds to go with their water instead of the ordinary six. "Go crazy, Mom," Cammie said.

"Yeah, I don't know what number the sin of gluttony is, but I'd give my right bicuspid for a big filet, medium well . . ."

"Baked potato with sour cream and chives . . ."

"Lemonade and a pile of those lousy, doughy rolls Ted used to eat right out of the cardboard tube . . ."

"I miss Ted. Remember, he used to eat butter, too? And cream cheese the way a person would eat yogurt?"

"I can't talk about food anymore," Tracy said. "It's like soft porn or something." Surprising themselves, they both laughed. "Besides that, I have to steer." And then they heard, rather than saw, Holly's approach. Step, drag, step, drag.

"Hi, Hols," Tracy said stoutly. She had examined her own face in the bathroom mirror last night, shocked that she had not noticed that her lower lip was crusted and swollen, that it had broken open, bled, and scabbed. Shocked that her nose was as raw as chopped sirloin. She hadn't forgotten to use sunscreen. Or had she? She could tell, and it frightened her, that bits of memory, and even time, were becoming slippery. But Holly, Holly looked ghastly. "Let me get you a blanket so it's softer on the seat. There's one over here that's maybe even more or less dry."

"You see, I had to come up," Holly said distantly, as if she were not awake and with them, but explaining something to someone they couldn't see.

"Of course, honey," Tracy replied.

"No, I had to. I was dreaming. I thought I'd had a dream. Because the funniest thing happened. I went into Olivia's cabin to get a book, that's right, a book. She was in the bathroom. Before I came out here. And I found these," Holly said, holding out a handful of wrappers, neatly folded, and a stack of what looked like candy bars. "Her mattress had slipped, and a few things went fluttering out onto the floor," she went on. "So I picked them up and looked. Cammie, go watch the wheel for a minute, hon. I don't want you to listen right now. Will you please go instead of Mom, and not argue? Will you please send Olivia down?" Something unstinting in Holly's level gaze galvanized Cammie, who turned and hurried for the steps.

Slowly, within moments, Olivia picked her way down the stairs from the cockpit, exchanging places with Cammie. "I thought my head would explode from you guys pounding up there," she said.

"We saw another plane when we were nailing, Livy," Cammie said as she passed. "Maybe we're getting closer to an airport. That's twice in two days."

"Let's hope, darling," Livy said. Cammie closed the cockpit door behind her.

"Now, Olivia," Holly continued, instantly more present than

she had been in days. "Let's tell me . . . no, let's tell Tracy and me what these are."

"I assume," Olivia said, "they were Michel's. He kept them in a plastic box in a drawer built into his berth."

"And what are they?" Holly asked, her eyes molten.

"They're . . . energy bars, I suppose."

"They are, Liv! Good! They're energy bars. They're loaded with vitamins and calories. They're meant for people who are using up . . ." She paused for breath, and Tracy heard the slight crackle from Holly's chest. "Tons of calories exercising, like doing marathons. Or for old people who aren't getting proper nourishment. Or for people who are starving, whose food was ruined or thrown away by some goddamn criminals, on a boat, and who had to find some way to survive on what little was left."

"And?" Olivia asked, gazing at the horizon.

"There were twenty-four bars in the box. I found the box, too. Folded flat. And each of the wrappers, folded, under the mattress, except for these last six. And I thought I would show them to Tracy and you."

"You didn't eat them, Livy," Tracy pleaded.

"A few, I suppose."

"About eighteen, I suppose," Holly said.

"Lenny may have eaten some of them. And Michel."

"What if he did? We've been without food for days, basically. I know I'm the only one who's sick, and it's not because of lack of food. But what about Cammie and Tracy? They've been lifting and cleaning up glass and running the bilge pump by hand and making sails and breaking open cans and everything else a human body can do, for the sake of all of our lives. Do you think they might have been able to use an energy bar?"

"I certainly don't think you needed it, or Tracy. You both could have lived off, well, your stored—"

"Don't insult me, you bitch. Answer the question."

"I'm small. I don't have Cammie's youthful reserves of energy. I felt that if I could contribute anything, I needed the extra nutrition."

"And still, you didn't contribute anything. Not one fucking thing but a few Valium," Holly said.

"Tell me," Tracy begged, "you didn't just find those bars and decide they would be your personal stash of calories."

"I didn't want to take anything away from the rest of you! And I couldn't stomach all that fried fish and bread and butter Holly and you were stuffing down the first days. I'm not built that way."

"How are you built?" Holly asked quietly. "For example, what did the Wizard give you in place of a heart? You'd think you'd at least have felt some responsibility toward the young one, toward Cammie—"

"Oh, can it, Holly!" Olivia screeched.

"No, you can it, Countess. We all took your orders in high school, but this is over the top, even for you! What I should do is what I did to that poor kid."

"You're some hero all right!" Olivia said.

"We're scarcely moving," Cammie said, hopping down from the cockpit. "What's all the screaming about?"

"These," said Holly, holding out the handful of wrappers and bars.

"You found energy bars! Aunt Holly! You're amazing! How did you . . . What's wrong with everyone now? I thought we all sort of agreed there would be no fighting anymore."

"I didn't find them. Olivia, the *contessa,* hid them under her mattress. That's why she looks so good, Cammie. Why she isn't trying to live on a spoonful of cereal and a nut. She's had these all along."

"No," Cammie said. "No way."

"I told them. I can't eat that . . . fried slop or canned garbage. I'd have died by now. I don't have any fat tissue. . . ."

"That's so fucking right! It's all been sucked out!" Cammie cried.

"I'm naturally small," Olivia said. "So are you. Did you want me to completely cave in, like Holly?"

"Did you want me to?" Cammie retorted. "I'm nineteen years old. I've never even been in love. I've never had a real job or gone anywhere but . . . right here. To hell. You've gone everywhere! You've had enough money and sex and plastic surgery for ten lifetimes!"

"Cammie, it must be painful to be so jealous of someone twice your age," said Olivia, the vitriol in her voice snapping and spitting like hot oil.

"I'm not jealous of you! I feel sorry for you! You're so totally desperate! If you think all the face work doesn't show, you're so mistaken. You look like someone pulled all your skin up and wrapped a rubber band around it and cut it off!"

"Camille, I had a touch-up while I was still young so I wouldn't have to have some drastic measures taken when I was older. It's important to preserve your looks, Cammie. You have good genes, and that helps. You're lucky you're not going to grow up and look like your mother, with freckles and wrinkles and—"

"What in God's name are you talking about, Olivia?" Tracy asked incredulously. "Why are you talking about the relative merits of face-lifts? Now?"

"She accused me—"

"You said my mother was the best person you know!" Cammie cried.

"She is, but there's a difference between good and good-looking. Good means a guarantee that people will take advantage. People have been taking advantage of Tracy all her life. She thinks it means she's good. She is good. But good doesn't always win. Naturally, if your father could have had me, he would have, but one time was enough. . . ."

"What are you talking about?" Tracy asked.

"About Jim. About Jim and me."

"Jim. And you?"

"A little tryst, which I assure you meant nothing to me, while you were off banging balls up and down a basketball court in the cornfields—"

"You slept with Jim?"

"You know about it, of course. Well, if you don't, what does it matter? We agreed at the time not to tell you. You were already engaged."

"You're lying, Olivia."

"Okay, I'm lying. I'd be lying if I said Dave wasn't right there waiting his turn, too, although Chris seemed a little bit unsure about the sexual side of things."

"You're lying!" Cammie shouted. "You couldn't get anyone but some old man you married for his money."

"Franco was a good man. But in Europe, a young wife is afforded certain liberties, Cammie. I assure you, I've had a full and satisfying life in every way. And I intend to continue."

"You showed that back in St. Thomas!"

"I did, because there are things more alluring than youth, darling. There are things I know about pleasing a man—"

"You never slept with Jim," Tracy said, her voice trembling. She would have begun to cry, but she had no tears to shed.

"Well, I suppose you can ask him. It was during sophomore year, which would have been just before I left for Italy and just before I met Marco. I'm afraid that went a little too far, but you aren't unhappy about that, are you, Tracy?"

"What's wrong with you?" Tracy asked.

"We were talking about food theft," Holly put in. "There's no reason to take this further. It's ugly enough."

"Except I'm so tired of seeing you two acting like a woman who has an ounce of femininity is some kind of disease! I'm tired of you acting like big firefighters and heroes, heaving the ho and pumping the bilge and treating me as though I'm excess baggage.

I'm tired of listening to Holly lecture me that I'm not doing my share when all she's done is cook some crap and lie in her bed. I'm dirty and sunburned, and I want to go home, and I never wanted to come out on this bloody stupid—"

"You shouldn't have come. You just hurt people! You've never done a kind thing for anyone in your life, have you? Except send me things because you probably were too busy screwing around to raise children of your own!" Cammie shouted.

"I chose not to have children. I saw that most of them turn out to be ungrateful and thoughtless. Nothing I've seen since has ever proved me wrong. But when I got pregnant with Marco, I was still a self-sacrificing little Catholic girl, and I decided to give my baby to a good Catholic couple. And I just happened to know one."

There was a breathless, interminable silence in which Tracy willed time to reverse itself. It did not. She reached out and found Holly's strong, spatulate fingers and was comforted, deep in her primate brain, when their hands entwined. But when she looked at Holly, Holly nodded as if to tell her, *Steady now, steady; it's all right.* But Holly's eyes darted, unblinking, from Cammie to Olivia and back. Tracy turned away, toward the extravagant, unbroken nullity of the sea. The tiny aquamarine tips of the waves winked slyly.

"You're my *mother?*" Cammie finally asked, releasing her breath as if she had been holding it underwater. "You . . . you're my real mother?"

"You never guessed? You are rough around the edges. But a great beauty. Brains and talent, too."

Cammie stared at Tracy. "You should have told me a long time ago. I asked and asked, and you never told me."

"She made me swear," Tracy admitted, miserable. "She wouldn't give you to me otherwise."

"So you listened to her. And you kept me wondering. I suspected, Mom. You know that? I thought about it. I just couldn't imagine it. Well, Olivia, does this mean I'm the little Countess

Montefalco? Do I get a big inheritance and a car? I like Alfa
Romeos. . . ."

"I'm afraid not, honey. When I gave you to Tracy, you became
a gym teacher's daughter, with a father who draws factories and
additions to people's houses. Legally a Kyle. Camille Kyle. Now,
there's a moniker." She reached for the red wine and began to
uncork it, but Holly's hand snaked out and snatched it from her.
Olivia shrugged. "Not that I didn't regret my choice. You'd certainly have been . . . well, better off. But I didn't know what lay
ahead for me when I was only twenty. And we all thought Tracy
could never have a child, because of her abortion."

"What abortion? Mom?"

"It was an ectopic pregnancy, Cammie. Dad and I were going
to get married then, but I lost that baby."

"So you see," Olivia went on, "I would have been utterly cruel
to renege. But then, along came big old Teddy! And isn't he just
the picture of your mom? Do you think that's maybe, just maybe,
why you and Tracy don't get along so well?"

Cammie looked from one of them to the other. "I never
thought it made any difference."

"That's because it doesn't, Cammie!" Tracy cried. "I put wash-
cloths on your head when you had fevers. I was the one who
taught you to walk, and to read. Daddy saw that you had a genius
for math. Ted adores you; you know that. . . ."

"But I'm not who I thought I was. . . ."

"You knew that you were adopted," Tracy begged. "You knew
that made us love you even more."

"I didn't know I was the daughter of the town whore," Cammie
said. "You must have worried that genetics would all come true,
Mom. That's why you watched me so close."

"Cammie, please . . . I watch you so close because you're my
child," Tracy said, dissolving visibly, quaking. "You're my heart."

Camille walked up and over to her cabin and closed the door.
Tracy shook the handle. It was locked.

"What's the matter with you? Why would you hurt her and me this way?" Tracy shouted down at Olivia.

"I meant to give her hope, Tracy. I meant to point out that she wouldn't have to grow up looking like a broomstick with a pillow tied around the middle."

"You hate me," Tracy marveled. "You hate me. I knew your childhood was lousy. But the rest of it . . . You must have had an absolutely horrible life, Olivia. I feel the way Cammie does. I feel sorry for you. You're not going to be able to take my daughter away at this late date. You heard what she said. The best you can hope for is that, for a few weeks or a few months, she'll feel some kind of self-loathing she doesn't deserve. You delight in being evil. It was funny when we were kids. It was jokes and naughty tricks. But you *liked* excluding the other girls. You took pleasure in their sadness. You liked making them feel inferior. But they weren't really inferior to us, Olivia. Cissy Hewlett was a nice girl. Mary Brownell was cute and smart, smarter than any of us. Even Peggy Ojewski was a nice girl. But you chose us. Why us? Why me? Why Holly?"

Olivia, bristling like a terrier, glared up at Tracy. "I'll tell you why. Holly had a foul mouth. She made me laugh. She was the girl everybody wanted to goof around with, the cheerleader, one of the boys. I wanted her to be with me, not with her dumb jock friends. I wanted the boys. If I wanted Janis, who was stunning and also had boys following her in packs, I had to accept you, too. Your mothers wouldn't have had it any other way. And after I got to know you, I did admire how bold you were. How you would always do the dirty work to get my approval. If anything had to be stolen or sliced or knocked over, you'd do it, so I wouldn't take away your status as a Godmother. Everyone wants slaves, Tracy. I never thought I'd really *have* them, though I did, later on. But well, it was high school. . . ."

"You'd like me to hate you, wouldn't you, Liv? But I don't. Every time I look at you, I see a trace of the thing I love most on earth, except for Ted and Jim. Something you're never going to see. Someday you're going to be a lonely old woman, Olivia. Joey has his kids. Your mom has Joey and her grandchildren, and the memory of your old bastard father, Sal. Who will you have? Some young guy like poor Michel you pay for companionship? I'd rather have my size fourteen ass than your size six life anytime, Olivia," Tracy said. "Take it to the bank."

Olivia turned to stalk away. But Tracy stepped in front of her. A cloud passed. When the moon reemerged, Tracy's face was as empty as an open hand. "Go steer the boat. If I have to hurt you to make you do it, I will."

Day Sixteen

"Will you call me the moment you get there?" Dave asked Janis for the fiftieth time.

"David! I'll call you when I call you. I'll call you when I have something to tell you!"

"That's what Tracy said."

"Honey. In the freezer there are casseroles that anyone who can work an oven could heat up. I made five in case. I don't care if they eat pizza five nights straight. Take it easy. Don't work too hard. Don't tire yourself out."

"They said there was nothing you could do."

"But I can't do nothing, Dave! The way Tracy and I grew up, we weren't like cousins, we were like—"

"Sisters, I know. And I'll look out for Jim. He's a basket case."

"Well, we talked it over and agreed that having both parents and his sister gone would be way more than Ted could take. I have to go, David. There's no other choice. What if something happened and I could have helped them?"

"Do you have everything?"

"The old lady said I didn't need anything but jeans and shorts and a jacket. And a swimsuit. As if I'd be taking a dip!"

"She's going out there to find them when they have perfectly good Coast Guard cutters and helicopters?"

"Lenny is this older lady's friend. Lenny owns the boat. They're apparently a very loyal little community. She's put off heading her boat to the Hamptons to help find Lenny."

"But you promise to let her and her partner go? You're not set-ting foot on any boat. Do I have your word?"

"Dave, you just reminded me. I finished Tracy's purse. I'm going to run up and get it, and then I have to get to the airport. When I see her, I want to give her the birthday present I fixed up for her. It makes me think that I'll really see her. Emma will be here any minute to drive me to the airport. Please wish me well." Dave held her close and kissed her upturned mouth.

Janis ran upstairs and lovingly placed the little evening bag she'd finished just the previous night into her carry-on. Emma honked the horn. She and David kissed again, and Janis shoul-dered her bag.

Twelve hours later, she stepped on board *Big Spender*. With Sharon Gleeman and Reginald Black, she promised Meherio Amato and little Anthony that they would find Daddy, and they set out from the marina in St. Thomas.

Tracy set her experimental sail. When it filled, her first impulse was to call out in triumph to Cammie. But Cammie had come out of the cabin only to drink her water and eat a few bites of cereal. She unlocked the door that night to admit her mother. When Tracy looked in on her, she was asleep, or was pretending to be asleep. The cabin virtually stank of tense, speechless hostil-ity. It fell to Tracy to make sure that Holly swallowed something, even if it was only a mouthful of water with a teabag dipped in it and some sugar or honey mixed in. Tracy was stretched thin as an elastic band, yet trying to balance a medicine ball on that narrow band alone. For the first time in her life, she thought she might snap. Yet the work and exhaustion staved off the anxi-ety. She could sometimes forget for hours at a time that her fam-ily might now have cracks that would no longer withstand any sort of pressure. The cracks would deepen into ravines. Cammie would spin off onto a lonely trajectory of avoidance. Jim's heart would break.

And all this, only if they lived to tell.

She had not said a word to Olivia, and she would not. But Olivia had been skillful. She had placed the barbs carefully and well.

After her last watch, she'd locked the door to her cabin. She would not come out, either.

That left Tracy alone, Holly barely able to speak, Cammie and Olivia sequestered. And so, her mind her only companion, she could not rein in her thoughts: *Did* Tracy feel closer to Ted because he was of her blood and Jim's? She did not. If anything, Cammie had been the brass ring, the prize, the most beloved, the sprite always just beyond Tracy's reach. If anything, Tracy had taken Ted's good humor for granted. Had she wished she had given birth to Cammie? Of course she had. But to Cammie, not some other child. Had she ever meant to tell Cammie? Yes, she had planned to tell Cammie this summer, this very summer, when she turned nineteen. Then Franco had died; and Olivia had announced her decision to come back to America; and Tracy had weakened, frightened—yes, frightened of the resemblance between them that would be so obvious now that Cammie was a woman. What had she feared? Olivia was glamorous and exotic. Tracy was . . . plain and, as every mother is to her own child, ordinary. Was she fearful that Cammie would want more than an "auntie's" relationship with Olivia? Or had she put off the discussion she had planned—a low-key intimate talk—for fear of the bonfire it would ignite, given Cammie's volatile age and state of mind? She had never been able to bear a confrontation. Damn it. Jim knew it. She went along with everything Jim wanted, always had.

What was done was done. Tracy shook out her shoes, mentally, and gave all her perseverance to the sails. And once they were moving, her spirits lifted.

Any progress was better than the endless slow drift. Alarmed as she was that the compass showed they had drifted back substantially in the direction from which they had come, now they were making time. Occasionally, Tracy saw a sprig of some kind of land plant on the water. She felt like Noah. Perhaps they would see land soon, or a vessel, anything. Perhaps they could find some nameless island, tie up, and fish, because Tracy had read in the reef book that fish sometimes played around the bottoms of boats if they were stationary. Perhaps they would build a fire and eat their catch.

Her forehead was so chapped that no amount of lotion could soothe it, and she feared she would have to have some kind of skin grafts on her nose. It was beyond recognition—like an artificial nose, raw and clownish. She kept it slathered with petroleum jelly, and still it ached, even to sneeze. Her hands, never kempt, now bled even when she coated them with shortening scooped from the tin vat. Her hair was impossibly tangled with wind and salt water. She had not even tried to run a comb through it. The hats were all sodden or blown to bits, except for the tied straw affair Olivia wore each time she came out of her cabin. Even her eyes stung behind her sunglasses, and her vision blurred periodically. One of her eyes had something that had blown into it and danced like a period in her line of sight. She was dizzy when she stood up, and her tongue was a bit swollen, the skin on her hands loosening, signs of dehydration she recognized from sports.

In ordinary life, Tracy often drank half a gallon of water a day. The four-ounce ration had had less of an effect on Olivia and Cammie, Cammie perhaps because of her youth. But Tracy knew she had to conserve her own strength. Without forcing anyone, but with stern determination, she simply walked away from the cockpit every four or five hours, and either Olivia or Cammie took her place. Although Tracy longed to reach out for her daughter, she did not. Cammie would need to come to terms as best she could with the facts of her biological parenthood. This ugly way of revealing something once cherished was in keeping with the nightmare voyage. Tracy hoped, perhaps too optimistically, that all of it might one day be an ordeal to be analyzed when it was safe to do so.

Cammie was more mature emotionally than she had ever been challenged to reveal. Tracy could pray and she could hope. But she could not alter Cammie's stubbornness or her quite natural burden of disenfranchisement. Her world had been reconfigured. It would take time to see that the recast world had not blasted the essential underpinnings of the person Cammie was. Tracy tried to imagine how she herself would react given the same news, and if she were honest, she knew that while she would not have lashed out, she would have made a psychic cave for herself and burrowed in, just as Cammie had.

Tracy did not blame her child, only Olivia.

She dared not think past the next hour, the next gust of wind. She had never felt more alone, more like a pinpoint of breath in a strangled world. One of her friends was . . . well, if she was honest, perhaps dying. One of her friendships, forged with a unique bond, was dead. Her relationship with her child was on life support, and there was no guarantee they would be found before . . . before it was too late. And the energy bars she held in her hand. She had crumbled off three pieces that morning and fed them to Holly with her morning water ration. She'd eaten the rest of the bar herself.

The remaining two would be for Cammie.

Cammie would survive.

Day Seventeen

What was that?" Cammie cried out.

Tracy stirred, too spent to answer.

"I felt something, Mom, like maybe a big wave."

"Go up and look, then. Up in the cockpit."

"Is Olivia up there?"

"No."

"No one is up there?"

"No."

"Then . . . what are you doing?"

"I'm dying. I haven't slept. I don't know how long it's been. So shut up and let me sleep."

"The boat is under sail. It could fuck up everything."

"Because I'm too fucking tired. Leave me alone," Tracy said.

"Get up, Mom. I felt something."

Tracy rolled out of the bottom berth and, with Cammie following, stumbled out onto the deck.

Together, in disbelief, they felt the wake of the freighter as it swept past them, a mountain moving like a river.

"Get the flares! Cammie, get the flares!" Tracy ordered. "It's not going to hit us. It has to be two hundred yards away. But maybe there's a watch on the back end. Get the radio!"

Cammie lit and threw flare after flare high into the air, until only a pack of six remained. Tracy shook the radio, which seemed perversely unwilling to revive, and screamed, "This is the sailing vessel *Opus*! Mayday! Mayday! . . . The batteries are dead, Cammie!"

Cammie fumbled to fetch and force open a new package. By the light of the battery-powered lantern, they flipped the old batteries onto the deck and reloaded. "This is the sailing vessel *Opus*! Mayday! Mayday! Do you hear us?"

After interminable moments, a voice answered in blunt Slavic syllables.

"English!" Tracy sputtered, trying to remember every foreign language phrase she knew. "*Anglais! Nous etes l'Opus! Vir sind der Opus!* Cammie! Is that German? Is that German he's speaking?" The voice, more faint, seemed to be reciting numbers, coordinates.

"Give me it," Cammie insisted. "Mayday! Mayday! Everyone understands that. Why isn't he listening?"

"For God's sake, Camille, did you think you could say it more fluently than I did? We can hear them, but they can't hear us," Tracy said. "Don't you get that? I have no idea why. We have to be on the same frequency!"

"You're right, but I can't accept that," Cammie answered, bursting into dry sobs of fury. "I would break this goddamn stupid thing to bits if I could, but it's the only goddamn stupid fucking thing we have!"

Both of them turned to watch the lights of the freighter as they grew smaller and smaller and then seemed to go over the edge of the world. Then Cammie looked up at the cockpit. "Mom," she said slowly, "the boat is still sailing with no one steering it . . . and we're in a shipping lane now."

Tracy bounded up the slippery stairs. "Olivia!" she called. "Olivia!"

"I'll take it," Cammie said. "I can do it. You find her."

"Olivia!" Tracy yelled, pounding on the cabin door. "Come out. We're being rescued by a freighter. It's all over!"

Olivia threw open the door, and Tracy grabbed her arm. "You

have let me steer this boat until I fell asleep on my feet and we almost hit an ocean liner. Now, you're not going back in there. There's more ammunition for that gun."

"Let me alone, Tracy."

"No. You're going to help save your birth daughter's life, Olivia. You're going to help save my life. I was the only friend you ever had."

"I'm not going to sit for four hours and stare into nothingness for you. If you're determined to try to starve me, I'm going to sit here and save what little energy I have. I'm not going to do a single thing. You can count on the fact that I'm going to live. There's more of what I found where that came from. And I'm not giving one bite of it to you, and I'm not showing you where it is, and you'll never find it." She smiled with a gracious air of victory.

"You don't want anyone to forgive you, Olivia. Even Cammie?"

"You made it very clear that she is your daughter, and you are the mother bear protecting her cub. You provide for her."

Tracy had never struck another human being. She drew back her hand and slapped Olivia's face.

"Why, for the adventure," Sharon Gleeman answered, to Janis's question. "Money? Oh no. My father spent his days screwing poor garment workers out of their daily bread. It's been more than enough to provide for me, for my entire lifetime. We take people out for fun. Sometimes they're fat cats. Mostly they're people who couldn't afford another boat, huh, Regin?" Sharon turned to her partner. "We've had inner-city kids from the Boston slums come with their teachers. We've had families we've had to pay to fly here. It's fun. You'd be surprised what the sea gives to them. And then, of course, it's beautiful. It's beautiful now. But it can turn on you, as life does. In an instant. And I must admit, I like that, too. It challenges me. I could be sitting on my porch, with biddies, planning charity events for snobs. Not me." Sharon peered into Janis's eyes. "Don't take that the wrong way, dear. I'm not looking for adventure now. I'm looking for Lenny and for that dear boy, and your sister. And we'll find them, I promise you."

Janis laughed, and Sharon stared at her. "No, nothing is wrong," Janis told her. "It's just that, what you said, that's what I do. Plan charity events for snobs."

"I never meant to be in any way disrespectful."

"Oh, you weren't. Not at all. It's the snobs who get the credit, though, not the planners."

"Just so," Sharon agreed.

Sharon Gleeman was a marvel of agility. Janis watched her scramble up ladders and heft heavy jugs and cans of gasoline with the strength of a man—and a man half her age at that.

Reginald Black was the architect of the details. It was he who had put together a makeshift map, from Meherio's description of the route Lenny would follow. While Janis chafed with impatience, Reginald had taken the extra hours to gather blankets, water, simple provisions, and information from everyone who'd spoken with Lenny or Michel before they set out. She knew they would need all of it. She *hoped* they would need all of it. But she could not rest until *Big Spender* was motoring past Norman Island and out into the open water. They would not need the sails, Sharon had told her. Sailing was for pleasure, motoring for speed.

"If you're thinking starvation, don't worry. Lenny keeps a hefty amount of canned goods on board for emergencies, including canned water. And if they haven't encountered weather, which I hope they have not, they should still have plenty of frozen food. In the worst case, they should have plenty of water in the tanks and can use the water maker if they need to."

"What are you worried about, then?" Janis asked.

"Let's just head on, dear."

"No, tell me."

"Well, you force me. It seems someone Regin spoke to thought he saw the little tender from Lenny's boat, like our little motor craft, you see, but theirs is a bit larger, blue, quite distinctive."

"Spotted it?"

"Spotted it adrift. He was in a rush and the weather was foul, so he didn't investigate. But he had the impression that it was unmanned. If there was anyone in it, he was lying down, which would make sense, of course."

"Which means . . ."

"I have no idea. Probably nothing at all. The line on the tender could have unraveled. Lenny would have gone in after it. He might be in the tender. He might have missed it and they've towed him back to the boat. Most likely he and Michel are with your friends. A drifting tender doesn't mean an accident. It doesn't mean anything on its own. I can't count the times people have lost their tenders. They wash up someplace. Someone else grabs and tows them in. All is well. Still, it's better safe than sorry," Sharon continued. "You know, when I met Lenny, I never thought he'd last. The only boat he'd ever sailed was in a bathtub, I thought. You can't count the navy, walking about on great flat cities that float through the sea. But he was a fine diver, one of the finest. And he was patient. He learned from everyone he met. No matter what's happened, Lenny can handle it."

"Tracy, my cousin, is very resourceful," Janis said.

"Well, there you have it. I wasn't looking forward to the beginning of the dull season back on Long Island in any case. We'll all be laughing about this in a few days."

"What if Lenny is hurt?"

"It would take a great deal of bad luck to get Lenny in a jam."

"What if?"

"Well, let's let each day's evil be sufficient unto that day. My mother said that."

"Something else is bothering you."

"No, nothing."

"Reginald. Mister Black, what else could happen?"

"Miz Loccario—"

"Janis, please."

"Janis, Sharon is the most relentlessly optimistic person on this good green earth. I've known her since she was ten years old. My family moved from North Carolina right next door to hers. It was thought we would marry. In a sense, I suppose we have."

"But?"

"But she doesn't like to dwell on the grim."

"And you do?"

"I'm more of what the kids call a downer. I've earned my last name over and over throughout the years, they tell me, and spared this fine woman a world of woe, I must say, when I turned out to be right."

"What are you getting at?" Janis finally asked.

"At this time of year, not all the boats out here, and there aren't many, are sailing for pleasure. Some are heading toward winter destinations. But others, ones we don't see, are, you might say, doing wrong. They're sorry folk."

"You mean pirates?"

"Well, there are modern-day pirates, I suppose. Robbers. But the people I'm talking about don't want to be seen. They're bringing drugs into coastal areas off the United States. Drugs that came from Costa Rica or El Salvador through Honduras or other spots. Very profitable and very dangerous work for them."

"But also dangerous for anyone who runs into them."

"Yes, and the people who run into them usually are agents from the Honduran navy who put the screws to them in short order. And that's the end of that."

"But not always."

"Almost always. Not always. Pretty near always."

"Reginald," Sharon said, "I, for one, am very hungry. Go cook something, please. No one wants to hear these tales of tourists. . . . Janis, there has never been a single case of anyone being harmed by these rascals."

"Sharon, darling, you know that's not true. There was that couple who were boarded, and they humiliated the woman, I'm very sorry to say, and the man was badly injured."

"No one has been killed. Not for ten years or more. Please don't let my gloomy partner here fill your head with more worries."

Janis looked out at the wide, gently ruffled, and forgiving expanse of depthless blue. *Icy rum drinks with pineapple slices and paper umbrellas. Old stories, Motown music, and suntan lotion.* "I didn't need him to. I was thinking about it already, Sharon."

And while human beings are not like animals, which can sense the approach of a storm or a predator, or even death, Janis and Tracy had been wheeled through the zoo by their mothers in a single baby stroller. They had slept, head to toe, in one crib, then in one double bed. Janis had never had premonitions. But as she stood in the sunlight on *Big Spender,* she felt Tracy, and Tracy's distress, and the exigency in it.

"It's not all right," she told Sharon.

Day Eighteen

At last, a torpor fell over all of them, like a caul.

The deaths would have been a horror. But had they had enough food and water, guided by Lenny's example, they might have gone on. Licks of luck had been given them: They had drifted off the sandbar. Tracy had sewn a sail. Even the armed men . . . at least the fact that they had held them off was a sort of piteous victory. But the vicious encounter between Holly and Olivia, Cammie's hurt, perplexed withdrawal from all of them, Olivia's naked spite: Taken together, it was too much.

Planes and boats and, as far as Tracy knew, trains and goats would pass them by. They were invisible in the inexpressible vast-ness of the imperturbable sea. Nothing would happen but the end. And if anything happened before the end, it would be dreadful.

Day turned into evening before Tracy woke.

It was the day after Holly and Olivia had gone at it.

It was the night of that day.

She had been asleep for more hours than she had ever slept in her entire life. Her hand still stung from the slap she had given Olivia. She thought, I have no urge to use the bathroom. Brush my teeth. Eat my almonds. And then she thought, I don't care anymore. She had not steered that night. She had no memory of lying down on the storage lockers, her head pillowed on a life preserver. But as Tracy had lain asleep, the shores of Jamaica had slipped past. The last of *Opus* would not have been able to turn with enough skill to master an approach to that destination if any of them had seen it. It was perhaps better that they had not. On the shore they passed, there were virtually no inhabitants, only treacherous rocks and shallows.

Cammie's reflections were parallel to her mother's.

Steering the boat . . . to where? Drinking . . . to what end? Nourishing herself with bits of food her body might not survive long enough even to use? She thought of the condemned, able somehow to disassociate and eat a *last* meal. I would ask for hemlock, Cammie thought. She had often wondered, How do people know when it is the last time they will ever make love? When it will just simply not occur to them to do it again? How do they know they will never again see their parents? The last time Dad or Ted gives me a kiss? Everything that will happen to me probably already has, she thought. But she needed to get up and find Tracy. She needed to do that much. She had used the words *real mother* to describe Olivia. She had stepped on a crack and broken her mother's heart. If she truly had to die, it would not be weighted by the shame she felt for those two words.

Holly lay upright in her bunk, because breathing had become difficult, a slow and deliberate labor. She could hear her chest fill and empty to a sound like small pebbles tumbled in a distant glass. She had heard it often before, at the hospital, in quiet rooms where DNR orders were tacked to the doors. But the people who lay and breathed their rattling last were most often old, surrounded by those who had loved them long and well. And if they were alone, nurses took special care to comfort and soothe them. She knew that death was neither painful nor difficult. Shock was a kind of pleasurable release, so she had been told by those who had come close to death—the source of legends about welcoming lights and euphoric entries into a real and visible kingdom. Would there be a kingdom? Would there be a kingdom for someone whose last act had been the mistaken murder of another mother's son?

Olivia munched on her mocha bar and drank brackish water from the taps. She was nauseated and weak. Her belly above her bikini bottom was flaccid. She had determined not to come out again, not to open the door of her cabin at all. Let them all beg her. She would survive and thrive. That she had spawned that little Jezebel, in all charity and pain, was bitter gall. That even Tracy had lashed out at her was impossible to comprehend. Olivia had learned a bitter lesson. No one, *no one* was to be trusted. In Europe, they considered these great, thick, loud American women a sort of joke. Olivia didn't belong among them. She had never belonged among them. She was like a changeling child, peasant-born by chance. Perhaps, one day, Camille would come searching for her. Olivia would receive her graciously and warn her about the ineptitude of fools.

After the sun went down, Tracy and Camille met at the door of their cabin. Tracy, who knew that despite her apathy she was still a mother, and that mothers did what needed to be done, was coming to claim her child. Camille, who had remembered that the only truly secure place she had ever found on earth thus far had been her Sunday mornings as a child in her parents' four-poster bed, had come to find her mother.

They regarded each other warily.

They did not fall into each other's arms. But when Camille opened her mouth to speak, Tracy put a finger to her own lips. If it was the last thing she did, she would not allow Olivia to hear her and her daughter speak the things that belonged only to the Kyles, to their family.

Silently, Camille hauled up the bucket her mother had so recently scrubbed and poured water into the machine. She longed to grab the first drops and swallow them all, but she thought, First I have to make sure Aunt Holly has hers. Holly had not opened her door since the previous night.

When there finally was a full cup, Cammie carried a third of it to Holly. Gratefully, her eyes heavy, Holly accepted a few sips. Then she patted Cammie's hand—a gesture that so reminded

Cammie of Gran, her father's mother, who had done this very thing days before she died, quietly and without protest, when Cammie was nine, that a thrill of fear for Holly rushed through her. Holly's hand had the same faint, papery touch that Gran's had. The same sweet but unpleasant smell surrounded her.

She and her mother each ate six almonds. They could have counted the nuts that remained in the bag. Finally, Cammie allowed herself to slake her own murderous thirst.

Cammie could not remember a day in her life she had passed without speaking. She passed this day entirely that way. She worked at seeing to today's water and tomorrow's. She sealed the water in a clean jar she found in one of the cupboards. She wrote a long letter to her brother on the backs of successive postcards, apologizing for being a bitch to Ted, jealous of the way Ted seemed to do everything right and fit in perfectly where she never had, saying that she hoped he would remember her as the big sister she had been when he was a little kid, who let him put toothpaste in her hair as mousse and taught him to ride a two-wheeler as a Father's Day surprise. And then she lay down inside and tried to read. But she could not read, and the demarcation between waking and sleeping was not clear. The two ways of being were no longer so different.

Tracy did not want to slip back into an oblivious sleep. When she went up to the cockpit, she took a lantern and unfolded her ancient plastic sleeve of wallet photos. One by one, she shook the photos loose. The thickness of photos of Ted and Cammie had created a bulge almost too fat to accommodate her cash and her single credit card. Somehow, when school picture time came, she could never bear to relinquish the previous year's sweet or silly pose, so she simply slipped the current snap in front of the others. There were a dozen of Cammie, culminating in her glamour head shot as a St. Ursula senior. There were more of Ted, because Tracy kept his sports photos, too, and the occasional snap from other occasions, cut down to fit.

Here was Ted, missing teeth in his second-grade soccer picture.

Here was Ted in his first suit at the winter dance in ninth grade.

She remembered that night—a loud gaggle of boys, six or more, all of them spreading sleeping bags on her rec room floor, running outside after midnight darkness to throw rolls of toilet paper into the trees at Angela Sheridan's house, while Tracy watched indulgently from her darkened window. The next morning, she had flipped endless stacks of golden pancakes, while they ate and ate and ate yet more, talking about this girl and that girl—none of whom they had the courage to speak to, much less ask to dance.

Tracy gazed at the photo of her and Jim at their tenth anniversary party. They had danced until one in the morning. Tracy's feet, crammed into unaccustomed heels, were so swollen the following day that she couldn't shove them into her bedroom slippers. Jim had teased her about being one of Cinderella's stepsisters. She was glad that she and Jim, along with Holly and Chris, had taken that ballroom dancing class at the community college. It made Jim proud to waltz her around the floor that night, with other couples applauding.

Cammie's generation didn't dance. To her daughter's vocal shame, Tracy had chaperoned several of Cammie's high school dances. "Couldn't you get someone else to do it?" Cammie had pleaded, livid. The kids seemed to grind each other into the walls during the fast dances and swayed back and forth like cattle attached at the pelvis during the slow songs.

Ted would be able to dance.

Over his protests, Tracy had taught him the rudiments of swing and a credible waltz. She supposed he would spend his sixteenth year grinding and swaying, too. But one day . . . he would be grateful. He would remember them laughing as he trod all over her feet in his size fourteen Nikes.

He was old enough that he would remember her.

That hurt.

When it came to losing parents, a child was better off very young or old enough to have someone to stand in, not in the middle of growing up. Tracy's parents were still alive and energetic, and Jim's dad still took a daily run, although his mother had died of a congenital heart problem when Cam was little. She supposed that Ted would be okay, although . . .

She had to save Cammie.

Somehow, she would find a way to save Cammie.

When she could no longer bear her solitude, Tracy slipped away for a moment to Holly, giving her water by the teaspoonful, playing music that seemed to please her on Lenny's disc player. She talked to Holly, who did not answer but nodded occasionally. She had not moved from the bed since the attack, except once to lean on Tracy's arm and use the bathroom.

The same switch had been shut off in all of them.

But Holly's light had already been flickering. Her roaring show of defiance at Olivia had been pure will. She used the bathroom less and less often, sometimes not even once a day.

Tracy talked about Ian and Evan, about their returning to school, about the turkeys Tracy would bake in the double ovens on the night following Christmas Day, for a formal meal after everyone had spent the previous morning opening gifts and going to church with their families. Tracy hosted all who would come, from Jim's parents to Olivia's mother, Anna Maria. She always had.

She talked about her memories of Holly's mother, Heidi. Of Heidi's kitchen, smelling of cardamom coffee cake and the incomparable spritz cookies. She told Holly about the potato dumplings that left Tracy's stomach literally protruding when she got up from the table to go home. Heidi had died only two years earlier. Often, she had told Holly that she was the old maid, forty-one years old when she gave birth to Holly, forty-three when she gave birth to Holly's sister, Berit.

"Now, in the old country," Heidi would say, "it would have been scandal that I should marry when I was so old. But I came here with my parents, and I meet your father. He didn't tell me his age. He was only thirty years! That he should die before me was impossible." Yet he had. Evan's name was spelled Even on his birth certificate in honor of Holly's father, who had lived until the boys were five. And Holly, in her turn, had married a Norwegian boy, the son of immigrant grandparents. They had landed in Westbrook only through a casual acquaintance with Tracy's father. A Jaycee of the first order, Frank Loccario sang the praises of their suburban home, with lawns that seemed vast to families who had grown up in tenements and then apartments, with swing sets and streetlamps and streets where children rode their bikes until their parents called them home for dinner at sunset.

"Darling Holly, don't leave me," Tracy begged. "Holly, you're my family as much as Janis is. Holly, listen to me. Evan and Ian need you. Christian needs his wife. I need you. Do you hear me, Hols? Don't leave me alone out here. With Olivia. Help me." And once in a while, Tracy thought that she felt Holly give her hand a soft squeeze.

Finally, after covering Holly with the light quilt, even though the whole and every stitch of cloth on it was damp, Tracy went back to the cockpit. She fell asleep with her head on her arms. No one heard the radio crackle to life and the determined woman's voice that called out, "This is the sailing vessel *Big Spender* out of St. Thomas, Virgin Islands. Do you hear us, *Opus*? . . . This is Captain Sharon Gleeman. Please answer, *Opus*. Do you read us? . . . Does anyone have news of Lenny Amato's sailing vessel, *Opus*, missing since June fifteenth? Over. . . ."

Day Nineteen

Cammie dreamed of her bed. She dreamed of her bed as it had been when she was a child, her soft white comforter sewn by Grandma, light and sheltering as a bird's wing. She dreamed of opening her closet and seeing the bright racks of her clothing, arranged by length and color, not the fierce blacks and browns of her young adulthood, but pinks and greens and yellows, stripes and flowers. She was angry at Jenny. Jenny had an American Girl doll party and pretended she was going to invite Cammie but then invited Rachel instead. Rachel and Jenny, always thinking they were better than Cammie. Cammie didn't care. Daddy would take her to the children's museum. They would play with the machine that made real shadows on the walls, shadows of you that stayed when you walked away. She smelled waffles baking and syrup heating. In her dream, she argued with herself, One more half hour of sleep? Or a waffle fresh instead of reheated? What if Teddy got all of them? Cammie jumped up.

"Teddy!" she called. "Teddy! Don't you eat my waffles!" Teddy was only three.

"Cammie?" Tracy said hopefully. "Cammie honey?"

"No, no, no, no, no," Cammie mumbled. "I don't want to."

"Cammie?"

"Ted will never remember me as a good sister, Mama," Cammie said, weeping in the strange dry way they all did now. Her speech was slurred. "He'll always think I was a jealous bitch. And I was.

Was I, Mom? Was I jealous of Ted because he was really, really yours and I wasn't? Is Teddy grown up now?"

"Cammie, let's get up and drink your water, honey." Instead of being moved by Cammie's sudden slide back into girlhood, Tracy was alarmed. Was Cammie mentally affected? Permanently or from fluid loss? "Do you know where we are? . . . Cammie?"

"Home?" She kept her eyes closed, determined, against the sunlight that bayed in the open door like a predatory thing.

"Where are we, Cam?"

"We're . . . no, no, no, no, no, no . . . I know where we are, Mom. I know. We're in the middle of nowhere; and Lenny is dead and Michel is dead and the other boy is dead, and Aunt Holly . . . Mom, I wish I was dead, too."

"No, you don't."

"Yes, I do. Mom, we're going to die. Anyway. We're going to die. Aren't we? Tell me, Mom."

"You aren't going to die, Camille."

"Aunt Holly is going to die. And then I'll kill Olivia myself. I'll kill her myself."

"It won't be Olivia's fault. She has nothing to do with this, except that she withheld the food. I think Aunt Holly has some sort of infection in her blood. And the antibiotics haven't been able to get it."

"I hate Olivia."

"Don't. It's too much effort. Think of it that way. She's not worth putting forth any effort," Tracy said.

"Still, how could she do this to us?"

"Cammie, we're right here. If we don't want this to change us, if we just want this to be another piece of information in our lives, that's okay, do you see? Your great-grandfather, my grand-father, lived in Italy during the time of Mussolini. He was a little boy. He saw freedom fighters shot against the walls where the masters had painted murals. Cammie, your father, James Kyle—and I don't mean Olivia's one-night stand—his grandparents were Dutch. The Dutch all wore yellow stars in support of the Jews. The Kyles were the Conklings then. Your grandfather changed the name to make it sound cool, American, like a pop song. Grandpa Loccario was a fireman. You come from brave . . . Cammie." Christ, Tracy thought, in her ordinary personality, her daughter would be laughing in her face, mocking her forensics.

"But I don't, Mom. I really come from bitch—not brave. I was selfish and rotten and mean to my brother, my good-kid sweet little brother, who loved me all my life. And now I know it's because I'm related to her."

"No. You did it because you're a hot reactor, Cammie. You feel things in a mighty way, all the way through. Anger at me. Irritation at Ted. Admiration for Dad. For Michel, love. Lust. All that."

Cammie began to cry again. "Will I get another chance, Mom?" She reached up and touched her cheek. "You washed me. I remember now. Thank you, Mom. But, my face is dry. Why aren't I . . . why can't I cry?"

Tracy said nothing.

She went up to find the jar of water Cammie had patiently made the previous day. It was empty. Revolted, she poured her daughter half a glass of wine.

Sharon spoke to the Honduran navy officer, who spoke excellent English. He had apprehended Ernesto Flores in a stolen motorboat fifty miles or so off Choluteca. Flores had not been roughed up, simply taken to port and given into the hands of local authorities after questioning. He admitted the smuggling and said he had been forced into it by an American he could identify if authorities set up a dummy run. He was a poor man, who had long supported a sick wife, now dead, and his cousin Carlo's entire family of children. He was illiterate, and work was scarce. An American teenager had approached him about the drug sale, telling him that he would bring home thousands of American dollars. He had never done anything like this before. Asked about the opals in his pockets, he said he'd been given them by some women in a broken-down sailing ship. Given to him willingly, when he'd helped save their lives from his cousin Carlo, who had tried to rob and rape an American girl. He and Carlo and the American teenager had found the girl and her mother somewhere between Santo Domingo and Honduras. Ernesto had to fight both of them off and finally had to use the gun given him by the man named Chief. He had never owned a gun. Several of his cousins came into the military compound to say that Ernesto was speaking the truth.

Janis listened as Sharon noted the area for the last sighting of *Opus*.

Sharon said, "Bravo!" when the Honduran officer told her that the navy would cooperate with the United States Coast Guard in alerting vessels and sending rescue ships to search for *Opus*.

"Now, this is something like!" Sharon said. "Regin, turn this boat west. We may be able to reach them by tomorrow if we travel through the night. They could easily get to them before us. I hope they do. But wouldn't it be fun if we could? You see, Janis? We know that your cousin was alive less than twenty-four hours ago, and so was her daughter!"

"What about your friend?"

"Lenny wasn't mentioned. This man, this drug runner, well, it was just as Regin said. Lenny might have been . . . well, restrained by this partner of his, or the agent simply didn't mention him. In any case, we'll see soon, won't we?"

Sharon tried to keep her spirits up for the sake of this decent young woman. She knew that Lenny was dead. Lenny would never have allowed anyone to board *Opus*. The thief's story stank to high heaven. She feared what she might find on *Opus* if they found her, but it was not in Sharon Gleeman's nature to fail to see something through that she had begun. She owed Meherio this much. And that sweet boy Michel, who called her "madame." She owed him, too. He was part of their confederacy, and those who sailed the turquoise seas that bled one into another would be poorer for the losses. Of course, there was a chance. Strange happenings were everyday currency in the Caribbean. Lenny might be making his way home by now. Michel may have been resting, battered by exposure but alive, when the tender was spotted.

Janis leaned forward, as if to urge *Big Spender* to proceed fast, faster toward Tracy. "Sharon," she said, "there's no way that they could drift away from the position they were in when the . . . accident happened? The sea is so calm. . . ."

"Here, dear, but perhaps not where they are. The winds are building, it's going to get choppy out there. And the currents are always crossing. In one latitude, you might have breeze. Just a degree south, nothing. Fine for Regin here to row in. Regin rows single sculls for exercise, in the Long Island Sound."

"So, they could drift. . . ."

"Janis, anything is possible. Let's hope for the very best."

"Have to go with her there, Janis. Let's keep a hope," said Reginald. "I'm going to make us a nice omelet. We'll have a snack on the fly."

"I see land, Mom," Cammie said. "I see land through the window of the cockpit."

"Sleep, honey," Tracy answered. She had spent another two hours wringing two pints of water from a gallon of sea. She had dragged Holly out of her bed, which was sodden with sweat, only long enough to air it. Holly's breath was racking and for long moments seemed to stop altogether. The water Tracy placed on her tongue, on a soaked cloth, dribbled from the cracked corner of her mouth. Tracy had to sleep, to block that picture from her mind.

"I see land, Mom," Cammie said again in a mechanical voice. She tried to pull Tracy out of her berth. Tracy opened her eyes, which clicked and ached as if she had been struck. It hurt to blink. "I see land."

Tracy hauled herself to her feet.

Cammie saw land because . . . there was land.

Not a spit of sand with a rock and a stick.

Tracy saw land with trees. There was a beach. And—she could barely make it out through a gust of morning fog—what could be a building among the trees. Rapidly, the *Opus* was drifting past it. It could be deserted. It could be inhabited by beasts like the ones who had come to murder them. Was there a way she could tack back? Tracy ran up onto the deck and successfully reset the sails. She was able to turn the boat slightly, sailing slowly, surprisingly upwind. But not enough. What was the alternative plan? What improbable course of action was left to her?

She took hold of Cammie's shoulders and said, "Make water every day. Promise."

The island began to recede farther. It had to be now. Tracy grabbed a life jacket and leaped up onto the deck, where she untied the inflatable's straps and stood back as it sprang to a huge, flapping, orange being, shuddering in the breeze. Strapped to the interior were a liter bottle of water, blankets, and harness. More gear she couldn't decipher. Oars and oarlocks were snapped securely to the sides.

"Take care of Aunt Holly," Tracy said. "Make sure she drinks whatever she can. Try to make her walk. Try to make the boat tack. Keep switching the sails with the wind, like I did. Go back and forth, Cam."

"Mom! Don't leave me!"

"Cammie, this may be our only chance. Help me throw it over. I'm strong. I can row that far. I'll take the big flashlight."

"It has to be a mile! Who knows who's out there? What if no one's there and I drift away, alone?"

"Hurry, Cammie!"

They struggled to push the inflatable to the end of the deck and lowered it into the water, holding on to the lines. As she descended the stairs, she caught sight of the device Lenny had shown them, the one that could direct rescuers to a sailor overboard. A tether, she remembered, attached the submersible device. It would send a signal from someone stranded in a life jacket. Would it work on the boat? She had no idea how but knew Cammie could puzzle it out.

"Honey, the thing with all the letters. ERPID or something. Find it and strap it on and dip it in water. Put a life jacket on and hang from the ladder with your body in the water. Do it as often as you can. This thing shows where you are."

"Why didn't we do this before?"

"I . . . don't know. It seemed every day we might make it to some kind of safety. And we had our hands full. The truth is, I forgot about it."

"You take it, Mom! . . . Mom!" Cammie called as Tracy disengaged the oars and leaned forward. She began to row. "Mom! At least take the radio. If you don't, I'm coming in after you."

"Throw it, then," Tracy instructed her, and Cammie pulled back her arm and aimed with all her soul and mind. The radio landed in the bottom of the inflatable. As far as Cammie knew, this radio was the one that still had fresh batteries.

"Listen to me," Tracy called out. "Look at me. Put the device on and don't take it off. Find the tethers. Give one to Olivia and get one on Aunt Holly. If the wind gets stronger, attach the tethers to the D rings! If it blows hard, lower the sails so they don't blow out."

"To what?" Tracy's voice was growing faint. Cammie strained to hear her.

"To anything!" Tracy shouted. "Attach yourselves to anything that has a hole in it and won't break free. I love you, Cammie!"

"I love you!" Cammie shouted, but her shout was caught up and carried toward the sky.

As darkness fell, Sharon and Janis leaned close to the radio and watched the radar. "If it's anything out there, it's a little rain. Not a tropical depression. Janis, that's the precursor to a hurricane. I'm telling you it's not that. It's a little rain, that's all."

They waited for contact from the Coast Guard, and finally it came. They were suspending for the evening. They'd spotted nothing and would resume in the morning. "We understand. This is the sailing ship *Big Spender*, signing off."

"We've alerted all available vessels in the area or close by, Captain Gleeman. They may be able to go on searching through the night. Over."

"Good on," Sharon said.

"Do you leave the radio on all night?" asked Janis. "And why would they go on searching?"

"For the sport, dear. And yes, of course, I'll leave the radio on if I'm running all night, to chat if you fall asleep, if for no other reason. Someone's always awake for a chat. In a while, I'll let Regin take over, and you should get some sleep. I will."

"I don't think I can sleep."

"Well, then Regin will have company. He'll like that. Be prepared for long stories about his sheltered southern boyhood."

"I don't mind. I like hearing him talk."

"So does he," Sharon said with a smile.

"I haven't prayed so long and hard since I was a girl taking my First Communion. I was afraid for my soul then. And I am now, too."

"Well, I've always felt closer to God here than anywhere else. Perhaps He will hear you."

Janis went on, "I keep thinking that if I hadn't been such a weenie and stayed behind, I'd have been able to help them. Although I'm utterly useless around any machinery except a word processor."

Reginald came up, wearing a pullover sweater over his pajama pants. A cloth fisherman's hat was stuffed down over his bald head.

"No word," he said.

"Nothing yet. I'll turn in," Sharon said.

"Get some sleep, Janis," Reginald suggested.

"I can't."

"Well, lie down, then, here on a canvas chair. When I was young, I had trouble sleeping. My father never locked the doors, and we lived far, far out, past the last house on the street. Not a streetlight to be seen, but this big gutter with a manhole cover right outside our front door. I imagined that something would creep out of that manhole into my room in the night and kill me. Slither right on up. Not that anything could have got past my aunt Patricia. She lived with us, and Lord, that woman was ferocious. . . ."

Janis was asleep, and Reginald smiled.

Cammie read the instructions for the EPIRB. She had to pull a loop to activate and get it in the water. She tied it to a tether, tied the tether to a life jacket, pulled the loop, and threw it overboard, waiting to see if it came up to float. A light pulsed from it so she could keep her eye on it.

A light and then a heavy rain began to fall, but the wind was bearable. Cammie did not think there was anything left that she could not bear. Except one thing. She thought of her mother, rowing through darkness. "Tracy is like the North Star," Olivia had said just before she betrayed Tracy. And Cammie had betrayed Tracy. Why had she wasted months and years on spite and rebellion? Why had she wasted even one day? She had been such a dumb kid. She set out the two buckets to collect rainwater.

After giving some of it to Holly, although most of it dribbled out, Cammie ate the last of the almonds. Olivia still lurked behind her locked door, with, Cammie knew, all the water Cammie had made the previous day. To her surprise, as she sat rubbing Holly's shoulders, Holly spoke.

"Cam," she said, "it's slowing down. The world is slow."

"It is, Aunt Holly," Cammie answered softly, dreading that she knew what Holly meant. "You should try to get up and walk."

Holly did, giving it her best effort. Her leg was bloated and splotched with red, thick and bulbous as an uncooked sausage.

"Do you remember," Holly asked slowly after she lay down again, "coming to stay with me when you were little? When I worked the PM shift and you went to half-day kindergarten?"

"I remember the grass," Cammie said, lying on the bunk beside Holly. They had spent hours together lying on the grass, watching the ants determinedly build their homes. Cammie would stagger up to Holly's door under the weight of her backpack, which felt enormous, and Holly never failed to greet her with a joke.

"Are you married yet, Cammie?" she would ask without cracking a smile, or, feigning a look of terror, she would stop Cammie before she set down her backpack and whisper, "Don't move. I'm going to try really hard to get that great big spider off your forehead before it bites. I can't promise anything, but I'll try. . . ."

Then she would snatch up Cammie in a hug that was big and splendidly yielding and cuddly. She would give Cammie things that Cammie had never realized existed in the world—Twinkies and marshmallow pinwheels, Kit Kats and Starbursts, treats health-conscious Tracy had never allowed Cammie even to glimpse. One April afternoon, when Cammie was mourning that she would never again be able to play in her sandbox, that summer would *never, ever* come, Holly simply took her hand and hauled her outside. Using the garden hose, she made Cammie a mud hole, where Cammie rolled and sculpted for hours. Unable to resist, Holly sat in the mud beside her. Tracy showed up just as they were making their way to the back door. Horrified, she threw down her huge duffel bag and demanded to know why Holly hadn't called her at work to tell her Cammie had fallen and been hurt. Cammie remembered Holly's brush-off: "Dirt is not an injury. You keep a kid too clean, you're going to raise an anal retentive. She's washable, Trace."

Cammie stroked Holly's tranquil face. Did it hurt? Cammie prayed it didn't hurt. How many times had she come home from college and contented herself with beeping out the window at Ev and Ian as she drove past? Too busy to go in and visit, even for a half hour? *Aunt Holly*, Cammie wanted to shout, *don't sleep! Don't sleep until you can't wake up.* Cammie's mother was careful, resourceful, protective, and gentle. But Aunt Holly was fun. Holly let seven-year-old Cammie sit on the couch and hold Ian and Evan, just a week old, one under each arm, like little footballs, again reassuring Tracy that babies were basically made of rubber, and as long as Cam didn't shake or drop them, they'd be happy for the contact.

She'd given Cammie her first tampon (Tracy feared toxic shock) when Cammie was twelve. When Cammie was sixteen, Holly had given Cammie her first beer. "Tastes like piss, doesn't it?" Aunt Holly had asked. "Well, that's the point." It was to Holly that Cammie had confided that no one had asked her to the prom. It was Aunt Holly who had suggested the totally classy solution of dressing up in a big, old-fashioned, fairy princess gown with a crinoline (all the other girls were wearing identical strapless sheaths) and talking Jim into renting a tux with tails. Cammie had taken her dad as a date and been asked to dance by about fifteen boys and got her picture on the front page of the local as well as the school newspaper.

Aunt Janis was great, but she was like a clone of Mom.

Aunt Holly did it her way.

Now Holly noticed that Cammie, while not having moved a single muscle, was looking at her. "Poor baby," she said.

"No, Holly," Cammie said.

"You know what's happening to me. And your mom knew, too."

"*No!*" Cammie covered her ears.

"Listen, Cammie, no one ever leaves who was loved, because of . . ." She paused and struggled to breathe deeply. "Of memory. Help Evan and Ian remember. I'm not being a drama queen. They need you. They're just kids. And, you remember, too. Everything that happened to us out here doesn't mean that life is bad. It means the exact opposite. Life is . . . wonderful, Cam. Keep fighting. Forgive Olivia. You're the only good thing she ever did. Forgive me for letting you down."

"You didn't let me down! You didn't let me down!" Cammie cried.

"I should have known sooner. . . ."

"Aunt Holly, no!"

"It's how it is, Cam. And I'm not scared now. I love you, Cam."

"I love you, too."

"You go to sleep, and I'll see you in the morning."

Cammie left her, taking Lenny's tools, his hammer and crowbar. Systematically, she began to rip the beautiful varnished paneling from the steps of the cockpit and its roof. She tore the benches to shreds and ripped off their backs. With bleeding hands, she tied all the boards together, the small splintered pieces on top of the largest board, the padding from inside the cushions on top of that, and then bound them with a line so they would float next to the boat. She sucked out a scant quart of fuel and found a quarter bottle of Haitian rum, the last liquid on the boat except for the few inches of rain. When the rain stopped, Cammie soaked all the debris as best she could, in booze and gasoline.

As soon as it got dark, she climbed down the ladder and set the wooden pyre on the water. Then she threw lit kitchen matches at the pile of boards and fluff until it caught. The flames soared and crackled as they drifted. Somehow the line went taut, and the boat didn't catch. It was still burning when Cammie lay on her mother's bed, wrapped herself in Tracy's blanket, and cried in her new, curious dry way, until she slept.

Day Twenty

Janis woke, breathless, a bird beating against her ribs. Had she missed something? But Reginald was gone, and she could smell fresh coffee. Sharon was at the wheel.

"Do not feel guilty, missy," said Sharon. "We're making fine time, and you were desperately jet-lagged and worn out. Don't you think stress always tires us?"

"I suppose," Janis said. "I know you'd tell me if there had been any news. . . ."

"Actually, there has. There was a signal, an electronic signal, seen about one hundred miles north of Honduras off and on, and a U.S. Coast Guard cutter is heading that way. Also, a sailing ship, I believe it was called Sable, out of Belize, heard a weak radio transmission late last night. A Mayday from someone in an inflatable. A life raft, if you will. Someone else, in a light plane, a corporate plane, saw a fire, something burning, around the same place."

"Is that Tracy?" Janis cried, leaping out of the chair. "Is that their boat on fire?"

"I can't hear," said Sharon. "Wait. . . . Fine. Over." She turned to Janis. "I'm not sure, and neither was the pilot or the captain. But whoever sent the radio message was a woman, and she said that she was approaching an island she thought was inhabited."

"So it could have been Tracy?"

"It was a woman."

"How could you not know whether an island was inhabited?"

Janis asked. "Aren't they either inhabited or not, and isn't that on the map?"

"People have private islands, dear. Rich folk or poor folk. The rich folk are living there in seclusion, and the poor folk might be living there illegally. Either way, they don't want their locations on charts."

"I see," Janis said. "A fire? A signal? I don't mean to be rude. All this. Why didn't you wake me?"

"Well, what would you have been able to do? We're just heading that way, and now we'll have some coffee and breakfast and see what the day brings us."

They were eating when a static-riddled radio voice asked for contact with the sailing vessel *Big Spender*. Sharon snatched up the radio.

"Captain Gleeman, we have successfully located *Opus*, and a rescue operation is in progress. There are three aboard, and three apparent fatalities, I'm very sorry to report. Over."

"Carry on," Sharon said. "Over."

"Reports are one passenger also missing. We are bringing the survivors to Hospital General San Felipe on Honduras for evaluation, where the navy, which intercepted the drug smuggler who seems to have attacked these women, will arrange transport to . . . Corpus Christi. Yes, to Texas Lutheran in Corpus Christi. We'll report when the evacuation is complete. The vessel is to be abandoned. Do you wish to arrange for her towing? Over."

"Yes, I do. I'll do that on my own," said Sharon. "Thank you for most gallant service, sir. Over."

"You're entirely welcome, Captain Gleeman. This is Telecommunications Officer William Thane signing off."

"Fatalities?" Janis asked softly. "Did they say it was my niece? Tracy? Or your friend?"

"Of course, that's what we fear. But we do know that one of the smugglers died. Perhaps the body—"

"You know it was one of them."

"Yes, dear. I hope, for your sake, that it was not your cousin. I know how you cherish her. I hope for my sake that my friend is alive. But one of us is going to lose."

"All of them . . . on the boat . . . are dear to me. I never knew Lenny, of course. But I know from what you say, he must be, or have been, a fine man. But we've been friends since we were girls. Olivia spent the last twenty years or more living in Italy. She fell in love during junior year abroad. She was studying art. She married a wealthy older man, a lovely guy, Franco Montefalco."

"The winery? I've enjoyed those wines for many years. I can't handle a Chianti, except drinking that Montefalco is like drinking perfume."

"Well, he died from pancreatic cancer, quite horribly, last year. And Livy sold the winery, and the cruise was to welcome her home, you see . . . we'd all been to her wedding, in the vineyard. There was an arch of flowers, all magnolias. She wore Franco's mother's wedding dress. . . ."

"You sound very fond of her," Sharon said.

"Actually, she and Tracy were the ones who were so terribly close. I was a hanger-on. But yes, wherever Livy went, something exciting happened. We all knew something wonderful would happen to her, and it did, for a while. She was like a fairy princess. But now, I don't know. She's hard. She always was, not cold, exactly . . ."

"I know that kind of person. Aloof, you might say."

"That's almost it."

"And so, if someone has died, you hope that it's she."

"No!" Janis cried. "I wouldn't wish that on Olivia! But Tracy is my . . . She's more than a cousin to me. We grew up together, and except for when she was in college, we've never lived more than a mile apart. Our children . . . my daughters and Cammie are more like . . . Cammie is my niece, in my heart, rather than my cousin. I love them very much. And Holly! Holly's heart is just as big as her head. Everyone loves Holly. She has twin sons only twelve years old." Sharon Gleeman squeezed her lips together and shook her head. "I wanted so much to go on this trip, but I couldn't. My husband was ill."

"I hope he's better now," Sharon said politely.

"He is."

"I suppose you're glad you didn't, given how things happened."

"Actually, I'm not. I wish I'd been there. I wish I could have done more. I wish I had been with Tracy, if Tracy is . . . hurt. I think she must need me," Janis said. "It had to have been Tracy in the inflatable. Livy would never have gone. She's not used to work. Tracy would never have allowed Cammie to be at risk in a little rubber boat. And Holly's tough, but she just isn't as strong and fit as Tracy. Tracy was an athlete. She still teaches gym class."

"Then I would imagine she made it to land."

"I pray that she did."

"I will pray with you, if you like. An old renegade Presbyterian's prayer might not be quite the thing. But there's a sailor's prayer I recall. It goes, 'Though my sails be torn and tattered, and my mast be turned about, let the night wind chill me to my very soul, though the salt spray might sting my eyes, and the stars no light provide, just let me another morning light behold.'"

"That's beautiful," Janis said, and unable to prevent herself, she added, "In the name of the Father and the Son and the Holy Ghost, amen."

"Amen," Sharon said.

Cammie lay on the deck in the sun. The sun felt healthful, as if it might give her some kind of nutrition. Didn't it have vitamins? She knew it must. That was why sunscreen could be dangerous. No, it wasn't. It was the IV rays. No, the UV rays. Was it vitamin A or vitamin D?

All the sunscreen was gone.

She wished she could lie on the ground, in the grass, even the grass on her front lawn or the hill leading up to her dorm, lie in its strong and motionless embrace and cling to it. Earth. Just solid earth. The geography of her world had been deconstructed.

Aunt Holly, she thought.

She had known the moment she'd opened Holly's cabin door. Holly's limp arm was still warm.

Cammie raced for the portable defibrillator. When she could not rouse Holly, she cracked the mirror in Holly's bathroom with her fist and, using one of the larger pieces from the sink, held it to Holly's still, blue lips. No mist formed.

"Oh Aunt Holly," Cammie cried, shaking and shaking the dear, still shoulder in its T-shirt that read nurses do it all night. She began to sob, leaning deep into Holly's chest as if Holly would somehow find a way to reach up and comfort her. She laid two fingers against Holly's wrist. Not a flutter. The tip of Holly's nose and her fingers were already cool. All Cammie could do for Holly was weep without tears for her two little cousins, all unknowing that they were now motherless. Very likely she, too, was a motherless child. Her still not quite adult mind could not fathom this.

A memory coalesced in her mind of Ian's and Evan's third birthday—just before Christmas, the year she was ten and Emma and Ali just a year or two younger.

For some reason, Holly had sewn matching outfits for all of them—not only her boys, but all of them. The girls wore red knit skirts with striped red-and-black tights and black velour long-sleeved shirts. Teddy and Ian and Evan wore rompers with little straps over the shoulders. At nineteen, Cammie could see now that these outfits actually were cute and still current. At the time, she wanted to be boiled rather than put hers on.

Over and over, the parents begged and cajoled all of them to stand up straight and smile once—just once—and then they could all fall on the cake and devour it.

But in every picture, Emma slouched, or Cammie pouted, until finally Holly turned off the camera.

"Listen, brats," she said, "I worked on those outfits until my fingers were like pincushions. And I don't care if you like them. And I don't care if you like this. But you stand up and give us one good picture of you or I'll give that sheet cake to the dogs." So they all did, brightly, frightened by something in Aunt Holly's tone of voice. "You don't know it, but someday you'll look at that picture and be glad you have it. You'll be glad you had a picture of all of you, at just that time, all together, before you grew up and went your ways. And you'll look at pictures of your folks and not be able to remember that we were ever so young. It's the way things go. I know."

At Christmas, Holly had given every one of them a copy of the photo in a strong pewter frame. Cammie's was still stuck at the back of her bookcase, her outfit in her "mem" box, saved for Cammie's own little someday daughter. She wished she had the photo now. She wished she could hold it to her now. Aunt Holly wasn't really old. She still had half her life ahead. Neither was her own mother old.

Aunt Holly was right. Except that Cammie would never be old enough to marvel at how young her parents had looked. . . . Very likely she was as old as she would ever be. If she lived, she would be good to Ted and help him make his way. She would love her father and comfort him. She would help Ian and Evan remember and be their big sister.

But who would comfort her?

Gently, she pulled out a clean blanket and laid it over Holly's face. "You're a good egg, Aunt Holly," she whispered. "You're a good egg. You believed in heaven, and if . . . if my mom is there, you'll find her right away, in those plaid shorts. And you'll be able to hang out together. And I'll do the same things for Ev and Ian that you did for me. I'll teach them how to get the girls, but not too soon. I'll teach them how they don't have to be hurt because someone picks on them . . ."

Olivia peeked in, rattling the door.

"She's dead," Olivia said dully.

"Go away," Cammie warned her without turning around. "Go away before I do worse than my mother would have done to you."

"Is she dead?"

"Go to hell," Cammie said.

"Is she dead? It's bad luck for us to be on a boat with a dead body. Remember what they said?"

"Olivia, you asshole. We've been dragging a dead man's bones all over creation. Don't you want to pray for Holly? If she's dead, she's in heaven. Don't you want to cry? Why am I asking you? You're a stone."

"I'm not," Olivia said, her eyes welling. She still had tears, Cammie noted bitterly. "I'm afraid, Camille."

"Well, so am I. But you're afraid for you! I'm not afraid enough to steal food and water. I hope Mario or whoever it was who got it on with you and made me was a halfway decent person, so I have at least a chance of being normal. For your information, my mother—my real mother—left yesterday in a rubber boat, a rubber boat that could already have been cut by coral or chewed in two by a shark, to try to save Holly and me, and even you, you skanky bitch. Stay away from me, or you'll wish you had."

"I know that. I saw her."

"That's because she's a person, and you're a thing."

"Cammie, I know what I said was wrong. I'm as desperate as you are. Holly was, too. But I am the person who gave you life."

"Thank you," Cammie said. "Go put makeup on, Olivia. You'll make a better-looking corpse. You know, think about it. You took away stuff that might have kept Holly alive long enough for someone to find us. And she was a nurse. She knew things that we don't. You might have killed yourself with your selfishness, you fucker. So, you'll be the last one alive on this boat. You'll die alone, of thirst. That's a really horrible death. If I start to get sick or weak, I won't show you how to work the water machine. I'll rip up the directions."

"Forgive me, Cammie."

"Oh, I do. Holly asked me to. I forgive you because you are so nothing. Now, I want to be alone and think about the person who saved my life and the one who would give her life up for me."

So Olivia retreated, her concession to all she knew of love made and spurned.

Cammie tried not to think of dying. You felt nothing. She knew that. She looked down at her belly, her chest and legs. She could not have imagined a person so dark and dry and wizened, like a mummy with patches of skin peeled and parched. She lay on her side and tried not to be afraid. There was no reason to be afraid. It would all end soon.

She thought the voice that woke her was God.

It was huge and from the sky.

Cammie squinted and saw a tall man in a military uniform, standing on the deck of a big white boat. No, it wasn't a uniform, more like a blue jumpsuit. He had no face. Goggles covered his eyes, and his head was hidden in a helmet. He might have been God. He was speaking through a megaphone. Was God American? Or did everyone simply hear God in her own language? Cammie closed her eyes. She was hallucinating. She knew that was part of the end, too.

"Can you stand, miss?" the hallucination called. "Ma'am . . . can you stand?" God was very annoying. Cammie pushed herself onto all fours, then stood. "Are you uninjured? May we come aboard?"

"Who are you?" Cammie cried.

The man seemed not to hear. Cammie walked down to the

cabin where Aunt Holly lay and got Lenny's gun. She came back out and pointed it at God.

"Whoa, miss! Is that loaded?"

"Yes!" Cammie shouted.

"I'm Captain David Hodges of the United States Coast Guard, Miss . . . Kyle? Are you Tracy Kyle?" Cammie hesitated. "Please lay down your gun, Miss Kyle."

Cammie dropped the gun. What did it matter, in any case? He was probably not real. She hadn't had any water in what seemed like forever, though it had been only . . . hours? A day and a night? The man and another man threw out a large metal hook and pulled *Opus* toward them, then a metal bridge unfurled mechanically. Gingerly, God-in-blue stepped across to Cammie and gave a thumbs-up sign to the others on the boat, who all were his twins or triplets. Possibly archangels.

"Good. Now, we'll secure you and over we go," said the trooper, the guardsman, the savior. He used a wide webbed belt to secure Cammie to his side and walked her into the arms of another goggled God.

"Am I hallucinating?" Cammie asked the second man. She clung to his arm.

"No, you're alive. This is real."

Beneath the grime, he saw she was a real dazzler. She had gone through hell, by the look of her. Poor kid.

"If you're hallucinating, we both are," said the man. "You gave us a scare."

On the boat, Cammie accepted the packet of liquid yogurt already torn open for her and asked, "Where are we?"

"You're off the coast of Honduras, ma'am."

"How far is that from St. Thomas, Virgin Islands?"

"Maybe twelve hundred, fifteen hundred miles."

"We drifted that far?"

"You're here," he said.

"There are two other women over there. My godmother Holly

and another woman. My godmother died last night. My mother was with us, too. . . ." The man's face fell.

She looked over and saw Olivia already on the deck, waving a zipped carryall in one hand. Once Olivia was brought over—carried, Cammie noticed—and settled into a seat, she sucked on a slender packet of Gatorade. Then two of the men in uniforms spoke quietly to the captain. Cammie heard them say that they needed a bag and a sling. The sling was the hammock into which they gently placed Holly, after zipping a white cloth covering around her.

That sight was so unbearably definite.

All of it had really happened. She could never wake up from Michel and Lenny and Holly and her mother and the smugglers. Cammie began to flail and shriek, and one of the officers removed the headgear. It was a woman, who sat beside Cammie and held her arms in a hug both tender and forceful.

"Don't you want her to be laid to rest at home?" she asked Cammie. "Don't you want to be able to know that, at least, she came home? You were very brave. You set a fire; you sent a signal. You managed to save your mother."

"My mother is out there!" Cammie shouted, trying to free her hands to point out into the distance.

"Wait!" the female officer said to one of the others, who had begun to wheel away. "She says there's another passenger."

"She's not on the boat. She took the lifeboat and went for the land, a little island we saw, before our boat . . . stopped. Why did the boat stop?"

"It's hung up on a sandbar."

"Well, she rowed. She's strong. I'm not leaving here without my mother."

"Be still," Olivia said.

"You be still! Push her over! Let her drown! I'm not leaving here before I find out where my mother is. I know my mother is alive. Listen, you have to listen. She had a radio. She would have called to someone. Please, my mother is lost out there! This woman is not my mother!"

"We need to get you to the hospital," said the young guardsman who had helped Cammie onto the cutter. "Our orders are to get you to the hospital on Honduras immediately. Your condition is good. But you need fluids and observation. Your mother here needs fluids and observation. Please understand."

"This is not my mother! My mother is Tracy Kyle. My mother is Tracy Kyle, and she's in a rubber boat!"

The cutter roared toward the marina in Honduras, and *Opus*, with its sad remnants and burdens, undulated gently in the immense waters that bled toward the sky.

Day Twenty-one

*J*anis sat drumming her nails on the table in the saloon on *Big Spender*. As she heard Sharon approach, she tried to fake a rally, if only out of a semblance of politeness. She didn't want to appear ungrateful. She owed Sharon a debt: Sharon and Reginald had trusted her, a stranger, to accompany them. They had helped her—for reasons of their own, but also out of simple compassion. If nothing else, she could tell Cammie and Ted and Jim that she had tried. She could tell Tracy's mom and dad that she had tried. What she would tell her own husband, she could not imagine. Dave must know by now that she wasn't waiting sweetly by the telephone in a safe room at the Golden Iguana. Well, the man knew whom he'd married.

Sharon finally asked, "Do you want to know what happened?"

Janis said, "Yes," and Sharon shared with her the mixed tidings of the Coast Guard rescue and the fact that, within hours, her young niece and her friend Olivia had been evaluated for injuries and then flown to a hospital in Texas. Holly's sister, Berit, was on the way to help Holly begin her last journey home. Tracy was nowhere to be found. She had taken the inflatable and, unaccountably, left Cammie aboard *Opus*.

What Janis understood as real was ripped forcibly into before and after when she tried to comprehend that she would never again see Holly, listen to Holly cuss, or roar with laughter at her own dirty jokes, or rag on her boys. No. This was not permitted now. There would be a time to mourn. She had to focus on the hope of some sort of collective redemption, some aperture of fortune through which a blessing, in exchange for this human sacrifice, might slip. Her mouth filled with saliva, as it had when she was newly pregnant.

"Put your head down on your lap," Sharon Gleeman said gently. "You look peaky." Janis did.

"You'll go back now?" Janis asked when she had gathered herself. Her question skated an edge of anxiety that she hoped Sharon could not quite detect.

"I don't think that I will quite yet," Sharon said. "What do you think, Regin?"

"I think we should go and bring Lenny's boat home. He would have done the same for us, Sharon," Regin said. "Meherio might be able to collect on the insurance, or even repair and sell her."

"No one will want to sail on *Opus* again, Regin, do you think? People will think it's cursed after what's happened, or might have happened. Of course, that's foolishness, but there's so much superstition that surrounds anything having to do with the sea."

Regin answered from the cockpit, "Don't you be so sure. I've heard the house where Lizzie Borden took an ax—"

"Spare me," Sharon said dryly.

"Well, it's a bed-and-breakfast inn now. Some people could have a yen for a boat with a bit of history, even if it's the grim kind." He stopped and turned toward Janis. "Y'all please forgive my manners. I realize I'm talking about your family here."

"And your good friend," Janis said. "No apology necessary."

"Well then. People move into houses they think have haunts all the time. My grandmother did. She said she never sat down at her dressing table but she saw a woman in white walk past the door behind her. Saw her in the mirror, plain as I see you. Never felt any harm coming from her."

"Why are they always women in white?" Sharon asked of no one in particular. "Why don't they choose a nice navy or a red cloak? It makes the whole business of being a ghost a bit tedious."

"Sharon, people used to be buried in *shrouds*," Regin said. "Shrouds were white. That house was more than a hundred and fifty years old. Couldn't expect a lady in a striped Chanel suit and high heels—"

"Well, this is all extremely titillating. But let's get to the business at hand. Now, by my reading, we should be close to the coordinates I've worked out. This is nearby to where the electronic signal came from. We should be there within the hour. Do you think we can tow *Opus*, Regin, if we find her?"

"We'll need to put in for more fuel. On the way back."

"But she won't swamp us."

"Not us."

"Well, that's what I'd prefer to do, then," Sharon said. "Do you mind if we do this errand for our friends?"

"You mentioned the radio transmission," Janis pointed out. "Do you think that . . . Are you hoping to find my cousin, too?"

"It's not out of the question," Sharon said. "Of course, we'll have a look around. I didn't want to bring it up. But you didn't think we wouldn't try, did you?"

"I thought you'd give up. It's only sensible. After the cutter failed to find her . . . the chances are almost nonexistent."

"They found the others. Just because the cutter failed to find her doesn't mean that we will. And it doesn't mean that we won't fail. Nothing ventured, Janis."

Surely, carefully, Sharon Gleeman made her approach to what seemed to Janis an impossible dot of needlepoint on her maps. How did people *do* this? Find an impossibly indistinguishable handkerchief in a voluminous and shifting sea on which a boat might have rocked hours earlier, using a series of graphs and lines on a paper and dots on a screen? Janis knew from going camping how quickly currents could carry craft away. But though this made their quest seem even more foolish, she grew more alert and avid as Sharon neared the place where the Coast Guard cutter had rescued Cammie. She picked up Sharon's binoculars and sat on the stern of the boat, in the hammock Tracy had described, which felt more to Janis like a trampoline. She scanned the seamless sea, back and forth, back and forth, as the day turned to its gloaming.

That was the moment in which she saw the light.

Two bright bursts and then, in a moment, a third. Two bright bursts and then again, in a moment, a third.

She rose slowly. She did not want to fall.

"Sharon," she said when she reached the cockpit, "look at that."

"Mmm," Sharon said. "I've been watching it for some minutes. Trying to figure out what it is. The Honduran officer said they call that Bone Island."

"Are there cannibals there?" Janis asked, thinking, Now they know you are a complete fool.

"No, legend says it belonged to a recluse with the unfortunate name of Mister Bone. His home is still there, that much I do know. I believe that I heard, and, oh, this is all lore, there was a son, who didn't want the house but didn't want to give it up. And gradually, this huge house, built with bricks shipped over from England, and with formal English gardens that were maintained by Spanish servants, fell to ruins. . . ."

"Someone is there. That light."

"Yes."

"Are you going in?"

"I'm not sure who it is," said Sharon. "I'm going to circle back behind it and see if there's any kind of natural mooring. It's less than a mile across." She motored away from the light, at right angles to it; and Janis saw it begin to blink furiously, on, off. On, off. On, off. "Well, it appears that the only place to put in is right about where that light is. There's a sort of indentation, Janis. What we'd have to do is for you and me to take the tender over and moor to one of those big trees. At least one, and bring the lines fast. I suppose it's best to try calling. . . .

"This is the sailing vessel *Big Spender*," Sharon spoke into her radio. "Who is there? Who is that?"

No answer came.

"The batteries could be dead," Janis said.

"Or someone could be trying to lure us into a world of trouble," Regin commented.

"The likelihood of that happening twice in a week is the likelihood of your growing a full head of hair by the time we get back to Charlotte Amalie," Sharon said. "Don't be so bleak." She paused and said, "Ah. Now I see her."

"You do?" Janis cried. "You see her? I don't see her!" She thought that Sharon meant Tracy.

"I see *Opus*, a mile or so to starboard," Sharon said. She picked up the binoculars. "Christ, she's a mess. There are wires and rags hanging all over. And a bunch of burnt lumber. On the other hand . . . I've seen worse. That ship was partially burned when Lenny bought it."

"Seems to me more like a couple of miles, Sharon. Visibility is fine out here."

Another report came. The fatality on board was a woman called, according to survivors, Holly Solvig. There had been no evidence of the violence the younger woman described and no sign of the crew, lifeboat, or tender.

"Len left his boat," Sharon mused.

"He wouldn't have," said Regin. "Maybe in a crisis."

"Funny how she stayed. She must be hung up on something below the surface. Do you think we can float her off if the tides . . ."

"Maybe. Depends on what's got her. It'll be a chore."

Janis thought that thirty years of living in a twenty-foot-square space together had given Sharon and Regin a kind of telepathy.

"So let's motor on over there, and try to avoid whatever she's on. . . . Maybe it's only a sandbar, Regin."

"Sharon, Sharon, wait! Look at the light," Janis pleaded.

"I am looking. It's impossible to see behind the light," Sharon explained. "It could be a beacon of some sort."

Then the radio crackled. A harsh voice rasped, "Help me." The words were indistinct and garbled, the voice thick. "Help. Tracy Kyle, of Westbuh, Illinois. I am on . . . with a—"

"Tracy!" Janis screamed. "That's my cousin. Sharon, that's my cousin, oh, that's my cousin!"

And within fifteen minutes, tall Tracy was limp in the arms of Janis, eight inches shorter and seemingly so caffeinated with elation that she might have been able to lift Tracy and carry her back to Chicago. Tracy's face was a welter of infected bug bites, bruises, and peeling skin. Her shirt was missing a sleeve, and her short hair was matted flat, like a wicked small boy's. She cradled one wrist, the left one, on which her hand hung limp. Burns had gone deep. To Janis, Tracy's nose looked as though it had been held to a grill instead of exposed to the sun. Her legs were scored with deep scratches and were swollen, purpling below the knees. She was the most fantastic sight Janis had ever seen.

"I found you. I found you," Janis whispered as Tracy collapsed, weak-kneed. Between them, Janis and Sharon half carried, half dragged Tracy into the tender. "I found you."

Tracy's lips and tongue were so cracked and swollen, she couldn't speak. Those words she spoke to call us would have been her last, Janis thought. She motioned for water.

"A little," Sharon said. "Too much all at once will make you sick." She wet a clean cloth and let Tracy try to suck on it, but even then she could not fully close her mouth. Sharon ripped open a sterile package of lemony moisturizing gel, squeezing it onto Tracy's tongue and smearing it over her lips.

Tracy worked hard, but no sound came. Sharon gave Tracy a sip of Gatorade. Finally, making a sound that reminded Janis of gears grinding, she said, ". . . me." Regin helped them get her aboard *Big Spender*.

"I won't let you go. You're safe now," Sharon said. "Lie down on the berth." Regin pulled back the coverlet and revealed crisp striped sheets. Tracy fell back, motioning Janis to lean down beside her. Janis did, and Tracy reached up, her dirty hand like a paw. "Cammie," she whispered. "Holly."

"She's safe, Trace. She's safe in a hospital in Texas," Janis said, careful not to mention Holly. "They're coming for you. Sharon's called. To take you to Cammie." Tracy nodded and made a noise Janis took to mean "good."

Janis stood up from her crouch and hugged first Sharon, then Regin. "Thank you for sparing me what would have been one of the most awful tragedies of my life, and my family's," she said.

"When the cutter comes, you go now, with her," Sharon said. "Go take care of your family. You earned it, you hung in there."

Janis was quiet and thoughtful for a moment. Then she said, "If you don't mind, I think I'll stick it out. You said it would be a chore to get the *Opus* free. I'm no sailor, but I'm relatively young and tough, and I can help. I think I owe Lenny that. I don't know what happened out here, but I know that if he was your friend, he must have been a fine guy. I'm guessing he would have done anything to save them. I think what happened must have been one of those things that are like being sideswiped by a car. You're doing everything right and one thing goes wrong, and then everything goes wrong. Fate, I guess. He doesn't sound like a man who'd leave his boat."

"You're right there," Regin said. "Lenny had a heart as big as his head. And a strong sense of responsibility. Sailing is like flying, Janis. It's safe, but it's not forgiving."

"So, I would like to do him the honor of helping you in any small way, to bring the *Opus* home to Lenny's wife and little boy."

Sharon smiled. "I like that in a person, Janis. Spirit. Welcome aboard."

An hour later, a nurse opened the door to the darkened room where Cammie slept under light sedation.

She had fought like a wolverine to get out of her seat for the whole trip to Texas. The Spanish nurse who sat beside her spoke gently, but her accent only made Cammie cringe away from her. She could hear only Ernesto requesting that she remove her clothing. Spoiled brat, the nurse thought. Yanqui bitch.

At the hospital, they had marveled at Cammie's sheer strength. It had taken a doctor and a burly nurse to drag her out of the emergency room, where she had been examined, again, for fractures and internal injuries—this time with a set of X-rays. There was no cosmetic surgeon on staff, but someone located a physician, a woman who was known to have good hands, who was willing to come in on her day off. She gave Cammie twenty milligrams of Valium, anesthetized her deepest cuts, cleaned the edges, and repaired the wounds with the precision of a pointillist. She was a beautiful girl. It was a beautiful leg and a pretty hand. The infection that had begun would have gone downhill fast, but IV antibiotics would chase it out within a matter of days.

The doctor, whose own daughter was fourteen, anointed Cammie's burns and applied gauze to the worst of them. A strong young immune system was on her side. This much damage was difficult to reconcile with having been out only three weeks. A great deal had to have gone wrong. After all, they'd had the protection of the boat, though the doctor had heard it was disabled. The doctor remembered a family she had once seen, a mother and two children, brought in by cutter from an inflatable where they'd spent three weeks exposed to the sun in the Gulf after their rented monohull flipped in Hurricane Daniel. How they'd managed to *avoid* running into land had been a mystery. The father, a Brit who'd once crewed on a racing yacht, was with them. One of the infamous bareboat captains, he'd been arrogant enough to attempt a long sail with skills that had been peak ten years earlier. He'd learned that sailing wasn't like riding a bike. To his credit, what little water he'd managed to save he'd given to the children. Still, he and his younger child had died within hours, the child of hypothermia. The doctor saw the mother's agony and thought, without charity, what a fool this woman had married.

After the doctor had finished her work, satisfied that Cammie was stable and at least physically sound, she gave her over to two nurses. They did their best to sponge Cammie down from head to toe like a baby, avoiding the bandages and the worst burns. Somewhat subdued by the pain of being touched, she quieted. They mourned her long thick hair, which would certainly have to be cut. Finally, they tucked Cammie's long mane into a surgical cap. They forced her down onto a clean bed. She promptly pulled back the sheets and got up, demanding her mother, dislodging her IV, demanding a phone to call her father. They forced her back down. She got up again. They gently held her down. She got up the moment they turned away. Finally they strapped on restraints, and exhaustion won out.

The Spanish nurse stamped out of the room after Cammie yelped. In her place came another, one of those who'd helped bathe Cammie earlier. She shook Cammie's shoulder lightly. "Honey," she said in a melodious Jamaican accent, "I have a phone message here for you from a Janis Loccario. She says your mother is doing well."

"How many times," Cammie asked dully, her eyes closed and fists clenched, "do I have to tell you? That woman who came in with me is not my mother. She's my birth mother. My *mother* adopted me. My *mother* is Tracy—"

"Kyle, of Westbrook, Illinois. Your mother is coming soon. Your aunt Janis and Captain Sharon Gleeman and the crew of the boat *Big Spender,* they found your mother. I know what I'm talking about, little girl. She was brought to Honduras by a fishing boat they hailed. In a few hours, she will be sent to this hospital on a jet. A fast one." The nurse laughed. "They're all fast, aren't they?"

Cammie lifted the nurse's hand and pressed it to her tattered lips.

When Tracy Kyle was finally brought in by ambulance, the doctors and nurses who worked over her determined that she had broken her wrist scrabbling up onto the shore of Bone Island, as the inflatable, having veered into an underwater reef, shrank from flimsy to flat. She was filthy, but they sponged her clean enough to slice away necrotic tissue from her burns. Some of the burns on her shoulders and nose would eventually need grafts if they were not to be disfiguring. She was dehydrated, but fluids would soon remedy that. Her electrolytes were out of whack. Her lips were lacerated, but lips healed. One badly swollen and infected eye required salve, a patch, and the best possible hopes. There was nothing more for that. They set her wrist in a cast that left her fingers free and started a drip of fluids, glucose, salts, antibiotics, nutrients, and sedatives.

All in all, she was in pretty good shape.

Finally, they wheeled her into the darkened room where Cammie Kyle lay sleeping and shifted her onto the second bed.

One of the nurses began to draw a curtain around her.

"No, no," said the Jamaican nurse. "What we got to do is push this bed next to her baby. So when she wakes up, she sees Cammie." So together, they maneuvered the metal nightstand from between the beds and pushed Tracy's bed as close to the other bed as the cords that connected her to monitors and the call button would permit.

In the night, Cammie woke and, her eyes adjusting to the gray gloom, her body protesting from the pain, looked around her. She reached up and felt her hair, her beautiful hair. It would have to be shaved, like Sinéad O'Connor's. Someone had tried to comb it out. Her stitches throbbed. She had cut her hand smashing the mirror in Holly's bathroom. And she was about to press the call button for more medication when she noticed her roommate, a still shape under a light blanket. Through the window blinds, moonlight shined just enough for Cammie to make out the distinctive profile, her mother's short brown hair.

"Mom," she whispered. "Mommy." Tracy didn't stir.

Cammie prodded the call button. A nurse answered efficiently, "Yes. How can we help you?"

"I'm in a pretty fair amount of pain," Cammie said. "And I want someone to tell me if my mother is in danger, please."

"I'll be there in just a moment, Miss Kyle."

Cammie watched as her mother slept, measuring the slight rise and fall of Tracy's breath. When the nurse came, she shined a penlight on Cammie rather than turning on the fluorescents. She shook Cammie's IV bag and injected a potion into it that immediately spread like salvation through Cammie's aching body. As she turned to leave, Cammie whispered, "Is my mother at least reasonably okay?"

"She's got a broken wrist and some bad burns, but the worst thing is her infected eye." The nurse saw alarm in Cammie's rolling glance and said quickly, "She's going to live and be fine, Miss Kyle. And her eye won't be damaged permanently, I don't think. She'll be fine, really fine. Don't worry."

Cammie began to cry, the sting of actual tears on her raw cheeks a perverse comfort. "I love my mother," she said softly as if this were a magic rune, a healing spell.

"I love you, too," Tracy rasped, and reached out so that the tips of their fingers touched.

Day Twenty-two

In a sensible skirt and a white lace shirt, Meherio Amato waited for the sight of her husband's boat. She stood straight-backed, the tiny bulge at her waistline apparent only because she was so slender. She stood alone, impassive. Her sister had taken Anthony for the day, and Meherio had refused her sister's offer to accompany her.

As *Big Spender* motored into the harbor, towing *Opus*, a crowd slowly gathered, keeping a respectful distance behind Meherio. There were Marie, the baker, and the barkeep Quinn Reilly, the jeweler Avery Ben, and Abel, the knife grinder, as well as the owner of the dive boat for whom Lenny and Michel had crewed. All of them held to themselves mortal thoughts. They stood silent as Sharon Gleeman leapt ably over the side and Reginald tossed her the lines and then gave a hand to the woman none of them knew, who wore jeans and large sunglasses, her short auburn hair swinging forward to hide her face. Quinn Reilly wished he had opened the store on Sunday. The jeweler wished he had given Michel a better price on the necklace. Marie remembered Lenny's foolish jokes and Michel's quiet smile. And Abel, the knife grinder, considered whether it might be time to go home to Arizona and spend time with the granddaughter he knew only from a photo.

Meherio stepped forward and offered Reginald her hand and accepted Sharon's hug. An ambulance parted the crowd, and a small white parcel was loaded quietly into the back. "My dear, with the help of the fisherman who found us, I wrapped him in the mizzen sail from *Opus* and sewed it closed. I didn't know what you'd want to do."

Meherio looked out, across the water. "I think that in a few days' time, my brother and I will take a small boat out to where the porpoises play."

"Will you want us with you?"

"I would like that, Sharon. I would like to bring hibiscus, which we wore on our wedding day."

"I'll arrange for it, two woven wreaths," Reginald said. "It will be our small gift. He was a good man, and we will miss his friendship."

"The sea doesn't like us, sometimes," said Meherio. "She would rather we leave her alone."

"That's very possibly true," said Sharon. "But I will not like this so much without Lenny. I may not want to do this any longer. This has taken something from it. I should tell you, Meherio, that Janis stayed with us, to honor Lenny."

"Thank you, Janis. I am sorry for your dear friend, and glad to the heart for your sister and her child. Is there any word of Michel?"

Sharon shook her head ruefully. "I'm so sorry, Meherio. I know that you will help your babies to know their father."

"Yes, in memory. Or if I love another one someday. This doesn't seem possible now; but Lenny would wish that I have a father for his children."

"Will you sell *Opus?*" Janis asked.

"I don't know," Meherio said. "My brother has said he might like to own her, with me. And a part of her belongs to Michel, if Michel ever should come home."

"How could you ever stand to see her sail away again?" Janis cried before thinking.

"Many women have done that," Meherio said.

*   *   *

Cammie ran down the hospital corridor into her father's and brother's arms, and Tracy insisted on walking, although she had a cane.

For three days, husband and brother had taken turns at the bedside, but this was different. They were taking whole people home, whole people dressed in new plain khakis and shirts that hung on them as though they were scarecrows (Jim had bought the customary sizes at the local Dillard's) but felt, to Cammie and Tracy, like designer rags.

Ted was missing a baseball tournament that day. Instead, he sobbed in Tracy's arms as though he were six years old instead of two inches taller than her.

"I'm not going anywhere, honey," she said as Ted tried to control himself and failed. "I'm not going anywhere anymore. Not for a long time."

"I guess I'm a big pussy," he said. "Sorry, Mom."

"No, you're wonderful," Cammie said. "Girls think guys who cry are sexy." Ted beamed at her. "Come here." Ted started toward her, then stopped. "Come here, Ted, my cute little bro. I love you so much." And she hugged her brother around the neck so hard, her feet lifted off the floor.

Jim helped Tracy and Cammie carefully into the taxi they would take to the airport. They could see in his face a journal of the way their injuries looked to someone from the world. Jim marveled at how a description over the telephone had failed to depict the reality and tried to master his reaction. The burns on his wife's legs were as shiny as pink plastic. Her face was ravaged. Cammie's magnificent black hair was cut to a cap of feathers that lay flat against her skull. Jim touched it softly. "My baby," he said. "Your beautiful hair."

"Dad, at least they didn't have to shave me bald. There was no way they were ever going to get the matting out of it unless they cut it. It'll grow back."

"That will take years."

"At least I've got years now."

"We have to hurry up, honey," Jim said. "The taxi's double-parked. What's Janis doing again?"

"She'll be home in two days," said Tracy. "She stayed for Lenny Amato's memorial. He'll be buried at sea tomorrow. In spite of everything, Jim, you know she loved it, the island. She did. She saw what it was that made it magical. Magical and treacherous."

"And Olivia?"

"Well, there's that," Cammie said.

"What?" Tracy asked.

"She . . . it's okay, Mom . . . came into our room the night we got here, right before you came, Mom," said Cammie. Tracy stopped. "I was kind of out of it. . . ."

"What did she say? And why didn't we talk about this? As a family?"

"I didn't feel the need to have her in . . . our family. I was going to tell everyone. She said she was checking out of the hospital. She was fine. We knew that."

"That's not all, and you know it," Tracy prodded her.

"Of course, she said she was sorry for everything."

"And?"

"That someday if I wanted to see her, I could find her at this address on a slip of paper she gave me, her wire address or whatever."

"Of course you can," Tracy said, and Jim nodded.

"Well, I know I can. But I threw the address out, because . . . the truth is, I'm glad this happened. I'm not glad *this* happened. But I'm glad this happened the way it did. I saw her for real. How she is. I used to imagine her as a real princess, Mom, when I was little. She sent me beautiful things, and she lived in a castle. She promised I could come for the summer when I was sixteen, although she never asked me. If you'd told me, I might have wanted to know her better."

"It would have been like, Come into my parlor . . . ," Tracy said.

"Said the spider to the fly," Cammie finished. "Kind of."

"So you weren't scared?" Jim asked. He'd heard Tracy's account and spent an unnecessary hour apologizing for not having come directly to Honduras: His passport had expired, despite Tracy's constant reminders; and his wife and daughter were in Texas by the time he got an emergency exception to fly out.

Now Cammie scoffed, "Scared? I told her to leave my room before my mother came because she had no right to be there. I told her she was nothing to me. And that I didn't have questions about my 'heritage.'"

"Where do you think she went?" Jim asked.

"Europe, she said. Back to Europe." They all sat quietly for a moment, imagining Olivia wandering from resort to resort, a phantom in Michael Kors.

"We'll need to go to Holly's as soon as we're home and see Chris and the boys," Tracy said softly.

"We've been there, and they're doing as well as they can," Ted told them.

"But *we* need to go," Cammie said, tears suddenly brimming.

"What's wrong? What is it?" Jim cried. The taxi driver jumped in his seat, startled.

"We really need to see Chris and the boys, on the way home from the airport, even if it's late," Tracy said.

"I was thinking that, too. It's like we're leaving her," Cammie explained.

"There's time," Jim tried to reason. "Tracy, you need bed. You need your own bed. Your face is raw. Your arm is in a sling. My daughter looks like a truck ran over her."

"But the strange part is, really, we're not that badly hurt at all," Tracy said.

"And even weirder, it wasn't completely awful," Cammie said, her sobs diminishing, her voice ragged as she gasped for breath.

"An experience like that puts your life in . . . place. If you almost die, you really, you know, you live. I know that sounds like a greeting card. I had some of the most wonderful things . . . I can't explain. . . ."

"You had a lifetime's worth of bad luck," Jim said. "Honey, don't try to transform it into something that transcends what it was."

"But I learned things," she objected.

There was no point trying to explain; her father was simply too pragmatic.

Cammie tried to codify those lessons, things she couldn't explain: secrets and what leaks out of secrets, limits and what lies beyond them, death and what might be worse than death, love and what might have been love, wrenched away.

"I learned I love the sea, and I hate the sea," she said simply.

"It's a bad place to be alone," Jim said.

"It is, but it's a good place to be alone, too," Cammie told him. "Aunt Janis called, and said Meherio told her that we go into the sea because the sea is in us. It's what we're made of."

"John Kennedy said that, too. And someone before him. That's woo-woo crap," Jim said. "You two nearly died."

"Okay," Cammie said. "You're probably right."

But he wasn't, she thought. A snapshot of Michel, his lion-colored hair pulled into dreadlocks by salt water, shot across Cammie's mind; Michel leaning over her, the careless stars and diffuse gray clouds of night framing his bare shoulders. Suddenly, Cammie realized she couldn't recall the color of Michel's eyes but could still feel his hands and smell the lavender on his neck. She saw Holly, her rifle cocked, and Ernesto cowering in the leaking boat, and the huge, sparkling sails the first time they filled. She had promised herself to try to hold off thoughts of Michel until she could be alone and take them out of their tightly tied bundle, examine them one at a time. She recommitted herself to that promise now.

Her father hadn't been there. She loved him and was glad he

hadn't been there. But she was also, perversely, sorry for him and what he would never know.

Chris opened the door to them. Tracy thought she must be as shocked by his appearance as he was by theirs. He was easily ten pounds thinner, perhaps more. "Chris," she said softly, "we won't stay long. Please let us come in."

"Trace, you're always welcome here," Chris said formally. His face, like a film in time lapse, worked from a ritual smile through a grimace and then fell, the demeanor of an older man. "Tracy," he said, "thank God you're okay. Come and see the family."

With a deep breath, all four of the Kyles walked into a room filled with Holly's relatives. There were perhaps thirty people. Tracy realized with a shock that tonight had been Holly's . . . oh, dear God . . . tonight had been the wake, and tomorrow was Holly's funeral. Tracy recognized Holly's sister, Berit, though she had not met Berit's husband and children. She was introduced to aunts and cousins, all with solid Norwegian names—working names, as Holly had said, that sounded like the names of tools: Kelsvig, Haaldag, Brotte. The men stood. Berit finally shook herself, as if waking up, and walked over to take Tracy, briefly, into what passed in Holly's extended family for a hug but would be considered an accidental nudge on a bus.

"Berit," said Tracy, "I'm so sorry. Holly was my best friend."

"And mine," Berit said.

"I know that you don't expect this, but I apologize for my part in this," Tracy said to the room at large. "I wouldn't blame you for hating me. If she hadn't gone—"

"No one hates you, Trace," Chris said, "except the boys. And they don't, really. Children . . . they see things in such black and white."

"Where are they?" Cammie asked, stepping out from behind her father. She heard the simultaneous gasp and the attempt to cover it with the clatter of spoons and cups when people got a good look at her skin and her hair. Food was everywhere, from heavy noodle dishes swimming in meat juices to powdered pastries built on air around a thimbleful of fruit that, Cammie knew, would crumble into a lapful of sugared flakes at the first delicious bite. The collective offerings could have fed this room three meals and the block for another day. Bereavement evidently scooped out a hole that demanded to be filled, but words simply fell into it like so many pebbles. Food, especially Holly's food, was at least consolation. Cammie's mouth watered for a moment, but then the sight nauseated her. The nurses had warned her that overeating would be a temptation and a danger in the first days. She was to eat slowly, and good plain food, no spices, no pizza.

Berit and the others quickly made a plate for Ted and cups of coffee for Tracy and Jim.

So Cammie went to find Ian and Evan. They were nowhere about. She wandered through the kitchen, out to the back porch.

The memories and very smells—starch, yarn, detergent, cardamom—combined to tug her back and down into childhood. This house, like her own, had a personal scent, undetectable to those who lived there. But Cammie had read that smell was the most potent of the senses. She expected to see Holly everywhere. In the breakfast nook, she stopped to look out at Holly's pride— her shining inground swimming pool. She pictured the two of them out there when the pool was only a patio with a plastic picnic set on it—small Cammie with her hair in braids, Holly pointing out that long division was only a trick, once you learned it. A small whimper escaped her lips. Would she ever forget the sight of the sailors carrying the surprisingly little cocooned form over the bridge into the cutter? Aunt Holly, she thought, please be here. A hollow slapping sound caught her attention.

Evan and Ian were at the back of the yard, alternating shots into their soccer net. Ian would guard the goal, then Evan would guard. Ian's hair was long now. It looked good on him. He was tan and already taking on the structure of a teen. Evan simply looked pallid and stooped, like a little kid who had done nothing for days except watch TV in dark rooms. How much they had changed since Christmas.

"Hey," Cammie called softly through the screen. She pushed open the door and sat on the steps of the porch. Evan gave the ball one vicious last blast and shuffled toward her, head down. Ian turned glacial blue eyes on her. Holly's eyes.

"Your hair is all gone," Ian said.

"You like it?" Cammie asked.

"It's okay. It was pretty before," said Evan.

"They couldn't get the tangles out. You don't remember, but I would cry when your mom brushed my hair out. She would say, 'You have to suffer to be beautiful.'"

"Yeah," Ian said briefly, cutting her off.

"Sit down by me," Cammie said. "Just for a minute."

Nervously, conscious as they never had seemed before that Cammie was a girl with breasts and other attributes, the boys complied. Holly had always explained that they were fraternal, not identical, though no one could tell them apart. Now, Cammie could see it. Ian would be fairer, taller. They looked like siblings now, alike but distinguishable.

"So . . . you guys . . ." What did she want to say? She had wanted to hold them, but they were too old for that now. "Well, I guess all I can say is that this sucks. There's nothing I can tell you that will make it better at all. And even more than it sucks now, I think it'll get worse for a while. And I can be here for you, and your dad can; but it'll still suck. There was nobody like my aunt Holly." Evan put his head down on one hand. Ian stared out into the night, where the yard lights gave way to a dark, thready tangle of lilacs. Cammie paused. Then she asked softly, "Can I tell you one thing?"

Neither boy said a word. Finally, Ian shrugged.

"Out there, we were boarded by pirates," Cammie began.

"They were drug smugglers, two South American guys and an American guy around my age. They had heroin in an old boat. They tried to rape us. Not the American boy, because we got the feeling he didn't have his heart in it. But the other guys were horrible. Like beasts. And right at the end, they decided they were going to take me with them. They were going to take me with them and rape me and kill me."

She glanced from one side to the other. The boys were looking at her, not exactly interested, but no longer enclosed in their stupor or numbed by the endless rote of the soccer drill. Cammie hesitated. She didn't want to make this an adventure story. She did want to convey . . . something. Trust yourself, she thought. You can do this.

"We had held them off for hours and hours, almost a day, before that. We were giving them a bunch of whiskey to drink, so much that they passed out. But finally, they were holding on to me, and it was the end." Cammie drew a wavering breath. This seemed so long ago. She could not contact the girl who had witnessed this thing. With every step back into her own life, that girl receded from Cammie with the speed of a kite.

She went on, "All this time, no one knew where . . . where your mom was. Your mom was already sick. She had blood poisoning, from a bite or a cut. That was something that could have happened to any one of us. But it happened to her. Anyhow, she was sick, and she was lying down in her cabin. We were all praying she wouldn't come out. But what she was doing, Ian, Ev, she was putting together the rifle the captain had. She knew how to do that. Sick even like she was. She broke the lock on a metal chest with a hammer, and she got out that gun and put it together and loaded it. And just when they were about to pull me over, she crawled out. Before they could do anything, she shot the guy who was holding me; and she shot the other guy . . . and then she shot a hole in the boat. She never missed once."

The boys' faces were unreadable in the dusk.

But then Ian sat up, squaring his shoulders.

Cammie, emboldened, pressed on. "Now, I don't know that I'm worth so much. I'm not telling you it was a trade. She loved you guys more than anything. She never wanted to leave you. But she saved all our lives. She was so brave. And she said, she said I should tell you . . . that luck was bad . . . but . . . life . . ."

"Is good," said Evan, and he began to cry, not sobbing, simply making no attempt to wipe the tears from his face or the rivulets from his nose.

"Ev, Ian, it doesn't help. I can't really be your big sister. I'll try my best, and I'll be there for you. I promise you that. But I'm going to miss her all my life. You will, too. I just want you to know, she was a hero. She was a total hero. That's all."

Cammie drew up her own knees and let the sobs she had held in, held hard in her like a knot of cloth, unravel. She wept until she gasped and shuddered, crumpling against the screen, panting for her breath. As the darkness grew thicker, first Evan and then Ian awkwardly placed a hand on each of her shoulders. This is all backward, Cammie thought.

But it didn't matter.

Holly wouldn't have minded.

August

Two identical flat white cardboard envelopes arrived together, one for Tracy and one addressed to Camille Kyle in care of the Kyle family. Tracy was alone in the dining room, assembling her list of materials for the new Lifetime Fitness section of her middle-school class, when the postman rang the doorbell.

"Nice to see you doing so well, Tracy," he said. He brought the mail to the door every day now, though he never had before.

"Thanks, Denny," she told him, as she had every day for six weeks.

Flipping through catalogs, the telltale glassine of insurance bills, a postcard from Janis at a dental convention in Puerto Rico, she stopped, startled to see the outline of the bougainvillea blossom on what she'd assumed would be an advertisement for shampoo or family photos. After peeling open the tab, she let the contents fall onto the tabletop. Her good eye welling, the other stinging behind its patch, she studied the eight-by-ten in gaudy color. She remembered it now, a shot taken by an Asian man on a bicycle who had patrolled the docks. It was just before they had boarded *Opus* for the first time.

She looked away, but not quickly enough.

She had seen them. There they all were: Holly with her thumbs cocked at her full breasts, her T-shirt with the bright blue legend nurses make it feel better; Tracy not quite prepared, as usual, her sunglasses half-on, half-off, making her look not so much batty as tipsy—a gangly British spinster on her "hols," her long white legs stretching away from those wretched plaid Bermuda shorts. Tracy had stuffed them and all of her salvage-able clothing from the trip (along with everything else Cammie adjudged "frumplitch") into a donation bag weeks earlier. So thin now that nothing in her closet fit except her wedding dress, she still—despite the myriad bruises and strains that grabbed her unexpectedly with bites of pain—felt better than she had since she'd worn that wedding dress for the first time. She and Jim made love three, four times a week; they saw movies; they were having an inground pool installed. Poignantly but proudly, they hosted Chris and the boys for barbecue. Together, they visited a therapist—the same one Cammie was seeing—who helped Jim through the task of witnessing Tracy's account of her terror. The doctor had suggested that they initiate a ritual of "checking in" with each other each day for fifteen minutes—not with problems, necessarily, or compliments, just keeping each other foremost in the business of living. This moment of communion had the effect of refreshing a marriage that was already better than most mar-riages they knew.

It was better than any Tracy knew, except the marriage Chris had had with Holly.

Tracy studied honey dissolving lusciously as she splurged on a second cup of tea. She broke her toast into tiny bites and savored each crumb—something Jim came to realize she might do the rest of her life. Tracy stood, mesmerized—until Jim interrupted—by the smells of vegetables crisping in oil, by the juice from the sliced orange or watermelon, the melting of butter on corn. It took her half an hour to eat a meal.

And it took everything she could muster not to shout at Ted for letting the tap run while he brushed his teeth. Tracy shook the bottles of milk until every drop collected in the bottom of a glass and washed and reused jam jars until Jim began calling them "our stemware." Always neat, she rearranged her drawers, strok-ing her clean T-shirts and bras. She placed every photo album in date order, with labels. For fifteen minutes, she quaked in shame before taking the first step of her first run, and then she ran for a mile, falling down into the grass on Hale Hill, then stopping to swing on the swing set at the playground until her sweat dried, walking home slowly, listening to the human music of voices from every yard. Real music, even old Broadway tunes, brought her to tears. And she played an Emmylou Harris CD again and again until Jim threatened to run over it with the car. Although weeks passed before Tracy could bring herself to drive, much less enter a store, when she finally did, it was to savor with her fingers the differing textures of fabric as if she were blind or newborn.

And she woke, shuddering, stunned to find herself anchored in a crisp expanse of dry, clean white cotton, as her dreams—damp and dank, stained and smelling of sickness and sweat—rocked away into the night, endlessly rising and falling.

Even with that, even with the memories that leapt up each time she drove past Holly's corner or mistakenly began to dial her telephone number, life was unutterably sweet in its every moment.

Tracy was almost reluctant to study the photo.

Finally, she did.

There was Lenny, making a big production of shading his bald head with a newspaper, and Olivia, a blur of cream-and-black voile and creamy flesh, her huge sunglasses flashing like black ice, turning toward Cammie. Oh, Cammie—smirking and cutting her eyes at Michel, who was feigning a strongman's bare-chested pose. Cammie's long dark hair looped through the closure of her Chicago Cubs cap. She wore the aqua bikini top they'd cut away. Here it was, brand-new again, not the filthy and blood-spattered rag they'd given to Jim in a hospital bag, a bag he'd tossed in a waste bin outside, while a photographer from a local newspaper snapped a photo.

Before she could stop, Tracy caught herself thinking how

beautiful Cammie had been when she was . . . and realized she had been about to think "when Cammie was young."

What foolishness!

Cammie was nineteen.

She was still only nineteen.

None of them was older than she had been six weeks before. Yet they felt as though they had aged. It was right, what the thinkers said, that there were different kinds of time—for lovers, it rocketed past with cruel speed; for those who waited, it shuffled.

What manner of time had held them, suspended, for seventeen days and an eternity?

Nonsense, Tracy thought. Cammie was looking more like herself every day. Her daughter had gained ten pounds. Her eyes no longer stared up haunted at Tracy when Tracy looked in at night, checking on her almost as if Cammie were a child. Cam invariably would still be awake, her fingers clasping the unbroken white sheet, her body barely rumpling the surface, a new mystery novel open and unread on the slight hillock of her belly. She still didn't like to sleep at night. People who didn't know—was there *anyone* who didn't know?—liked Cammie's gamine cap of dark feathers, though they rolled their eyes at Tracy and said, "That's kids for you," and asked, "How could she have cut that gorgeous hunk of hair?" And therein lay a tale that Tracy tried, usually without success, to avoid telling.

Yes, Cammie looked beautiful—yes, she did, with her great eyes, like mythical moons, under that pixie thatch.

She looked, Tracy realized in that moment, exactly like Olivia.

Tracy squeezed her forehead between the palms of her hands.

"What's that, Mom?" Cammie murmured, wakened by the doorbell, coming into the kitchen. She often stayed up late, then slept well into the afternoon, often in Tracy's bed on the shaded side of the house. Once a week, usually after therapy, she told Tracy that the psychologist assured her that the fantasies that

kept her awake would dissolve over time. Right now, it was normal for her to rewind the film and then try out different endings.
It was what happened to so many crime victims or survivors of
disasters. It was, Cammie said, a process that was part of healing. Cammie would go back to school in the second semester. By
then, some of this would have receded to a pinpoint of memory.

But not yet. Now the distance was real only when she was
awake. In sleep, she was there, pleading under a blasted sun on
Opus.

"Oh, Aunt Holly," Cammie crooned, tracing the curve of the
beloved face. "Mom, look how beautiful and young she was—"
Cammie seemed to bite off her sentence and was absent for a
moment, as if concentrating on a sound in the distance she was
trying to identify. Then her eyes snapped back. She said, "You
have to frame this, Mom."

"In time, I guess I will. You have one, too," Tracy said.

"Do you think Meherio sent it?" Cammie asked, sitting down,
rubbing her forehead with the tips of three tapered fingers. Still,
Tracy noticed, no polish and no "squovals." Cammie's nails were
cut straight across and filed only enough to keep them from snag-
ging her clothes.

"The photographer, I suppose."

"But the envelope is from the *Opus*," Cammie pointed out,
tapping the return address. Tracy noticed then that a label with
a telephone number, handwritten, was attached to Cammie's envelope that hadn't been to her own. She stifled a desire to snatch
it from her daughter's hands.

"I imagine they pay the photographer to do that with every
one of the boats," Tracy suggested, her body thrumming, edgy
with impatience.

Cammie opened her envelope. When she tipped it, not only
the big photo but also a small square envelope—with a pale,
lime green watermark—fell with it. It was not sealed. Cammie

pulled out a snapshot, a dried flower, and a single folded sheet of stationery.

Michel smiled at her from the depths of a white dress shirt that seemed to engulf him like a prizefighter's robe. His fingers were arched, as if at play on the padded arms of the wheelchair—and his feet, in carefully laced shoes, hung with a telltale carelessness from the enormous cuffs of khaki pants, one toe dangling off the footrest.

"He's . . . alive," Cammie breathed, as if she were alone. She reached up and made a fist around the tiny cross and the necklace of shells that she had never removed.

Tracy crossed to Cammie's side of the table. "He's so thin, and look, he's badly hurt," she said.

"Do you think . . . ?" Cammie asked.

"I don't know," said Tracy.

"I should go to him," Cammie said.

"No," Tracy said. But then she added, "I don't know, really. Do you want to?"

"He would want me to," Cammie said.

"But to send you this picture, with no word, what is he trying to say?"

Cammie said, "There's a note." She touched the flower—bougainvillea, the blossom he had tucked behind her ear that day in St. John—with her fingertip. It crumbled, as a mounted butterfly wing would have crumbled, removed from its pin. Tracy sat down expectantly. "For me," Cammie told her gently, and took the sheet and the photos into her own room.

"Dearest Cammie," she read:

Meherio and my mother are fierce nurses, and I am no longer scheduled to die as I was when I frightened an old Basque fisherman nearly into his own grave. He thought that I was dead when he found me. The rock I crashed into on the tender tore it apart. I didn't feel this, but I will never go climbing up the mast again. I am lucky it wasn't more damage, as it is my legs, but not more. The doctor says I will still be able to be a father one day, though I can't imagine a woman who would want this ghost. Perhaps we are all ghosts, of "Opus," Meherio and Sharon and Regin and Lenny and me. Meherio and her brother are hard at work repairing the boat, and sometime soon, it will be a party and wedding boat. She says I am a partner, of course, but it may be that my days of going to sea are ended. I write to tell you how sorry I am, beyond my ability to say, and how happy that you have survived and that one day this will all be as if a bad dream. Meherio sends her best wishes, and I remain,

> Yr friend,
> Michel Eugène-Martin

Cammie turned the sheet over and examined both sides for another word. There was none, only the handwritten number on the larger envelope. Was that his number? Was it an office phone? Did he mean her to call? "Yr friend . . ."

He did not mean for her to call or to come to him. He was ashamed. No one would have been more shamed by such helplessness. Oh, Michel, she thought. She let her mind's cascade of pictures fall open: Michel climbing the ropes, his careless, athletic grace, his back roped with the kind of musculature no gym ever made. Holding the picture facedown on her lap, she thought of his shameless, wide smile on the night she'd come wading out of the surf. She saw herself, impossibly naive and, yes, lovely, a hopeful Venus from the foam. Where was this Michel? He had written of the ghosts of *Opus*. Was she one as well?

Cammie examined the photo again and saw things she did not remember. There was a snarling blue-and-red tattoo of something, a dragon, perhaps, on Michel's exposed forearm—such small forearms now, small as a teenage boy's. A tattoo! Cammie didn't know boys who had tattoos, except boys who'd been in the military. She didn't . . . date boys with tattoos.

In the end, as Michel had said, he was a different species.

She could not deny the turbulence of pity and relief and gratitude, of regret and sweetness. And guilt. A long stain of guilt. All unintentionally, in exchange for a game, a little game of passion between a boy and a girl, Michel had paid so much. She had paid, too, although her debt would not last forever—oh, it wasn't possible! Michel! Cammie wanted to pound her fist into her hand at the endless injustices of the *Opus*. She was just young enough to imagine that going on, without eyes, or hearing, or after the loss of a leg, was mere existence, a pitiable trap a person endured for the sake of others. Was he even glad to have survived, having lived so fully in his body? His body. She swallowed a dangerous lump in her throat. It was gone. What he was, was gone. She thought of Olivia, of Franco's neediness that had so repelled her. Was she, Cammie, such a coward? So reptilian, absorbing warmth but unable to return it?

No. But she could not lie.

She could feel herself, tiny, swept up in Michel's arms. He had been thin but so strong, holding her against him in a way that demanded and defended her. She'd been as pliant as a fresh leaf. That was the only moment of unambivalent lust and possession, of being possessed, that Cammie had ever experienced. Had it been a bottomless pool, she would have, at that moment, stepped into it and allowed it to subsume her. Now the recollection was as flat as the snapshot. She didn't know who Michel really was. And she was not equal to this. She had to extract herself from this, carefully, as she would an earring caught in the weave of a costly sweater.

The shame was hers, too.

But neither of them owed an apology.

Someday, Cammie hoped, a woman of the island, a friend, an old lover, would give him children, help him, cherish him, say sweet words to this sweet man who deserved at least this. A hot needle prodded her as she considered this. But she forced it away. Would he even want to see her? To have her see him? He would not. A heady moment between two healthy young animals: It should have been no more than that. Of course, it had been what followed, the merciless accretion of wicked luck and desperation and drama, that had given it heft and contour, had fashioned each word and touch into part of a sculptured story Cammie clung to with both hands, those blazing days on the boat and even later, in her bedroom, in her cool, shuttered dreams. But at the moment that Cammie saw Michel's photo, the substance of the story began to dissolve into a shape that pressure would reduce to particles.

Was she merely rationalizing her fear?

If she was, it amounted to the same thing as truth.

She let herself taste the mixture that had been her and Michel; and the taste was the taste of seawater, or of tears.

Gently, she slid Michel's snapshot and note back into their small envelope, then back into the large cardboard sleeve, along with the big photo. She walked into their computer room and deposited it, all of it, deep into the recesses of her father's commodious wastebasket, covering it so Jim would never see it. Then she went back into her room, closed the door, and lay on her bed. Instantly, she was asleep.

Tracy woke next morning to the sound of the garbage trucks.

It happened all the time.

Garbage day had been changed now from Monday to Friday; and it threw her. Ted, who had a honey, had begun to stay out late. Half the time he hauled out the large bin but forgot to collect the liners from the household cans. Shouting a warning from the back door, Tracy ran around grabbing up plastic bags from the bathrooms, the office, her bedroom and Ted's, tying them on the run. She didn't bother with Cammie's room, knowing Cam would sleep until noon, only to nap again later. Down to the curb Tracy sprinted, to hand the bags up to the young men balanced on the lip of the garbage truck who were just emptying the larger bin into the maw.

Then she saw Cammie run out of the house, wearing only boxers and a cutoff T-shirt, screaming, "No! Did they take the trash?"

"Yes," Tracy said, "except these couple of things. . . ." She had just handed up the small cluster of plastic bags.

"Put that down!" Cammie shouted over the roar of the garbage truck. "I'm sorry! Please put those bags down! Give them back!"

Shrugging expressively, the men let the bags drop onto the lawn.

Cammie fell to her knees, ripping open the bags. Disposable razors and crumpled tissues and spent soap wrappers flew onto the grass of the parkway. The truck, with a massive bleating of its brakes, stopped at the next house. Tracy glanced around her. It was 7:00 a.m. and there was no sign of neighbors. She quickly fetched a leaf bag from the garage and began to gather up trash as fast as Cammie tossed aside one bag and began shaking out another. More crumpled paper, wrappers from granola bars, blueprints.

Finally, Cammie spotted the edge, with the imprint of the bougainvillea blossom, and grabbed at it. The handwritten label with the phone number in the corner was not smudged, still legible. Sitting in a rubble of paper towels and apple cores, she held the big envelope first to her breast, then, closing her eyes, to her cheek. Tracy moved quietly around her, gathering up trash before it could blow away. The wind was picking up, the leaves showing their undersides. That, and a metallic smudge of scent in the air, hinted at rain in the offing. She didn't want her parkway strewn with sodden wads of tissue.

Cammie seemed to waken and glanced up into the branches of the chestnut tree her father had planted when she was born.

Her body presumed it had been months and months—a season, a year—since she'd walked out into the early morning. Her body presumed it should be cold by now, school weather. It was not: The air was warm, muggy; and the grass smelled freshly mown. The tree was a glossy, full-bodied umbrella, with just here and there a furled tint of yellow, a handful of shells and crisp brown leaves at the base. Impossibly, it was only August. It was still summer.

Trembling, Cammie opened the white cardboard sleeve: Although she had shaken the bags with all her strength, she had not lost it, the small, pale green envelope nestled deep inside.

Reading Group Guide

Between the Devil and the Deep Blue Sea

By Jacquelyn Mitchard

It just seems true that everything important in life happens in the space of a breath—from falling in love to a car careening around a blind corner to the birth of a child. And that is why I called my novel *Still Summer*. For the women on the *Opus*, a single moment and a rash decision would set in motion a chain of events that would change their lives. And those lives would be changed, not just for the duration of a crisis, but forever—in events that happened in a space of time so short that the leaves on the trees hadn't even changed to the colors of fall.

Still, at the end of the day, *Still Summer* is a story of strength and survival. The events are undoubtedly terrifying and even tragic. There is despair and disillusionment on the journey. And yet, strong relationships grow stronger; love outlasts death; learning surpasses fear. The four women who board a sailing boat for a pleasure cruise discover themselves as warriors who will not let the elements, their own inexperience, and even human predators take away their only chance to make their way home.

And yet, why did I choose to put such ordinary, happy people in peril?

Only villains deserve such a fate.

Couldn't they simply have bickered, and Olivia's secret have emerged through some sort of drama to lay to rest the ghost that haunted Tracy's life with her daughter? Why did the events that stranded the sailing ship *Opus* have to be so extreme—so much so that some critics said they could not have happened? (Ironically, in fact, I had to pull back on what *really* might have happened in the circumstances because the horror stories told me by those who live on boats would have strained my credibility budget!) The choice to make *Still Summer* an adventure was not only to give my readers the kind of read that would pin their ears back, but to examine the behavior of people at the very limits of endurance. In the same sweet, sunny silence they came to the Caribbean to find, they nearly met their doom. And it has always been my belief that people under stress reveal themselves—even find themselves—in ways they might never do with an escape hatch at hand or even with a comforting prognosis. The unknown is the most fearsome of all.

Of course, Holly didn't deserve to put her life on the line. Lenny's death was the loss of a blameless and good-hearted man (Lenny Amato is a real person, by the way—the skipper of the sailing ships *Opus* and *Slipstream* out of St. Thomas—and was very moved by his own demise). But fate is no respecter of its targets. Early on in the crisis, Tracy and Holly vowed that, of them all, nineteen-year-old Cammie had to survive. She was the seed corn, and more than any of the others, although all of them were relatively young women still, she deserved her chance to experience life.

And so I had to pose questions about how far the others would go to protect Cammie and themselves, how well we really know our friends, our families—even ourselves. A gym teacher with a placid life, Tracy Kyle would never have imagined fighting her way to a deserted island. Spoiled, cherished Cammie thought that she'd truly suffered when a boy broke her heart. She had no idea how great her capacity for passion was, nor her courage and ingenuity under fire.

I also wanted to make a point about women and their strength and endurance. Too often, books that even touch on relationships among women are dismissed with a phrase that's so cute it's become de trop and overused: chick lit. But anyone who can read *Still Summer* and consider this novel of suspense a bonbon box of words has never known either love or fear. When my friend Andre Dubus III read the book, he confessed that he shocked his wife by bursting into tears, and another reader, thriller writer Craig Holden, said that the action nailed him to his seat.

Perhaps stories, and even the critical brief passages of life, are essentially comprised of those moments that show the difference between people who face their fears and people who don't. The women on the *Opus* were forced to face their past and their uncertain future in one hundred square feet, trapped together in time and space, trapped without sustenance or apparent hope, in the midst of a featureless ocean, and had to choose to give in to fear or to go down fighting.

All of them, even the least gallant, chose the latter. Their losses were huge, but as Cammie explained later in the novel, not everything that they learned in those harrowing days was ugly or bad. Some of it was the very essence of being alive.

A Q & A with Jacquelyn Mitchard

Q. When did the idea for this novel come to you—and why? Did this concept give you a chance to explore anything new in your writing?

A. I wanted badly to write a novel of suspense and survival but not to forsake the stake I have in writing about the essential connections that bind us. It came to me, truly, as the result of a betrayal by someone very close to me. The hurt and anger was immense, staggering. It stalled me for months. Finally, writing gave me both a way to explore the roots of that personal pain and to examine betrayal and loyalty in fiction.

Q. How did you go about expanding your original idea into a gripping, sometimes terrifying, story? Did you dream about it? Jot down notes? Keep a clipping file?

A. I went to sea! Lenny Amato really is the skipper of the sailing boat *Opus*, and I taped four days of interviews with him, hearing many of the tales and perils of a seemingly benign voyage—and how they go wrong all the time. Lenny believes that many of the modern Bermuda Triangle stories, for example, really are stories of piracy, with no trace left behind. Unlike my other novels, each of the major characters is based entirely on a real person, and I combined the chemistry of those people to see what would blend . . . or combust. Even my cousin Janis, who went with me, is one of the saviors of the *Opus*.

Q. This is very much a "woman's book" in that the husbands remain offstage, the love interests are killed off or gone missing, and other male characters are pirates, drifters, or just plain badly behaved. Now that's interesting. Can you tell us why the men don't "stay afloat" in this novel?

A. It might be a woman's book, but it's not a "chick" book. This isn't the mascara wars; it's a true fight for survival in which modern women have to use every ounce of their strength and savvy to try to make their way to safety against all odds. I didn't want any knights with white chargers to happen along and save them. I wanted to let them do all the heavy lifting. It's no disrespect to men—just a way of putting a twist on the tradition of women in jeopardy.

Q. Friendship is perhaps the most important relationship depicted in *Still Summer*. How important are women friends in your own life? Do you still have friends from high school?

A. Absolutely. I've known two of my closest friends for more than thirty-five years and one of them, who has multiple sclerosis, was the model for Julianne in *The Breakdown Lane*. We remain very, very tight. They're the sisters I never had.

Q. On your Web site (www.jackiemitchard.com) you respond to questions with a great deal of humor, wit, and laugh-out-loud zingers. But the tone of *Still Summer* is dark and intense. Your body of work nearly always focuses on painful and challenging situations, and humor is not a major element. Why?

A. I think there is always humor in my books. Always. Stephen King has said that I manage to infuse the darkest situations with something absurd and true-to-life. But it's not when we're at a beach picnic or reading in bed that our most essential selves are revealed—it's when the face we show the world is peeled back and not one of us escapes without having the trapdoor open under us in life. That said, I'm working on a novel I think will be funny indeed.

Q. Do you ever write comedy? Have you thought about creating a lighthearted book for adults—even one of nonfiction?

A. You betcha. I love to make people laugh. I've thought of writing about my *Please Don't Eat the Daisies* life—with the seven children (the eldest living in the basement in a bedroom made entirely of sheets, the youngest upstairs in his trundle bed), two Cyldesdales, the Saint Bernard puppy, the Indy track around which three little boys race from the kitchen to the living room each day on their Big Wheels . . . and I've thought of putting a single woman in an utterly impossible situation when she falls in love with the photo of the sperm donor she used to have a baby . . . I think of these all the time.

Q. You have said you like to scuba dive, and you certainly used that knowledge to create realistic scenes in the novel. Do you also sail? Have other special abilities and interests of yours appeared in your work?

A. I love to dive. It's because of my friends, authors Beth Gutcheon and Patricia Wood, that the sailing details are correct in *Still Summer*. I couldn't sail in my tub; it wasn't "done" growing up on the west side of Chicago. My only true talent—and it's major and you can test me—is that I know the lyrics of every song I've ever heard exactly, whether it was written in 2008 or 1908. I just described my life . . . Where would you see the opportunity for hobbies? I love to bake and cook for my kids. I love to study wildlife, especially bats. And of course, everything I know, from teen habits to competitive cheerleading to homemade pasta, shows up in my books.

Q. The British Virgin Islands also figure hugely in this book, but your portrayal reveals a very different place than that seen in the tourist brochures. Did you have a mixed experience in your travels there or is your depiction of the other side of paradise from your imagination alone?

A. No, Lenny shared fully with us that BVI is paradise with a shadowy side. One of the truest lines in the novel is that everyone who is there (besides the tourists) is either wanted or unwanted. That was the inspiration for the young man with no name who has signed on with the drug smugglers. Island life is ravishing, but also very solitary.

Q. Your worldview seems to include such themes as "stuff happens, now deal with it" and "bad things do happen to very nice women." Can you tell us a little more about the way you look at life?

A. I believe life is like a bran muffin: Much of it has to be slogged through, but there are raisin treats every so often and it's generally good for you. I'm a very happy person. I wake each day singing and look for good things to come even out of the bleakest of situations. But bad things happen to everyone. In my life, I've lost a brother, father, mother, and husband. I'm not unique. Survival of the spirit is a choice renewed every day.

Q. Which character in this book best embodies your outlook and philosophy?

A. Oh, Tracy, for sure. She's the self-sacrificing mom with the cherished child. There is no point at which I would not drop everything to walk to Banff, barefoot, for one of mine.

Q. What or whom did you draw on to make the youngest character in the book, Cammie, so authentic?

A. I have three sons who are teenagers or very young adults. They're all attractive young men with many female friends. And, you know, I was a Cammie once, though not quite so lovely—fully as bratty, however.

Q. You wrote in *Still Summer*, "Olivia snorted, 'Love at first sight!'" (p. 131). Christopher Marlowe wrote, "Who ever loved, that loved not at first sight?" So which is it? Can love at first sight happen—and endure? Or, evaluated through the lens of experience and life lessons, would it seem that instant love is simply chemical attraction?

A. Well, I met a guy one day and married him five weeks later. That was ten years ago. I personally think that if a relationship requires *too* much work (as opposed to care, which is altogether different), perhaps it was a mismatch. And I also know that I have known instinctively most things I needed to know about people within the first fifteen minutes of acquaintance—unless I was trying to second-guess myself or unless they were sociopaths.

Q. You wrote about your previous novel, *Cage of Stars*, that you achieved "a story that mattered, told simply, with the fewest possible and right words." Is that true of this novel too?

A. It is. I don't believe in long passages of rumination and description for the sake of showcasing the writer's ability to conjure with words. The narrative is the regent and, ideally, it should be both lush and spare.

Q. Cammie and Tracy have a relationship that is both loving and fraught with tension. Do you think this is true of most mother/daughter relationships? And do you think that it is maturity and/or adversity that draws mothers and daughters closer? Or perhaps other elements?

A. I think Cammie and Tracy's relationship is not atypical of a child who was much wanted and much loved. In most cases, it is growth and time that teaches a child to see the world through the eyes his or her parents use to see. But for Cammie, that dimension of maturity had to happen in a short time—and she was astonished at how much she had grown when it was, well, "still summer."

Discussion Questions

1. Friends to the end—or not! This book focuses on the friendship of four women and how it is tested. Which of the friendships in this book prove to be the strongest? What qualities are they based on?

2. The friendships of these women began in high school. What is the importance of them calling themselves "the Godmothers"? How have the women changed over the years? Do people usually turn out as you believe they will?

3. How do friendships end in this book? In your own experience, what are some reasons for the ending of a woman's friendship with another woman? Has the demise of a friendship ever changed you or your outlook on life?

4. "Life is not fair." How does that truism emerge in this novel? What patently "unfair" things happen in this story? What point do you think the author is making?

5. Several characters get killed off in this novel and some of these deaths certainly come as a surprise. Who dies and why do you suppose the author "offed" them?

6. The outward or surface appearance of many things or people in this book clashes or contrasts with the reality beneath. This dichotomy or deception leads the characters to make some huge mistakes. Pick one or two to talk about.

7. Does anything happen in this book that cannot be avoided (fate) or is everything that occurs dependent on a character's choice? How much control do you think we have over the outcomes of our lives?

8. Olivia says in the book, "Your mother told me luck could be bad, but life is good" (p. 107). Do you agree?

9. Talk about Cammie's relationship with her mother, Tracy. Is it typical? Is it extreme? Do you think its depiction is realistic?

10. Speaking of motherhood: Tracy is Cammie's adopted mother. Olivia is her birth mother. What did you feel shaped Cammie's basic character: nature (her genes) or nurture (her upbringing)?

11. In your own experience, how important is it for an adopted child to know her birth parents? Is blood "thicker than water"?

12. Why do you suppose the author set the story on a boat? Can you think of another setting where the same kinds of things could have happened?

13. What do you think about the portrayal of men in this story. What might be the reason they are "offstage," missing, dead, or the bad guys?

14. What is your response to the love story between Cammie and Michel? Do you believe they fell in love? Do you believe they have a future?

15. Cammie says, "An experience like that puts your life in . . . place. If you almost die, you really, you know, you live" (p. 291). Do you agree? This is fiction, but do you think the survivors would have responded the same way in real life?

16. If you were given permission to rewrite this story and keep one of the characters from dying, which one would you save? Why?